DARK ARTS

Shalindra couldn't afford to let astonishment shake her concentration, but the ghostly figure hovering before her was extraordinarily sharp and clear. His eyes were sly, and he was actually smirking.

Well. A real amateur, observed the ghost. *You need practice, missy.*

He giggled, and Shalindra jumped. She had never thought to accomplish so much.

Better close your mouth and mind your concentration, little girl. You're not very good at this, are you?

"Good enough to bring you here," she replied without thinking.

Presumptuous chit. I CAME, of my own free will. The Deathmaster knows no constraint. Hasn't anyone ever taught you ANYTHING?

Her head was spinning, she could barely stay on her feet. "I called you here because I want you to send a message to The Librarian, on Fruce Isle. That's all I ask. That's—"

Do you take the Deathmaster for a carrier pigeon?

"Please—I need help—"

That you do, little girl. Clotl could help you. If he chose. Heh. IF. I've decided to grant your request. You needn't thank me. Farewell for now, songbird. Clotl leaves you with a word of advice. If you must practice necromancy, next time try to get it RIGHT.

Also by Paula Volsky

ILLUSION

THE WOLF

OF WINTER

Paula Volsky

BANTAM BOOKS
New York Toronto London Sydney Auckland

This edition contains the complete text
of the original hardcover edition.
NOT ONE WORD HAS BEEN OMITTED.

THE WOLF OF WINTER
A Bantam Spectra Book

PUBLISHING HISTORY
Bantam trade edition published December 1993

Bantam paperback edition / January 1995
SPECTRA and the portrayal of a boxed "s" are trademarks of Bantam Books,
a division of Bantam Doubleday Dell Publishing Group, Inc.

Map design by Laura Hartman Maestro.
All rights reservd.

Bantam Books are published by Bantam Books, a division of Bantam
Doubleday Dell Publishing Group, Inc. Its trademark, consisting of the
words "Bantam Books" and the portrayal of a rooster, is Registered in
U.S. Patent and Trademark Office and in other countries. Marca Registrada.
Bantam Books, 1540 Broadway, New York, New York 10036.

PRINTED IN THE UNITED STATES OF AMERICA

OPM 0 9 8 7 6 5 4 3 2 1

TO JANE BISHOP
ECCENTRICITIES OF
GENIUS

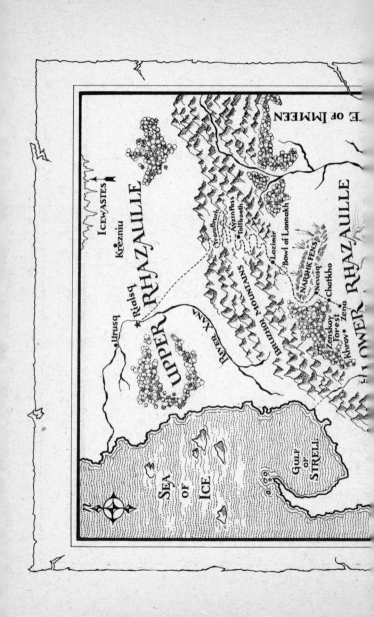

PART ONE

The White
Wolflings

PROLOGUE

IN THE NORTHERN land of Rhazaulle, society is shaped by two great influences; the severity of the climate, and the sometimes disruptive activity of the necromancers. The hunger of winter personifies itself in the legend of the fabulous Ulor. Heraldic beast and national symbol of Rhazaulle, the Ulor is a gigantic, white, winged wolf, whose yearly flight from mountain lair, across the realm and back again, marks winter's onset. Flight concluding, the Ulor returns to its nest, there to slice its own throat open upon a shard of ice. White blood spurts from the wound. Each gout striking the snow swells, sculpting itself into the form of a winged wolf cub. The parent expires. Throughout the long winter, the cubs thrive and grow upon a diet of ice. When they are old enough to long for stronger meat, they turn upon one another, killing and devouring until at last the strongest alone remains alive to become the new Ulor, an assumption of power traditionally bringing winter to an end. So firm a grip has this legend taken upon the national imagination that Rhazaulle's ruler is officially known as the "Ulor."

1

"AT THIS TIME, to announce my choice of the Noble Landholder Pire Zelkiv as new Minister of Diplomacy," the Ulor Hurna XI concluded. Pire Zelkiv beamed and bowed. The courtiers applauded. A battery of curious eyes turned upon the Ulor's youngest brother Varis, whose face, as usual, revealed nothing at all.

Tactless. Remarkably tactless of the Ulor. Minister of Diplomacy was a position traditionally held by members of the ruling House of Haudrensq alone. Selection of the aristocratic but nonroyal Zelkiv outraged custom, and presumably outraged the Ulor's sibling Varis as well. Young Varis, after all, had spent years mastering assorted civilized and not-so-civilized foreign tongues in anticipation of future diplomatic responsibility. He knew the history of every nation, and the literature of most. He had even troubled to familiarize himself with the intricacies of countless alien customs, habits, rituals, and taboos, arcane oddities of every sort. And now all that great spate of solitary study stood revealed as so much wasted effort, for Varis had been passed over once again—and in brutally public fashion, at that.

Yes, Hurna XI had displayed a total want of family
feeling, not to mention respect and esteem. And yet, all
things considered, who could truly blame the Ulor? For it
wouldn't do to forget that the Minister of Diplomacy occupied a highly visible position; as royal counselor, as con-
duit of influence and information, as ultimate authority
upon all matters pertaining to the accommodation of visiting dignitaries and their entourages, their servants, concu-
bines, monkeys, and lapdogs. At times, in a sense, the
Minister actually served as his master's personal representative. This so, the Ulor's decision was understandable,
almost inevitable.

The contrast between the two candidates verged upon
the ludicrous. Given such a choice of potential proxies,
who in his right mind would not have preferred Zelkiv?
The Noble Landholder, after all, was a splendid specimen
—tall and broad, magnificently garbed, with an air of easy
confidence, and a full set of blindingly white teeth—altogether fit representative of a monarch, and not unlike the
Ulor Hurna himself. Whereas Varis—

Varis was another matter altogether. Hard to believe
he was the Ulor's own brother, the two were so dissimilar.
Almost the younger man might have been taken for some
sickly changeling, but for his Haudrensq family characteristics of height, sharp-peaked hairline, and large eyes of
hazel—a distinctive shade of brown-speckled green, lightening to the yellow that ringed each pupil—the famous
"Haudrensq Corona." Proof of royal lineage notwithstanding, those eyes were Varis's downfall. Abnormally acute
and morbidly sensitive, blind in the glare of afternoon
sunlight, burning and watering by day even within doors,
they condemned their owner to perpetual shadow, barring
him from the Ice Kings teams, from the sleigh races, from
the White Bombardment matches, from all the standard
communal athletics that might have made a normal, comprehensible Rhazaullean out of him. He had lived his life
in twilight or worse, and it showed—showed in the flour-

paste pallor of hollow-cheeked face, in the weedy etiola-
tion of long and spindle-shanked frame, in the lankness
of lustreless black hair, the tired pessimism of hunch-
shouldered stance—showed drearily in everything. Ill
health and general puniness might have been offset by
conviviality of manner, but this advantage was likewise
denied the Ulor's youngest sibling, whose bookish isolation fostered a peculiar, somehow otherworldly remoteness.

Never any telling what went on in that odd if undeniably clever dark head. The present instance was a perfect
case in point. If Varis experienced any normal sense of
outraged justice—resentment—disappointment—humiliation—no sign of it showed upon his gray-white mask of a
face. There he stood, stoop-shouldered and somehow con-
spicuously self-effacing in his plain garments of gray,
doubtless feeling the pressure of multiple covert stares,
but composed and expressionless as always. Well, perhaps
not altogether expressionless. Unfolding the dark-tinted
spectacles that ordinarily shielded his eyes against light,
he slid them on, and the defensiveness of the gesture was
more telling than he could have known. Before the spectacles settled into place, the Haudrensq hazel eyes jumped
briefly to the exit, as if their owner contemplated flight
from the Ulor's audience chamber; but this was impossible. Rigid courtly etiquette demanded the presence of the
Ulor's brother; demanded it throughout the stupefying sequence of oaths and affirmations that accompanied the
new appointment, throughout the ritual succession of congratulations to the new Minister of Diplomacy, the renewed vows of loyalty to the Ulor, the paeans in praise of
Rhazaulle the Motherland, the requisite patriotic excesses
and ecstasies, all designed to uphold the questionable authority of a dynasty intriguing and murdering its way to
power, in the not-so-distant past.

Whatever his internal state, Varis played his part well.
He whisper-chanted, dipped, heart-clutched, and cheered

along with the best of them. When the time came to render the traditional Handclasp of Solidarity to the new Minister, he didn't hesitate an instant, and his grip, if neither warm nor fervent, was adequately firm. Pire Zelkiv responded with a too-hearty grasp and a practiced flash of awesome teeth. The congratulatory rites continued, and a line of fur-trimmed courtiers inched forward, nudging Varis on as far as the dais surmounted by the ivory Wolf Throne. The Ulor's youngest brother performed the obligatory obeisances. Hurna XI leaned forward in his great carved chair to lay a hand briefly upon his sibling's shoulder.

"Needed a more experienced man, youngster," the Ulor murmured, presumably by way of explanation. Perhaps there was even a touch of apology there; or else pity.

Varis glanced up quickly, then lowered his eyes, as if unable to sustain the dazzle of the other's natural golden radiance. He might have remarked upon the Noble Landholder Zelkiv's utter lack of practical diplomatic experience. He might have pointed out that he himself was now twenty-two years old, and thus no "youngster" by any standards. He did neither. Dutifully inclining his head, he rose and backed in silence from the Wolf Throne.

Bows. Genuflections. Oaths and vows, mumbles and ringing declamations, multiple repetitions. The rites lumbered on interminably. Droning voices, stylized marionette gestures. Dark richness of velvet robes, banded in sea-sable, snow-cat, marten, black fox. Old-fashioned voluminous caftans bulking alongside modern silver-laced coats and knee breeches. Bewildering dance of light upon gold, jewels, paillettes, metallic embroideries. Flash of light glancing off polished marble, gold leaf, rock crystal. Stab of merciless light from the great pier glasses. Voices, bodies, and light, light everywhere. Behind the dark glasses, Varis's eyes began to sting and water; an involuntary response to strong illumination that no effort of will could control, yet certain to be misinterpreted by all observers. For a moment or two, the impenetrable lenses would conceal his weakness, and then the tears would stream down his cheeks, and the familiar snickery whispering would start up. All avoidable, of course, could he but manage to exit quietly, to reach the sanctuary of his own blessedly dim and solitary apartment, with its book-lined walls and its windows velvet-shielded against the light; to get out *now*—

Not so easily accomplished. The ceremonies were not nearly done. His own early departure might be viewed as an insult to the new Minister of Diplomacy, and thus an implied criticism of the Ulor's judgment. Hurna XI's easy manner masked an iron authoritarianism. Opponents deceived by the surface geniality were wont to recognize their fatal error atop the Public Funnel. Still, the need was pressing, and the perpetually twilit apartment beckoned.

Varis's unobtrusive drift toward the exit was arrested by the pressure of a hand upon his shoulder, the second such pressure within minutes. Suppressing a start, he turned to confront a slightly dilute version of Hurna XI. The middle brother—Breziot, Duke of Otreska—shared the Ulor's regular chiseled features, his tawny coloration, and his effortless assurance. Breziot, however, lacked something of his older brother's height, breadth, and muscularity. In place of the Ulor's powerful raw vitality, Breziot possessed surface polish; in place of the older's impetuosity, a studied nonchalance; in place of Hurna's broad joviality, a somewhat waspish wit. Self-appointed arbiter of elegance, builder of palaces, and patron of dramatists, this second royal son aspired to a level of civilized refinement sometimes thought alien to the national character. Beyond doubt, it was alien to Breziot himself. The layer of self-conscious sophistication thinly masked an essential crudeness verging on barbarism. The facade was shiny and weak as shellac; from time to time it cracked. And then true nature found outlet, and Breziot ran wild, seeking relief from the tyranny of the tasteful in the grossest of diversions. These irregular fits were apt to coincide with bouts of heavy drinking—strong spirits, in place of his usual exquisite wine—and a powerfully alcoholic reek now surrounded the Duke.

"Infamous," observed Breziot. He spoke in a discreetly low tone, with his customary precision. Only a slight exaggeration of emphasis suggested the influence of alcohol. "You have been shamefully used, youngster."

Varis shrugged minimally. His face was still. He neither shook off the other's unwelcome hand, nor objected aloud to the patronizing term "youngster" employed by this brother some twelve years his senior.

"It is an insult, a disgrace," Breziot insisted, exhaling inflammable pollution. "Hurna has blundered."

"He thought it for the best, no doubt." Varis's voice, flat and monotone, was as unrevealing as his face.

"He thought—pah! He has blundered. Zelkiv is a fool. You at least are not that—whatever else may be said, no one can call you a fool. Hurna will soon perceive his error."

"If so, he is unlikely to declare it."

"You could hardly expect so much. He is Ulor, after all. Shall he compromise his own dignity?"

"Far better to sacrifice mine, in public." Varis's face remained expressionless, but his weak sore eyes watered uncontrollably, and now the tears slid down his ashen cheeks.

"Just so. That is only the way of the world, youngster. Unjust, but unchangeable. Well, our brother will come to regret his choice. Let that thought console you."

"That is comforting beyond expression. The pure fruits of moral victory are always sweetest, if rather less than filling."

"Well said. And that being so, you've nothing to cry about." Breziot finally withdrew his hand. "Do control yourself, youngster. Where is your dignity? You are carrying on like a girl, before all the Court."

The slightest tinge of color darkened Varis's corpselike complexion. "The light in here is too strong for my eyes," he said.

"Ah, the eyes again? Still harping on that old complaint? Very well, if you insist. But you can hardly permit yourself to be seen in this condition; you'll disgrace us all. You had best retire at once, before you're noticed. Come, I'll go with you."

"No need. The new Minister's ceremony—"

"Is tiresome, tasteless, and worst of all, tepid. I've had all I can stomach. Hurna will excuse my departure, when he learns the reason. In fact, as I'm sparing him an embarrassment, he'll thank me. What could be more convenient? Come along, youngster. And do try to get a grip on yourself."

Varis said nothing. No use in pointing out the purely physical nature of his ailment—Breziot never had and never would believe it. Moreover, the watering of his eyes had set his nose to running, and his voice, should he attempt to use it, would emerge a ridiculous nasal croak. This he knew from dismal experience. His vision swam and blurred. The faces and figures about him smudged beyond recognition. Suddenly they were anonymous, identical, save for a few anomalously short ones. Dwarves? Here? He blinked, restoring momentary clarity. Children. Of course. There was the widowed Ulor's three-year-old son and heir, holding the hand of his nurse. And there were Breziot's son and daughter, standing beside their handsome mother. The son—offhand, he couldn't recall the boy's name—was watching the ceremonies, or pretending to. The girl—a couple of years her brother's junior, all hazel eyes and black hair—was studying her Uncle Varis in frank curiosity. She was old enough to have learned better manners, but somehow her scrutiny wasn't offensive. The child (What was her name? Something with at least three syllables) had an intelligent look; inquisitive but distinctly sympathetic. Uncommon. Breziot's wife

looked down, caught her daughter staring, and frowned a
reproof. The little girl's eyes dropped. The scene swam out
of focus. Passively Varis suffered his brother to steer him
from the Audience Chamber. A small localized buzz of
speculation accompanied their exit.

They stepped out into a gallery devoid of contemporary gold and crystal bedizenments. Reflecting the original, old-style architecture of the palace, (or, as it was more
properly known, the House Uloric) the long passage was
low-ceilinged, massively wooden-arched, windowless, and,
for those possessed of normal vision, inadequately illuminated. Varis paused and sighed almost inaudibly. Drawing
forth a handkerchief—an accessory regarded as laughably
effete, but for him, a necessity—he wiped his streaming
eyes, mopped his brow, blew his nose, and settled his dark
glasses back into place. For a moment he stood blinking.
When the pain in his eyes subsided, he set off down the
gallery at a quick pace, heading for the refuge of his own
apartment, his solitude, his friendly books.

Breziot, however, was unready to part. He could
hardly have failed to note his brother's distaste, yet some
drunken spirit of perverse mischief seemed to impel him
to cling. Falling into step beside Varis, he suggested,
"Slow down, youngster. Now is not a time to go crawling
back into your burrow. You will be taken for a glum her-
mit—sullen, mopey, and odd to boot."

Varis's shrug conveyed indifference.

"Come, are you resolved to disgrace us all? It won't
do, youngster. Remember, you are Haudrensq."

The ghost of a bitter smile touched Varis's colorless
lips; the sole indication that he had heard.

"Bad form, youngster. Execrable, in fact. You need
something to stiffen your spine, something to heat that
sluggish blood of yours. Fortunately, I've the wherewithal." Breziot reached into the pocket of his superla-
tively tailored brocade coat to bring forth a hip flask.
Drawing the stopper, he took a patently unnecessary swig,

then extended the vessel to his brother. The anise-pine tang of double-distilled vouvrak wafted from the flask.

Varis shook his head without slackening his pace. He never touched spirits.

"But how dull you are, youngster. How fearful and staid. You are like an ailing old woman. Come, I say you must sample the vouvrak—it is sure to lift your spirits." Breziot's insistent hand descended once more upon his brother's shoulder, and Varis halted reluctantly. "You shall not budge until you drink. I insist. Come, it will do you some good, if anything can. I tell you, I insist."

Varis's shoulders sketched another minute shrug. Argument seemed bothersome. Breziot, capable in his cups of infinite obstinacy, wouldn't desist until he got his own way. Best to drink and get it over with.

"Very well." Accepting the flask, he took a half-unwilling swallow and immediately regretted it, for the liquid filled his mouth with fire, burned its way down his throat, and set his stomach to smoldering. His eyes predictably watered, and for a moment his breath stopped. Discomfort was brief, however. The internal fires swiftly abated, leaving him suffused with a pleasurable tingling warmth, and temporarily fortified against the worst drafts of the chilly old palace.

"There, that is better, is it not? I'll swear our Rhazaullean vouvrak is the stuff of magic—it's actually put a trace of color in your face, and I didn't think anything could do that."

Varis came close to smiling. His brother's patronage, usually so annoying, somehow failed to irritate him now. Perhaps it was the unfamiliar warmth flooding his veins, perhaps the equally unfamiliar sense of relaxation soothing his brain, but somehow his mood had improved.

"Have some more," Breziot urged. "Drink up, youngster."

Varis complied, intending only another swallow or two, all that he could safely consume. But the warmth and the relief of inner tension were so agreeable that he drained two-thirds of the flask before handing it back to its owner. He found himself a little unsteady on his feet, but the sensation was not unpleasant. Later on, within hours, he would doubtless suffer a headache of blinding intensity, bouts of nausea, copious eye watering—his body's invariable response to alcohol; but for now, he didn't care.

"There, that is what you need. Have some more, youngster."

Varis noted that Breziot's expression combined affability and a certain sly amusement. He recalled then his brother's lifelong penchant for practical jokes, to which he himself had repeatedly fallen victim. There had been, for example, that long-ago game of Sightless, wherein the seventeen-year-old Breziot had led the blindfolded five-year-old Varis up to the highest parapet of the palace, and there abandoned him in the full glare of afternoon sunshine, leaving the panicky light-dazzled child to find his own way down. There had been the episode with the purgative-laced jam tarts. There had been the staged haunting of the younger brother's bedchamber. There had been—but there was no point in recalling all such incidents. They were too numerous, and they had continued until such time as Varis had learned, years earlier, to allow his middle brother wide berth. Breziot had matured since then; but under all the acquired elegance, his nature remained unchanged.

"No more." Varis resumed his interrupted progress, on legs that wobbled slightly.

"Don't lurch off like that, youngster. You have received a setback, but you mustn't give way to gloom. I am resolved to cheer you, at any cost. I will provide diversion to chase the troubles from your mind."

"Diversion?"

"There's a revel at Stratkha's, presently entering its fourth night. I will carry you there in my sleigh."

The marathon routs of the Rhazaullean great, designed to counteract the ritual-ridden stultification of the imperial court, were infamous throughout the world. Extravagant, immoderate, frenetic, and excessive, they generally continued for days or even weeks on end—continued, in fact, for as long as the strength of the revelers and the resources of the host held out. Occasionally, an entire family fortune was squandered upon a single gargantuan binge; the overly generous host thereafter sinking into genteel poverty. Thus, the revel at the mansion of the Noble Landholder Stratkha, whose wallet was reputedly bottomless, upon this fourth night remained in an early phase of its development.

But the prospect of lights, din, overheated rooms, unbridled gluttony, suicidal consumption of vouvrak, and an almost dogged devotion to debauchery held little appeal. Varis shook his head.

"But Stratkha has promised a bear baiting," Breziot urged, as if he imagined the prospect alluring. "Lareevo's troupe of children will be there to stage their erotic tableaux. Something extra in Lareevo's pocket, and the little villains will stage a good deal more. . . . And listen, this should tempt even you—I have it on good authority that Stratkha has dug up a sorcerer somewhere. There's going to be magic."

"Stratkha cannot count even upon Hurna's favor to ward off the storm, should the Venerators catch wind of that," Varis observed, interest finally snagged.

For reasons of health and public safety, magic was proscribed in Rhazaulle. Practicing necromancers were, after all, notoriously prone to violent episodes; and the Spifflicates were worse yet. Even so, the nobility—acknowledging no law other than tradition and the will of the Ulor —might openly have defied the ban, but for the power of the Venerators, whose near-religious zeal in defense of the dead's sacred dignity fired rabid opposition to necromancy. The Venerators, with their exaggerated deference

of the deceased, their elaborate rituals of respect and propitiation, commanded a considerable idiotic following.
More than once, their pious fulminations had been known
to set off public riots; and their enemies—the necromancers, the grave robbers, the flippant, and the profane—
were wont to suffer colorful misfortune. Even the Ulor
respected the force of pure fanaticism; and Rhazaullean
magic, while never quite suppressed, was generally practiced in secret.

"Oh, Stratkha does not concern himself—he relies
upon the discretion of his guests."

"And of his servants, his hirelings, his entertainers as
well? Trusting nature, hasn't he?" Varis inquired.

"Pah, shall a Noble Landholder trouble his head over
trifles? Stratkha must amuse himself, come what may.
Now let us be off, youngster. Lareevo's delights await."

"Your Grace will enjoy them without me."

"How vexing. But I am not to be fobbed off so easily.
I have made it my mission to cheer you tonight, and
cheered you shall be, whether you like it or not. If
Stratkha's revel will not serve, there are alternatives. Ah, I
have it—I know where to take you. Perfect. Youngster,
come with me. No arguments, now. I am quite determined." Taking the other firmly by the arm, Breziot set
off down the gallery.

Varis allowed himself to be dragged. His brother,
while shorter than he, was far heavier, stronger, and
drunkenly resolved. Resistance would have been difficult;
and in any case, why resist? Who could say that whatever
form of mindless entertainment Breziot intended might
not prove unexpectedly agreeable? Perhaps the novelty
might do him some good, might even serve to pry his
thoughts from this evening's latest humiliation. It would
be a change, at least. His brother, it was true, still wore
that disquieting look of sly amusement; but the cold familiar voices of caution and judgment were temporarily

muted. Double-distilled vouvrak seemed to have opened new worlds of possibility.

They altered course once to collect warm garments; fur-lined woolen cloaks, fur-lined gloves, mufflers, and hats. While Breziot sported a characteristically stylish shako, the younger brother's hat was an eccentric affair, unfashionably broad-brimmed to shade its wearer's eyes against the light. The sun having set, such protection was now unnecessary, but Varis never altered his headgear.

A brisk hike through a warren of ill-lit, ill-ventilated corridors brought them to one of the back exits. The guards at the door made way, and the brothers stepped out onto the rear portico of the House Uloric. A blast of frigid air drove grit and fine snow straight into their faces. In temperate lands to the south, autumn still held sway; but here in Rhazaulle, the long winter had already begun. Neither brother so much as flinched beneath the bitter wind that would have set a southerner to shivering.

Scores of lamps illuminated the Zalkhash, or royal enclosure. Their light yellowed the packed snow underfoot, wavered upon the ice-glazed prominences of the living quarters, banqueting halls, council chambers, and chambers of state that edged the central courtyard; glinted upon fanciful twisted spires surmounting conical rooftops steep-pitched to shed snow; upon ornate window shutters, built to withstand arctic gales; upon stone carvings and decorative grotesques, gilded and colored to echo their wooden counterparts of yore. Before the House Uloric awaited Duke Breziot's newest sledge—pagoda-roofed, stained glass-windowed, enamelled in gleaming crimson, curlicued in gold, and drawn by four perfectly matched white horses—an extravagance extraordinary even by the standards of his Grace's notoriously luxurious tastes. Breziot glanced at his brother, in search of a suitably awed or incredulous reaction. Varis's pallid lips were set in a faintly amused curve. He said nothing.

A few yards from the sledge, the Duke's driver

hunched over one of the glowing braziers that served as lifesavers for servants condemned to wait upon their masters' pleasure in blood-chilling temperatures. Breziot clapped his hands once, and the driver abandoned the fire to resume his post. Sotto voce instructions were issued, and the brothers entered. Snap of a whip, jingling of harness bells, and they were off; horses's breath pluming on the frigid air, sword-edged runners sliding frictionlessly over the packed snow. Beneath the little pagoda roof, the atmosphere was almost tropical, for the sledge was equipped with every modern convenience: perforated metal hampers filled with radiant coals, fur-wrapped heated bricks to serve as hand- and foot-warmers, even little glass vials of perfume to scent the air. Breziot settled back in his seat with a gusty sigh of contentment.

Within moments they passed through the vast main gate in the wall that surrounded the Zalkhash, emerging into the icy streets of the Ulor's capital city of Rialsq. Down a broad avenue lined with cone-roofed mansions sped the sledge. Winter was young, and the way was still entirely clear. Not for another several weeks at least would pedestrians resort to the fetid enclosed walkways affording passage even in the worst of blizzards. At the bottom of the street they came upon a great turreted townhouse so brilliantly illuminated that Varis's eyes stung and swam at the sight of it. Its windows were wide open, despite the weather. Through the windows, frenzied bacchanalian activity was discernible.

"Stratkha's," Breziot explained unnecessarily, and added with a touch of longing, "You're certain you wouldn't care to—?"

Varis shook his head.

"Pah, you are still prim and stiff. Here, let this thaw you." Breziot proffered his flask. The younger brother, preoccupied with his disordered vision, accepted absently, drank almost unconsciously.

The sledge hurried on, beyond the region of opulent

townhouses, through the more modest neighborhoods of the solid craftsmen and shopkeepers, and on into the malodorous realm of the poor. But even here, in the midst of filth and squalor, where the frozen ordure mounded in the gutters, and the perfume vials served so useful a function, the old tenements were stoutly constructed: the walls thick and well caulked, the window shutters solid, all chinks stuffed with rags, with mud, or straw, or moss, or anything capable of excluding the cold.

On glided the sledge, and by this time Varis might have been wondering about the destination, save for the curious lassitude slowing mind and body, damping curiosity; beyond doubt the effect of the vouvrak, but not an altogether unwelcome respite.

On they went, and now the city buildings were thinning around them. On past the dank quasi-crypt of a prison known as the Rialsq House of Correction. On past the Public Funnel, adjacent to the Correction, where condemned malefactors were publicly bled to death. On past Nightfields, last resting place of criminals, lunatics, Spifflicates and necromancers, suicides, debtors, anonymous mendicants. On past the White Level, site of the annually constructed House of Ice, whose frozen foundations were already laid, and whose transparent walls were already rising. Past the White Level, nearing the edge of the city, and now there could only be one destination.

Varis turned to face his brother. "You are bringing us to the Wrecks," he said.

"Ah, you have found me out, youngster." Breziot guffawed, spraying vouvrak-sharpened spit.

"Then tell the driver to turn this gilded behemoth of yours around."

"I'll do nothing so tiresome. Come, where is your sense of adventure?"

"I've no interest in ogling Spifflicates."

"Oh, I daresay you imagine such pleasures quite beneath you, youngster. Not nearly up to your intellectual standards. But how do you know if you've never tried them, eh?" The sly amusement gleamed again in Breziot's eyes. "I'm told that Neemoff has something special on for tonight. You may as well resign yourself—you are quite my prisoner, you know."

There was some truth to that. The pagoda-roofed sledge barreled on unstoppably. Varis sat speechless and rigid in the too-soft seat. Presently the vehicle slowed to a halt before an ancient, gray stone fortress of a building—Rialsq's Public Hospital of Mercy, commonly known as "the Wrecks." Every major city had its Public Hospital of Mercy, originally designed to confine the obtrusively insane, but in latter years given over almost entirely to the housing of Rhazaulle's growing population of Spifflicates. The various Public Hospitals were more or less alike in the corruption of their administrators, the cruelty of their warders, and the misery of their inmates. Some were worse than others, however; and Rialsq's Wrecks was oldest, ghastliest, and most notorious of them all.

Before the Wrecks paraded and postured a gang of Venerators, equipped with the usual paraphernalia; the tall wax tapers, the scrolls, potions, amulets, sacred diadems, and all the rest of the gewgaws they were wont to employ in their elaborate ceremonies of penance and propitiation. Such a ceremony was now in progress. Some long-haired, wild-eyed zealot, garments concealed beneath a loose white robe resembling a glorified bedsheet, was flourishing a wand and droning out ritual questions; to which his equally outlandish followers, supposedly speaking on behalf of the dead, wailed and moaned their ritual responses. This in itself was not unusual. The Wrecks, with its large population of the spifflicated, mind-blasted former necromancers, remained a constant focus of Venerator attention. For necromancy, an affront to the dignity of the dead, an offense against the human spirit itself, was the most abominable of crimes, far worse than murder. The fanatics always clustered about the hospital, chanting their litanies, yelping their slogans, demanding the extermination of the Spifflicates immured within. They were always there complaining, but tonight seemed particularly noisy and numerous, as if they, like the Duke, had heard that something uncommon was afoot.

"Absurd, are they not?" Breziot's lips curled contemptuously.

Varis did not reply. He sat motionless, staring frozen-faced through the stained-glass window.

"I said, do you not think they are—" Breziot glanced at his brother and broke off, surprised. "But what's the matter with you? You're looking even greener than usual. Are you sick? What are you goggling at—those Venerators? You are not afraid of those capering imbeciles, are you? Gad, I believe you are. I verily believe that you *are!*" The Duke roared with laughter.

"No. But I dislike them."

"Then perhaps it is the Spifflicates you fear? Is that it? I seem to recall—"

"No."

"What a joke! Well, if you are not afraid, then you must prove it, little brother. Come along. And *enjoy yourself!*" He laid hold of the other's arm.

Varis was plucked forth from the sledge and propelled resistlessly through the chanting, grimacing ranks of the Venerators, up a short flight of stone steps and into the Wrecks.

Massive double doors groaned shut behind them, and the voices of the Venerators faded away. They stood in a dim, grim antechamber, not differing noticeably in temperature from the outdoor air. Hurrying forward to greet them was a heavy-jowled, thickset man of middle years, with grizzled hair and mustache of military cut; very spruce, with every brass button upon his coat gleaming— Dr. Neemoff, Governor-General of Rialsq's Public Hospital. "Doctor" by courtesy alone, for the Governor-General was in fact a former officer cashiered for brutality; given the standards of the Imperial Army, an almost unheard-of occurrence, but one confirming Neemoff's qualifications for his current position.

The Governor-General bowed civilly enough, but without subservience; very much like a provincial Noble Landholder upon his own soil, within whose bounds his whim was law. "You are here for the conclave," he stated.

"Ah, so it's definitely on, then," Breziot replied. "To-night?"

"Beyond doubt."

"How are you so certain?"

"I know my business, and I know my creatures."

"Admirable, but——"

"They've been restless for days—snappish, off their feed, hard to handle. It's been building all month, and tonight it comes to a head. Be certain of this," Neemoff crisped.

"Excellent. Explain to my little brother, then. He is all innocence and ignorance."

"Not quite all. I read," Varis observed dryly, apparent nonchalance belied by a rigid tension of stance. "Tonight is the dark of the moon. Granted a favorable configuration of stars, it's upon such nights that necromancers gather to work in concert. I'd hazard a guess that here in this place your Spifflicates do likewise, or at least attempt as much."

"More than attempt," Dr. Neemoff pronounced. "They haven't forgotten all their old tricks."

"Even yet?" Varis was, impossibly, paler than ever.

"Even yet. That's what's got the Venerators out there worked to a lather. They know that tonight my creatures may actually manage to drag some bedraggled protesting old shade up out of the grave."

"And then?"

"And then invention fails, and the Spifflicates sit around dithering in a frenzy, while the ghost flitters, and the Vens squawk outside. It's a sight."

"Then show us, by all means, my dear fellow," Breziot suggested. "Entertain us."

Neemoff looked at him, and the Duke produced coins.

"Right. Two for the standard tour and an extra fifty brazzles apiece for the conclave. A bargain at the price. And now before we go in, here are the rules. One—you stay close behind me at all times. Don't go wandering off on your own. Two—you touch nothing and nobody. Three —you don't talk directly to my Spifflicates, no matter what they may say to you. Four—you don't give or take anything to or from anybody. That includes food, money, notes and messages, keepsakes and gimcracks, or anything else you can name. Five—never stick your hand through the bars, or you're liable to lose it. That's it. Not much to remember, but the first time anybody steps out of line, I pull him straight out of my wards. Understood?"

"Oh, quite. Absolutely, my dear Governor-General." The Duke of Otreska had apparently chosen to grant Dr. Neemoff the license of a court jester.

"Armed, either of you?"

"No."

"Good. You carry a weapon, one of them will find a way of lifting it off you."

A muted snort of amusement escaped the Duke.

"Gentlemen, follow me. Be on your guard, and don't forget the rules." Dr. Neemoff made for an iron-strapped oaken door at the far side of the antechamber.

Varis advanced on stiff-jointed legs. He was shaky, and it was more than the effect of the vouvrak. He had spoken truly in disclaiming fear of the Venerators. But the broken beings on the other side of the door affected him strangely, inspiring a cold horror not devoid of attraction. In childhood, the spectacle of a trainer with a troupe of performing Spifflicates had once sent him fleeing for the safety of the royal nursery, to the loud amusement of his two brothers. They had teased him about it for years. Later, he had learned to camouflage such weakness, but it had never truly left him, and the old dread was strong upon him now. A curious dull roaring filled his ears. Imaginary, he assumed; but the noise intensified as he advanced, and he knew then that it was real, and that it came from the other side of the door. Resisting the urge to twist his arm free of Breziot's grip, he followed the Governor-General on through.

Instantly the clamor swelled. An infernal chorus of groans, shrieks, sobs, and joyless laughter shuddered the foul icy air. Varis's eyes traveled. He stood in a vast, murky chamber. The feeble light of the twin lanterns burning overhead barely illuminated weepy walls and a high-vaulted ceiling of gray-black stone. Verminous straw carpeted the stone flags underfoot. Upon the straw reclined or squatted or crouched a scattering of the Governor-General's favored clients; favored in the sense that their restraints were limited to manacles and anklets of moderate weight, affording a certain freedom of movement—not that many availed themselves of the privilege. Most sat inert, slack of jaw and vacant of eye, with only the occasional jerk of a limb to betray the presence of life. Others lay motionless in their own filth as if tranced or already dead. So profound their stupor that the countless fleas feasted upon their bodies undisturbed, and the flies that lighted upon their eyelids rested unshaken by so much as a blink.

By no means were all of the inmates similarly inactive. Some were engaged in quiet, harmless pursuits; weaving straw, shredding rags, picking lice, pitching pebbles, sculpting feces, massaging genitalia. Others, less tranquil, bellowed and wept, jittered and shook in strange fevers; and these sported heavier fetters, short-linked and iron-weighted. Several wore rust-reddened iron collars, linked to staples sunk in the floor. Some were ankle-anchored to iron cannonballs, about which they orbited in perpetual tight circles. A few such satellites, entangling themselves within their own bonds, lay wrapped in chain like flies in a spider's larder.

Such were the comparatively fortunate. Others were unluckier. Several, presumably singled out for disciplinary action, hung vertically spread-eagled upon huge granite pillars. A few raged, struggled, spewed bloody froth; most sagged limp, naked starveling bodies suggestively crisscrossed with cuts and welts. But even these were not the wretchedest.

The two long walls of the great rectangular ward were lined with steel-barred compartments, too low to stand upright in, too short to lie full length in, equipped with rusty-hinged doors opening only to permit removal of corpses or installment of new tenants. Empty of furnishings—devoid even of straw and slop bucket—these cages and their fetter-freighted occupants were fully exposed to public view. Here, all but lost in perpetual shadow, existed the most fearsome and pitiable of those human wrecks whose experiments in necromancy had brought them to the crashing mental collapse commonly termed "spifflication."

Much of this scene Varis absorbed in his first glance. His stomach lurched, and he drew a deep breath that was almost a gasp.

In the face of such misery, even Breziot could not remain unmoved.

"Faugh," spat the Duke, and lifted a pomander to his nose.

Their entrance roused considerable inmate interest. Apparent corpses returned to life, suddenly wide-open eyes glinted, hitherto silent throats erupted. Formerly somnolent figures leapt and bounded, clanking their chains. Unruffled, Dr. Neemoff turned and plucked a coiled whip from its peg beside the door. Loosing the coils, he snapped the lash sharply, and the chained scarecrows dropped to their knees. A second crack of the whip, and a charged hush fell over the chamber.

"Gentlemen, here are the Spifflicates." For this one moment, the Governor-General did not need to raise his voice to make himself heard. "You see the state to which their dabbling in forbidden arts has reduced them. You see the price they have paid for their brief term of magical power. I leave it to you to judge the worth of their bargain." He spoke his lines smoothly, pauses and emphases practiced but lifeless. Clearly, he had delivered this speech hundreds of times.

After that, the horrors accumulated. Neemoff led his customers through the ward at a leisurely pace, halting here and there at exhibits of particular interest, allowing the visitors time to gawk their fill, too much time. Despite an overpowering revulsion, Varis found he couldn't look away. Impossible not to stare at the elderly man clinging upside-down to the bars of his cage, long white hair sweeping the filthy floor. Impossible to disregard the addled wretch methodically cracking his skull against the walls. Impossible to ignore the screamers, the gabblers, the flesh-pluckers, the crazed acrobats, the whisperers.

"Stay. Stay here."

"With us."

"You belong."

"Brother."

"Welcome home."

Repressing a shudder, Varis threw a quick glance at his companions. They seemed not to have heard. Breziot was blithe, Neemoff indifferent. Enviably impervious, they strolled through the ranks of the damned.

The trio completed a slow circuit of the huge room, and it seemed that the endless tour was drawing to its close. But then Neemoff led them through another door, and now they were in the ward of the female Spifflicates— less than the men's ward in dimension and population, but every bit as noisy and malodorous—with shrill, jungle-screeching voices knifing a rank, jungle-humid atmosphere. Here, the sights and sounds of the previous chamber were repeated; but the bodies that shuffled and cavorted were female, a novelty affording much diversion to his Grace, who often paused to inspect and appraise.

The entrance of two male strangers inspired a number of distaff inmates to strip themselves bare of their rags. Filthy tatters sailed through the air to pelt the Ulor's brothers. A cooing uproar arose—lip smackings, singsong obscenities and endearments, half-mocking solicitation—punctuated with high-pitched, yelping laughter. Naked women wiggled and jiggled, flexed and posed, extended dirty arms in a parody of invitation; a sight to inspire his Grace's uproarious mirth. While his brother stood grinning and blowing juicy burlesque kisses to the most repulsive of the surrounding harpies, Varis contemplated flight. A quick break for the exit, and he could be free of this place, out of doors under the stars, where the fresh, icy breezes would clear his clouded vision and his vouvrak-muddled head. Before he had taken a single step, however, the Governor-General's lash snapped, a path through the ranks of the women opened, and the trek resumed.

Ugliness upon ugliness. And then the surprise discovery, behind a high straw mound, of a naked couple vigorously copulating. Somehow, one of the male Spifflicates had managed to smuggle himself into the women's quarters. A warder came running to wrench the erring pair apart. The woman whined and scuttled away on all fours; her paramour was permitted no such escape. The warder plied his truncheon fast and hard, until the culprit's howls subsided to gurgling moans. Even then the thrashing continued, eventually piquing Breziot's curiosity.

"Gad, what a pother," murmured his Grace. "Why not simply let them have their fun?"

"Ignorance. My creatures breed true," Neemoff informed him. "One of the females whelps, and the offspring's born spifflicated. Always. Let 'em multiply, and soon we'll find ourselves overrun. Then it will take a full-scale pogrom to clean up the mess. Gelding and spaying's

the answer, of course, but for now the law won't allow it.
The sooner that changes, the better."

Breziot nodded thoughtfully. Varis found himself
drenched in cold sweat and increasingly queasy. Incipient
migraine was beginning to squeeze his brain. The vouvrak
had all but run him to the ground.

The warder carted his victim off toward the men's
quarters, while the Governor-General led his visitors
through a third door to the final rarest and finest exhibit.

They entered a reeking ward much smaller than the
preceding two, but otherwise similar in design, with the
same dank walls, vaulted ceiling, and double row of steel-
barred cages. The atmosphere in this place was particularly foul, dense, and dark with the smoke arising from a
small fire that burned on the floor at the center of the
room.

"Phew—faugh—you allow them to play with fire?"
Breziot demanded.

"Ordinarily not. Around conclave time, though,
they're so hot, there's almost no controlling them,"
Neemoff told him. "We could chain 'em, maintain constant watch, all of that, and a few would still manage to
dash their own brains out against the walls. Temporary
indulgence makes better sense."

Some two dozen Spifflicates, both male and female,
were kneeling around the fire. All were naked, their rhythmically swaying bodies marked with scratches and bite
marks, scabs and splotches of dried blood. Their arms were
draped about one another's shoulders, linking a circle.
They were chanting or groaning something in unison. The
words, if any, were indistinguishable and probably meaningless, serving only to promote tranced group consciousness through endless unvarying repetition.

The visitors watched expectantly. The chanting and
swaying continued without pause. Heads lolled, eyes
rolled, saliva dribbled down slack chins. The minutes
passed. Nothing happened. Breziot waxed impatient.

"That's all?" his Grace demanded. "That's the entire show?"

"Quiet. Watch," Neemoff ordered.

"Your impudence amuses, fellow, but I advise you—"

The door behind them opened, and the Duke's complaint broke off. Into the room came trouping a raucous merry band led by a warder. Many of the newcomers were masked and fantastically costumed—as ghouls and goblins, wraiths and revenants, Snow-spirits and satyrs, these last accompanied by nymphs whose tawny litheness marked them as Turo dancing girls. Some of the men had lost or discarded their masks, and among these were recognizable several Noble Landholders of the Ulor's court. One such Landholder bore upon his shoulders a brace of tiny green-haired sprites, presumably members of Lareevo's juvenile company, for this was a delegation from Stratkha's mammoth revel.

Breziot greeted the revelers with delight. "—nearly perishing of boredom!" he cried.

"Come to Stratkha's, then!"

Mutual salutations were effusive, with embraces, hand-pumping, back-thumping, kisses from the nymphs. A few of the merrymakers greeted Varis, with some constraint, for nobody ever knew quite what to say to the popular Duke of Otreska's eccentric younger brother. The majority found it more comfortable to ignore him.

Devoirs completed, they crowded in close, jockeying hard for the good positions affording an unobstructed view of the spifflicatic conclave. Varis found himself jostled, shouldered, shoved, and squeezed. Somebody's elbow was digging into his ribs. One of Lareevo's well-schooled sprites was clinging to his leg, and not, he suspected, by accident. A kick and a couple of well-placed jabs would have freed him of encumbrance and encroachment alike, but somehow he couldn't work up the energy. His headache was worsening by the moment. Nausea churned his stomach, dizziness warped his vision. Before him, the Spifflicates moaned and swayed, their woozy oscillation sickening to behold. Varis pressed cold fingers to a clammy brow. There was something wrong with his breathing; he was suffocating. His ears were failing as well, or so he surmised, for the babble of conversation died away, and the spifflicatic voices swelled—moaning manic gibberish somehow resolving itself to something akin to an alien chorus; plaintive, insistent, hovering upon the verge of intelligibility. And when it seemed he could all but understand the words, the import of which loomed increasingly vital—when he sensed the imminence of a vast revelation—then the chant crescendoed, and the promised spectacle materialized at last.

The chorus splintered to shrieks, barks, random crazed yammerings. The circle broke and boiled, its members rending themselves and one another in indiscriminate frenzy. Teeth flashed, talons raked, cries of pain and ecstasy tore the air. Blood welled, spattered faces, coursed down jerking bodies, while the visitors whooped and shouted their approval. Presently the sorcerers rose to prance about the fire; a leaping, shambling straggle of grotesques, entertainingly ridiculous. Howls of mirth greeted their antics.

Unconscious of observation, the Spifflicates danced on. As they went, they shook their lacerated limbs, to rain droplets of blood upon the flames.

A cloud of lead-colored smoke arose—far more smoke than that minor sprinkling might ordinarily have accounted for. The vapor whirled and billowed, the Spifflicates shrilled and keened, the audience hooted and cheered. Then the volume of shouting rose, for there in the midst of the seething mists, a figure was taking shape —faint, indistinct, insubstantial; but unmistakably human, and unmistakably there.

A ghost. Dragged from deathly repose by necromantic art.

Success.

The Spifflicates went wild. Excitement, triumph, or mad exhilaration sent them spinning about the ward. Some leaped and kicked up their heels, others twirled and chattered frantic gabble. Several flung themselves to the floor, writhing and foaming in powerful convulsions. In the midst of it all, the captive shade floated and wavered, tugging this way and that against psychic restraint like a balloon on a string, wringing its transparent hands and grimacing miserably.

Once it had been a man. Identity was long gone, and circumstances of life forever lost, but one thing was certain. The ghost, whoever he had been, had died in a state of extreme mental disquiet; else would have fled the physical plane at the moment of death. Only unquiet spirits lingered on, inexplicably bound to the environs of their mortal remains. So much was common knowledge. Ordinarily, such ghosts slumbered. Sometimes, for reasons beyond human ken, they woke spontaneously. Far more often, forbidden magic restored unwelcome consciousness. Rhazaulle, with its ancient, if illicit, tradition of necromantic investigation, and its correspondingly accomplished practitioners, contained within its borders the world's highest concentration of wakeful spirits; of which the wretched creature hovering above the fire was a fairly typical example.

Most of the spectators found the performance vastly diverting. To Varis, it was anything but that. The bile rose in his throat, and moments later he bent double to vomit, the contents of his stomach spewing forth to smirch the green locks of Lareevo's clinging sprite. The infant relinquished its grip and retreated, cursing fluently. Varis dropped to his knees and thence to the floor, overcome with dizziness and humiliation. His collapse did not go unnoticed.

"Oh, gad." Breziot's familiar voice somehow cut through the din. "What a nuisance." A pause, and then, "Here, you—Neemoff. Give me a hand. My baby brother cannot lie there underfoot. Lareevo's little demons will pick him bare in seconds. We must put him somewhere out of the way."

"Empty cage," suggested the Governor-General.

His Grace assented. Varis felt hands upon him, and then he was lifted. The room tilted and rocked. Nausea, and a sour taste in his mouth, but nothing left in his stomach to lose. He closed his eyes. Brief, bumpy progress. Protest of rusty hinges as a door opened, and then Varis was brusquely set down. The shock of contact with a wet stone floor snapped his eyes open in time to see the steel-barred portal swinging shut. The lock caught with an audible snap. Alarmed, he tried to sit up, and failed.

"No fear, youngster. You will do well enough here, for now," Breziot promised gaily. And turned his attention again upon the Spifflicates.

Varis stretched forth a hand, fumbled with the door, which was securely locked, and allowed the hand to drop.

Thereafter, time lost meaning. A merciful fog blanketed his mind. Outside the cage, the uproar continued, but Varis scarcely heard it. Brain-crushing headache, nausea, feverish chills and sweats occupied his awareness. He did not notice when the distraught ghost finally made good its escape, nor did he notice when the Spifflicates, drained by their labors, began one by one to collapse in exhaustion. When next he opened his eyes, the ward was comparatively quiet. The conclave was over, its membership largely unconscious. The visitors were drifting exitwards, trailing laughter. Evidently, they had forgotten him.

Varis rattled the bars of his cage. No one noticed.

"Breziot," he said, syllables emerging faint and dull. Then, louder and sharper, to send the white pain lancing through his skull: "Breziot."

His Grace heard, and turned to look. "Awake, eh?" he inquired.

"Unlock this door."

"Oh, impossible." Breziot spread his hands helplessly. "No key."

"The Governor-General."

"Wandered off somewhere."

"The warders."

"Nowhere about."

"*Unlock it.*"

"Oh, I cannot do that—I am on my way to Stratkha's. They have implored so prettily, how was I to resist? You will not accompany me, and what are we to do with you? Best you remain where you are, for tonight." Breziot's regretful expression cracked. He burst out laughing.

Varis's eyes slid swiftly about the ward in search of assistance, of which there was none. He said nothing.

"Oh, the look upon your face, youngster! Too rich!"

No reply.

"Well, I shall leave you now," his Grace announced, perhaps a little disappointed by his victim's impassivity. "I wish you a good night's rest. No doubt you will find yourself much the better in the morning. Adieu for now, and sleep soundly, youngster. Rest well." His Grace exited, cackling.

Following the Duke's departure, Varis lifted his voice in repeated shouts for help, which went unheard or else ignored by all save a handful of inquisitive Spifflicates, who clustered about the cage, jabbering and clutching at the motionless occupant.

Finally he gave it up. His throat was raw, and his skull was crammed full of pain. His outcry ceased, and he sagged to the floor, compressing his spindly frame in accordance with the limitations of the cell. For a time he lay sunk in a horror-tinged apathy, observing his drooling observers, with whom he felt an instant's hideous oneness. An intolerable sensation. He willed himself to think of other things. His mind shuffled images, and his brother's face rose to the mental surface. Breziot's laughter rattled through his brain. There had been a moment—it had come during that laughter, Varis recalled—when he had experienced an urge that was unexpected, unfamiliar, and shocking in its intensity; the urge to kill. More than he ever wanted anything in his life, he had wanted to strangle Breziot. He had never realized that he possessed such impulses. The discovery was unsettling, but not uninteresting.

The Duke's image blended and merged with the spifflicated visages beyond the bars. The faces blurred, wheeled, spun out of existence; and vouvrak-flavored darkness swallowed all.

2

A WARDER FOUND him there in the early morning, and recognizing the error, unlocked the cage. The low barred door did not permit upright exit. Varis, still suffering alcoholic aftereffects, crawled forth on his hands and knees. The warder assisted him to his feet, led him back to the foyer, and out of the Wrecks.

The double doors closed behind him. He stood at the head of the short stairway, still littered with squatting Venerators. The fanatics had lost much of their earlier enthusiasm; perhaps their exertions had exhausted them, or else the bitter chill of night had sapped vitality. Now they huddled dully about the portable braziers set up on the stone treads. A few glanced up as the demolished-looking young man in the eccentric wide hat dragged on by. Two or three raised their voices in half-hearted, almost perfunctory exhortation. Most took no notice.

Varis descended. Before him stretched the empty snow-smoothed street, just touched with the gray light of dawn. The Zalkhash stood on the far side of the city, a distance of many miles, and there wasn't a public sleigh in sight. He began walking.

The cold was brutal, but as a Rhazaullean, he was used to that; in fact, hardly felt it. Of more immediate concern was the consistency of the snow underfoot—hard-packed, slick as oiled glass—the kind of surface with which the famed Rialsqui spiked boots were designed to deal. But he wore no such boots. The soles of his shoes were of smooth leather, and each step demanded attention. The distraction was welcome, blocking all thoughts of last night's debacle from his mind, for a time.

He walked on. Charcoal dawn matured to drab gray morning, and the city awoke about him. Lamplight glowed through the tiny view-slits in shuttered windows. The smoke of newly replenished fires curled from scores of chimneys. Shopkeepers, craftsmen, and artisans began to hang out their various emblems; the symbol of each trade fixed by Uloric ordinance, and therefore consistent throughout Rhazaulle. The matinal appearance of such emblems was often the sole indication that seemingly life-less establishments, boarded and shuttered against the winter winds for months on end, were in fact open for business.

Presently pedestrian and runnered vehicular traffic appeared upon the street. By the time he reached the White Level, the laborers were already there, at work upon the House of Ice. The architectural plan was always a close-guarded secret, but rumor had it that this year's House was a particularly ambitious undertaking—a mansion designed in frivolous Aennorvi style, graced with life-sized ice sculptures of characters from the Winter Wolf cycle of verse drama. Varis scarcely wasted a glance upon the rising structure. On he trudged, retracing last night's route, until he came to the Rialsq House of Correction, outside of which he managed to secure a shabby sleigh-for-hire; open, exposing the passenger to public view, and devoid even of such basic amenities as wind guards and lap rugs. This unappetizing vehicle carried him all the way back to the Zalkhash.

His arrival drew little notice and less curiosity. Few observed Varis cross the courtyard to enter the House Uloric. His progress along the corridors was deliberately inconspicuous, and he succeeded in reaching his own apartment without exchanging a single word with another human being. Once there, he dismissed his servants; and when he was quite alone, drew a deeply relieved breath.

Relief faded as last night's sights, sounds, and sensations came flooding back. Pire Zelkiv's appointment; the whispers of the courtiers; vouvrak and Venerators; stench and Spifflicates; revulsion and nausea; steel-barred door swinging shut in his face; Breziot's laughter. He had wanted to strangle Breziot. He still did. Last night's fury and disgust burned in his brain. He hated the Ulor's court, and everyone in it, he realized. Brothers, Noble Landholders, attendants, and hangers-on—he wanted none of them. He hated the entire city of Rialsq. Above all, he hated his own sickly, unsuccessful, infinitely ineffectual self.

Self-loathing was pointless and profitless, probably the lingering result of vouvrak poisoning. Sleep and solitude would doubtless improve his outlook. A few hours of rest, and this unaccustomed impulse to remove himself from court and capital would surely evaporate, along with the last of the alcohol polluting his bloodstream.

He washed and then had his rest, a long, unbroken span of dreamless peace. But when he awoke around noon, it was to discover the urge to flee still with him; if anything, stronger than before. He made his decision then, and once resolved, moved swiftly.

Preparations were few and simple. Recalling one of the servants, he ordered his personal sledge provisioned for travel and readied for immediate departure. He packed a single valise of clothing. He penned a letter announcing his withdrawal, and dispatched the missive to the Ulor. He forced himself to eat a light meal.

The efficient Zalkhash stablemen completed their

commission promptly. Varis, carrying his own valise, exited his apartment in the midafternoon. He had half-expected that the note to Hurna would draw inquiry, a demand for explanation, even a summons to the royal presence. But no word had come from the Ulor, who evidently viewed his youngest brother's parting with indifference, or else satisfaction. Varis passed from the House Uloric in silence and seeming invisibility.

In the courtyard awaited his sledge, a vehicle very unlike Breziot's pagoda-roofed extravaganza; simple and sleek in its lines, designed for speed, durability, and comfort. The sledge was coated with fifteen flawless layers of black enamel, waxed and polished to perfection—an uncharacteristic concession to vanity, but one that Varis never regretted, for that wicked anthracitic glow never failed to please his eye.

He issued instructions to the driver—his sole attendant, unwanted but indispensable, for Varis himself could not take the reins during the day. Even shielded by dark glasses, his eyes could not endure the glare of sunlight upon the great white expanses stretching between Rialsq and his destination. He entered the sledge. Inside, it was warm and beautifully dim, the walls swathed in gray brocade, the seats upholstered in black, the windows curtained and shuttered against the light. A few faint rays poking in through the peepholes provided all the illumination needed or wanted. Outside, the driver cracked his whip, the horses snorted, the harness jingled. The sledge moved off smoothly, without a creak or rattle.

There remained several hours of daylight—enough time to put a satisfying number of miles between himself and Rialsq. He would spend the night in some public hostelry; so might he expect to spend an indeterminate number of nights, anywhere from optimal half dozen to disastrous double dozen, depending upon conditions of travel. But conditions now, in early winter, were at their best. The roads overland were frozen, the mud turned to cement, but not yet buried in snow. Better yet, the River Xana was now hard-frozen and fit to bear individual sledges, if not armies, and that long, icy passage was smoother and finer than any highway ever cleared by the hand of man. He might expect to make excellent time.

He did so. At the northern edge of the Zalkhash, the Winter Gate opened upon the Xana Incline, gently graded to ease royal traffic down to the frozen river. A few sleighs plied the ice. Here and there rose wooden sheds and merchants' winterbooths; structures of necessity temporary in nature, yet often colorfully elaborate, with painted emblems and colored fretwork. Among the booths wandered an assortment of well-bundled pedestrians; not enough of them, however, to impede the progress of Varis's sledge. He was clear of the city within the hour.

Beyond Rialsq, the surrounding landscape seemed to flow by. Village, white-cloaked farmland, coniferous copse, and empty, snow-glittering waste alternated without variation and seemingly without end. But gradually, the terrain was losing its flatness, and much of its population. As he proceeded south, the white intervals between villages lengthened. Hummocks and hollows undulated the land. The hummocks swelled, sharpened, and presently the frozen Xana was passing through a shallow valley, quite uninhabited. The fourth night of travel Varis spent in a cone-shaped warmstop. One of the countless tiny public emergency shelters scattered across the length and breadth of Rhazaulle, the warmstop was bare of all save firepit and fuel. Accommodation was always free, but the one duty of any departing traveler was replenishment of the wood pile —an obligation regarded as sacred.

The journey resumed in the morning, and now there were no more villages, no more inns, few amenities of civilization. He had reached the desolate foothills of the Bruzhoi Mountains. Here, the Xana took an undesirable westerly curve. Abandoning the thoroughfare of ice, the sledge returned to the overland route and followed it up into the mountains.

The Bruzhois were steep and windswept, dark-clad in pine and fir. Here was neither village nor farm, but only the occasional hunter's lodge or trapper's hut, usually buried out of sight among the trees. The tortuous old road—the only trans-Bruzhoi route for hundreds of miles about—ascended at a taxing grade, dictating frequent halts to breathe the horses. Within weeks, the TransBruzh would become impassibly clogged with snow, remaining so until the vernal thaws. This annual blockage effectively cut the land of Rhazaulle in two. Circumvention of the mountains involved so arduous a journey that only the reckless or desperate dared undertake it. Commerce between the northern uplands surrounding Rialsq and the gentler southern lowlands all but ceased for months at a time. During these hiatuses, the ancient city of Lazimir became de facto southern capital, governed by its arrogant cluster of hereditary Highworthies.

Another night in another warmstop. Then off again at the break of a dawn so somber and clouded that Varis for once unshuttered a window without risk of ocular discomfort. He could not see much, however. The tall conifers, green-black boughs freighted with snow, crowded to the very edge of the road, curtaining the world from view. Before him, the TransBruzh angled steeply, to lose itself in the gray mists of morning.

The dawn aged and brightened. The mists dispersed slowly, and Varis closed the shutters. The TransBruzh wound its slow way through the mountains, and the sledge climbed. Around noon, the coniferous roadside curtain drew itself aside. The forests thinned and faded, presently straggling out of existence. At this altitude, the northern slopes of the Bruzhois bared themselves to the skies. The thin stony soil supported only the hardiest of scrub vegetation, and the wind moaned ceaselessly amidst naked outcroppings of granite. Here the sledge left the road, to follow a narrow lane up a grueling slope to the summit of a cliff overlooking the Ayzin Pass—a sheer-sided rift so stingy and daunting that the TransBruzh seemed to cower between its walls.

Atop the cliff, commanding the pass, rose the crenellated ramparts of Castle Haudrensq, ancient family seat of the Haudrensq clan. Its masters' systematic extortion of funds from TransBruzh travelers had earned this structure its bitterly humorous nickname of "The Tollbooth." And it was, in fact, the strategic position of the stronghold, combined with a blithe willingness to exploit its advantage to the fullest, that accounted, above all other factors, for the rise to preeminence of Clan Haudrensq. Safely ensconced behind the castle walls, even the smallest of garrisons might control the flow of troops and traffic across the Bruzhois; and had often done exactly that during the civil wars of preceding centuries.

But the union of Upper and Lower Rhazaulle, coinciding with the accession to the Wolf Throne of the first Haudrensq Ulor, brought internal strife to a halt. Lasting peace ended Castle Haudrensq's utility. Its garrison dispatched elsewhere, the old fortress fell into disuse, then into disrepair. Successive owners, luxuriously housed in Rialsq and little concerned with this grim old relic of a ruder age, allowed the property to moulder quietly. Certain portions of the structure were actually verging upon collapse at the time that Varis first took an interest.

Imagination caught by the gloomy grandeur, historical significance, and above all by the utter isolation of the site, he had sought the Ulor's permission to restore the crumbling stronghold. To this odd request, Hurna had readily if amusedly assented, even offering to deed the useless property over to his youngest brother, upon two conditions—that improvements include modernization of the castle defenses, and that title should revert to the Ulor in the event of military necessity. This last precaution was legally redundant—in time of war, the Ulor possessed authority to commandeer all national resources, at his own discretion. Agreeing without demur, Varis proceeded apace with his designs.

That had been three years ago. Now the project was complete, and Castle Haudrensq stood once more fully habitable—equipped with every modern comfort, yet its original archaic, brooding character perfectly intact. The place had become his personal refuge, to which he was wont to retire at least semiannually, remaining in residence for weeks on end. This time, however, he meant it to be different.

At the head of the lane, where the ground leveled, the sledge picked up speed, rushing on under the tunnellike archway that pierced the great outer wall, and into the courtyard. The servants of Castle Haudrensq were few, but well-trained. One emerged at once to attend his master. Varis briefly stated his intentions and requirements, then walked into the old donjon and climbed the stairs to his apartment. As far as he was concerned, he had come home.

Life at Castle Haudrensq was solitary as the most ardent of misanthropes could have desired. The old fortress was all but deserted. Varis ate alone, slept alone; rose, dressed, and filled the hours as best he could, alone. He saw no human faces, heard no voices, other than those of the few resident servants, who—to him, as to any other Rhazaullean of rank—scarcely seemed more than two-legged beasts of burden. There came no word from Rialsq; no news, no expression of regard, no personal inquiry. At first he was glad of this, for he had wished to separate himself absolutely from the life of the Zalkhash, and the silence signaled his success. Gradually, however, this latest slight began to rankle. It seemed that his brothers and their cohorts had scarcely noted his departure. Typical of them, of course; consistent and predictable, but galling nevertheless. He found himself watching for the royal messenger who never came; found himself continually frustrated.

Even when winter's tightening grip had effectively settled the matter—when the accumulation of snow and ice had annihilated the TransBruzh, cutting Castle Haudrensq off from all the world—the anger still festered.

He had the time, now—the quiet, uninterrupted stretch of time that he had always longed for. He had the time for his beloved books, for his literature, his mathematics, and natural philosophy. There was time to write that monograph he had so often contemplated, the analysis of Hurna VI's brilliant foreign policy in the last century. Time to study music, architecture, military history. Time to sketch, to sculpt, to conduct experiments in chemistry.

All the time in the world.

Immersing himself in his studies, he found satisfaction there for a little while. But the weeks passed, winter's chill deepened, and gradually he became aware of a growing discontent, an inner emptiness. It couldn't have been simple boredom, or so he assured himself. He had always believed that an active mind was capable at all times of occupying itself, and he wasn't about to abandon that conviction. It was only a question of discovering new interests.

In one of the large ground-story chambers lay scores of crates, filled with books carted in from Rialsq over the course of the last three years. The walls were lined with shelves built to receive the volumes. The task of unpacking, inspecting, cataloguing, and arranging the huge collection was sure to demand time and care. Just the sort of diversion he wanted.

He commenced with great zest, initially losing himself in his work. His spirits improved, and for the space of several days, he thought himself clear of the doldrums. Then he awoke one frigid morning to discover the prospect of sorting books all at once futile and utterly meaningless.

A library? In the midst of a mountain wilderness? For whom, and for what?

Why bother?

The books could wait.

Similarly, he began and then lost interest in a survey of Vonahrish neoclassical drama. A study of Immeeni reptiles. An analysis of Belevian Logic.

His experiments in chemistry were somewhat more absorbing, but ultimately irrelevant. Pointless. Useless.

He began to have trouble sleeping. He would wake in the middle of the night, to lie alert and jangle-nerved for hours. Sometimes he would sit up, reading by candlelight until his stinging, streaming eyes forced him to his rest at three A.M.—only to wake listless and depressed at the break of dawn.

The day that he woke up disinclined to rise from bed because there was nothing he wanted to do, nothing that seemed worth doing—the day he woke brimful of direst darkness—he recognized at last that his customary pursuits had palled beyond redemption. Something different was needed to alter his humor. Companionship might have helped, but there was none of that for him at Castle Haudrensq; or anywhere else, for that matter.

Physical activity, perhaps. It was worth a try.

There was little sport he was fit for, with his spindling, sickly body and his abnormal eyes. He might work to strengthen his slack muscles, however. That much he could do. Thus, that same morning, he commenced a program of mild exercise—bending, stretching, repeated climbing of stairs, lifting and carrying of crates half filled with books; for a full crate he could not manage. Amazing how little of this it took to exhaust him, at the beginning. But simple fatigue carried its own benefits; he slept soundly at night.

It wasn't long before he noticed changes. The exercises were becoming easier. His strength and agility were growing. He took to hoisting a full crate of books; then a larger crate. He lengthened the daily span of his exertions; lengthened it again. His appetite increased, and he even put on a little weight, which he had badly needed. He remained pallid and lean, noticeably undernourished by robust Rhazaullean standards, but no longer a walking skeleton.

He slept better, ate better, and his spirits improved, although an acrid residue of anger remained. Physically, he had never been so well in his life, and sometimes he wondered why he hadn't embarked upon such a program of self-improvement long ago. Fear of ridicule had hindered him, perhaps. His brothers would have found his efforts hilarious. Frequent illness—in the populous, often fetid House Uloric, ailments of one kind or another had plagued him continually; but here in the clean isolation of the mountains, he enjoyed uncharacteristically good health. Then, there had been his own prejudices. Barred from athletic competition, he had cultivated a quiet defensive contempt for all pursuits other than intellectual. But that was changing.

He added walking to his regimen of exercise. At the beginning he walked the chambers of the old donjon, but soon the building seemed too small to contain him. Then he ventured out upon the battlements, despite the bitter weather; or perhaps because of it, for he found a grim satisfaction in outfacing the mountain winds. From the high vantage point, he gazed out over a vast sweep of countryside jagged and glittering as broken glass. Across the paralyzed peaks and valleys, he could trace the course of the TransBruzh, following the ice-throttled curves for miles before losing them in the shadows of deepening twilight. The condition of his eyes precluded daylight excursions, but this limitation imposed no hardship. At this time of year, in these latitudes, twilight lagged only some three hours or so behind noon; a lingering twilight that blackened at its leisure. The climate encouraged a brisk pace. The entire circuit of the walls could be completed in minutes, and presently the battlements became confining.

He took to wandering the cliffside above the Ayzin Pass. Soon his explorations took him farther afield, into the coniferous forests that clambered high up the southern slopes of the Bruzhois. The snow had drifted deep and soft amongst the trees; he needed snowshoes there. Sometimes, late in the afternoon, the shadows pooled so thick and dense beneath the green-black needled boughs that even his super-sensitive eyesight failed, and he would be forced to light the lantern that he always carried with him upon these treks. The forests were silent, pristine, uncannily wakeful. The peasants imagined such places inhabited by tree sprites and human ghosts. There was even a local legend that these woods had once witnessed the visitation of a Snow-spirit, one of those vastly potent, icicle-crowned mystery-beings of national folklore. Varis encountered no such supernatural manifestation, but once he came upon a wolf—a white one, huge and motionless and all but invisible against the snow. He halted. He was unarmed, and the animal stood not twenty feet distant. He gazed into eyes that were greenish, shading to yellow about the pupils—eyes not unlike his own. Eyes that spoke, eyes that he felt he knew.

"Ulor," he whispered. "Ulor."

The wolf's ears flattened at the sound of the human voice. In silence, it faded away into the darkening forest. He stood looking after it for a long while.

Utterly solitary in his ramblings, he thought the area quite devoid of humanity, but in this soon found himself mistaken.

Dusk, and an unfamiliar section of the forest, a place where the trees grew thin and short, as if reclaiming territory once cleared. Twilight, and darkening skies—but not so dark that he failed to note the plume of smoke curling above the pines. A fire nearby. Fellow men. A novelty. Intrigued, he followed the smoke to its source.

A quick walk brought him to a small, roughly circular clearing, site of a tumbledown hut, presumably once the dwelling of some woodcutter. The hut was old and pitiable, with a crazy-hanging door and a partially caved-in roof. Such dilapidation suggested long-term vacancy, but the place was occupied. Smoke rose from one of the holes in the roof, and faint light glowed under the door.

Varis walked to the door and paused to listen. Within, a faint pattering, a rodential chittering. He knocked. Pattering and chittering ceased. Silence reigned. He knocked again. No response. He hesitated; then, depressedly indifferent to possible danger, pushed the ruined door open and stepped into the hut. The air inside was hazed with smoke, foul with the stench of filthy bodies, excrement, and rotting food. He gagged on it. He did not notice as the door, counterweighted in the usual Rhazaullean style, swung shut behind him. For one instant, he imagined himself transported back to the Wrecks.

The weak glow of a starved little fire reddened some dozen or so crouching forms. There were three or four adults, and a gaggle of subtly misshapen, unnaturally quiescent children. Listless with hunger, an observer might have supposed, for the faces were uniformly pinched. But the eyes that gleamed through matted elflocks held none of starvation's languor—rather, they shone with an unnerving brilliance; the same glare that pierced the gloom of Rialsq's Public Hospital wards. Moreover, the flesh visible beneath the layers of dirt possessed the unblemished, almost waxen appearance characteristic of one condition alone.

Varis's skin crawled. He had never seen spifflicated children before; they were a rarity all but unobtainable even to the professional handlers of performing troupes. And here in one room was a whole gang of the little monsters, each varying in style and degree of deformity, but all similarly repulsive. The children shared a family resemblance that manifested itself in sharply receding chins and foreheads, accentuated by thrusting high-bridged noses. Beyond doubt, they were siblings. The adults—one male, a couple of women, and one adolescent female of about thirteen in an advanced state of pregnancy —likewise sported emphatically convex profiles. More than likely, they, too, were siblings; their family characteristics refined and concentrated by relentless inbreeding.

Human blight. Ugliness indescribable and unexpected in a place he had thought scoured clean by the elements. Danger, as well. For these sylvan Spifflicates, like their counterparts of the Wrecks, were doubtless capable of tearing an intruder limb from limb. And here were no warders to restrain them. Behind his back, his hand sought the latch.

A feral glittering of mad eyes signaled intention.

A trio of snaggle-toothed urchins sidled toward him. They were clutching rocks.

"Do you know what's really happening here?" A sharp snapping of fingers punctuated the question, and the children stopped dead.

Countertenor voice and finger-snapping came from a smudged-out corner. Varis's eyes probed the shadows.

"Do you know, or do you think you know? What do you know you think you know? Anything? Do you know at all? Do you think at all?" The inquisitor giggled thinly. The accent was Rialsqui, and educated.

Varis waited. The black bulk in the corner shifted, leaned forward into the light. A scrawny form materialized. There squatted an elderly Spifflicate, with explosive grizzled locks, billy-goat beard, smirking lips, cunning eyes filled with smug secret knowledge. Crisscrossing, star-shaped scars adorned his forehead. Carved beads and toggles clacked in his intricately plaited beard.

"Do you have any idea what I see when I look at you? Do you dream how much your every move reveals to me? Do you think you're safe? Tell me, since you happen to be here—do you think you're SAFE? Are *they* safe?" A sweep of a long-nailed hand took in the juvenile brood. "What's safe, anyway? Ever considered? Have you? SAFE. Think about it. Tell me what you think, if you think. Eh, boy?"

Varis paused, momentarily intrigued.

"Why are you here? Do you know who brought you here? Where are the answers? Are there any answers? I won't tell you; it's better if you figure it out for yourself." The decorated Spifflicate smiled, a sly pedagogue quizzing a backward student. "Need a hint? Here it is, then. Unity. Just that—unity. Think it over."

Varis's hand found the latch. The door behind him opened.

"Going, then? Good-bye," chirped the Spifflicate. "Good journey. Enjoy yourself. Don't stop and think about anything you leave behind. What's thought, anyway? Got an answer? That's all right, you don't care about the magic. You don't want to see, it doesn't interest you. Right? Right. Good-bye."

"Magic?" Caught again. Pointless and absurd to attempt conversation with a Spifflicate, but this particular specimen was unusually articulate, and the response had slipped out.

Magic. Spifflicated children and adults alike seemed to recognize the word. Heads turned, eyes gleamed wakefully, a brief low muttering arose and died.

"Everywhere. Always. Inescapable," proclaimed the family spokesman. "You want to see it? Look around you, pay attention. Really look. You know what that means? Look straight ahead of you. What do you see, or what do you fancy you see? Do you see *time*? Do you see interdimensional *resistance*? Do you see alternate *intention*? Are you really *looking*? Eh?"

"What can you tell me of necromancy?" Varis inquired, already regretting his misguided conversational attempt.

"Everything. Who better? Do you know who I am? You don't have to tell me who you are—I can take one look and see all of you, inside and out, present and past, clear down to the smallest raw nubbin of old disappointment. But do you know me? No, the eyes are empty. You are blind, boy, but I can teach you to see. I can teach you to fly. I can teach you everything. If I choose. I am Clotl." The old man's meager torso jerked and twitched. He seemed poised on the verge of one of those typically spifflicated foaming seizures. "Clotl. Clotl. Clotl."

"Clotl. Clotl." Squeaky little voices echoed. Several children of the tribe jerked in sympathetic spasms.

Clotl. A whiff of familiarity there. Varis's brow creased. There had once been someone—a famous scandal —decades earlier, prior to his birth. Accusation, furor, then a disappearance. And the name, similar to Clotl, but longer, more syllables, something like—

"Clotlenulev," Varis remembered. "The Noble Landholder Tiv Clotlenulev. Tiv the Fugitive."

"That's it. That's it. Clotl Ghost-Lord. Clotl Deathmaster. Clotl of the Shades. The name lives yet, lives always."

"Formally charged with necromancy, the sole Noble Landholder ever so accused. Hounded by the Venerators—"

"Scum, fanatical scum."

"Tried before the Ulor himself. Convicted and condemned, despite noble rank. Inexplicable disappearance prior to public execution—a great mystery, never solved—"

"Heh!" A high-pitched yap of merriment escaped the Spifflicate. "Clotl Deathmaster, greatest necromancer ever to fish a flopping ghost up out of the grave—greatest of them all. No competition, then or now, nothing resembling a serious rival. Did they think that locks and bars could cage the ultimate sorcerer? Such fools, such fools. Are you another fool, boy? Eh?"

"Probably. So you claim to be the Noble Landholder Clotlenulev, missing these forty years?"

"Claim? Is that what I'm doing? Can you *claim* an identity, if you see it running around loose? What if somebody else wants it? Or what if it wants itself? Eh?"

"As I recall the story, this Noble Landholder, reduced to despair by the loss of his wife, resorted to necromancy, in the hope of calling her spirit to him—"

"Xuvenia. Wonderful woman. Face like an ax blade, tongue like a stiletto. Mind like a subterranean labyrinth. And a voice—such a voice! Could have etched glass with it. We'd fight, for weeks, months at a time. She had the true warrior spirit. Never admit defeat. You could break her right arm, and she'd swing at you with her left. I speak from personal experience. Magnificent woman. And then, a fever carried her off in her thirtieth year." Clotl's face and body twitched at the recollection. Similar twitches yanked the limbs of his spifflicated listeners. "At first, I thought myself liberated. I ordered new garments, restyled my beard, and entertained myself with Turo dancing girls. All too soon, however, these diversions palled. Something seemed lacking; my life was inexplicably empty. At last I divined the cause. I missed the thrill of combat. I missed the violence, verbal and physical. I missed the heady stimulant of raw hatred. I missed my Xuvenia. Without her, existence was meaningless. And thus I resolved to call her back from the dead. Turning to necromancy, I discovered therein my own unequaled store of native talent, my genius—in short, I discovered Clotl Deathmaster."

The old Spifflicate appeared more or less lucid. For the moment, his wretched companions were still and quiet. Encouraged, Varis inquired, "And did you indeed bring back your wife?"

"Assuredly. I summoned and ruled her, for magic granted me a power over her in death that I had never possessed while she lived. Her submission was uncommonly bitter. She railed and stormed, to no avail. She threatened dire vengeance, and I laughed. For her, there was neither oblivion nor escape, but only servitude. Ah, her fury was sweet to savor! Life was full and rich again. Those were the days!"

Clotl sank into a smiling reverie. Several moments of silence followed.

"But those happy days ended—?" Varis prompted at last.

"Too soon—ah, too soon! I had thought Xuvenia reduced to absolute impotence, but once again, I underestimated that splendid woman. Somehow, she found means of alerting the Venerators. The fanatics set their spies upon me; they discovered my necromancy. The rest, you already know."

"I take it you fled Rialsq. Thereafter, where did you go? How did you live? How soon before the change came upon you, and what happened then?"

"Change?" Clotl appeared uncomprehending.

"Yes, your—" Varis hesitated. Diplomacy precluded the use of such terms as spifflication, disintegration, or ruination. "Decline in health."

"Decline. In. Health. DECLINE. Whoosh, and down goes Health, right down the slide! Eh? Heh! WHOOSH!" Clotl folded double, thin shoulders shaking. For a moment, he seemed prey to convulsions. Then the shrill giggles erupted, to be caught up and echoed by every member of the tribe.

Varis waited. When the crazy commotion abated, he asked, "Has there been no change? Think back to your time in Rialsq, and remember."

"Yes, a change—for the better. Better! Are you stupid? Use your eyes, boy—use your head! There and then, I was bound by rules and conventions, weighted with titles and possessions, encumbered with responsibilities. Here and now, I am free. There I was blind; here I can see. There I was a slave; here I am a king. Indeed I have changed."

"You don't feel you paid too high a price for your necromancy?"

"What price could be too high?"

"Though the gift was but a loan?"

"Ah." Clotl lapsed into smirking catechism. "But was it a loan? If it was given for life, is it still a loan, since life itself is a loan? What's a loan, and what's possession? Are either of them real? If not, is there any difference between them? You don't have to answer; I see you haven't reached that level yet. But think about it."

He was thinking about fresh clean air. He was thinking about solitude and sanity. But some species of revolted fascination held him fast. That, and an absurd desire to demonstrate his resistance to this crudest form of manipulation. "But surely the power was neither given nor loaned for life," Varis observed. "As you no longer possess it."

"Don't I? Don't I? Sure about that? Your nose for necromancy that sharp, eh? Or is the perfume a little too subtle for you, boy? Can't sniff out what you most desire when you're all but standing in it? Better try a little harder."

Varis's smile was skeptical.

"Heh. This puppy thinks he knows everything, when he knows nothing. Doesn't know Clotl Deathmaster, doesn't know necromancy, doesn't know life, most of all doesn't know himself. He might learn a great deal, if he deigns to listen, and if I choose to teach."

Varis didn't bother to argue. There was no point in baiting the old lunatic. All at once, he was surfeited with absurd conversation, with the foul hut and everything in it. The lifelong disgust of all things spifflicated was rising fast. The toxic atmosphere was stifling. Suddenly starved for fresh air, he turned to go.

But Clotl was unready to part. Quick as the weasel he somewhat resembled, the Spifflicate was on his feet and bounding across the room to seize the visitor's arm. Standing on tiptoe, he thrust his face near and whispered, "I can teach you, boy. I can show you. The power. You want it, don't you? I see you. You want it."

The decoratively scarred face was inches from his own. The eyes were incandescent, and a thin line of spittle trailed from one corner of the lips. Revolted, Varis shook his head. He tugged his arm, but the other clung.

"You don't believe. Do you know so much, with your hungry eyes? I can show you."

"Another time." Varis twisted his arm, and Clotl staggered, without relinquishing his grip.

Anger rippled the ranks of Spifflicates. Someone threw a rock. The missile grazed the crown of Varis's hat.

"Afraid, boy? Afraid of the truth?" Clotl smirked. "I can show you."

A writhing of bodies, a red smoldering of eyes. The angry Spifflicates muttered. Flouting their patriarch was clearly inadvisable. Varis inclined an acquiescent head.

"Come with me." Clotl pulled on the captive arm. "I'll educate you, boy. I'll open those bloodshot eyes of yours."

Varis followed the other from the hut. The Spifflicates snarled, but let him go. As he stepped outside, the cold struck him, despite his heavy garments. Clotl, wrapped in a tattered robe that scarcely covered his knees, went hatless, gloveless, shoeless, and apparently untroubled. Barefoot in the snow, gait improbably bouncy, the old man trotted north, toward Castle Haudrensq.

Those few brief minutes spent in the hut had deepened twilight into night. A thin sliver of new moon, hanging low in the western sky, cast a faint, chill light upon the snow. Varis made his way across the clearing without difficulty. At the far edge, however, in the shadow of the firs, even his owl's vision failed, and he paused, groping in his pocket for wherewithal to light the lantern. His companion divined his intent. A thin bare hand plucked at his sleeve.

"No light. No need. No need! Can't you tell where

we're going, boy? Don't you sense the power, doesn't it
pull at your mind, doesn't it lead you through the dark?
Eh? Don't you *feel* it?"

He spoke with such conviction that Varis actually
paused, senses straining for occult guidance. There was
nothing but darkness and cold. He shook his head, almost
smiling. For a moment, he had actually expected—what?

Ridiculous.

"This way. *This* way!"

Insistent tug on his arm. For reasons he could hardly
have explained, Varis allowed himself to be led. And it
seemed that Clotl actually possessed arcane perception, for
he never brushed a tree or rock, never so much as stumbled in the dark.

On through the woods, blackness occasionally pierced
by the fugitive stray moonbeam. Here and there, the faint
suggestion of light upon the snow; luminous patches subtle and elusive as wraiths. No stars visible overhead; no
wind in the trees, for the moment. Darkness and a silence
broken only by the sound of Clotl's continual, incoherent
muttering.

The trees thinned. The atmosphere lightened, and
Varis could see again. Now he knew where they were—not
far from the castle, walking a slope traditionally shunned
by family retainers and by soldiers of the now-defunct
garrison, who thought the place infested with ghosts. It
was understandable that they should think so. Not a hundred yards distant rose a vertical face of rock, at whose
base yawned the artificially enlarged opening to the natural cave that was the earliest family crypt of Clan
Haudrensq. The crypt contained the mortal remains of
several notoriously bloody local Haudrensq tyrants, together with three or four murder victims, and at least one
known family suicide. Such spirits did not rest easy.

Clotl was heading straight for the cave. Bemused,
Varis followed. No need now for the Spifflicate to drag
him; his interest was fully engaged. Probably the old

man's claims were so much random raving, yet the possibility existed—

And could not be ignored.

Across the last few yards of snow to the entrance. The heavy iron gate set into the stone arch hung ajar on its hinges, the lock ruined. No telling how long the neglected crypt had lain open to the invasion of the inquisitive. Ordinarily, this would scarcely have mattered; but it mattered in this case, owing to a certain circumstance of which Clotl might or might not be aware. Best to discover how much the old man knew.

Clotl pulled the gate open with the confidence of familiarity. He advanced, and the blackness swallowed him. A moment later, his voice rattled out of the void, "Well come *on,* boy! Or are you afraid?"

Varis feared neither Spifflicate nor ghost, but the danger of a stumble in the dark, a twisted ankle or a broken leg, was real enough. Accordingly, he lit the lantern. Weak warm light pushed the darkness back a few feet. Removing his snowshoes, he stepped into the cave. Three years had passed since his last visit, but the place hadn't changed. The air was motionless and dead, as always. Walls, floor, and roughly domed ceiling still glittered with ever-present frost. Rows of niches cut into the walls held scores of carven wooden coffins; in that frigid atmosphere, all but proof against decay. Three particularly consequential Haudrensqs presumably reposed in the three great freestanding sarcophagi topped with reclining effigies. Yes, all just as memory painted, with the exception of the pine boughs heaped on the floor at the foot of Celgi "Stoneheart" Haudrensq's massive marble tomb. Had Clotl gathered them? Did the old man sometimes sleep here? The restoration of iron gate and lock would hereafter repel all such illicit intrusion. In the meantime, had this spifflicated trespasser already discovered too much?

Varis eyed his companion narrowly. Clotl was drifting back and forth along the wall, counting niches and mumbling to himself. He displayed no interest in the crypt's rear recesses, and his indifference suggested ignorance, but did not prove it.

Locating the niche he sought, Clotl groped about the interior. A low hoot announced his triumph, and he brought forth a widemouthed glass jar with a tightly fitting metal cap. He groped again and pulled out a spoon. Uncapping the jar, he dipped the spoon and lifted a quivering mound of pale sludge. He swallowed the stuff without hesitation. A deep sigh escaped him, his eyes shut, and he stood motionless.

Curious, Varis drew near; bent his head to peer into the jar. The light of his lantern played upon a glinting mass of gelatinous matter. The substance was milkily translucent, touched with sparks of purest color, like impossibly jellied opals. He had never seen anything like it in his life.

Clotl's lids snapped open, and the lantern in Varis's hand jerked. Formerly, the old man's eyes had shone with the typically spifflicated intensity; now, they positively flamed. A hectic flush stained his hitherto colorless cheeks. In an instant, his face appeared to renew itself, flesh stretching and smoothing elastically over the sharp old bones. His spine straightened, and the years fell away from him. For a moment he luxuriated, flexing and preening, then bent a brilliant contemplative gaze upon his companion. Internal debate abruptly concluding, he proffered open jar and spoon.

"Your turn, boy," the old man invited. "Dig in."

For one lunatic instant, Varis actually found himself tempted. The stuff was probably pure poison, but its effect was startling. "What is it?" he temporized.

"Ah. What is it, he asks." Clotl addressed Celgi's marble effigy. "*What is it?* Does he desire philosophical enlightenment? A discourse upon the history, significance, capacity, and potential utility of the substance in question? Metaphysical-supernatural exegesis? Or does he want a recipe? Eh?" He rounded suddenly on the younger man. "Which is better, boy—words or experience? Listening to someone talk about it, or *doing* it? Eh? Go on, give it a try."

Varis shook his head. The scene was familiar, reminiscent of—what? He remembered. Breziot and the vouvrak, weeks earlier, upon the occasion of—

Best not to dwell on it.

"Just a smidgeon," Clotl coaxed.

"No."

"Tchah. Mollycoddle. Spectator. Observer only. From the sidelines, eh? Always from the sidelines, a lifetime of it. No more part of it all than the ghosts I summon from the grave—"

"If you mean to prove that claim, go ahead. So far, you've failed to convince me."

"Prove? And what's proof, boy?" Clotl went arch and coy. "The evidence of your senses—is that conclusive? Do your eyes, ears, and all the rest of the nervous paraphernalia perceive true reality? Will you trust them, gullible as they are? Ever thought about it? Ever stopped to consider—"

Disgusted, Varis made for the exit.

"Wait. Don't go. Watch, and I'll prove it." The Spifflicate's voice was suddenly subdued, almost sane. "I'll do it now. Watch. Watch me."

Against his better judgment, Varis turned back to discover the other seated cross-legged on the floor before the sarcophagus of Celgi "Stoneheart" Haudrensq. Clotl was muttering and swaying, as the crack-brained sorcerers of the Wrecks had muttered and swayed on the night of their conclave. But there the resemblance ended. The wretched captive necromancers, enthusiastic but undisciplined, had moaned, chanted, twitched, and fidgeted their way to success, almost as if by accident. Clotl, on the other hand, manifested an unexpectedly precise focus. Perhaps the influence of the opalescent jelly accounted for the change in demeanor. Certainly the—potion, drug, elixir, whatever the stuff really was—had boosted the old man's mental and physical energies to new levels. It was said that the greatest of necromancers found power to rule ghosts, single-handed in such a state of heightened vitality.

Clotl's eyes were closed. He seemed lost in another world or dimension, a place where spifflication reversed itself. For the moment, he commanded his magical faculties. His gestures were fluid and sure, his chanting sonorous. His body bent and swayed bonelessly, continuing so for long minutes. Then, quite abruptly, the waving torso froze. The chanting altered, rising in pitch, breaking and jumping in rhythm.

Response to this summons was prompt. Tendrils of vapor extruded from Celgi's sarcophagus. The tendrils rose, stretched and met, wove themselves into a cloud. The cloud thickened, darkened, shrank, and coalesced. A human form took shape; nebulous and transparent at first, but gaining in substance and definition with each passing moment. The figure was tall and broad, its bulk enhanced by vast fur swathings, antique in style. A face sprang from the mists. Strong features sculpted themselves, pearly ghost-eyes glinted, bushy hair and beard bridged form and chaos. Then it was complete, and Celgi "Stoneheart" Haudrensq, shaped and draped as in life, floated above his own tomb.

Varis watched, intent as a snow-cat. From time to time, throughout his life, he had witnessed illegal necromantic exhibitions, but never anything to equal this. Nothing that even came close.

The ghost of Celgi Haudrensq was all but opaque, each detail of face and form magnificently realized. The presence was nearly tangible, its personality immediate.

Celgi was unmistakably peeved. Beard, hair, and furs all bristled. His white eyes bulged, and his mouth worked, but the words that emerged were inaudible to Varis. Clotl, however, could hear. His head bobbed, and he giggled, bending double and clutching himself. Celgi raged in silence. Had he possessed corporeality, his voice would probably have rocked the cave, for his throat cords were straining, and the vein in his ectoplasmic temple throbbed. Drawing a ghost-dagger from his belt, he thumbed the blade suggestively.

"Tchah. Idle threats of a pettish phantom," Clotl scoffed. "You know better, Stoneheart. You are all empty bombast. I love to provoke him," he added, aside, for his companion's benefit. "He is the most choleric of spirits, and oh, how he hates me! Just like Xuvenia. Be at ease, Stoneheart, we just want some fun. Do a somersault for us, eh? Up and over, bum to the breeze. Come on, you can do it. Up and over, now."

Celgi mutely screamed and raved, spewing spectral froth.

"Now, then. No insolence." Waxing stern, Clotl rose to his feet. "Do it, Stoneheart. Just do as you're told."

Another soundless spate of vituperation, before which Clotl stood firm.

"Useless to stand upon your dignity, my friend. Didn't work for Xuvenia, either. Now, let's see that somersault."

The Spifflicate gestured, sketching circles. Unwillingly, the shade followed the spinning hands, burly form drifting slow and weightless as morning mist. The shaggy head sank, the feet rose, and presently Celgi hung inverted in midair. The furred robes slid down the legs, exposing pallid ghostly glutei. Clotl chortled and clapped at the sight, while his victim beat the air in helpless fury. The ghost-fist clenched about the dagger struck the sarcophagus lid, and Varis heard the all-but-inaudible scrape of steel on stone. Perhaps he had imagined the sound. Or perhaps it had been real, so nearly palpable was the weapon and so fervent its dead owner's desire to use it.

The prolonged somersault continued to its conclusion, and Celgi resumed his former upright posture.

"Bravo!" Clotl applauded. "Excellent! Now, how about a nice handspring?"

Celgi's contorted visage perceptibly darkened, as if the blood he no longer possessed had rushed to his face. His jaw was wagging, and he was obviously bellowing, his passion almost leaping dimensions. Varis thought to catch the merest whisper of sound, traveling across an unimaginable gulf.

"Here, now, Stoneheart," Clotl chided. "Is that nice? I'd hate to think you really meant it."

Another silent thunderblast.

"Best you keep a civil tongue in that insubstantial old head. Unless you want me to make you dance the djakasha, the way I did last time. Remember? Heh, but how you pranced it!"

The shade, evidently struggling to curb its wrath, appeared to remonstrate. Clotl listened, sometimes nodding, often tittering.

"What's he saying?" Varis asked at last.

"I'm not your interpreter, boy. If you're that interested, take some of this, and hear for yourself." Once again, Clotl proffered jar and spoon.

This time, Varis took it. Caution warred briefly with raging curiosity, and curiosity triumphed. Dipping a generous shimmery spoonful, he forced himself to gulp it down.

It wasn't nearly as bad as he had feared. Expecting detestable rotten-sweet flaccidity, he was pleasantly surprised to find the jelly flavorless. There was no perceptible odor, and the texture was firm, slightly resilient, like well-stiffened aspic. He wondered how long it would be before he felt the effects, if any. Perhaps he was simply not susceptible—

It struck with dumbfounding force and suddenness. His nerves ignited. A surge of wild energy swept through him, and he was whole, complete for the first time, alive as never before.

His senses were heightened a hundredfold. The cave and all its contents sprang into crystalline focus. He could sort a hundred separate scents upon the air; distinguish each individual hair prickling along his forearms. He could hear—everything; the rush of the wind through the trees outside the cave, tiny rustling of some mouse or woodchepe nesting in one of the wall niches, gallop of his companion's heart, hysterical ranting of a furious spectre—

The hoarse, yelling voice was now quite audible. Celgi Haudrensq was spitting a stream of threats and invective, all in the regional dialect of his own time. The archaic phrasing and accent, while odd, were generally comprehensible. But Varis scarcely heeded the hollowly echoing tirade. There were other matters to consider—

His mind. His body. They had never worked so well. Lifelong infirmity vanished in an instant. He could have moved mountains, swum oceans. And his thoughts—their speed, clarity, and power were stupendous. It was as if he had shaken off the stupor of decades.

As if he had discovered himself.

And all the sensations of the moment distilled themselves to one fierce throb of inordinate desire:

I want this.

DROOLING DEVIANT! FESTERING NAZHTAK'ASSI! I WILL HUNT YOU IN YOUR DREAMS!

Celgi Haudrensq, wildly emoting. Unimportant, now.

I want this.

IDIOT-MOONCALF, BEWARE YOUR SLUMBER! I WILL BUILD NIGHTMARES IN YOUR SKULL!

"Stoneheart, do you by any chance know how to do a cartwheel?"

To have it always.

A CRACK-PATED SLAVE TO FOUL THE HONOR OF THE DEAD! SVOKORZKE'VOI!

"Backflip? Headstand?"

To live at last.

"Xuvenia knew them well."

"Where did you get this?" Varis asked aloud. There was no response, and he jogged the Spifflicate's shoulder.

"Eh? Eh?" Clotl shrugged impatiently.

"This jelly, where did it come from? What's in it? Where can I get some?"

"Such urgency. Such intensity, all of a sudden. Well. Where did it come from? *Here.*" Clotl tapped his temple. "It came from *here.* I made it myself, I am the proud papa. What's in it? All that's necessary, and no more. Where can you get some? Right out of that jar you're holding. Help yourself."

"How long do the effects last?"

"Oh, you're good for hours at least, boy."

"And then?"

"And then— Whoosh." Clotl gestured a swift slide down a steep incline, an abrupt arrest at the bottom. "Heh— Whoosh!"

"Yes. In that case, I need the formula."

"Secret. Secret. Aren't the best things in life always secret? The philosopher's stone, perpetual motion, eternal youth, the consistently reliable love potion—aren't they always elusive? Part of their charm. My formula. My masterpiece, my crowning achievement, my own gelatinous baby. Mine. All mine. My secret." Clotl hugged himself fondly.

Perhaps a brief or not-so-brief sojourn in one of the Tollbooth's subterranean dungeons would alter the old loon's outlook. The vaults were equipped with varied implements of persuasion. . . . The thought sprang whole into Varis's mind, unexpected and disturbing. He had always deplored the more violent forms of coercion, one of the many eccentric inhibitions that roused the merriment of his full-blooded, more traditionally Rhazaullean older brothers. He had imagined himself beyond such barbarities; but then, he had never in his life wanted anything so desperately.

There were surely other ways.

"Keep your secret, then. I invite you to enter my service. You'll live in luxury at Castle Haudrensq. You'll be rich, safe, and honored. In exchange, you need only supply me with this substance of your invention."

"Shall Clotl Deathmaster sell his freedom for a bed and dinner? Shall the greatest necromancer of all time descend to *servitude*? Tchah!"

"You'll be free."

"I am already."

"Perhaps you boast," Varis suggested. "Perhaps you merely discovered the jelly hidden here. Perhaps you're ignorant."

"Could be. Never know, do you, boy? Uncertainty. Makes life interesting, eh? Now, don't distract me, or Celgi will slip away, and I'm not half finished with him." Clotl turned back to the shade. "Well, Stoneheart, what next? What shall we play?"

SVOKORZKE'VOI! CHAKS'TA ALLA VESHENKI!

"Just so. Celgi, do you know the Turo girls' Dance of the Vanishing Veils? Stimulating, eh? Like to perform it?"

The ghost fulminated, its summoner persisted, and presently a reluctant disrobing commenced. While Clotl hummed the old Veil Song, stamping and clapping to keep time, the phantom furs dropped one by one, each hovering a moment upon the air before floating away into nothingness.

"Now quiver and shimmy, while tossing your hair to and fro! Yes! Very pretty!"

The Spifflicate was altogether absorbed. Varis queried and cajoled, to no avail. At length he laid his hand upon the other's shoulder.

"Deathmaster, state your price."

"Not now! Look, he's down to his linen!"

"Deathmaster—a moment of your time—" Varis's grip tightened.

"What?" Clotl's attention was finally arrested. "Oh,

let me alone, boy! I tell you—" He looked up into the younger man's eyes, and his face changed. "*Heh!* What's this? I'm seeing, it's coming to me. I smell your thoughts, don't think to hide that kind of wanting. Clotl sees. Clotl is clothed in power. Dungeon walls cannot contain him. Steel blades shatter upon his breast. Ghost-slaves guard him, you cannot harm him—"

"I intend no harm. I only want—"

"To take, to pillage and plunder, to steal, to murder."

"To pay you."

"With what? What will you pay for my power, my knowledge, my freedom, my life, my soul? Eh?"

"Calm yourself and listen—"

"To false promises? Or to the true inner voice counseling self-preservation? Clotl sees."

Varis withdrew his hand. The gesture failed to reassure.

"Celgi!" Clotl's countertenor thinned to a whetted edge. "Guard me! Defend me! Kill him!"

Kill him? The old man had lost his last hold on sanity. No doubt his power had fled as well.

Not so.

The ghost of Celgi Haudrensq flickered and wavered. *HIS BLOOD IS AS MINE. HE IS HAUDRENSQ,* argued the shade.

"And?"

I CANNOT HARM MY BLOOD.

"Try," Clotl suggested. "Do your best. I insist, Stoneheart."

PUTRID OFFAL! L'UVUSK'ST! Unwilling, but helpless to resist, Celgi advanced driftingly upon the designated victim.

"Faster!" Clotl commanded. "Faster, faster, faster!"

The violent thrust of the necromancer's will drove the ghost through the air with the sudden speed of a flung missile.

Varis backed deep into the crypt. Celgi's shade boiled

the air between himself and the exit. He perceived his ancestor's compunction, he sensed potential support, but knew not how to engage it.

FORGIVE ME, KINSMAN.

Celgi came on fast, dagger fist low and slightly extended. Lantern light struck hard sparks off ghostly steel. The blade flashed in a snake-quick arc that sliced through multiple woolen layers, and Varis recoiled, one hand pressed to a bleeding gash in his arm. Cold, searing cold, despite the welling blood. Astonishing that a phantom weapon could wound perfectly solid flesh; but there was no time to ponder the phenomenon, for the ghost was upon him.

"Now finish him, Stoneheart! Do it! Do it!"

This thing, with its dagger of smoke, could kill. The frigid wetness under his sleeve told him as much. Varis retreated, and the shade pursued.

FORGIVE ME, KINSMAN. I AM COMPELLED, IF YOU WILL NOT FIGHT HIM.

"Shut up! Shut your mouth, you old wisp of nothingness, you rag of ancient fog, you!" Clotl shrilled, and the ghost fell silent.

Fight him? How? Clotl stood safely out of reach, half the length of the crypt away. Before him, Celgi lowered like a storm cloud. To Varis's enhanced vision, the blade in the nearly opaque hand seemed to glow with its own supernatural light. The ghost was silent, in accordance with its summoner's commands. But at that moment, some hitherto-unsuspected faculty of perception—probably jolted awake by the artificial stimulant of the gel, combined with the natural stimulant of alarm—afforded Varis hazy insight into the nature of Celgi's susceptibility to living influence.

A luminous, formerly unperceived tangle of steely spider-silk tied Celgi Haudrensq to his sarcophagus. Similarly relentless delicate strands glistened between the wretched shade and the walls, ceiling, and floor. For the first time, Varis perceived old Clotl's hold upon the threads. There was nothing here so crude as manual manipulation; the Spifflicate tugged with his mind and his malice.

The same threads that bound an unwilling spirit to the physical world for centuries on end could be yanked like the strings of a puppet by a perceptive necromancer. The stronger the sorcerer's concentration and determination, the stronger the pull upon the incorporeal ties. Training and practice would doubtless augment native ability; but it was, above all, a matter of raw will.

Too many threads, too many knots and tangles, too confusing to sort through it all in an instant, and Varis did not try. Instinctively, he pushed with his mind, shoving it all away from him. The entire gossamer network trembled, and Celgi Haudrensq's advance abruptly halted.

"Eh!" Clotl grunted as if punched. "Eh?"

Again, Varis pushed. This time, he encountered the resistance of Clotl's will; still formidable, despite its aged and worm-eaten condition. The old man possessed much experience and a certain deranged intensity. He used them both to good effect, and Varis sensed vise-pressure upon his own mind. His concentration flagged, and then Celgi was coming at him.

"Heh." Clotl smirked.

Celgi's knife gleamed, fast and bitter. No time to attempt a mental deflection. Varis dodged, and the flying ghost-blade barely touched his jaw. Blood welled, but the wound was deadly cold.

This was a duel he was hardly equipped to fight, but a possible source of aid was close at hand. Varis focused his thoughts and will upon his ancestor's lips, then shot the command like an arrow—"Speak to me. Speak freely."

Spider-silk wreathing Celgi's shaggy head loosened, and a psychic gag disintegrated.

"Eh?" Clotl blinked. Surprise must have shaken his

concentration, for the attack ceased, and the ghost checked in midlunge. "You want to *chat* with him?"

DEFEND YOURSELF, MY KINSMAN, counseled the shade.

"Tell me how."

FREE ME, AND I WILL GLADLY KILL HIM.

"How shall I free you?"

CUT THE THREADS THAT BIND ME.

"Cut them with what?"

THE SWORD OF YOUR MIND.

"That's enough out of you! Just you keep quiet, Stoneheart!" Clotl scowled.

FREE ME, KINS—

"Not another word!" The Spifflicate's fists clenched on air, and Celgi Haudrensq's dead voice died.

The sword of his mind? Varis exerted his untrained mental force; it was more of a push than a slash. The ghost went shuttling off across the cave, but the threads held. For an instant, the path to the exit was clear. Before he had taken a single step, Celgi was back upon him, phantom blade flickering.

Phantom blade. Into Varis's artificially expanded mind sprang the image of a sword, broad and massive in the outmoded medieval style, too huge and heavy for any normal mortal to wield, with a luminous blade honed to impossibly keen double edge. He made the image real, more real than the cave in which he stood. Intellect and sword were one.

The two-edged blade described a mighty arc. The myriad threads binding Celgi Haudrensq fell away, severed at a single stroke. Incredulity stilled the ghostly face.

A startled, almost aggrieved squawk escaped Clotl.

AT LAST. Incredulity yielded to savage joy. Celgi wheeled to face his erstwhile tormentor.

Clotl shrank back, plucking frantically at loose, disconnected ectoplasmic threads.

USELESS, YOU MAGGOT. IT IS FINISHED. CHTARVA'ASK!

Clotl turned to run, and the shade stooped like a falcon. The ghost-dagger plunged, and the living blood jetted. Clotl's expression was purely astonished. He fell, and his life gushed away within seconds.

Varis stood motionless, amazed and unexpectedly exhilarated. His eyes slowly rose from the Spifflicate's corpse to the ghost hovering sated overhead. Perhaps it was imagination, but it seemed that his ancestor was dwindling in bulk and solidity.

IT WAS GOOD. VERY GOOD. I THANK YOU, MY KINSMAN, AND I BID YOU FAREWELL.

"You return to your tomb?"

NO. YOU HAVE CUT THE TIES THAT BOUND ME TO THIS PLACE. NOW I DEPART.

No doubt about it. The ghost was fading. The big body, formerly verging upon solidity, was now quite transparent.

"Where are you going?"

ELSEWHERE. FAREWELL.

Thin as a bubble, now.

"Stay a moment."

FAREWELL.

Gone, before the hollow echo of his voice had died. Varis stood alone in the crypt. The blood sang in his veins, but mingled with the sense of pleasurable stimulation there was confusion and profound revulsion. His eye fell upon the glass jar still sitting open on the floor before Celgi's sarcophagus. A couple of long strides carried him to it. Intentions destructive, he grabbed the jar—and paused. For a moment he stood there undecided, then capped the vessel and returned it to its former resting place in the niche. Clotl's invention—if Clotl's it truly was—merited respect. Shameful to destroy so rare a piece of work, in the very presence of its alleged creator. He wouldn't do so. But he'd never touch the sorcerous sludge again, never look upon it, never more meddle in necromancy. Of that, he was certain.

Quite certain? Eh?

He could have sworn he heard a voice. The Spifflicate's staring sightless eyes held his. Varis turned his back on the eyes. Suddenly he was starving for solitude; real solitude, unvisited by ghosts. Taking up the lantern, he hurried to the rear of the crypt whose secret old Clotl might or might not have known. The back wall was jaggedly irregular. A casual observer would have noted no sign of human workmanship there. Varis's fingers ran over the bumps and hollows; pressed hard here and there. An unseen mechanism grated, a lock snapped, and a hitherto invisible door swiveled upon its central pivot to crack itself a few inches open. Varis pushed, and the aperture widened. He stepped through, closing the door behind him. The passage in which he now stood, a marvel of antique engineering, ran underground all the way from the family crypt to the deepest cellar level beneath Castle Haudrensq's donjon tower. Its existence was known to family members alone. And Clotl's potential threat? Fortunately, Celgi Haudrensq's intervention had solved that particular dilemma.

Long frame hunched to clear the low ceiling, Varis made his way swiftly along the narrow passage. Minutes later, he emerged into the donjon cellar and climbed the winding stairs to his own apartment without encountering a soul.

Sleep was out of the question. It was too early, and he was wide awake—wider awake than he had ever been before. He was still ablaze with uncharacteristic excess energy, too much to burn off in a lifetime. Perhaps he would never need to sleep again. Dimly, he was aware of the cuts upon his arm and face, but he felt no pain, only wonder. A ghost-dagger, devoid of physical reality, had slit his perfectly solid flesh. The paradox demanded explanation.

His mind seethed. Ideas and images boiled to the surface by the hundred, by the thousand; extraordinary new ideas, disturbing images, coming and going almost too swiftly to be grasped. He paced feverishly. The lamp in his chamber burned all night long.

3

WHOOSH.

Just as mad old Clotl had predicted—a swift slide down a steep incline, a jarring arrest at the bottom. Jarring? Shattering.

He had enjoyed a night and a day of intense vigor. He'd been filled with energy, strength, confidence, and, for the first time in his life, a sense of well-being. Even his eyes had improved. He'd actually ventured out into the courtyard, at noon, without his dark glasses and without the slightest discomfort. There he had stood for half an hour, heightened senses drinking the sights and sounds of the unfamiliar sunlit world. Diamond clarity of air. Astonishing blue infinity overhead. Sun on the snow, splendor beyond imagining. He was alive as never before, as he was meant to be—or so it seemed.

Until the end of the day, at which time exhaustion abruptly overtook him. Within the space of seconds, limbs and eyelids went leaden. His racing mind stumbled. It took enormous effort to drag himself up the stairs to his own chamber, where he collapsed into bed and a deep dreamless slumber that lasted well into the next afternoon.

Varis opened his eyes, and the daylight slanting in

through the window stabbed at his nerves. He threw an arm across his face a moment too late. Already, his eyes were starting to burn and water. Rising to stagger blindly from bed to window, he drew the black curtains. His flesh sensed the merciful shadow, and he let his arm drop. The room was comfortably dim, but his eyes stung yet. And that was scarcely the greatest of miseries. He had slept for hours, but remained deeply tired, wobbly, and nauseated. A headache battered the back of his skull. The ghost-dagger cuts upon his arm and jaw, formerly painless, now ached icily. He'd have to bind them. The state of his body echoed the state of his mind. Gone were yesterday's optimism and satisfaction, the sense of hard certainty shoring confidence. His thoughts had slowed and darkened. He had simply reverted to his former condition, but now normality seemed penitential.

Whoosh.

Returning to his bed, he lay inert for hours. Necessity finally drove him back to his feet, and back to his life. His first consideration, upon arising, was securement of the iron grillwork gate guarding the entrance to the Haudrensq family crypt. He needed a new lock. The most readily available replacement, presently hanging upon his clothespress door, was flimsy and unsuitable. Better than nothing, however, and it would do for the moment. Varis visited the crypt at twilight, pausing only long enough to switch padlocks. He didn't enter the cave. He didn't want to confront old Clotl's corpse, doubtless frozen solid by this time. Sooner or later, the body would have to be disposed of, but the condition of the rock-hard, snow-covered ground precluded immediate burial. Clotl would have to wait for the spring thaws.

A dead Spifflicate was no great matter. Of far larger consequence was the glass jar, sitting in its niche, and exerting an attraction that he felt across the intervening barrier. If he opened the gate, the pull would grow stronger, much stronger. He hiked away from the crypt as fast as his snowshoes would carry him.

Over the course of the following days, he forced himself to resume his usual activities. But the exercises, experiments, and endeavors formerly claiming his attention failed to divert him now. Nothing caught him, with the possible exception of the books.

There was still the library to complete; the hundreds of volumes, the treasure-trove, as he had once regarded it. All that time, effort, and expense, expended upon so many books. He really ought to complete the project.

Accordingly, he returned to the crates, the empty shelves, and random accumulation. In sorting through the countless uncatalogued works, he came upon the cache of folios—clandestinely acquired years earlier, and since that time all but forgotten—containing a brace of necromancers' notebooks. Mere possession of such proscribed lore constituted a criminal offense. But for an avid bibliophile who happened to be the Ulor's brother, there were ways of cheating the law. Despite the outrageous price he'd paid for the writings, he had never before found time to examine them. He found the time now, however. He couldn't keep away from them.

One of the notebooks supposedly belonged to Yelnyk of Krezniu, infamous necromancer of the last century, who had avoided spifflication and lived to a healthy old age; the other, to the contemporary Sesz Nishko, current deranged resident of the Public Hospital of Mercy in Lazimir. If they were genuine, the notebooks were extraordinarily revealing. Each contained accounts of assorted sorcerous experiments, including details of method and procedure, together with lists of essential materials, their required quantities, sources, and even, in some cases, prices. Thirty years ago, a pouch of Crimson Ellodi, sometimes available from itinerant Turo vendors, had sold for about one hundred brazzles. Presumably the price was higher now, but an aspiring necromancer had no choice but to pay. Crimson Ellodi was so often called for that it qualified as a necessity.

The lists, the ingredients, and methods of preparation varied widely, yet the objective was always the same—concoction of some stimulant to concentrate the user's vitality, imparting temporary power to summon and to rule the dead. Old Clotl's opalescent jelly had been an exceptional specimen of its type.

Difficult to avoid thinking of that jelly, and the way it had made him feel for a night and a day. Hard to forget the lost power and glory. Impossible to forget that the jar still rested where he had left it, tucked away in a niche in the crypt. Thanks to the secret passage, he could lay hands on that jar in a matter of minutes . . .

Exactly what he wouldn't do. He'd vowed never to touch the stuff again. Having made that decision, he would put the matter from his mind once and for all.

Back, then, to the interrupted regimen of exercise, the projects and chemical dabblings, with renewed determination. Back to the long, solitary treks, though he never again approached the Spifflicates' disintegrating shack. Back to the calisthenics, the dogged lifting and shifting of heavy objects, and now the physical improvement was so unmistakable that nobody, remembering him from the Rialsq days, could have failed to note the difference. The ghost-wounds had healed, but the short scar upon his jaw remained almost luminously white, noticeable even against his uncommonly pallid complexion. Still lean to the point of gauntness, he was now fit and agile, all wire and whipcord. Once, such progress would have pleased him. Now it seemed insignificant, almost a mockery, by comparison to that rush of power he had experienced only once, but could not forget.

Of course he wouldn't forget so remarkable an experience, nor should he try. He needn't assign the incident undue importance, but there was no harm in remembering. Or so he assured himself, as he lay wide awake in his bed through the winter nights, with the north winds screaming outside his window, and the memories clamoring inside his head.

The library project was not going well. The necromantic folios were to blame for distracting him. The arcana they offered consumed hours and days.

Techniques for summoning ghosts—the words, the rhythms and gestures, the combinations. Imposition of the living will. The nature of interdimensional resistance, the mutability of which explained the effect of Celgi Haudrensq's ghost-dagger upon living flesh. Dominance, deception, spectral dysfunction. Alternate intention. Elasticity of the ectoplasmic bond. Forn and the universal Greej pattern. Crimson Ellodi substitutions. Ten warning signs of spifflication. The Shernivus family of stimulants, and their side-effects.

Mesmerizing, all of it. Surprisingly easy to assimilate and retain; he seemed to possess a natural affinity for such material. He thought then of Clotl's discovery, at a relatively advanced age, of native necromantic talent. He remembered his own success in breaking the ties that bound Celgi's shade—and that feat accomplished without benefit of any training whatever. Was it possible, Varis wondered, that he, too, possessed—?

He wouldn't put it to the test. He was no Tiv Clotlenulev, hell-bent on spifflication. No harm, of course, in simply perusing the notebooks, provided it went no further than that, and provided that his illicit research went undiscovered. This last thought gave him pause. It wasn't likely that he would be observed. No stranger was apt to intrude upon his ice-bound stronghold at this time of year. As for the servants, they were few, closemouthed through loyalty or fear, and entirely illiterate. On the other hand, they were doubtless inquisitive. Best to protect the priceless, proscribed writings; best to lock them away out of sight.

The thought of locks carried his mind back to the Haudrensq crypt. For weeks now, the gate had stood secured by nothing more than a flimsy little padlock. Not good enough. He wanted a solid lock on that door.

Unwilling to entrust the task to a servant, he searched through the cellars and storerooms himself. An old trunk yielded the required article—a massive padlock, rust-free, and probably strong enough to withstand cannon fire. It would be the work of minutes to set the lock in place. Already he was cloaked and gloved against the bitter chill of the fireless cellar; no need of additional wrappings to visit the crypt. No need of light, for he had brought a lantern. No need to wait.

Down the winding stairs he hurried, down to the lowest subterranean level, and straight to the southeast corner. Sweep of a gloved hand over the rough stone wall, knowledgeable pressure here and there, and the hidden door creaked open. Then he was in the passageway, dead air heavy in his lungs, pace quickening as he advanced, until he was almost running; and yet the way seemed endless.

Creak of a second concealed door, and he stepped from the passageway into the crypt, where his lantern was unnecessary. It was well past midday, and the shafts of sunlight slanting through the grillwork gate at the mouth of the cave illuminated the interior. Varis's eyes jumped instinctively to the niche concealing the glass jar. It was not for another moment or two that his gaze traveled to the marble sarcophagus of Celgi Haudrensq, and thence to the corpse on the floor.

Clotl lay on his back, arms outflung and skinny legs bent, as he had fallen. No predator had disturbed the body, which was frozen solid and perfectly preserved. The old man's dying look of astonishment remained intact. Varis met the wide dead eyes, which seemed to reflect awareness, recognition—mockery? Pure fancy, but disturbing. He looked away. Clotl could not lie unburied indefinitely. Probably best to place the body outside the crypt, then let the castle servants deal with the logistics of removal and disposal. Perhaps he would order them to cremate the remains, then scatter the ashes upon the wind. There was something reassuring in the thought of so total an annihilation.

Key in hand, Varis made for the entrance. As he approached, the daylight that had seemed moderate intensified and set his eyes to watering. He hadn't thought of that. Arriving by way of the passage, he had come without his dark glasses, without even his usual wide-brimmed hat.

By the time he reached the gate, his eyes were burning and streaming. Vigorous blinking failed to clear them, and he knew from experience that rubbing would worsen matters. Averting his face from the light, he shut his eyes, thrust an arm through the bars, fumbled blindly with lock and key.

No good. Sightless, he was all but helpless. He'd have to go back for the glasses after all. The quick flare of fury was inappropriately intense.

Into his mind sprang the image of the snow-mantled courtyard, glittering in the light of the midday sun, as he had viewed it just once in his life; viewed it without the slightest discomfort, through eyes fortified with Clotl's concoction. One swallow, and his eyes would function perfectly. He could do what needed to be done—

He moved without thought, without volition, without even full consciousness of his own intentions. He moved like the ghost of Celgi Haudrensq, yanked upon invisible strings. Almost to his own surprise, he found himself standing beside the niche, glass jar and spoon in hand. As he uncapped the jar and dipped a mounded spoonful of jelly, a sense of inevitability filled him. He lifted the spoon and swallowed. On some level, he had known all along that he would.

A moment's lull, an instant's doubt—*Will it happen?*

—and then it came flooding upon him. The miraculous rush of energy; the heightening of every sense; the surge of power and confidence that he remembered so well, that he had dreamed of every day and every night for weeks . . . He downed another spoonful.

Varis slowly raised his head to gaze out through the grillwork at dazzling sunstruck snow without blinking, and without pain. The unblemished whiteness furnished the canvas upon which his mind painted images; extraordinary images, highly colored, violent, exquisitely perverse, sometimes macabre. He had never before recognized the breadth of his own imagination, or the midnight depths. Sweat slicked his forehead, despite the chill of the crypt. He could have stood there, enthralled, for hours, but there was work to do.

Removing the light padlock, he opened the gate, then turned to consider the corpse. Small and scrawny, Clotl would be easy to transport. The dead stare held no terror now. Varis felt himself more than ready to meet the challenge of those glassy eyes.

Challenge. No doubt about it. He could almost hear the piping countertenor:

Think you're up to it, boy? Eh? EH?

Yes.

Really?

No doubt. And easy to prove it. The pages of the necromantic folios obligingly presented themselves to mental inspection. Yelnyk's crabbed black jottings, Sesz Nishko's elaborate diagrams and instructions. All perfectly remembered, as if the folios lay open before him. What point in acquisition of knowledge, without practical application? He realized then how eager for experimentation he was. Why live as a miser, hoarding his mental gold?

The muscles of his mind knotted. The syllables burst from his lips. The gestures, both physical and metaphysical, seemed to perform themselves. The power welled up within him, coursed through his brain, reached out to seize the thing he sought, and to drag it forth into the light.

The corpse appeared to contract. Ectoplasmic tendrils snaked from its every orifice. The tendrils interwove to build smoke, the smoke condensed to shape a colorless figure, and the ghost of Clotl, once known as Tiv Clotlenulev, floated above its erstwhile fleshly shelter.

The living and the dead regarded one another raptly.

Figured it out, have you? inquired the shade at last.

The voice was thin and distant, but still recognizable. Clotl himself, while transparent and more than a little blurry around the edges, was complete and unchanged down to the last detail of decorative facial scarring. Ghostly threads bound spectre to corpse.

So—now what? Overflowing with ambition, are we? Bursting with creativity? Can't wait to get started? Eh, boy? EH?

Clotl was Clotl still.

What's the matter, cat got your tongue? Infinite choice infinitely daunting? Mind a little too small to hold all those possibilities, boy? Are possibilities any different from responsibilities? Ever stop to consider—

Loony old windbag hadn't changed an iota. Dead for weeks, and still spewing crackpot mockery.

"Be quiet." Varis did not raise his voice, but annoyance stirred beneath the calm surface.

Quiet. QUIET. By 'quiet,' does he mean 'silent?' Does he mean 'tranquil?' Or does he mean 'unmoving?' Does he mean all of them, or none? Does he know what he means, or hasn't he thought about it? Does he—

Irritation sharpened to anger. The hot emotions exerted force; almost, it seemed, of their own accord. Power arced from Varis's mind, and the results were startling. Clotl hurtled backward the length of the cave to strike the rear wall, into which he sank like a traveler in quicksand. A sharp mental yank plucked him forth from the stone, sent him whizzing to and fro, wall to wall, floor to ceiling, spinning and tumbling helplessly in midair, to end where he had begun, floating upside down above his own frozen corpse.

Varis watched incredulously. He had done it. Unaided and self-taught. Himself alone.

With swimming motions, the ghost righted itself.

Heh. Clotl patted his garments, smoothed his beard, adjusted his trailing threads. *Just like Xuvenia. Heh.* Unexpectedly, he grinned and winked at his summoner. *Fun, isn't it?*

"Yes," Varis said slowly. "It is." Incredulity was giving way to novel sensations; triumph, and a fierce joy, hot and black as melted pitch.

And only think, boy, this is just the beginning. There's so much more, so much you've never dreamed of. What I could tell you, if I chose—

"The choice," Varis observed, "is no longer yours." Voice and face were expressionless. Behind the assumed impassivity, his emotions rioted. Power. This was what men fought and killed for. He had never tasted it before, hardly even dreamed of it. Now, all unexpected, it was here in his hands and mind, filling the void he hadn't known existed inside him. And now at last he recognized the nature of his own hunger.

Tchah. Very high and mighty, all of a sudden. This puppy thinks he knows everything. He knows nothing, he's like a child in need of guidance. Understand, boy, that Clotl Deathmaster is no commonplace, garden-variety ghost. He is not just any deadbody. The Deathmaster possesses occult insight, wisdom unparalleled, knowledge of multifarious secret practices—

"All of which he will communicate to me."

Will he? Will he? Perhaps, if he finds you worthy and humble—if he is in a communicative mood—if he is properly entreated—

"I do not entreat. I state facts. Clotl is gone, the Deathmaster's dead. As for his ghost—that thin rag of

identity is subject to my will." A retort worthy of his
brother the Ulor, delivered with all of Hurna XI's auto-
cratic inflexibility. Would the ghost rebel? Varis hoped so.
The power within him wanted exercise, screamed for it.

Clotl obliged.

Clotl Deathmaster remains—he is here! the ghost proclaimed. *You may twitch the strings that move his limbs as you
please—much joy may it bring you!—but his mind remains
inviolate. His necromantic knowledge is his own, now and forever. And none of your piddling, dilettante, rudimentary hocus-
pocus will ever change that, boy!*

Yelnyk of Krezniu had known how to deal with recal-
citrant spectres. Sesz Nishko had possessed almost equal
proficiency, in his time. Each sorcerer had recorded his
methods, and now Varis mentally re-read the pertinent
pages. The required procedure was internally strenuous,
but comparatively straightforward, involving the inner
recreation of a specialized Greej pattern, evasion of alter-
dimensional Blindnesses, psychic infiltration and im-
pingement; and after that, simple application of will.
Ordinarily, flawless recollection of an intricate Greej pattern might have proved all but impossible; under the influence of Clotl's jelly, however, it was easy.

Varis performed the requisite mental exercises with an
ease suggestive of great innate ability. In a matter of moments, his consciousness attained the spectral plane.
Clotl's ghostly awareness lay open to him—exposed and
defenseless as the mind of a living entity, shielded in tangible physicality, could never have been. Here was an almost pitiable vulnerability; spifflicated chaos, and a link
—or perhaps it could better have been regarded as a potential transference, a bridge—to an unimaginably alien
place, a dimension transcending and even encompassing
Forn. He could impress himself upon this consciousness at
will. There was nothing poor dead Clotl could do to shut
him out.

No time now for triumph, pity—even wonder—or any other distraction apt to shake the concentration that maintained necromantic control. Varis considered. Selecting a region of particular sensitivity—some lump of bloated delusion that seemed related to Clotl's sense of self —he pressed lightly.

"Tell me," he suggested, "everything you know of interdimensional resistance."

Go to a book, boy. Look it up. Or try hopping a few dimensions, and feel it for yourself.

Varis increased the pressure.

Ask me tomorrow. Maybe I'll tell you then, if I feel like it. Ask tomorrow.

More pressure, and he could sense the shape and texture of Clotl's resistance, the hopeless thin fragility of it. Pitiful, really. So easy to crush. But not too quickly. This sense of dominance, so novel, so delicious, was meant to be savored. Very delicately, Varis folded his will about the ghostly mind. Almost lovingly, he squeezed, taking care to avoid the sharp, sudden force that could end the game prematurely.

Heh. Not bad, boy. Clotl fidgeted and flickered, fading to the edge of visibility, but never quite escaping.

Python pressure upon the spectral presence, and it was lovely, it was exquisite, this first-time sense of utter mastery. It was emergence from the shadows; it was completion.

Gently. Slowly. Make it last.

Talented youngster. Confound you. Clotl's scowl conveyed petulant admiration.

A little more, a very little—and then, too soon, it was over. The ghost's resistance buckled, gave way altogether, and the words came squirting out like juice from a squeezed lemon. For the next several minutes, Varis harkened intently as Clotl disclosed his not inconsiderable understanding of interdimensional resistance. The listener's assimilation of sorcerous knowledge was immediate and complete, as if his brain had been formed by nature to receive and to store such information.

And there you have it boy. That's all there is.

It was clear he spoke the truth, so far as he knew.

"There are other topics. Alternate intention," Varis pressed, and a lengthy explanation followed. When the ghost finally ran out of words, a fresh inquiry presented itself at once. "The manufacture of the magical gel—materials and method. Explain."

Can't oblige.

"Certain?" Not reluctantly, Varis exerted force.

HEH! No good, boy. Not this time. The ghost grinned, displaying decayed, transparent teeth. *Can't dig it out of me if it's not there, now can you?*

"Then it was never your invention?" The sudden intensity of disappointment was almost painful.

Mine alone. Never think otherwise.

"And the formula—?"

Forgotten. Don't give me that fish eye, boy. I tell you, I don't remember the details. After all, it's been decades.

"I would have thought your memory excellent."

So it is. So it is! In spots. Let's see how YOUR memory's doing, fifty years hence. If you still have one.

"Your thoughts are open to me. I'll detect a lie."

Detect away.

A swift scan confirmed the ghost's veracity. Clotl's mind was full of malevolent whimsy, but there was none of the camouflaged resistance denoting deliberate falsehood. The essential recipe was indeed lost in the attic junkheap of dead memory.

Bad luck. Very sad. Oh well, that's the way it goes. Eh, boy?

But memories, while often mislaid, were infrequently destroyed. Somewhere, buried deep beneath the rubble of a spifflicated mind, the secret remained intact.

Somewhere, amidst a billion shattered, dusty recollections—

"It is still there inside you," Varis said.

Is it? Is it? Do I still have an inside, or an outside? Now that I'm dead, and bereft of my body, aren't "inside" and "outside" the same? If so, where's my memory? Inside or outside? Either or neither? Could be anywhere, couldn't it? Eh? Think you can track it down, boy?

"Eventually."

A universe of memories to sift through, one by one. How long d'you think that will take you?

Varis was silent, and the ghost's high-pitched giggles filled the cave.

By noon of the next day, he was ashamed of himself. The effects of the gel had worn off. He was exhausted and dispirited, afflicted with headache, smarting eyes, and a leaden sense of guilt. Yesterday's performance in the crypt, he now realized, had been a disgraceful business. He had enjoyed imposing his will upon that miserable ghost. He had virtually goaded it into defiance, then reveled in crushing its pathetic little resistance. His pleasure in winning that unequal contest had verged upon the obscene.

Yet winning was such a heady and unaccustomed joy . . .

No matter. He had erred, at some mental and physical cost. The rewards hardly justified the expense, and he wouldn't repeat the experiment. The best insurance of abstinence lay in the destruction of the gel, which, he belatedly recalled, he had carried from the crypt and concealed in his bedchamber for safekeeping; or perhaps for easy availability—yesterday's motives were hard to untangle. The glass jar now lay at the bottom of the wooden coffer in the corner. It would be the work of an instant to pitch vessel and contents from the tower window. Varis actually took a step toward the coffer, and paused. No need to go to such extremes, so suggestive of diminished self-control.

He had resolved to forgo sorcerous stimulation. He would simply abide by that decision.

For several days, he did so. The wooden coffer remained firmly locked, while Varis pursued his customary diversions. He was at all times acutely conscious of box and contents, but managed to refrain from touching either. This resolve might have continued intact indefinitely, had he not committed the error of consulting his necromantic notebooks upon the topic of transFornic vision. The conclusions of Yelnyk and Sesz diverged in several significant particulars. Sesz was the more modern, and probably the more objective observer; but Yelnyk had been gifted with inspired insight. It would be interesting to learn which of his two colleagues' methods Tiv Clotlenulev had favored in his day. It would be—educational.

Having taken hold, the idea was impossible to dislodge. Varis held out for another forty-eight hours, at the close of which he swallowed a double spoonful of jellied stimulant and hurried by way of the underground passage back to the Haudrensq crypt, there to raise old Clotl's manic shade.

How long, the ghost demanded upon manifestation, *are you going to let my poor old carcass just LIE there on the floor? Eh?*

"Surely it doesn't feel the cold."

Irrelevant, boy. The point is, it's not right. It's not respectful. I think it's pretty disgusting, if truth be told.

"The truth is just what should be told. I want to know—"

How'd you like it if it were YOUR frozen corpse sprawled out there for the rats to break their teeth on?

Varis repressed an urge to slam the ghost face first into the stone wall of the cave. The gel had reawakened his dormant passion for power, and this time, the desire was accompanied by an urge to inflict suffering. There was an old, hungry rage smoldering at the base of his brain. Perhaps it had always been there, banked and unnoticeable; but he noticed it now. The misery of others would feed the flame that he dimly recognized as a source of strength. Tempting, but there were surer ways of imposing his will.

"Give me the information I want, and I'll dispose decently of your body," Varis offered.

Heh. Leave it out for the wolves and crows, no doubt. Thank you very much.

"Cremation. Blued flame to char the threads and set you free." This procedure was set forth in Sesz's notebook.

Silver ring on the middle finger? Coins on the eyelids? A little bit of STYLE?

"Agreed. Now speak."

For the next half hour, Clotl held forth on the topic of transFornic vision. Varis listened, memory busily absorbing and recording. Beneath his preoccupation, a faint frustration flickered. Something was lacking. The information he wanted was forthcoming, but too voluntarily; he missed the gratification of mentally bludgeoning an adversary into submission. No matter. This way was actually far better. This way, Clotl was open, freely communicative, vain of his sorcerous knowledge. In fact, the old chatterer was showing off.

He had just cause for pride. His fund of information was immense, and his memory generally impressive, though subject to sporadic lapses. One such persistent lacuna encompassed the formula of the magical gel. Clotl might remember each twist and turn of the TransFornic Path, each and every whorl of the mind-boggling Fortieth Greej Pattern. The formula, however, he truly did not recall.

Disappointing, but not catastrophic. There were other means of heightening consciousness, innumerable stimulants. The notebooks outlined preparation of at least a dozen. That very evening, in the privacy of a windowless storage cellar, hastily converted to makeshift workroom, Varis commenced his experiments. The magical energy sang in his blood, and he labored tirelessly through the night. Hampered by the lack of essential ingredients, however, he found no success. The Crimson Ellodi, powdered shernivus leaves, roots, fungi, and rare metallic elements called for in all of the formulae were unavailable, and would remain so until the vernal thaws opened the TransBruzh to commercial traffic. In the meantime, fortunately, a substantial quantity of Clotl's gel remained.

There was no further thought of abstinence. The sensations were too rare and beautiful to relinquish; not now, when he'd barely tasted them. Perhaps later, when he'd drunk his fill, but not yet. He knew the danger of sorcerous excess. The Spifflicates of the Wrecks had taught him all he needed to know of that. But those reckless fools had destroyed themselves through grossest overindulgence, and he didn't intend to repeat their error. He'd exercise intelligent self-restraint, and he'd be safe. As Yelnyk of Krezniu had conclusively demonstrated, spifflication was avoidable.

Throughout the following weeks, there were repeated visits to the crypt, spaced at judicious intervals. There were numerous interviews with Clotl, and gradually, over the course of the bitter winter, Varis received and assimilated the bulk of the ghost's necromantic recollections. In exchange for cooperation, Clotl demanded funeral arrangements of ever-increasing grandeur; his requirements expanding to include various silver trinkets, an embroidered cloak, cakes and wine, a glazed urn for his ashes. All of these concessions were duly granted, and Clotl continued cheerily garrulous. The gel's formula, however, remained elusive.

There finally came a day when Clotl's mind, plumbed to the depths, had yielded all of its secrets. Perhaps forgotten knowledge still lingered, just beyond the limit of ghostly recollection; but such knowledge was inaccessible. For all practical purposes, the well had run dry. This so, the shade demanded its reward.

Varis did not demur. He might have continued his search through the spifflicated mind for the missing formula. He might have held Clotl indefinitely for that purpose, but chose otherwise. The spectre's presence, he noticed, was subtly oppressive. The lunatic loquacity, the shrill giggles and sly grimaces—all increasingly chafed his nerves. He wouldn't be sorry to rid himself of Clotl, once and for all. There was also, of course, the matter of his promises to the ghost. The influence of the gel had greatly reduced the significance of such details, but he had not entirely forgotten them.

Accordingly, Varis collected the gauds and trinkets, the edibles and the all-important urn. With his own hands he cut the faggots and stacked a funeral pyre in the snowy clearing before the mouth of the cave. On a bright, hard morning at the close of winter, he placed the suitably bedecked frozen corpse atop the pyre, and set torch to wood. The dried straw and kindling heaped at the base of the pile caught fire at once. The flames danced, and presently the unseasoned faggots ignited. A dense, strangling smoke arose, to billow through the clearing. Varis coughed a little and moved upwind; but his eyes, magically fortified for the occasion, remained dry and pain-free. Neither the glare of sunlight on snow, nor the cindery sting of the smoke, provoked a single tear. Drawing a deep breath and holding it, he performed the mental contortions required to lower dimensional barriers surrounding the flames. At once the fire took on the faint blue cast indicative of an ectoplasmic fuel supply. This "blued flame," promised to Clotl, would devour the threads binding spectre to corpse.

The pyre burned fiercely. The fire leapt and roared, the corpse at its center blackened and dwindled. When it finally ended, hours later, nothing remained but a dark spread of greasy ashes and a few charred scraps of wood and bone. Varis scooped it all into the big glazed urn. Wooden and human remnants mingled indiscriminately, but it scarcely mattered. He had kept his word, and Clotl was free to travel the unknown realms. Varis was free as well. His thoughts and mood lightened wonderfully. He had never quite realized the galling weight of the ghostly presence, until the burden was removed.

He shoveled snow over the blackened ground. He placed the sealed urn in a wall niche within the crypt, locked the gate, and departed with a sense of finality.

Winter was ending. Somewhere in the mountains, a winged white wolfling had fought and killed its way to power. A young Ulor had assumed sovereignty, and the world now began to renew itself. Or so the old folktales had it. On a more mundane level, the knife edge of the mountain wind was almost imperceptibly blunting itself, and the ice was reluctantly loosing its stranglehold upon the Bruzhois. The weeks passed, the snows abated, and gradually the serpentine curves of the TransBruzh redefined themselves. Presently, light traffic appeared upon the road; the boat-shaped runnered caravans of wandering Turos, the occasional commercial traveler hurrying between Rialsq and Lazimir. Such folk availed themselves of the annual interlude known as the Rift; a brief span—following initial recession of the snows, but preceding the massively muddy springtime thaws—during which travel was more or less possible.

It was the Turos that interested Varis. Such itinerant, irregular folk, known to deal in oddities of every questionable sort, presented a potential source of ingredients called for in the necromantic formulae of Sesz and Yelnyk. And it wasn't even necessary to seek them out. They continually deposited themselves upon his doorstep, demanding his attention and his patronage. He left orders at the gate to admit all comers, and soon a hawk-nosed Turo trader appeared in the Tollbooth's Great Hall.

"Bazikki," the fellow announced himself with a bow. "Your Lordship's humble servant."

Varis searched the visitor's face for mockery, and found there nothing but obsequious amiability. It had probably been an honest mistake. The Turo had not unnaturally assumed that the master of Castle Haudrensq must be a lord. The Rhazaullean Ulor's siblings, however, possessed no hereditary titles. Fraternal ennoblement was customary, and Breziot had received the dukedom of Otreska years earlier. But somehow Hurna had never seen fit to similarly honor his youngest brother.

"Show me your medicinals," Varis directed. "Herbs, essences, waters of d'Neef, your desiccations, bluepowders, granules, the Luminous Elements—all that you have."

"Gooth's Distillations?"

"Yes, but nothing less than fourth level."

"Ah, an educated consumer. A most informed gentleman. Your Lordship is fortunate. My present inventory is extensive and superior."

"Display it, then."

Bazikki spread his wares out. The collection of jars, boxes, bottles, flasks, and tubes covered a considerable expanse of tabletop. Varis inspected at leisure. The variety was admirable, and some of the items—if genuine—were impressively rare.

"Your price?" Varis tapped a bottle of Crimson Ellodi.

"Your Lordship's for a mere three hundred brazzles."

Varis nodded. Probably an exhorbitant sum, but it wasn't in him to haggle. "And this?"

"Oil of jurn, highest quality, guaranteed pure. Fifty brazzles."

"The extracts?"

"For your Lordship, twenty apiece."

Fifteen minutes later, selection completed, Varis said, "That will be all."

"Your Lordship is a connoisseur. In view of your Lordship's erudition and fine discernment, I offer an extraordinary opportunity."

"To acquire—?"

"A jewel, a prize, a wonder." One of Bazikki's numberless pockets yielded a small volume.

Varis briefly examined the book. Leather-bound, hand-lettered, with hand-painted illustrations—doubtless unusual and valuable. The title, in characters of gold: *Fatal Flora*.

"Poisonous plants?" he inquired.

"Identification. Preparation. Combinations. Presentation. Dosages. Symptoms. And more; much more. A treasure trove of useful information."

"Useful to whom? A physician, or a professional assassin?"

"It strikes me that his Lordship might wish to acquaint himself with the full potential of his various purchases. In any event, the volume itself is nonpareil. Note the beauty of the illustrations, the quality of the binding—"

"The price?"

Bazikki soon departed, a wealthier man. In the days that followed, others of his ilk appeared. Varis interviewed each at length, and, over the course of some three weeks, purchased most of the essential substances, even including an outrageously costly vial of powdered shernivus. He paid premium prices to anonymous transient traders. Perhaps some of these acquisitions would ultimately prove themselves counterfeit; time alone would tell. For the present, he possessed ample means of experimentation.

The world warmed, softened, and melted. The Rift closed itself, and Castle Haudrensq stood once more isolated, a high island in a sea of mud. Traffic ceased, and Varis gave himself over to necromantic research. His two notebooks pointed the way. In swift succession, he recreated nine of the twelve stimulants described by Sesz and Yelnyk, testing each upon himself. The results were at once encouraging and unsatisfactory. All of the stimulants were to some degree effective. All of them heightened physical strength and mental energy, all were exhilarating. Five of the nine speeded thought, two expanded the scope of consciousness. Of those last five, four induced prolonged illness, one of them confining him to his bed for the term of six days. One deadened all sensation in his limbs, and one was impossible to judge, for it gouged a thirty-six-hour hole in his memory. All required massive dosages, and none could truly duplicate the effect of Clotl's gel, although one or two of the strongest came close.

Thereafter, he embarked upon a program of experimental modification; altering the proportion of ingredients, adding and deleting, quantifying, improvising combinations. His studies were intense and consuming. He soon grew accustomed to magically enhanced existence, soon accepted it as the norm. The sharp, painless vision he now enjoyed seemed natural. The physical vigor and mental acuity seemed right. Surely this was the way that mind and body were meant to function.

Spring ripened and dried. The roads hardened, and travelers reappeared. Varis hardly noticed. Immersed in his studies, caught up in communion with the captive ghosts of his ancestors, the changing seasons passed him by. His power over the ghosts was growing; the result, no doubt, of internal transformation. He remained almost unaware of the change in himself until the morning that he bent over a washbasin to catch his own image reflected in the water. He saw a face older than the one he remembered, stronger, and hardened with a quality that he couldn't define; perhaps knowledge. And hungry, he realized. More than hungry. Ravenous, for something or other.

Whatever was missing was not to be found here, in the mountains. He needed rare books, proscribed necromantic writings, materials and instruments quite unavailable in this place. Far more important, he needed humans about him; dead ones upon whom to practice his new skills, and live ones to supply what had always been lacking.

It was time to return to Rialsq.

4

"IS IT TRUE what I've been hearing about Pire Zelkiv?" the Duchess of Otreska inquired of her husband.

"And what have you been hearing, Madam?"

"That Varis demolished him."

"Just so. Julienned him prettily, my baby brother did. Absolutely anatomized him. Gad, what a show that was!" Breziot roared with laughter.

"You mean, they actually fought a duel?"

"Certainly not. I spoke figuratively, of course. How absurd you are, Madam. What colossal ignorance."

"You'd be equally ignorant, were you mewed up *here*, as I am." The Duchess' expressive gesture took in the surrounding apartment. Located in a west wing of the House Uloric, the chilly ducal suite was decorated in unremitting black and white, in accordance with his Grace's preferences. A few rugs and wallhangings might have added warmth, but such adornments, compromising the stark elegance of the decor, were prohibited. The Duke's standards of excellence in design were sacrosanct, and the resulting domestic comfortlessness a price he could easily afford, in view of the rarity of his visits.

Ordinarily, there were better things to do. Tonight, however, diversion had palled, and for once Breziot ate with his family. Four of them—all suitably attired in black and white—sat at table in the black-and-white private dining chamber. The Duchess—over thirty years old, yet still youthful, handsome despite the vertical lines of discontent that etched her forehead—frowned and picked at her food. The Duke's son Cerrov—well-grown, sturdy, tawny as his father and his uncle the Ulor—fidgeted and kept his eyes fixed on his plate. The boy's younger sister Shalindra—fair-skinned and black-haired like her Uncle Varis, with startling black brows arching above the Haudrensq hazel eyes—studied her father with precociously analytical curiosity, as a naturalist might have eyed an unfamiliar species of reptile. Wife and children appeared unanimously ill at ease in the presence of the paterfamilias.

"I never go out. I hear the news at second hand from the servants, and half the time their tales are garbled," the Duchess complained.

"Your seclusion is modest, proper, and suitable, as befits my wife and the mother of my heir. What need have you of court gossip, or indeed, of anything that is not already yours? You have your needlework, your music, and a voluminous correspondence to keep you occupied. Above all, Madam, you have your children to care for—two healthy children, one of them a Haudrensq male. Does all of this not suffice to content you? Any reasonable woman would be grateful."

"Ah, but your Grace scarcely credits the existence of a reasonable woman. As a dutiful wife, I strive to fulfill my lord's expectations."

"How tiresome."

"Tiresome? Do you know what's tiresome?" The Duchess drummed her fingers. "It's tiresome to sit in here day after day without adult company and without variety. It's tiresome to waste my youth in prison, while life passes me by. It's tiresome to know that other women are laughing, dancing, gaming, enjoying themselves—"

"Petulance doesn't become you, Madam. Your voice takes on a disagreeably shrill tone, while that unattractive scowl adds at least ten years to your age. Perhaps fifteen. As for the tawdry diversions you covet, it should be clear to the meanest intelligence that such frivolities are the province of the young and the thoughtless—"

"You don't despise 'em for yourself, I notice. You certainly don't despise those Turo dancing girls."

"Madam, you surpass yourself. You plumb new depths of vulgarity. I've a position to maintain, if you'll recall. I am the Ulor's brother. My rank imposes certain social obligations, which I must fulfill as a matter of duty. And you, Madam, have duties of your own—the sacred obligations of motherhood. Remember your responsibilities," the Duke admonished soulfully. "Your babies need you."

"Oh, pish. Babies indeed. Cerrov's twelve and Shalindra's already ten. They don't need or want me hovering over them every moment of every day. There's certainly no shortage of servants to look after them for a few hours at a time, while I go out—"

"Servants," the Duke informed her, "cannot heal the wounds of a mother's neglect. I must confess, Madam, your callousness shocks me. I am astonished, and deeply saddened. Have you no care at all for your children's welfare? Would you go junketing off to pursue selfish pleasures, leaving your little ones abandoned, no doubt imagining themselves unwanted and unloved by their own mother?"

The Duchess had no immediate answer, but her young daughter did. "We wouldn't think that," said Shalindra.

"Quiet, child. Never contradict your father," the Duke advised, and returned to the attack. "If natural maternal feeling does not rule you, Madam, then I advise you to consider time-honored custom. The noble matrons of Rhazaulle are modest, retiring, self-effacing. Once wed, they retreat from public view, thereafter emerging from happy seclusion infrequently, and with great reluctance. In home and hearth, they find their paradise. It is my will that you do likewise; that is the Rhazaullean way."

"Not any more, your Grace," observed Shalindra. "Don't you remember that your own father abolished the Spousal Seclusion laws when he set about his national modernization? And don't you remember that your own brother, Uncle Hurna, officially called for the attendance of noble matrons at banquets and balls? And—"

"What did I tell you about contradicting me?" the Duke inquired.

"But, your Grace, our tutor gave us a history book, and—"

"Enough, you impertinent urchin. How dare you lecture me?"

"But—I didn't mean—but the book says—"

"Books! What does a girl your age want with books?"

"She is a very clever child," the Duchess remarked, deliberately drawing his Grace's fire back upon herself.

"Well, she doesn't need cleverness. Education will warp her character." Irritably, the Duke drained off his wineglass. A hovering servant instantly refilled it. "This is your work, Madam. You have failed to rear her properly, and now she is not only skinny and undesirably crow-haired, but rude, willful, disrespectful, and unladylike as well. Feed her books, and she'll grow up peculiar as Varis. She'll find no husband, she'll sour young, and we'll have her on our hands forever. Gad, what a disaster! And it's all the fault of your selfishness, Madam—your folly, your blundering irresponsibility—"

The Duchess regarded the wall stonily, while the tears welled up in Shalindra's eyes.

"Mother's done nothing wrong." For the first time since the meal began, the boy Cerrov lifted his eyes from his plate to fix his father with a very level gaze. "And there's nothing the matter with Shalindra."

"Contradiction again. Am I to be flouted by my own children? Intolerable. Your insolence validates my criticisms, boy. I await your apology."

Cerrov said nothing. Under the table, his sister grabbed his hand and held on tight. The silence stretched.

"Well?" The Duke bent a freezing glare upon his son. The boy's eyes did not fall, and it was the father who blinked. "Well? I am waiting. What have you to say?"

"Mother's in the right," said Cerrov. "So is Shalindra. And I won't say I'm sorry for telling the truth."

"Outrageous. Absolutely outrageous. This place is a madhouse, worse than the Wrecks. Where are the respect and affection due the head of the household? Here, I encounter defiance and ingratitude. Where is my loving spouse? My dutiful offspring? Here, I confront a peevish termagant and her brood of ill-bred, unruly, unmannerly little savages. It is too dreary for words. But I assure you, things are about to change. Cerrov—" the Duke snapped his fingers. "Stand."

Loosing his sister's hand, the boy obeyed. The Duchess and Shalindra exchanged apprehensive glances.

"You will stay where you are until we have heard your apology," decreed the Duke.

Silence. While his mother and sister prodded their untasted food about their plates, and his father ate, Cerrov stood motionless.

"Well?" the Duke inquired, some minutes later. "Exactly how long are you prepared to stand there like a tailor's dummy?"

"Forever, your Grace," Cerrov replied, with courtesy and absolute conviction.

"I see. It might be interesting to put that claim to the test, but this is neither the proper time nor place. I am the most liberal, patient, and forbearing of parents," the Duke observed, "but even my indulgence finds its limit. A child's faults require correction. It is my parental duty to provide it. Cerrov, you may go to my study, and select a switch. I will join you directly."

A network of welts and scars marking Cerrov's flesh beneath his clothes bore testimony to the Duke's paternal zeal.

The Duchess met Shalindra's stricken eyes. Her own expression was carefully unconcerned. When she spoke, she echoed her husband's negligent tone. "But how tedious. Surely your Grace cannot mean to interrupt dinner over such a trifle. The chef will be desolated. Tonight, in honor of your Grace's presence, he offers his finest. One of the courses includes a Vonahrish saffron soufflé, which will collapse if not consumed at its precise instant of inflated perfection. Should such a tragedy occur, your Grace's reputation as a connoisseur stands to suffer."

The Duke hesitated.

"Come," the Duchess suggested, "the matter scarcely justifies sacrifice of a culinary masterpiece. As for these wretched children—if the creatures vex their father, then of course, they shall be banished at once." Allowing her lord no opportunity to reply, she clapped her hands smartly. "Cerrov, Shalindra—off to your rooms, and no argument."

Brother and sister scurried thankfully for the exit. Their mother drew a relieved breath.

The Duke frowned after his fleeing offspring. "The boy wants discipline. The girl is a hoyden. Perhaps I will—"

"Another time. Later. Remember the soufflé. Come, let's find a more diverting topic. Tell me all about Varis and Pire Zelkiv. Your Grace adorns such tales with incomparable wit." The Duchess produced the creditable counterfeit of an admiring smile.

"You are very cozy all of a sudden. Don't think I don't see through you, Madam."

"Ah, your Grace is far, far too sharp for me. But the story?"

"Oh, very well. If you wish. Here it is, then. Hurna had called yet another of those ghastly, purgatorial planning sessions—"

"Planning sessions?"

"Gad, do you know nothing at all? Haven't you heard about Dasune's visit?"

"Yes," the Duchess replied quietly. "Even I have heard about that."

All the Zalkhash buzzed with news of the Aennorvi King Dasune's impending arrival. The visit of a foreign monarch was a rarity, an occasion of significance both social and political. The vanity and diplomacy of the host nation demanded a display of overwhelming hospitality. There would be banquets and balls, parties and Honor Guard parades, concerts, theatricals, a Snow Festival, fireworks and illuminations, sleigh rides and races, an Ice Kings match, a White Bombardment tournament, and more. In short, no trouble or expense was to be spared. Preparations had begun weeks ago, and of late, activity had reached fever pitch. The House Uloric itself was in a state approaching chaos, and the reverberations of assorted domestic quakes had made themselves felt, albeit faintly, even within the confines of the Duchess of Otreska's black-and-white prison. In the midst of this tumult, the unheralded return to Court of the Ulor's youngest brother had gone all but unnoticed—initially. The long, solitary retreat, however, had wrought changes; and in the few days following his reappearance, Varis had revealed a new talent for making his presence felt.

"Well, this particular session concerned itself with Dasune's reception," the Duke resumed. "Entry of the Aennorvi gang into Rialsq, arrival at the Zalkhash, greetings, ceremonies of welcome, lodging of royalty, and all that tedious slop. As Minister of Diplomacy, of course Zelkiv had to be there, and so was Varis—"

"Why?" interrupted the Duchess. "It doesn't concern

Varis, and I'd thought the Ulor considers him something of an embarrassment."

"You are behind the times as always. I gather you've not seen my brother since his return from his—retreat—meditation—sulking fit—whatever it was he was doing perched up on that mountaintop for the better part of the past year."

The Duchess shook her head.

"Well, you'd hardly recognize him. He's changed. In fact, he's quite transformed himself."

"In what way?"

"Every way. His appearance, for one thing. To begin with, he's abandoned that infernal weeping. His eyes are quite adequate, as I always suspected, so he's discarded the bizarre black spectacles and the ridiculous hat. He's gained a bit of weight, looks quite fit and altogether less like a shambling skeleton. And speaking of shambling—you remember the way he used to slouch around, head down and shoulders hunched, as if he were trying to make himself invisible? Well, he's straightened up at last. These days he carries himself like the brother of an Ulor. Miraculous as it may seem, he turns out to possess a certain idiosyncratic style, even authority. It seems he is a Haudrensq, after all. These days, Varis walks into the room, and people notice. Actually, they gawk at him, as if they took him for an Ice Kings champion, at the very least."

"Difficult to imagine."

"Believe me. But those are only the externals," the Duke continued. "There are other things. His speech, for example. Remember that monotone mumbling of his? Didn't matter what he said, it came out sounding dull. Now, it's as if he'd more or less—awakened. He's confident, forceful; in fact, he expresses himself rather effectively. Effectively enough to settle poor old Zelkiv's business, once and for all." His Grace guffawed.

"How?"

"As Minister of Diplomacy, Zelkiv was obliged to present at least a token selection of recommendations. If the poor simpleton had possessed a single shred of good sense, he'd have paid some clerkly flunky to compose a list for him. Unhappily, he'd been out drinking himself paralytic the night before, and thus neglected prudence.

"The afternoon of the meeting," the Duke recalled with relish, "Zelkiv rolls in bleary-eyed, green-faced, and half an hour late. He claims illness, makes his apologies, lurches on over to his chair, and more or less collapses into it. The Ulor, I might observe, is hardly transfigured with joy. Hurna doesn't mind a bit of jollification—provided it doesn't interfere with business. Nothing is said, however, and the session drags on wearily, until, without warning, the Ulor turns around, pins the semi-conscious Zelkiv with a very chilly stare, and demands the Minister of Diplomacy's suggestions. Zelkiv is taken entirely off guard, of course. The poor sot sits open-mouthed for a moment or two; then rallies, fumbles in his pocket, brings forth this miserable-looking crumpled scrap of paper, squints at it, and begins to mutter like a senile Venerator. It turns out that he actually does have a few ideas, after all—bad ones, but still, ideas.

"'An escort to guide King Dasune and his retinue through the streets of Rialsq to the main gate of the Zalkhash. Two dozen riders arrayed in violet and black, the colors of Aennorve's flag—a pretty compliment,' Zelkiv suggests, and people are nodding sagely, until Varis speaks up, very quietly and courteously. 'In Aennorve,' my brother announces, 'that particular color combination is set apart for one use alone. The pretty compliment you propose would be viewed by the visitors as a deliberate affront to their flag.'

"So much for that one. But Zelkiv tries again. 'A Rhazaullean banquet,' he suggests, 'consisting entirely of our native specialties.' And he goes on to name a few, including pickled lorbers, whereupon Varis speaks up

again, to point out the fact that the Aennorvis regard
lorbers as food for swine.

" 'Gifts of greeting,' Zelkiv attempts, and suggests
some sort of trumpery jewelry for the wives of the visiting
nobles. And Varis politely informs him that Aennorvis use
the term 'trinkets from strangers' as a euphemism for harlotry. My brother *knows* all this twaddle, you see. He studied for years, having nothing better to do, and now he's a
walking encyclopedia of alien trivia.

"And so it went on," his Grace summarized, "with
Zelkiv digging his own grave deeper with every word, and
Varis methodically shredding him. Gad, it was exquisitely
done—it was downright surgical. I could hardly keep
from laughing out loud, but the Ulor was not amused.
Hurna grew testier by the minute; finally lost his temper
altogether, called Zelkiv a drunken fool, sacked him on
the spot, and appointed Varis new Minister of Diplomacy
—which is what he should have done in the first place.
What a show it was! Poor Zelkiv!" Merriment all but
overcame the Duke. "Poor old Zelkiv! I could almost feel
sorry for him. Any other time, he might have gotten away
with it, but he chose exactly the wrong moment to parade
his incompetence. With Hurna's own personal stake in the
matter so high—"

"Personal?" inquired the Duchess. "How so? King
Dasune comes to push an Aennorvi-Rhazaullean alliance
against Immeen—to cobble a trade agreement of some
sort—to settle that wrangle over fishing rights in the
Straits of Bitheen—"

"Oh, that's the official line. Truth is, the old boy's
coming to peddle his daughter. Yes," the Duke answered
his wife's unspoken question. "Hurna's been a widower for
two years now. He's enjoyed his blessed respite from mat-
rimony to the fullest, but all good things must come to an
end. Time to choose a new Ulorre-consort, and you may be
certain there's no shortage of candidates. Assorted kings
and optimistic nobles have been dangling their marriage-

able girls under Hurna's nose for months now, and a most amusing spectacle it's been. Appalling creatures, some of them. Vast bulging bottoms, pocked complexions, hook-nosed snaggletoothed wonders—gad, such public eyesores should have been drowned at birth. Perhaps it's not too late to rectify the error. Excessive ugliness in women ought to be declared illegal."

"A truly progressive policy."

"Pah, you've no sense of humor, Madam. In any case, his Majesty Dasune arrives with a putatively virginal seventeen-year-old daughter in tow. A political alliance strengthened by marriage stands some fair chance of hold-ing up, and so, if the girl proves reasonably palatable, Hurna will probably take her. But he demands inspection prior to purchase, and that's what this royal visit is really about."

"Poor child," the Duchess murmured, but she was se-cretly smiling. A perfectly genuine sympathy for the Aen-norvi princess could not damp her pleasure in the prospect of her own impending liberty. The heavy emphasis upon the social aspects of the occasion was now explained; the utility of the parties and banquets self-evident. As young Shalindra had observed, attendance of noble matrons at such functions was encouraged, even demanded, by the Ulor. There would be dancing, beautiful clothes, bright conversation. She would enjoy them all, and this time, her husband could not prevent it. His Grace chatted on. The Duchess scarcely heard him.

The saffron soufflé arrived. The one-sided flow of con-versation faltered, and the Duke finally noticed his wife's abstraction. "What are you looking so smug about, Madam?" his Grace demanded.

"What? Oh, nothing. That is, just wondering—what do you suppose accounts for the change in your younger brother?"

"Maturity. Fresh mountain air. Both or neither.

Really, what signifies the cause? It is such a remarkable improvement."

Varis awoke sweat-drenched and wire-nerved. Another nightmare. Images . . . Mutilated bodies, screaming eyes and shattered mouths, black blood steaming upon moonlit snow . . . and worse things, that his waking mind blotted from memory; nearly forgotten things, whose stench somehow lingered in his brain. They came to him frequently, of late; it would seem that the close air of the Zalkhash bred nightmare. But did the term "nightmare" properly apply to visions evoking neither fear nor horror, but rather, a curious excitement? For there could be no denying the molten pleasure of those dreams. Hard to account for that. He could only suspect the influence of the varied magical substances currently maintaining his good health and untroubled eyesight. The sole means of testing this theory involved temporary sacrifice of the stimulants, a course he emphatically did not intend to pursue. In view of the benefits he now enjoyed, what mattered a few dreams?

Yet they seemed to be waxing in clarity and vividness, as if his consciousness was gradually losing its power or desire to shut out the ghastliest of visitors. And this latest dream, tonight's, surely surpassed them all in violence, perversity, and allure.

He was feverish, perhaps; almost suffocating. Varis sat up, flinging the heavy covers aside. The hand that reached out to pull the bed curtains open was shaking. Absurd. A draft of cold, comparatively fresh air rushed in through the gap in the hangings, abruptly chilling his damp flesh. He shuddered, and his head cleared. Confusion abated, lurid visions faded, but his breath came fast, and his heart still raced. He was wide awake now, and certain to remain so. No sense lying abed, open-eyed. He might as well put the empty time to some use.

He rose, wrapping himself in the quilted, fur-collared

dressing gown that warded off the bitterest chill of the
nighttime bedchamber. Making his way in the dark to the
stove, he poked up and replenished the fire; lighted a
splint, and touched the flame to a couple of candles. One
end of the chamber brightened to orange twilight. Varis
stood motionless, listening intently. His ears caught not
the slightest whisper or scrape of human activity. His few
personal servants doubtless slept. Nonetheless, he took the
precaution of bolting the bedroom door before fetching his
latest acquisition from its hiding place. A hollow space
beneath one of the floorboards yielded a fantastically rare
and illegal manuscript of Arkhoy's notorious *Memoirs,* of
which only four hand-lettered copies were known to exist.
Arkhoy, most infamous of necromancers, had terrorized
Rialsq during the reign of the Ulor Hurna III. So formidably armed a sorcerer could only, in the end, be vanquished
by a coalition of his disparate enemies; but not before
committing the catalogue of his singular accomplishments
to parchment. Popular legend painted Arkhoy as the
monster-murderer of no less than a hundred peasant children; whereas, if the *Memoirs* were to be believed, the actual bag stood nearer three hundred.

Varis sat reading, intrigued by Arkhoy's ornate, incongruously formal account of a ritual human sacrifice
wherein all bloodletting was performed by ghostly hands,
with the reluctant shades even compelled to participate in
the subsequent cannibalistic feast. The power of the necromancer over the ghosts that he summoned was bounded, it
seemed, only by the limits of inventiveness. The possibilities, as Arkhoy's example demonstrated, were all but infinite. . . . Varis read on, and the banished red fancies
came crowding once more to the forefront of his mind.
Alien yet familiar internal voices whispered insistently.
The images—Arkhoy's and his own—blazed through his
brain. His hands were clammy again, the fingers leaving
damp marks upon the pages. He'd smudge that priceless
ink if he weren't careful. He set the *Memoirs* aside; rose and

paced the chamber. His tension mounted. A headache pressed his skull experimentally. It was months now since he'd last suffered one of his headaches. Imagining himself quite free of that misery, he had almost forgotten the sensation. But he remembered it now.

Too many people about him. Too many faces, too close. Too many voices, too loud, too incessant. Too much noise and stir, for one grown used to silent solitude. He had not as yet reaccustomed himself to the bustling Zalkhash—that was all the trouble. Presently the hectic atmosphere would grow familiar, but in the meantime, he was jittery and sleepless.

The presence of the Aennorvi visitors was scarcely helping matters. King Dasune and his entourage had been in residence for nearly three weeks now, and the foreign element influenced all things. The constant round of lavish entertainments interspersed with conferences, negotiations, and discreet strategy-planning sessions was enough to tax almost anyone's endurance. Even the Ulor Hurna, so gigantically vital and tireless, was beginning to show signs of strain. Hurna—no fool, but uncomplicated, almost crude in the directness of his manner and methods—did not relish prolonged fencing matches with his urbane Aennorvi counterpart. Hurna wished the diplomatic shilly-shallying over and done with, the bargain concluded. He was frustrated, impatient, although still maintaining a jovial public face; and his irritation, all the more intense for its repression, was making itself felt among his luckless intimates. Uloric proximity was no pleasant business these days, not even for closest friends and kin. Not even for Hurna's youngest brother Varis, crept into remarkable favor these days, by reason of his impressive knowledge of Aennorvi affairs; his newfound, oddly ascetic distinction; and a hitherto-unsuspected flair for politics. Even brilliant, useful Varis occasionally suffered the blast of the royal temper.

Still, the vast court comedy was an engrossing spectacle, and some of the individual players, worthy of study. His Majesty Dasune, for example—surely an interesting foil to the Rhazaullean Ulor; Hurna's opposite in almost every respect. Middle-aged, middle-sized, soft-middled. Said to be balding beneath his peruke. Clever, dark, mobile face. Amused eyes, cynical lips, eloquent hands. Exquisite tailoring, exquisite courtesy, exquisite subtlety. Great charm of manner, refined appetite for pleasure, supremely civilized. No wonder Hurna couldn't stand him.

Then there was Dasune's daughter, the hapless Princess Olisi, scarce-considered pawn in this large game. A sad, rather touching young creature; quiet and introverted, quite lost in the shadow of her charismatic father. Tiny, pale, and always cold. Multiple layers of fabric and fur failed to shield her thin little body against the drafts of the House Uloric. Her gloved hands always shook, her teeth continually chattered, and nothing could induce her to distance herself more than a step or two from the stove in any chamber she chanced to occupy. A puny child was no fit competitor at the Rhazaullean court. Hurna would marry her, and she'd be annihilated, deprived of identity, swallowed alive. And judging by the look of perpetual melancholy clouding her small white face, Olisi recognized her fate.

There were others deserving of note, of course—various nobles and functionaries, of both nationalities; a number of their wives, companions, and attendants. Absorbing, as well as educational, to observe the interaction among these characters thrown by circumstance into unlikely propinquity for the space of a month or so. Aennorvi and Rhazaullean—hereditary rivals, traditional opposites in taste and temperament, often mutually uncomprehending without the aid of interpreters—were now busily forging friendships and political alliances, starting feuds, love affairs, and financial ventures. Some of the personal connections now established would influence diplomatic relations between the two nations for years to come.

Most of course, were transitory and insignificant, the mere fodder of gossip. To the latter category surely belonged all exchanges between King Dasune and the Duchess of Otreska, who, within a day of the Aennorvi arrival, had commenced a red-hot public flirtation.

Nobody really seemed to blame the Duchess. Her husband had kept her virtual prisoner for years; no wonder that a taste of freedom had gone straight to her head. Prolonged deprivation explained her current hunger for diversion, society, gallantry. And no doubt about it, his Majesty Dasune was gallant. What the King lacked in youth and good looks was more than balanced by rank, wit, polish, and flattering attentiveness. Dasune troubled to disguise neither his interest nor his purpose. He was the Duchess' constant dancing partner, dinner companion, cavalier. Always he was at her side, amusing and admiring. He was known to have sent her several valuable gifts, and such was his skill as a wily campaigner that his largesse included the lady's two children, who consequently became his allies—a stratagem admired by all spectators.

The Duchess was understandably susceptible. Following the guests' departure, she might pay dearly, but for the present, her life was the stuff of feminine fantasy. The Duke of Otreska was livid, but helpless; the royalty of the visiting predator precluded open resentment, much less retaliation. His plight drew more laughter than sympathy. Few pitied Breziot, bane of many an outraged husband, now tasting his own medicine at last.

Breziot wasn't taking it well. His efforts to maintain a casual public demeanor were unsuccessful. Just yesterday, for example, during the festivities at the White Level, when his Majesty Dasune had gracefully insisted that the Duchess of Otreska alone conduct him through the House of Ice—the Duke's dyspeptic expression had been wonderful to behold. Sitting alone in the orange murk of his chamber, Varis smiled at the recollection, and even that slight change in expression sent the pain slicing through his skull. His headache was intensifying. Another couple of minutes, and the first wave of nausea would hit. The symptoms were familiar, but tonight seemed worse than he remembered, almost unbearable, as if brain and body stood poised on the verge of violent revolt. Breziot's discomfiture and all such pleasant matters fled his mind. There was only sickness, and the misery of it. Judging by past experience, he might expect to find himself incapacitated for the next thirty-six hours, or so. And he had thought all that was finished . . .

Varis shut his eyes. Whiteness dawned behind his lids, and he saw once more the wintry courtyard at Castle Haudrensq. The noon sun flashed on snow and ice, but the light didn't trouble him—he was vital, invulnerable, filled with exhilaration—he remembered it well. He would always remember it. A sense of loss and longing filled him; a profound desire that ached and burned. He recognized it now. Strange that it should have taken him so long.

A moment later he was kneeling beside the floor niche. There were several necromantic notebooks stored away in that compartment, together with a small collection of glass vessels, spoons, and a measuring cup. The stoppered vials held the most successful results of his various experiments, but he didn't so much as glance at them. His hand flew to the lidded jar containing Clotl's gel; the first of the stimulants he had known, and still unequalled. He swallowed only two rounded spoonfuls. It was not easy to restrain himself, but the stuff was limited in quantity, and irreplaceable.

Varis resumed his chair. Expelling his breath in a quiet sigh, he leaned back and let the peace flow through him. The headache was gone, already forgotten. He was whole, he was himself again. His eyes were fixed upon the wall, onto whose blank surface his mind projected remarkable images. For a time there was silence as he watched, and then the voices started up again, whispering from some unmapped region deep inside him. They did not alarm him, now that he was fortified; indeed, he was hungry for instruction. He hearkened, while they whispered on and on.

"My dear, you give me very great happiness. Allow me to express my affection and my gratitude." King Dasune handed his companion a small velvet box.

The Duchess of Otreska felt the flush of mingled gratification and embarrassment warm her face. She adored presents, and this one was not the first she had accepted from him, but coming at such a moment, the offering's significance seemed open to some question. She regarded the box uncertainly.

"Do you not wish to open it?" Dasune inquired, amused.

The Duchess threw him a slightly anxious glance. Without its customary frame of artificial hair, his face looked older, almost unfamiliar. But his dark eyes, full of admiration and apparent candor, could surely be trusted. Such a change from her husband. She opened the box, and her breath caught. Her fingers shook a little as she drew forth a circular gold locket on a fine gold chain; an extraordinary piece set with diamonds. The stones edging the circumference were colorless; splendid, but conventional. The one in the center, however, was unique—a great black diamond, combining hard fire and unknowable darkness.

"It's—superb," she whispered, former disquietude fading. The magnitude of the gift clearly confirmed her value in his eyes. *Didn't it?*

"Then it is worthy of its new owner. I am delighted that it pleases your Grace. Allow me." Taking the locket from her, he fastened it deftly about her throat. "There—the perfect finishing touch to your very charming ensemble."

They both laughed.

"But truly, your Majesty is too generous—"

"Bah, my dear, do you not realize there is nothing in the world I wouldn't do for you?" he inquired easily. "Rest assured, I am your Grace's hopeless slave."

He said a good deal more, and time passed quickly until the clock struck, recalling the Duchess to reality.

"I must go," she told him. "Or I'll be missed."

"So soon?" Dasune touched her shoulder lightly. "May I not persuade you to stay a while longer?"

"Well—" The Duchess smiled. "Perhaps a little while longer."

Two nights later, Varis stood amidst lush greenery, listening to music and to his oldest brother's complaints.

"It's hot as a kettle in here. I'm sweating like a pig," the Ulor snarled, mopping his wet brow with a bare hand. "They've got this place tricked out like some sort of cross between a jungle and a whorehouse. It makes me want to puke."

Hurna's condemnatory sweep took in the whole of the Grand Ballroom, site of the evening's festivities—this time, a celebration calculated to dazzle the sophisticated Aennorvi guests, at any cost. Mere glitter would hardly suffice to achieve this aim; a degree of inventiveness was required. The household functionaries entrusted with the planning of the party had thought long and hard, eventually hitting upon a solution that expressed an essentially Rhazaullean concept of the flabbergasting—a wholly unseasonable taste of summer. Tropical summer, at that. Thus, a deployment of camouflaged stoves and braziers heated the ballroom to a swelter. Hidden tubs of boiling water added an exotic steaminess to the atmosphere. Potted palms arched overhead, vines dangled, creepers twisted, thickets of shrubbery greened the corners, and everywhere there were flowers—unimaginable masses of priceless hothouse blossoms, their languid perfume weighting the oppressive air. The buffet table was heaped with summer's all-but-unobtainable fruits. At the opposite end of the room, an artificial waterfall cascaded into a pool stocked with tropical fish. Butterflies looped amidst the flowers, while gaudy birds-of-paradise fluttered in the trees; this last touch pretty but misguided, for raucous avian voices warred with the music, and dollops of white excrement rained down upon the marble tiles faster than the harried servants could clean them.

"Whoever cooked this up should slake the Funnel. It's an assassination. I'm suffocating." Encased in the formal attire that he detested, Hurna XI tugged uselessly at his tight cravat. "So is everyone else in sight. Except you."

The statement contained a limited measure of truth. Alone among male Rhazaulleans, Varis appeared unaffected by the heat of the ballroom. His brow remained dry and clear, his dark garments impeccable. His compatriots, accustomed to arctic temperatures, were uniformly limp, damp, and rumpled. Their women—accorded the unaccustomed luxury of diaphanous, revealing dress—had fared better. Many actually appeared to be enjoying themselves. The sun-loving Aennorvi guests, of course, were in their natural element; content and comfortable as they had not been since their arrival in this cold, harsh land. The Ulor Hurna, perceiving his visitors as effete, incomprehensible, and not quite human, was serenely blind to their reactions.

"How do you contrive to stay so cool in this damned steam bath, youngster?"

Varis smiled faintly.

Hurna evidently expected no reply, for he continued, without pause, "There are the smart ones." He pointed. "I envy them."

Varis's eyes followed his brother's digit to a group of uproarious Noble Landholders, masked and clad in fantastic disguises. The maskers were clustered about the pool at the foot of the artificial cascade. One of them was actually in the pool, standing knee-deep in water. With the aid of silver forks lifted from the buffet table, they speared for tropical fish. Bellows of approbation greeted each success.

"They've come from a revel, where men know how to amuse themselves," Hurna continued. "They'll probably tolerate this overheated funeral service for another ten minutes or so, and then they'll go back to the revel. Lucky bastards."

"Strathha's?" Varis inquired.

"His annual. Said to be the best he's ever thrown. I've heard he's got a brace of red-haired drabs from Madam Wlav's, stripped bare, armed with razors, and primed to fight each other to the death. That I'd like to see. So would everyone else in this room, I'll wager."

"Perhaps not everyone. The Aennorvis appear satisfied. Your little princess seems content."

True enough. Olisi had bloomed in the tropical warmth of the Grand Ballroom. Relieved for once of the furs and heavy wrappings that had burdened her since her arrival, she was dancing the bolaska with a young Aennorvi noble. Her face had lost its pinched look, and a tinge of rose colored her cheeks. When she smiled up at her partner, she revealed an unexpected, childlike prettiness.

The Ulor, however, was not impressed. " 'My' little princess? There's a title of ownership you can keep, and welcome. What should I want with that pale-faced, thin-lipped, flat-chested mannequin? It'll be like taking a rack of antlers to bed. Boring, too. Namby-pamby, milk-and-water, prates of poesies and posies in that silly foreign accent. Really sad."

"Yes." Expressionlessly, Varis studied the sacrificial virgin. "It is."

"This one will be even worse than my last. At least the last Ulorre managed to squeeze out a few healthy brats before crypting it. This white little skeleton's scarcely like to accomplish so much. I tell you, youngster, I wish I were out of it."

"Do you so, Ulor? In that case, might I advise you to hold out for better terms?"

"A little late for that. Dasune and I have struck a bargain."

"Signed and sealed?"

"Tomorrow."

"Then not too late. Try telling his Majesty that you'll accept his daughter sans dowry."

"Brilliant. Next you'll suggest that I pay *him*."

"Exactly so. Offer two hundred thousand brazzles—"

"*What?!*"

"—In exchange for a one-hundred-year lease upon the Czennivhor Islands."

"Smoke and dreams, youngster. The Czennivhors include the nearest breeding grounds of the sea-sables. The profits from the harvesting of furs in two seasons exceeds that two hundred thousand figure you mention. And that's not even including the income from the flogae beds in Czenni Bay. You must take Dasune for a numskull."

"Far from it. But I take him for a debtor in severe financial straits. Were you aware that the Aennorvi debt to the Dhrevate of Immeen falls due one year hence? Or that the defense of the Aennorvi colony at Jumo demands complete refurbishment of an antiquated fleet, at immense cost? His Majesty's needs are pressing, his treasury all but exhausted."

"Where d'you pick up your information?"

"Wherever it is sold or given away. For example, the estimates of a dozen shipwrights and chandlers are filed for public record at the City Hall in Feyenne. The bids were submitted last year, but the contract has not yet been awarded. You may draw your own conclusions."

"Why has no one brought this to my attention? I'm surrounded by incompetents. Why did *you* not speak sooner?"

"The reports from Feyenne reached me today, Ulor. It is not too late to act upon them. Release from the dowry obligation, coupled with a substantial cash offer, may prove particularly tempting to his Majesty at this time."

"It might. It just might, at that. Hah. If it doesn't, I can always tell him to take his waxworks daughter to market elsewhere. I'll scarcely mourn her loss. On the other hand, if he bites—quite a coup, youngster. Quite a coup. I did right in appointing you Minister of Diplomacy." Hurna grinned. "No doubt about it."

Varis inclined his head a couple of degrees.

"I think I've got that old fox where I want him, well and truly snared. I can hardly wait to see his face when I put it to him. He's vastly underestimated Rhazaulle. Those Aennorvi twinkle-toes regard us as semi-barbarians, you know."

"I wonder why."

"Dasune's about to discover his mistake. Where is he now? I don't see the old boy."

"Over there." Varis gestured minutely. "Dancing with our sister-in-law again."

He might better have said "still," for his Majesty's choice of a partner had not varied throughout the evening. So undisguised a preference amounted to outright indiscretion, but neither the King nor the Duchess of Otreska appeared overly concerned with public opinion. The musicians were playing a slow trierge. Dasune held his partner unnecessarily close. The hand that should have rested upon the woman's waist was placed high, to press the smooth flesh bared by her low-backed gown. The two were smiling intimately into each other's eyes, occasionally whispering and laughing.

"So he is. Those two look about ready to drop linen and go at it on the floor." Hurna laughed hugely. "Poor Breziot! Anything sprouting out of his forehead, yet?"

"Forehead's clear," Varis reported, not without enjoyment. "But he's not looking easy."

"Where is he? Oh, never mind, I see him." Hurna's

merriment expanded. "I think our good brother's about to explode. This is rich."

The Duke of Otreska, unmistakably the worse for drink, stood glowering in a corner. His face was flushed and moist; angry, slightly unfocused eyes fixed upon the Duchess and her partner. Presently pushing himself off from the wall, he lurched toward the mutually absorbed couple. Whirling dancers impeded but did not halt his progress. His look of sullen alcoholic fanaticism was recognized by both of his brothers. That look invariably preceded violence.

The Ulor's grin vanished. "Fit for the Wrecks," he observed, and cursed softly.

Unaware of surveillance, Breziot advanced. His right hand was buried in his coat pocket.

"Armed?" Varis asked.

"Don't know. If he's got something, the damned fool's sure to use it. Cut him off."

Quickly the two of them pushed their way through the crowd to Breziot's side. The Ulor's hand descended upon his middle brother's arm. The Duke rounded furiously, recognized his sovereign, and controlled himself with obvious effort.

"Calmly, Brother," Hurna advised. "Remember where you are."

"Don't give me that! You think I'm going to stand gaping like a dolt while that Aennorvi ooze makes free with my wife?"

"Dancing and a little fooling." The Ulor shrugged. "Harmless."

"That slut smirches my honor. I'll whip her bloody. I'll sew that busy hole shut."

"Lower your voice, Brother."

"As for that foreign fop, I'll take those wandering hands of his off at the wrist. King or no, I'll call him out, I swear I will!"

"*Lower—your—voice.*" The Ulor's huge hand, still resting upon his brother's arm, tightened like a vise.

"*Ouch!* Gad!" Breziot winced, and his threats broke off abruptly.

"I want this drunken idiot out of here." Hurna's eyes sought his youngest brother. "Any idea what to do with him?"

"I won't go," Breziot muttered. "You cannot dismiss me like an unruly child."

"I am master here, and I will be obeyed." The Ulor's voice remained even, but his tawny brows lowered ominously.

It was never a safe thing to cross Hurna XI, but the Duke seemed beyond caution. He folded his arms. "I say I am not ready to—"

"Forgo Strathka's revel?" Varis broke in easily. "I don't blame your Grace. They say the Noble Landholder has outdone himself this year. We'll be the judge of that."

The Duke blinked. "Strathka's?"

"Redheaded razor-girls, this year."

"Turos?" Woozy interest sparked his Grace's bloodshot eyes.

"I believe so."

"Double-jointed? Oiled?"

"Quite likely. Your Grace is certain to find diversion. Shall we go?" Varis offered.

"Well—I'm not ready—redheaded? Oh, very well." The Duke's head bobbed. "Very well."

"Youngster, I am beginning to wonder how I ever made do without you," said the Ulor.

Varis nodded acknowledgment, and deftly steered his wobbling brother from the Grand Ballroom.

Breziot's sledge carried them. Sitting in the warm dimness of the pagoda-roofed vehicle, Varis could not avoid recalling last year's similar excursion. Then, as now, early winter; same ridiculous scarlet sledge and white horses; same two passengers, one of them preoccupied with his flask of vouvrak; same sights and sounds, same route through the ice-paved streets of Rialsq. Almost he might have imagined himself carried back a year in time, but for the profound changes that separated him from the wretched sickly boy he had been. That younger Varis had been passive, ineffectual, perennial butt and victim. That Varis could never have supplanted Pire Zelkiv, manipulated the Duke of Otreska, distinguished himself at Court, or indeed, even braved the pandemonium of a full-blown Rhazaullean revel. Not that he was looking forward to the rout. The noise, the crush of overheated bodies, the drearily repetitive excess held no jot of appeal; but now, at least, he could face them.

The sledge sped down an avenue lined with cone-roofed mansions. Just this way had it traveled last year, bearing him to the Wrecks, to horror and humiliation. Even now, he grew queasy at the thought of it. His brow was cold with sweat. Evidently his new assurance was not as impervious as he had imagined.

Beside him, avid as a nursing infant, Breziot sucked vouvrak from a hip flask. He seemed content, his domestic grievances momentarily forgotten. Such tranquillity was enviable, but his Grace's means of achieving it, crude. There were far better tools than alcohol.

Varis drew a small enameled box from his pocket. Placing two pinches of the brown powdered contents upon the back of his hand, he lifted the hand to his nose and inhaled sharply, twice. Anyone watching would have thought him devoted to ordinary snuff. In reality, he partook of the shernivus-derived stimulant unrevealingly christened SD-9b; one of the most successful of his creations, a substance rivaling Clotl's gel in power, but distressingly variable in its side-effects.

Returning the box to his pocket, Varis leaned back in his seat. Disturbing recollection receded. The strength coursed through his veins, and the voices started up in his head. The voices were particularly insistent tonight, but that scarcely troubled him. Something else did, however. It occurred to him that the various stimulants—designed to serve as sorcerous appurtenances, and nothing more—actually performed a far larger function. They alone supported his health, his mental and physical vigor, and recently, his equanimity. Perhaps it was unwise to rely so heavily upon an artificial support. Unwise, and even unsafe, for there had been times when the line between violent dream and reality smudged out of existence. Mornings when he'd awakened to find himself stretched full length on the workroom floor, numb and amnesic, with blood upon his hands and face, and no idea where or what it had come from. Such episodes were lately increasing in frequency; he could no longer dismiss them as freak aberrations. And for the first time, it seemed to him that matters might be slipping beyond his control. A disquieting sensation, for sorcery's chief seduction lay in the mastery it seemed to offer. Was it possible that sweet sensation was illusory—a cheat?

He could abjure magic; renounce the actual practice, if not the study. Safest, no doubt, to do it now, long before the spectre of spifflication darkened his horizons. Give up sorcery, stimulants, and all that they had brought him. Go back to what he had been this time last year; feed himself for the rest of his life upon the memories of lost power.

A life not worth living.

No.

And surely unnecessary to seek such extremes. It was not impossible to limit and control the practice of sorcery. Yelnyk of Krezniu had done so. It was only a matter of will.

No need to give it up altogether. Only govern it. And Varis shut his eyes, allowing the voices, ever stronger, to chase the doomful fancies from his head.

The sledge slowed to a halt.

"Ah, a warmstop," observed Breziot.

Varis opened his eyes upon the turreted, brilliantly illuminated townhouse of the Noble Landholder Stratkha. The windows were wide open, the activity within, bacchanalian—just as they had been, almost exactly a year ago. His pulses jumped, and time slipped for an instant. Time for another quick sniff of SD-9b? No.

The brothers alighted and entered the townhouse. Light, heat, clamor, and stench battered their senses. Smiling broadly, Breziot opened his arms. A host of shrieking merrymakers converged upon him. In an instant, he was surrounded and engulfed. They bore him off, and his Grace disappeared into the revel.

No such greeting of kindred spirits extended itself to Varis. The personal alterations that had won widespread respect in recent weeks had not lessened his aura of alien remoteness. No one knew quite what to say to the Ulor's youngest brother. That much had not changed.

The scene was unappetizing, even more so than the Zalkhash tropical endeavor. Activity was ceaseless and frenetic; the level of noise, literally painful. Varis wandered off in search of quieter air. Presently he came upon a darkened chamber given over to consumption of vouvrak and other spirits. Vouvrak seemed mild to him now. He remained there for a time, lulled by comparative quiet, until the alcoholic twilight palled.

Wandering again, through room after riotous room, and now the sights and sounds blurred, and the voices in his head clamored, until it grew difficult to distinguish between internal wild visions, and material world. The Strellian flame-dancers in the blue salon—they were real enough; likewise the redheaded razor-girls on the third floor, the communal mud wallows, the busy featherbeds. No doubting their substantiality, but other things weren't so definite. The spifflicated sorcerer conjuring ghosts, for example—dream or reality? And had he, Varis, actually summoned a complaining shade, permitting the incompetent Spifflicate to take credit for the deed—or had he imagined it? Unclear. Too many things. That half-clothed Turo dancing girl who followed him about so persistently —did she exist? And had he truly allowed her to lead him off to a silent, deserted garret, and a storage closet with floorboards masked in layers of sacking?

Reality asserted itself hours later, when he woke to discover the girl's torn corpse sprawled on the sacking beside him, and the taste of her blood in his mouth.

5

THERE WAS NOTHING to link him with her death. In the midst of Stratkha's monster revel, nobody would have noticed him wandering off with her, nobody would have cared. Hidden away in the closet, her body would probably escape discovery for hours; perhaps days. He need only remove himself from the site, and his own part in the incident would go quite unsuspected. And if by chance it did not—no matter. He was the Ulor's brother, while the victim was a nameless Turo dancer, of no more account than one of Madam Wlav's disposable redheads. He had only to walk away.

A scrap of sacking served to towel the blood from his face, hands, and body. He dressed hurriedly, raked his fingers through his hair, and chanced a quick glance at the dead girl. The light of a single candle flickered upon swollen features, gaping mouth, and protruding tongue. He had braced himself against a rush of remorseful horror. In fact, he was simply disgusted. She was repellent. Dimly, he recalled he had first thought her rather enticing. Hard to imagine that now. He wanted to be away from her. He wanted to forget she had ever existed.

Not an impossible feat for the Ulor's brother.

Varis exited the closet, bearing the candle with him. The corpse fell into shadow. The Turo girl vanished. She had never been.

He departed the revel quietly. In the old days, nobody would have noted his withdrawal. Now, it was observed, but nobody ventured to address him.

No questions, no accusations. No detaining hand upon his shoulder.

Out into the fresh air. Icy night breeze like a purifying agent. Strathka's behind him, a thing of the past.

Back by sledge to the Zalkhash, journey dreamlike and subjectively extended. Back to the House Uloric, his own apartment, his own bed. Swift descent into sleep vibrant with color. Jumbled, chaotic visions; fantastical, sometimes incomprehensible, and one recurring image of a seated figure—long and spare, perhaps himself—indistinct and veiled in fog.

He woke refreshed and filled with a sense of luxurious repletion. The heavy curtains shrouding the shuttered windows of his bedchamber maintained artificial night, yet his body knew that the morning was old. He was well, better than he had ever been, as if somehow renewed.

His mind strayed from dream to recollection. Last night's phantasmagoria. The distinction between fancy and actuality was not always clear, but in certain particulars, there could be no question.

Dead girl on the floor. Her eyes. Her blood.

Quite real.

The quiescence of his conscience was peculiar. In the old days—almost another life, they seemed—it would not have been so. Back then, guilt had often racked him for the pettiest transgressions. And now, there was nothing beyond a certain distant astonishment. Perhaps it was the persistent sense of fantasy that buffered his mind. He might have enjoyed the anesthesia, had he not too clearly recognized its origin. The various gels, powders, draughts, and concentrates so essential to magical practice were affecting him. That influence was unpredictable, and worse, uncontrollable.

Uncontrollable was unacceptable. It pointed the way to spifflication.

He decided then and there to rule himself. There would be no repetition of last night's ugly, curiously fulfilling episode. He'd limit his use of Clotl's gel, and all like substances. Perhaps he'd give them up entirely, for a time. It would be an exercise in self-discipline, a demonstration of control.

Desiring no witnesses to the experiment, he sent his personal servants away. Likewise he dismissed his secretary, who departed temporarily empowered to administer the Minister of Diplomacy's routine correspondence. Giving out the false intelligence that he had briefly departed Rialsq, he provisioned his own apartment, then repaired to its thoroughly soundproof depths.

For the next week, he faithfully abstained, and the results were disquieting. Initial intense longing soon gave way to sluggish apathy, and he thought himself past the worst pains of deprivation. Then his eyes began to fail; burning and watering resumed, as the old ocular malady, long in remission, reasserted itself. Throbbing joints, inexplicable qualms, internal upheavals, and above all, the killing headaches—all the old familiar ailments returned, in concentrated form, worse than he had ever known them.

But greater unpleasantnesses were to follow, as he learned upon the morning of the sixth day, when he opened his eyes to discover last night's vivid dreams thrusting themselves upon the daylight world. Nightmare beings filled his bedchamber. Creatures of ghastly imagining mingled indiscriminately with ghosts of men, ghosts of extinct animals and air-swimming fish, with sentient flowers shaped like viscera, strolling fungi, and black carnivorous moths. The Ulor of legend was there, its jaws lathered with the snow-broth blood of its brethren. There was the Zuviskya, mythical bird of fire and ice; the human-ursine Old Man of Twilight, with his grizzled pelt and his necklace of dried ears; and ice-tusked Foosk the Creeper. Folktales, impossibilities; yet looking decidedly substantial by day.

Old acquaintances were there too, hovering between floor and ceiling. Necromancer Arkhoy, and a clutch of his infant victims; Deathmaster Clotl—purely illusory, for Clotl's ties to the material world had perished in blued flame—yet there he was, smirking and winking; the Turo girl from Strathka's, bloodied and puff-featured, but aware and watching him . . . staring . . .

Delusions, delirium.

But inescapable. They crowded close about him, whispering gibberish. They dogged his footsteps from room to room, plucked at his garments, laid weightless fingers upon his face. Only once, he closed his eyes to blot out the sight, and in that instant, icy lips pressed his own, and he caught the unmistakable echo of the Turo girl's musky perfume. His eyes snapped open, and he did not shut them again.

The hours passed, and morning slid into afternoon. The visiting wraiths, evidently comfortable in the dimness of the curtained apartment, remained to warp reality. Varis observed them, almost apathetically. The initial thrill of horror had long since subsided, but he wished the oppressive presences gone. They wearied his mind. He valued privacy. Only as winter's early evening approached did he consider flight into oblivion. Black, dreamless slumber. They could not follow him there.

No need of magic, this time. An ordinary sleeping draught, purchased of a common apothecary, would serve his purpose. Already, he possessed such a draught; inconsistently efficacious, but when it worked, his slumber was empty and dreamless. This evening, to guarantee results, he would double his usual dosage. Thus, without reckon-

ing the effect of recent abstinence, Varis swallowed a full
goblet of syrupy potion.

He slept. There were no dreams. Consciousness was
annihilated.

When he woke, he was alone. He lay unclothed upon
the floor, a few feet from the cold stove. The fire was dead,
the bedchamber icy. Varis himself was numb and all but
frozen. He raised his head a little and gazed about him.
The room was clear of ghostly intruders; it was also a
shambles. A few weak shafts of daylight filtering through
torn curtains illumined massive wreckage. Furniture was
overturned and smashed; upholstery and hangings shred-
ded; windowpanes, lamps, and looking-glass shattered;
rugs wadded and darkly blotched. Similar red-brown
blotches marked the floorboards, the walls, and the bedding.

He sat up with difficulty. He was stiff and curiously
sore. He looked down at himself. His body was striped
with welts and deep scratches, spotted with bruises and
scabs. Broken crescents marked his hands and wrists.
Toothmarks. He stared at them without comprehension.
The metallic aftertaste of blood filled his mouth. His own
blood? The scabs were dry and hard, the bruises fading
from purple to green. They were not new. He looked at
his right hand. Dried, caked blood beneath the fingernails
explained the origin of his scratches. Slowly, he lifted the
hand to his face. The stubbly growth upon his chin was at
least two days old.

He dragged himself to his feet. He was weak, shivering with cold, and parched with thirst. His dressing gown
lay tangled among the bedclothes. He picked it up and
put it on. His water pitcher had somehow escaped break-
age, but its contents were frozen. Now he smashed the
pitcher to extract a chunk of ice, upon which he sucked
almost desperately.

The stale air was frigid, and there were no servants
about to light the stove. Laboriously he fumbled with

coal, kindling, tinder, flint, and steel. The dampers wanted adjustment. Thick smoke arose and gushed out through the grating. Varis breathed it and coughed. His eyes stung sharply. Tears blurred his vision. Automatically he rubbed his eyes, and the sting intensified to a ferocious burning. He blinked, and the tears streamed down his face. Still coughing, he turned from the stove to encounter Foosk the Creeper, or at least her ghostly simulacrum, back again. Through the haze of smoke, shadow, and salt water, he discerned the famous misshapen figure, crouched in a corner, watching him.

It was enough.

He resisted no longer. Opening the hidden compartment, he inhaled a massive dose of SD-9b and was himself again.

The experiment was concluded.

He did not intend to repeat it. Henceforth, however, he would be careful and clever. No more revels, no more lunatic risks. And when the dark thirsty urges came upon him, the impulses that would not be denied, he would deal with them discreetly.

It was not really difficult, he discovered in the weeks that followed. Not even particularly dangerous, provided he took a little care. The occasional discovery, in Rialsq's seedier alleyways, of some nameless trull's savaged remains scarcely roused great public outcry. And even if it had, the matter would never have been traced so far and so high as the Zalkhash itself.

As winter deepened, the snow piled high, and pedestrians took to the unmapped warren of enclosed public walkways, the sport waxed in challenge and satisfaction. Rarely did he pause to ponder his new appetites. He was well, his secret mastery of magic was increasing day by day, and he stood high in the Ulor's favor. He was respected for the first time, his alien remoteness perhaps a little feared. No need to question concommitant personal alteration.

Absorbed in novel enterprise, Varis scarcely noted the departure of King Dasune and his Aennorvi entourage, or the subsequent reincarceration of Breziot's wayward Duchess. The wedding of Ulor Hurna XI and the luckless little Princess Olisi, glittering event though it was, barely touched upon his awareness. His life was largely nocturnal. His waking hours, while often solitary, were rich and full. His diurnal slumbers were likewise full, of dreams and color. The nature of his visions varied greatly, and repetition was rare; only the one familiar blurred image of the seated figure continually recurred. The days passed, the vision came to him a dozen times, and gradually the hazy picture began to resolve itself. The outlines of the figure and the chair sharpened, the facial lineaments defined themselves, the enveloping mists faded out of existence, and Varis beheld himself, seated upon the Wolf Throne.

He did not know exactly when the idea—so long with him, but always submerged—finally rose to the surface of his mind. He could not have pinpointed the precise moment that he knew he would make himself Ulor. The desire had built gradually, over the course of many months, or perhaps years. When it finally impinged upon consciousness, it was as if it had always been there. And yet, when he paused to consider, the strangeness of the ambition was manifest. He had never sought glory, acclaim, the center stage—those things that seemed to belong by natural as well as by human law to Hurna XI. The traditional trappings of sovereignty—throne, crown, robes, ritual, and all the rest of it—he regarded as vaguely embarrassing anachronisms. Even possession of real power —delicious a sensation though it was—seemed but a means to an end. And that end? Difficult to define, and his current pastimes tended to discourage analysis. As nearly as he might have expressed it in words, he intended to take the Wolf Throne because his new sense of self demanded it; because his transformation required the ultimate confirmation; because he had to satisfy himself that he could.

Removal of the present Ulor was certain to prove a difficult undertaking, and in an immediate sense, useless. The Rhazaullean laws of dynastic succession were well-established and unvarying. In the event of the ruler's death, the crown passed to his immediate male issue, in order of birth; or, in the absence of sons, to female offspring. Hurna was father to a five-year-old boy, the little Ulorin Lishna. There were also twin daughters, whose birth had cost their mother her life, two years ago. Standing behind the Ulorin and two tiny ulorinnes in the line of succession was middle brother Breziot, followed by Breziot's son Cerrov and then his daughter Shalindra.

Seven lives between Varis and the Wolf Throne. Seven obstacles to eliminate. A considerable feat, but not impossible; not to a patient and determined predator. Not to a necromancer, whose mastery of magic went altogether unsuspected. He did not as yet contemplate final disposal of the various children. The prospect was distasteful, the necessity still remote. Far easier, for the present, to consider Breziot's disappearance; an infinitely pleasanter prospect.

He had hated Breziot for a very long time. He recognized that hatred at last, and it was like his hunger for the crown—as if it had always been there. Pretty that the satisfaction of one urge should further fulfillment of the other. He could appreciate the economy of it.

Breziot would be first to go. His murder would arouse alarm. His death by accident or suicide would not.

Suicide. Not infeasible.

He would need considerable ghostly assistance. He knew just where to find it.

On a still, bitter night in the dead of winter, a gleaming black sledge passed from the Zalkhash enclosure, out into the snow-packed streets of Rialsq. Varis himself handled the reins. His departure was observed, but that hardly mattered, provided nobody guessed where he was going, or what he intended to do when he got there.

The city had barricaded itself against the cold. Windows and doorways were so heavily curtained and so tightly shuttered that no stray beam of light escaped. The covered walkways were mantled in white and seemingly lifeless. Streetlamps, few and far between, were confined to the wealthiest neighborhoods. The night was moonless and empty of stars. Throughout most of the journey, the sledge lanterns—their light magnified by reflection off a marblelike pavement of packed snow—provided the sole illumination. This was sufficient, for the remission of his ocular ailment had not deprived Varis of uncommonly acute nocturnal vision.

Through the silent dark streets he drove at a moderate speed that scarcely approached the velocity of his thoughts. The horses' hoofbeats were muffled, and the beautifully constructed sledge glided on with never a creak or a rattle. Presently he reached the straggling outskirts of town, and there on his left rose the darkened bulk of the Rialsq House of Correction. Beyond the prison, lamplight brushed the distinctive contours of the Funnel. A little farther along the road, and he came to Nightfields, public burial ground where the dead felons, Spifflicates, and nameless paupers shared common graves. Having reached his destination, Varis halted the sledge, detached one of the lanterns, and alighted.

An iron paling surrounded the cemetery. Even in death, the tenants continued caged. The gate was unlocked. He opened it and entered. Before him stretched a broad, slightly sloping field; deserted, bare, and treeless, desolate beyond description. Here and there, the otherwise featureless expanse was broken by abrupt little mounds in the snow, revealing the location of the communal grave markers. No telling who or what lay beneath those markers. The forgotten wretched lay there in strata, the deepest sometimes dating back hundreds of years.

It was the custom of the cemetery custodians to dig vast pits, generally in the summer, when the soil was free of frost and relatively dry. Corpses, arriving shrouded in burlap sacks, were placed at the bottom of such pits, well-dosed with quicklime, and covered over with soil. This procedure was repeated until the hole was all but full, whereupon the last few feet were filled in with dirt to the level of the surrounding ground, and a new pit was excavated. It might take many months to fully populate a grave; but in time of pestilence, the task was sometimes completed in days.

He chose one at random. Whichever he selected was bound to contain the mortal remains of executed criminals. Men of violence, dying by violence; murderers would suit his purpose well.

He had already fortified himself with SD-9b. His mind was marvelously focused and limber. Almost effortlessly, he performed the mental exercises lending power to the words and gestures that summoned a motley graveful of ghosts from their rest.

They arose like a snowfall reversing itself; wavering white figures, initially a small drift of movement upon the white ground, all but invisible until they ascended to float weightless upon the still black air. There were perhaps a score in all, and they were not what he had expected. Among those ragged wraiths, he spied three or four of the kind he sought; burly translucent bodies, iron faces, lizard eyes. But the others? The weak rays of lantern light picked out a gaggle of wasted puny forms, many of them once female. He saw faces withered with the recollections of hunger, illness, disappointment. He saw scrawny gnarled limbs, swollen joints, twisted spines, spifflication, and deformity. Above all, he saw scared confusion. Incomprehension beamed from their staring dead eyes, shaped their fluttery gestures.

Very little here to inspire fear. Something of a disappointment.

Their voices were coming at him now, squawking and whining across the intervening dimensions. A screechy babble of overlapping queries, pleas, and plaints hammered at his mind. He concentrated, and the individual voices began to resolve themselves. A few of the shades were pleading abjectly for release. One, with the glowing eyes of a Spifflicate, dared to curse and rail. Most clamored for elucidation.

Varis raised a commanding hand, and the ghosts fell silent. He needed no words to make his will known to them, yet spoke aloud through force of habit.

"No doubt you are wondering why I have summoned you here tonight."

The hubbub resumed. He quelled it with a glance.

"I will inform you presently. But first, you will identify yourselves. You—" He pointed, selecting one at random. A starved-looking youth, rickety and narrow-faced, apparently about seventeen or eighteen years of age. "State your name, profession, and the circumstances of your death."

The chosen shade fidgeted, tugged against invisible restraint, and at last answered unwillingly, *Rigo Kulyin, pickpocket. Bled to death atop the Funnel, fifteen years ago. What do you want from me?*

"Obedience. And you?" He pinned another with his eyes. A woman, blowsy, gray-haired, toothless.

Iskhina Lovik, vagrant. Robbed and knifed, in the Correction, fifteen years ago. Who's asking?

"Your master. You?" The pointing finger shifted.

Zirv Eskorni, pamphleteer. Cap and scarf of a student, intelligent bespectacled face. *Bled atop the Funnel, fifteen years ago.*

They answered him each in turn. It was their various trades that chiefly concerned him. Petty thief. Forger. Coiner. Fence. Black marketeer. He had overlooked the hard Rhazaullean law that condemned so many minor, peaceable malefactors. His graveful of ghosts even included a sprinkling of prostitutes, drunkards, and debtors; small fry never consigned to the Funnel, but dying by violence in prison or the Wrecks.

Not exactly the dauntless killers he wanted. But they would have to do.

When he issued his homicidal commands, a not-unexpected outcry arose. These hopeless creatures, losers in death as in life, wanted no part of murder. Their protests were ineffectual, however; likewise useless their whining complaints, arguments, and appeals. Not troubling to argue, Varis merely restated his requirements. The sole objection he consented to refute was purely practical in nature. The threads binding ghosts to Nightfields, he informed his unwilling henchmen, had been stretched for the duration of a single night. Until the break of dawn, the shades enjoyed free range of all Rialsq; including, of course, the Zalkhash.

Where their quarry lay.

I've no quarrel with the Duke of Otreska. Complaint and implied criticism, from the pickpocket Kulyin.

Why don't you do your own dirty work? Outright criticism from one of the women.

Afraid to soil your own lily hands?

Where's your conscience, anyway? Haven't you got any MORALS?

"Silence. No argument. Fulfill your commission," Varis commanded, but his servants were decidedly fractious.

A current of reluctance, even resentment, stirred the floating white ranks. Spectral outlines wavered, blurred, and faded as various captives vainly sought exit. Escape was impossible, and presently the fretful chorus resumed.

I don't know how to do it. I've never done it.

Does anyone here know how to do it?

It's against my principles. I want to be excused.

Women should be excused.

Let's negotiate.

"Enough. About your business, else I bar you from your grave forever." A ghost, chained to the physical sphere, yet magically denied the oblivion of the grave, was condemned to everlasting insomnia; a gruesome prospect. Such a threat generally cowed the most rebellious of spirits, and it did not fail now.

An alarmed chittering arose; a swirling agitation. The spectral cloud seethed, and swiftly faded from view, its component members presumably off to fulfill their commission.

Returning to his sledge, Varis quietly departed Nightfields. His continuing necromantic link with the wandering shades informed him they were already halfway to their destination, and yet it was hard to shake the conviction that none of it was quite real.

The Duke of Otreska's bedchamber was separated from that of his wife by the entire length of the black-and-white apartment. It was an arrangement calculated to safeguard the master's privacy, yet his Grace, when present, invariably slept there alone. Not even the supplest of Turo companions had ever insinuated herself across his threshold; a state of affairs dictated less by Breziot's fastidiousness than by his fear of the Ulor's displeasure.

Thus he was alone when a curious noise woke him in the dead of night. It was not particularly loud. Most likely, the strangeness of it had penetrated his slumbers. Puzzled, Breziot lay listening for a time. He heard a delicate rattling overhead. *Clink. Tinkletinkle.* Unidentifiable. At last he sat up, drew the silver-spangled black bed curtains aside, and looked out. The nightlight burning beside the bed dimly illumined a chamber infested with ghosts. There must have been at least a score of them, floating and drifting everywhere. Never had he seen so many assembled in one place. And never, in all his experience of illicit—often spifflicated—necromantic performances-for-hire, had he ever beheld ghosts so substantial, so visible and tangible, so completely *present*. Beyond doubt, however, these were spirits; their buoyancy and faint transparency marked them as such.

Breziot wondered if he could be dreaming. Perhaps all that vouvrak had caught up with him at last.

He blinked and knuckled his eyes. The ghosts remained. They looked busy.

A blanched gang clustered about the great crystal chandelier that depended from a short chain attached to a hook sunk into the silver-starred black ceiling. The ghosts —pallid forms nicely visible against the dark background —shoved and tugged at the shivering branches. And here was revealed the source of the noise that had awakened him; the faceted lusters rattled and clinked under the onslaught.

The visitors looked to be having a hard time of it. Their power in the physical world was real, but limited, and their full combined strength was required to shift the position of the massive crystal-and-silver contraption. Overcoming initial inertia was their greatest obstacle, of course; but presently they got it going. The chandelier began to move, swinging in tiny arcs. Gradually, the arcs widened. Velocity built, and soon the visitors' task became easier. To and fro flashed the chandelier, glittering at the end of its short chain. The creaking and rattling increased. A few flying lusters tapped the ceiling.

The ghosts appeared to confer. Transparent mouths worked vigorously. Breziot heard nothing, but evidently communication was achieved. Upon the pendulum's next descent, the spectral gathering pushed, and that communal force sufficed to lift the chain from the ceiling hook. An instant later, the chandelier crashed to the floor. Shards of broken crystal flew, and a startled curse escaped his Grace. The wraiths turned to the sound. A white tide flowed toward him.

Wonder gave way to fear, then. Breziot grabbed for the bellpull, which hung within easy reach of the bed.

Before his fingers closed upon it, the dangling silken cord was gone, carried ceilingward by one of the visitors. No matter; at least half a dozen servants lay within earshot. He took a deep breath. Before the intended cry escaped his lips, they were upon him—a crowd of chilly, foglike, all-but-weightless wraiths, whose combined efforts were disorganized but surprisingly effectual. They laid their hands across his mouth, his eyes, ears, and nose. Cold mist dimmed his vision, invaded his throat and lungs, stirred in the depths of his belly. That icy touch froze mind and voice. The belated cry that broke from his lips was faint and muffled. If the servants heard it, they heard too late. The sharp click of a bolt sliding home signaled the exclusion of assistance.

Breziot fought with hysterical strength, clawing at his own face, flinging himself violently about the bed. The wraiths were hard put to control him, until half a dozen of the most ingenious detached a bed curtain and flung the heavy fabric over their victim's head.

His Grace was blind and all but breathless. The vigor of his struggles waned, and a swarm of ghosts succeeded in pinning his limbs. While Breziot lay helpless, transparent fingers fiddled with the heavy silver cording that scalloped the tall tester. Eventually, the cord fell free. Inordinate effort fashioned a gleaming noose at one end. Raising the cord to the hook in the ceiling was easy, but tying the knot wasn't. The intruders jittered, fluttered, dithered inaudibly. A full fifteen minutes passed before the rope was properly secured.

Thereafter, their course was clear. The full ghostly gathering converged about the bed to levitate the body of the Duke.

Breziot sensed the jerky, laborious ascent. He squealed, writhed, and thrashed. The startled ghosts loosed their hold, allowing their velvet-wrapped burden to drop. His Grace struck the white-carpeted floor heavily, lay motionless for a fraction of a second, then tore the enveloping layers of fabric away. Fresh air reached his lungs. His vision cleared, and he glanced about him to encounter a host of staring spectral eyes. Directly overhead dangled the silver noose. He understood.

There was time for one scream—a good, loud one— before the dead hands fastened once more upon his face, his body, and limbs. This time they got it right, bearing their struggling victim aloft with minimal confusion. Quite deftly, they slipped the noose over his Grace's head, adjusted the knot one last time, then drew back to observe the ensuing spasmodic ballet.

Presently, all motion ceased; and the ghosts, their commission successfully completed, were free to seek the comfortable oblivion of their grave.

The Duke of Otreska's death was accounted something of a mystery, for the circumstances surrounding the apparent suicide were odd. To begin with, in the weeks following the departure of the Aennorvi guests, his Grace had displayed no signs of melancholia; quite the contrary, in fact. His health was excellent, his fortune sound, and there seemed little reason or explanation for self-slaughter. Quite apart from the puzzle of motivation existed the question of method. That his Grace had died by hanging was certain, and yet the mechanics of this feat remained obscure. How, for example, had the Duke managed to displace the heavy chandelier, secure the cord to the hook in the ceiling, then slip his own head through a noose suspended some twelve feet above the floor, without benefit of ladder, stacked furniture, or any other obvious means of ascent? Had he looped the noose about his neck, shinnied up one of the tall bedposts to the tester, sat there, and slung (with fabulous aim) the free end of the cord over the hook, somehow contrived to knot cord to hook, and then—launched himself from the tester, as some supposed he must have done? Not absolutely impossible, and therein lay the theory's greatest charm—it could not be conclusively disproved. And yet—was it probable? Who, possessing a grain of sanity, would choose such a method? Never, throughout the course of his career, had the Duke of Otreska displayed the smallest aptitude for rope tricks or for acrobatics.

The question of foul play inevitably arose. The servants were minutely interrogated. Those belonging to the Duchess, sleeping at the far end of the apartment, had heard nothing. The cook, his minions, and the various household drudges, dreaming upon their pallets scattered across the kitchen floor, were likewise ignorant. A little more enlightening proved the testimony of the Duke's own personal attendants, disposed about his Grace's antechamber. There were five of them, and their accounts coincided in every particular; difficult to doubt such consistency. Four out of the five had been awakened by a loud crash, apparently the sound of the chandelier hitting the floor. The fifth was roused by scurryings and whisperings within the antechamber itself, as the occupants flew to press their hungry ears to the door. All of them heard thumps, thuds, the creak of bedsprings, and one full-throated scream. After that—silence.

They had knocked and pounded upon the door. They had yelled, pleaded, exhorted, and eventually run for aid. In the end, they had broken down the door, to discover the Duke's corpse twisting at the end of its rope overhead. The room was otherwise uninhabited. The door and the windows had been locked from within. No other means of ingress or egress was known to exist. So much for all thought of murder.

He must have killed himself. No other reasonable explanation existed. Unless—certain devout Venerators muttered of ghostly intervention, prompted by impious necromancy. Venerators always gabbled of such things; this time, however, there actually were grounds for suspicion. The circumstances suggested supernatural intervention, and yet, ghosts were tenuous creatures, handicapped in the physical world. A hostile shade might scatter the coals of a dying fire, splash in a washbasin, fling loose documents about. But murder? Of a healthy, doubtless uncooperative victim? No. There was no ghost strong enough for that.

The death of the Duke transcended normal limits. Either it was suicide, or else it was something sorcerously astonishing.

The Duchess of Otreska scarcely paused to consider the source of her liberation. Her husband was gone. Her father was dead, she had no brothers, her son was underage; there were no male guardians for her Grace. She was a widow, moneyed, and unfettered at last. It was enough to know; it was paradise. She might paint the black-and-white apartment scarlet, if she chose. She might paint all of Rialsq.

There were, of course, a few preliminary formalities to be endured, and these included the obsequies of her husband. Thus, upon a dingy day late in winter, the Duchess and her two children found themselves standing in the great vaulted chamber of the royal crypt, whose black stone bulk—separated from neighboring structures by a wide expanse of black flagging—rose at the northernmost extremity of the Zalkhash. Upon a black-draped bier rested Breziot's coffin. One of the many niches built into the wall stood open and ready to receive it. The gray marble slab, inscribed with appropriate titles and dates, awaited its final placement. About the bier stood scores of mourners, arranged in ranks of decreasing status. Immediate family members, including the Ulor, occupied positions nearest the coffin. Behind them clustered black-clad friends and associates of the Noble Landholder class, and then the gentry of lesser quality, all the way down to servants and assorted paid subordinates, who were obliged to wait in the snow outside the crypt.

Hurna XI delivered his brother's eulogy. He spoke simply, affectingly, and at some length. While the Uloric bass rumbled on interminably, the Duchess of Otreska stood shifting her weight from one foot to the other, and back again. The Duchess was tired of standing. Her feet ached, and the continual decorous bowing of her head had produced a crick at the back of her neck. The air in the crypt was dankly dead. She was uncomfortable, and unutterably bored. She wasn't the only one, she noted. A few feet away, Hurna's heir apparent, the little Ulorin Lishna, squirmed and fidgeted, unintimidated by the frowns of his iron-faced old battle-axe of a nurse.

The Ulor spoke on. The Duchess diverted herself with thoughts of the excursion she would make to the Aennorvi capital city of Feyenne, as soon as she could decently doff her widow's weeds. His Majesty Dasune had painted glorious word-pictures of Feyenne, urging her to visit, and to bring her two children along. Cerrov and Shalindra would enjoy the novelty—the sunshine, the exotic sights—

Her lips began to curve. Just in time, she remembered to suppress the incipient smile. She was, after all—bereaved.

The Duchess' reverie was interrupted by the tingle of gooseflesh along her forearms, and the sudden sense of being watched. She looked up, and her eyes flew unerringly to the face of her younger brother-in-law. Varis stood beside the Ulor. He was watching, yes, but she herself was not the object of his attention. The unwinking hazel eyes were fixed upon her son, Cerrov.

Cerrov, the new and underage Duke of Otreska.

The Duchess felt an instant's icy, almost sickening, qualm. She could not have said why. There was nothing obviously alarming or repellent about Varis. Rather the contrary, in fact. The spare, upright figure bore itself with much distinction. The lean visage was angular, austere, intellectual—quite an arresting face, if overly pale. His coloration should have won her favor, for it was identical to her daughter's. Moreover, he and Shalindra even displayed a faint suspicion of family resemblance in the modeling of their features. And his expression? Unrevealing, at best. Composed and grave far beyond his years; for her brother-in-law, she had to remind herself, was not yet twenty-four. Somehow he seemed much older than that. There was no longer the slightest trace of boyishness about him; if, indeed, there ever had been.

Varis must have felt her eyes upon him, for his gaze lifted to her face. The Duchess managed to repress a nervous start. Quite unthinkingly, she placed a protective hand on Cerrov's shoulder. Varis inclined his head in ceremonious commiseration. Nothing menacing there. His courtesy was unexceptionable. Nothing to explain why the sight of him, studying her son so attentively, should have chilled her to the heart.

The weeks passed. Winter gave way to soggy spring, and gradually the curiosity surrounding Breziot's death subsided. New topics of interest presented themselves, gossip shifted focus, speculation died away, and presently his defunct Grace of Otreska was all but forgotten by nearly everyone.

With one notable exception. The Ulor Hurna had not forgotten. In fact, the Ulor thought of his middle brother's ending a good deal. It had been disquieting. The suddenness and strangeness of it had conveyed an unpleasant reminder of the human vulnerability to which even royalty was subject. What if it *had* been murder, an extraordinarily clever one? And if the Ulor's own brother could fall prey to an assassin, what of the Ulor himself?

Hurna XI, while neither impressionable nor timid, was not reckless. He thought to consult an astrologer, and the results of his conference with the gifted Dr. Faribendo were not reassuring. The vernal stars, it seemed, danced in sinister configurations. The Ulor stood at risk. The night skies threatened, treachery poisoned the very air, and a sudden fall from high estate was imminent.

Hurna heard, heeded, and accordingly altered his

course. He took to wearing a protective vest of steel mesh beneath his clothing. A couple of bodyguards trailed him everywhere. Sentries stood watch before the Uloric apartment throughout the night. Tasters sampled every morsel of food destined for Uloric consumption. No precaution could guarantee perfect safety, but he had made himself a difficult target.

Uloric inaccessibility hardly troubled Varis, whose imagination was fertile, and whose patience was exemplary. He was quite content, in fact, to bide his time. Too close a conjunction of fraternal Haudrensq deaths would rouse suspicion; best to wait a little while longer. In the meantime, the days passed not unpleasantly. His mind was entirely fixed upon his goal, and it seemed that such intense focus of intellect and will purged him of lesser, undesirable urges. Massive doses of sorcerous stimulants maintained his health, his composure, his necromantic power; while the thirsty red needs that formerly ruled him now subsided to manageable levels. At present, the back alleys and covered walkways of Rialsq yielded no more distinctively torn corpses. This was well—he was master of himself and his own powers. He was in control, and he would remain so. He knew the secret now. It was only a question of well-directed mental force. Concentration. A task to tax his mind and keep him occupied. That was what he had needed all along.

The air warmed and dried. Summer came to Rhazaulle. The days were long and comparatively soft. City windows unsealed themselves, boats and barges plied the unfrozen Xana. The gardens of Rialsq adorned themselves, and human bodies emerged from their shapeless winter cocoons of fur and wool. Nature's relaxation, however, inspired no corresponding relaxation of the Ulor's caution. Upon the advice of Dr. Faribendo, Hurna XI maintained his barriers of steel mesh and steeled flesh. He had no way of guessing the uselessness of such precautions.

Varis waited for beautiful weather, for the luxurious

temperatures that struck most Rhazaulleans as vaguely decadent, if not downright immoral. Upon one of the balmiest nights of summer, a night so gentle that windows yawned wide all over Rialsq, he made his way from the House Uloric, across the Zalkhash courtyard to the royal crypt. The world slept under black velvet skies. The air was silken and still; the dreaming silence so deep that the buzz of the nightlappers in the gardens beyond the Zalkhash wall was audible. The click of his heels upon the black flags seemed to fill the courtyard. He made no particular effort to conceal himself, and yet, he was certain, his progress went unobserved.

The crypt was as it had been upon the occasion of his last visit, months earlier. The atmosphere was moist and stale as ever. A stray shaft of moonlight, slanting in through the circular skylight, defined the contour of curved basalt walls rising to a coffered domed ceiling; gleamed upon the fresh polish of the marble square marking Breziot's last resting place. For the eyes of Varis, such fugitive illumination sufficed. The candle in his pocket was redundant. Not troubling to light it, he went to work.

The knowledge was ripe in his brain. The words, inflections and gestures that focused mental power were all but second nature to him now. A controlled convulsion of mind and body, a transference of conscious will, generated power to summon the ghost that he sought.

The air shivered, the ectoplasmic tendrils wafted, and the remembrance of Breziot issued from its tomb. Pallid threads knit, and presently the Duke's image formed itself in midair; as always the case with Varis's summonings, a remarkably sharp, complete, and tangible image.

The translucent lips moved, and a ghostly voice issued. It was faint and distant, yet Breziot's voice still:

I see many things more clearly, now. You sent them to my room. It was you.

"Myself alone."

*Alone, yes. You have always been alone, always will be. You
contemptible little grotesque. You ridiculous, pathetic monstrosity.
You were a freak of nature from the very beginning. A few
kindly souls pitied you, but most simply laughed. No doubt that's
still true. And how you hated us for our normality! You hated in
your own particularly damp, morose style, and probably thought
your bitterness went unremarked. Wrong. We laughed, all of us.*

*Did you ever know the names we made up for you? Hurna
and I, and some of the others? Did you know that we always
referred to you as—*

Varis held up one hand, willed silence, and Breziot's
tirade broke off in mid-taunt. His brother's words woke
no anger, but only a curious sort of depression. There was
no conscious need to inflict punishment, but Breziot must
be made to understand that such commentary was imper-
missible. Varis's mind, or some obscure part of it, was
already at work, its secret speed actually outstripping his
awareness. Before he had fully realized what he meant to
do, the Duke's pallid outlines were changing. Arms, legs,
neck, and torso stretched and thinned like ductile wire,
drawn to impossible lengths. The ectoplasmic substance
was wonderfully pliable, easy as twine to bend and loop.
Almost automatically, Varis's mind began tying knots.
Boneless giraffe-neck twisted over and under elongated
left leg, ends pulled tight.

The shade shrilled.

Right leg crossed over left arm, looped and doubled
back, ends pulled tight.

Hysterical ghostly yammering that almost seemed
loud enough to make itself heard upon the corporeal
plane. Distracting. Annoying.

Mental yank and twist, and a length of infinitely flexi-
ble arm wrapped itself about Breziot's head, circling again
and again, until the entire skull was lapped in ectoplasmic
coils that muffled outcry. A push brought the shrouded
head down to waist level. Additional limb-wrapping followed, and the dead Duke's voice died. Thereafter, Varis

continued looping, knotting, tucking loose ends, until the entire mass of ghostly substance took on a roughly spherical form. For a few moments, he studied the floating, faintly translucent globe; then his mind clenched like a fist.

Mental pressure compressed the yielding ectoplasm, and the sphere shrank to snowball dimensions. A potent thought set it spinning upon its axis. Varis watched almost bemusedly. Prior to that moment, he had not fully recognized his own level of sorcerous expertise. Presently, however, the novelty began to pall, and he permitted his control to slacken. The sphere slowed to a halt, gradually expanded to its former size, painstakingly unknotted itself. Endlessly elongated limbs slowly resumed their original proportions, and his Grace's ghost, once more recognizable, hovered several feet above the floor.

Gad! What was left of Breziot appeared inexpressibly shocked.

" 'Oh, the look upon your face, youngster,' " Varis quoted softly, but his brother seemed not to recognize the allusion, and he continued in a neutral conversational tone. "I am remembering a game of Sightless we two played, nearly twenty years ago. I was blindfolded. You led me to the rooftop of the House Uloric and left me there. Does your Grace recall this?"

The shade stared uncomprehendingly.

"The sunlight upon the snow was particularly brilliant that afternoon. I'd ample opportunity to observe it when I stripped the blindfold away, for I'd left my dark glasses behind. By the time I found my way down from that roof, my eyes were seared and all but sightless. They remained so for some weeks, and several physicians pronounced the condition permanent. Eventually, my vision restored itself, yet that interval of blind uncertainty remains to this day one of the most enduringly vivid of childhood recollections." Varis paused, tacitly inviting reply.

A joke, merely!

"An inspiration."

The ghost opened his mouth; reconsidered, and shut it again.

"It is to your Grace's wit, invention, and quick fancy that I owe such memories," Varis continued expressionlessly. "I can but hope these qualities persist beyond life, for I find myself compelled to call upon them now."

Divining the imminence of retribution, the ghost distressfully billowed and fluttered. Escape, however, was impossible.

When his brother's efforts ceased, Varis resumed, "Years ago, you led one brother to the House Uloric roof. Tonight, you will perform the same service for the other."

What, for Hurna? There was no reply, and the ghost demanded, *Why?*

"Moments ago, you claimed you saw so many things more clearly, now."

And I do. Yes, I know your malice now, you worm. I won't help you.

"You've a choice?"

There's always a choice.

"In theory." Varis considered his own history. "Choice is often less than it seems. Let us put it to the test." Again he exerted his will, this time not troubling with ectoplasmic distortion, knots, or magical pyrotechnics. This time, in the manner of the great necromancers, he simply ruled natural force.

The living possessed advantages over the dead. Breziot was helpless; his will buckled at once. Without further argument, his troubled shade sped from the crypt.

Varis stood motionless, curiously drained. He could sense his middle brother's progress; knew that time was limited. Still, the minutes passed before he could bring himself to move.

Some sixth sense of danger woke the young Ulorre Olisi. Or perhaps it had been the creak of the bedsprings, and the shifting of her bedfellow's weight. Which could only mean one thing. Her huge and relentlessly vigorous husband was about to set upon her again, for the third time that night. Behind closed lids, the tears warmed Olisi's eyes. She didn't think she could stand it—not again. She was still sore from the last time, covered with bruises, filled with desolation and a sense of defilement impossible to wash away with soap and water.

There was no question of refusing him, however. He was her husband, as well as Ulor of Rhazaulle, and he had his rights. If she didn't give voluntarily, then he would simply take, as he was doubtless entitled to do, and that was far worse—painful and unspeakably degrading. Within hours of the marriage ceremony, she had learned the futility of open resistance.

She had also learned, however, that subtler forms of dissuasion had their merits. Her assumption of some particularly unappetizing demeanor would often repel him, provided his urges were not overly pressing. Still feigning slumber, she gathered the saliva in her mouth, let her jaw sag, and allowed the spittle to dribble thickly from her lips. Flopping over on her back, she vented a series of wetly snuffling snores. Sometimes, this was enough; sometimes not.

The suspenseful seconds passed, and she did not feel his hands upon her. At last Olisi lifted her lids a hairbreadth and risked a furtive glance. Owing to the unusual mildness of the weather, the bed curtains were open, and the chamber windows likewise gaped wide. Moonlight flooded the room. By that pale light she could see her husband quite clearly. He was wide awake, lying there rigid, and he was not looking at her. Understandably, his astonished gaze was fixed upon the white form floating a few feet above him. Despite its faint translucency, the ghostly form was perfectly recognizable.

Breziot, recently deceased Duke of Otreska, had come back.

A startled gasp, impossible to repress, escaped Olisi. No point any longer in pretending unconsciousness. Eyes wide, she shrank back, clutching the sheets to her. Her husband scarcely noticed. The ghost was similarly preoccupied.

Breziot's expression conveyed a curious mixture of urgency and distress. His lips moved, but the words that issued were inaudible.

"I can't hear you. I don't understand," the Ulor observed evenly, and his young wife jumped at the sound of his voice.

The ghost harangued in eerie silence.

"Why are you here, Brother? What do you want of me?"

The Ulor displayed not a trace of fear, and for the first time, Olisi perceived in her lord a quality other than pure loathsomeness. It was not much; but it was something.

The ghost's utterance waxed in vehemence, if not intelligibility. His gestures, however, were eloquent. Repeatedly, Breziot beckoned. Beyond question, he desired his brother to accompany him, somewhere.

Hurna rose at once from the bed, wrapped his nakedness in a dressing gown, and without a glance to spare for his cowering bride, confidently followed the ghost from the bedchamber.

Olisi was not disposed to chase them. Immediately following her husband's departure, she curled her small body, nose touching knees, and pulled the sheets up over her head. The world was temporarily excluded, yet thought persisted. She wondered, for the thousandth time, whether her father had known or cared what she was consigning her to, when he married her off to the Ulor. She wondered how the folk of Rhazaulle endured the presence of their remarkably intrusive dead. And finally she considered her own future prospects; wondering, miserably enough, whether she was trapped in this horrible place for the rest of her natural life, and perhaps, beyond.

In the antechamber outside the bedroom waited the Ulor's two massive bodyguards, one awake and one asleep. Upon Hurna's emergence, the wakeful guard sprang to his feet, saluted, and turned to rouse his companion. The Ulor's sharp gesture halted him. Breziot's ghost was shaking his head, pantomiming an emphatic negative. Evidently, the bodyguards' attendance was unacceptable.

At the entrance to the royal apartment, the sentries stood commendably eagle-eyed. A word from Hurna chained them to their post. Unaccompanied, the Ulor followed his brother's ghost down the corridor, around a corner, up a tightly winding flight of stairs, and up, and up.

Hurna emerged at last onto the highest rooftop of the House Uloric; a lead-sheathed confusion of flats, slopes, catwalks, fanciful domed turrets, and innumerable chimneys. The place seemed deserted. He looked about him, mystified. The ghost was nowhere to be seen. He called his brother's name. No response. A joke? Was Breziot still addicted to practical jokes, even now?

A flash of white caught his eye. Something small and pale lay at the very edge of a level expanse of roofing. He walked toward it, and as he drew near, saw that it was flat, rectangular, and weighted down with a couple of pebbles. Folded paper—a letter? From Breziot? He hurried to the verge of the roof, stooped, and reached for the white rectangle. Intent upon his goal, he never sensed the human presence behind him. A tall form stepped forth from the shadow of a chimney. A firm shove sent Hurna XI hurtling from the summit of the House Uloric.

He plunged some six stories to the courtyard below, and the impact of his large body upon the stone pavement was loud enough to wake sleepers. No doubt the inquisitive would shortly begin to converge upon the spot, yet for long moments, Varis could not bring himself to move. He stood very still, gazing down at his brother's splayed form, and found himself equally devoid of triumph or remorse. He felt nothing, in fact, beyond a faint astonish-

ment at the speed, ease, and finality of the deed. The Ulor
was dead. There his corpse lay, bathed in moonlight, and
still it seemed unreal.

One of the servants, bearing a lantern, came running
out into the courtyard. Real enough. The sound of the
fellow's yells broke the spell. Varis quietly retired, making
his way back to his own apartment without mishap. His
own few attendants still slept. They had noted neither his
departure nor his return. Once safe in his bedroom, he
exchanged his dark garments for a dressing gown, but did
not seek his bed. There was no point. Within minutes,
some messenger would be pounding on the door of the
dead Ulor's only surviving brother. They would discover
him awake, immersed in a book; for him, nothing unusual.

Varis selected a volume, sat, and stared unseeingly at
the pages; waited, and in his mind's eye watched his
brother's body plummet, again and again. So quickly
done. So easily accomplished, and this time, by his own
hand. Clotl and Breziot had died by supernatural agency,
but this time, he himself had done the deed. Extraordinary. Unreal?

It seemed an eternity before the urgent knocking commenced. He sat motionless. Presently one of the servants
roused himself and responded. There was a flurried exchange, and moments later, a minor commotion outside
his own bedchamber, whose threshold no attendant passed
without the master's express permission. Varis set the
book aside carefully, rose, and walked without haste to the
door.

Hurna's demise, like his brother's before him, was fraught
with mystery. This time, unlike the last, accident seemed
the best explanation. The Ulor, wandering about the roof
in the dark, had lost his footing and plunged to his death.
Simple mischance.

But what had he been doing up there in the middle of

the night? Here, the accounts of several witnesses provided some information, if not insight. No fewer than four guards had observed the Ulor following a fleet, wraithlike figure. The little widow, Ulorre Olisi, even claimed to have recognized the ghostly form and features of her husband's middle brother, but this story was largely disbelieved. Olisi was, after all, only a young girl; probably hysterical, an unreliable observer, and Aennorvi to boot. Moreover, Breziot's involvement in the Ulor's death was difficult to credit; the two had always been on excellent terms.

In any event, it was certain that the Ulor, for once refusing the protection of his guards, had chased a ghost up to the roof, from which he had fallen or jumped. Or been pushed.

Suicide? Hurna XI, with his gigantic appetites, his high spirits and huge vitality? Difficult to believe.

Even less believable was the homicide theory; for who could have predicted Hurna's visit to the roof upon that particular night, and who could have waited there for him? A few Venerators had an answer to that question. The necromancer responsible for the ghost's presence could have predicted, and waited, whispered the devout; but these people were fanatics.

In the end, the relatively palatable verdict of accident was accepted, and the Zalkhash busied itself with the business of interring the dead Ulor and enthroning his successor. Hurna XI was duly laid to rest in the royal crypt, alongside his first wife. As for the second wife, the pale little Ulorre Olisi—she, being childless, husbandless, and foreign, was now deemed superfluous at Court. Offered the option of return to her native land, she accepted with almost unseemly alacrity, and a mere six weeks following her husband's funeral, Olisi embarked for Aennorve. The arrangements for her departure were overseen by her surviving brother-in-law, who had likewise orchestrated the interment of the dead sovereign, and the prompt installment of the Ulorin Lishna. These matters were handled with praiseworthy dispatch; and Olisi, departing Rialsq forever upon a limpid morning late in summer, knew she would always remember Varis, and the debt of gratitude that she owed him.

The competence and energy that won the widow's admiration did not go unnoticed by courtly observers. Moreover, Hurna XI's youngest brother was the little Ulor's closest living male relative. Thus it seemed logical, indeed inevitable, that Varis preside over the Council of Regents set up to govern Rhazaulle until the juvenile Ulor Lishna V should come of age. The Council consisted of eight men, great Noble Landholders all. The office of Chairman, while pleasantly prestigious, carried no special privilege, for all eight members were equally empowered.

Varis recognized but scarcely grudged the limitations of his new eminence. The situation, after all, would shortly change. But not too shortly. Breziot and Hurna had both died within the space of a few months. Best to allow some time before others followed. Best, for now, to busy himself publicly with Regency, and privately with illicit research.

His books, his necromantic notes and folios, his various gels and powders—he could occupy himself with these things for months or years on end. Or so he supposed. In reality, the matter was not so easily managed.

Something was interfering with his concentration. As he sat up alone through the lengthening nights, poring over crabbed and ancient pages, he couldn't rid himself of the sensation that he was not alone. Almost it seemed that unseen companions hovered beside him, peering over his shoulder as he read. They were diffuse, almost nonexistent, yet their illimitable enmity bridged dimensions.

Ridiculous. Distempered imagination. And if by chance something other, then he was qualified to deal with it. He spoke certain words, completed certain procedures, designed to clear the immediate area of unsummoned spectres. The effort tired him—necromantic activity was debilitating, always a drain upon body and mind—but it was worth the price. The inimical intruders were gone.

Two nights later, however, they returned. Varis felt the icy prickling at the back of his neck, felt the chill of hate in the air; knew at once they were with him again.

He sent them away. For another two nights.

Once more he banished them, this time at so high a cost that he lay abed until noon of the next day. His apartment remained clear for five nights; at the end of that time, they came back. He could chase them off again, but the personal expense was high, and the results unsatisfying.

There were already many with cause to hate him, but this spectral persistence suggested intensely personal animosity.

Breziot? Hurna?

No matter. They might hang about as long as they pleased, rattling his nerves if they could; but otherwise, they were powerless to harm him. He could afford to ignore them.

But it was worse than he'd expected. Not so bad during the daylight hours, when he was busy, and there were people about him. At night, though, when he lay in bed, and the hate hung heavy in the motionless air, and the memories welled in his brain—then it was hard to get to sleep, harder yet to stay asleep, and he often woke to find himself clench-jawed and sweat-drenched, alone and not alone in the haunted dark.

Hungry for rest, he resorted to a narcotic draught. He slept deeply, but even in slumber did not escape unwelcome visitation.

His dreaming self beheld a scrawny form, a plaited beard, scarred face, familiar sly smirk.

So—how's it going, boy? Enjoying life? inquired Clotl.

"I sent you away," said Varis, in his dream.

Is that your idea of a welcome? Where did you learn manners?

"Unreal. You are not here."

I beg to differ. Heh. You've got it wrong. For all your drudging, there's still a lot you don't know. Example—you never actually sent me away. I mean, as in BANISHED. You merely charred the threads, thereby freeing me. For which, by the way, I thank you. Now I can come and go as I please.

"Then go."

And miss the show? When the best is yet to come?

"Out of my sight, and never return."

Heh. Very masterful, very necromantic. Good effort. Trouble is, it doesn't work when you're asleep. But never mind, you'll learn. You see, I believe in you, boy. I think you've got the spark of talent, and being your first instructor, your mentor and your inspiration, I take a personal interest in your career. I'm going to follow it through to the very end. From this night on, I'll never be far from your side. Yes, boy, make no mistake about it—you've found a friend.

"Leave me," sleeping Varis commanded, but the shade disobediently lingered, forcing the dreamer to retreat. Varis managed to jolt himself awake. He lay alone in a quiet, dark room. There was no sign of Clotl, and if Hurna or Breziot lingered nearby, the presence was undetectable.

Nightmare. None of it real. Clotl had passed to the unknown realm, months earlier. He could not return.

Moments passed before his breathing eased. Then he rose from bed to pace the chamber, for he wanted no more of sleep and dreams.

The dreams and fancies were ungovernable. His imagination was running out of control. Intolerable.

He recalled the salutary effects of concentration. The comparative aimlessness of his present existence was taking its toll. He needed a goal to work toward, to focus his mind upon—it was at such times that he was at his best, altogether his own master. He needed to resume his interrupted march upon the Wolf Throne.

Five lives still in his way. Five nieces and nephews. The little Ulor Lishna V, and his sisters, tiny twins incongruously titled Grand Ulorinnes. But their father was scarcely cold; it was too soon for another Uloric death. Moreover, there was something in him that recoiled a little, even yet, from infanticide. Hurna's children were condemned; but, almost unconscious of his own qualms, their executioner delayed the stroke.

Breziot's offspring, on the other hand, were scarcely babies. Their destruction was essential, and it was upon these next two targets that Varis's attention fastened.

The boy, Cerrov.

His sister, that black-haired youngster. Shalindra.

6

A LIGHT HAND shook her awake, and Shalindra knew at once that something was wrong. It was the dead of night, not even close to dawn; her windows were shuttered and curtained, but she could tell. Her mother—fully dressed, cloaked, gloved, and bearing a single candle—knelt beside her bed.

"Time to get up, darling," whispered the Duchess.

"Whaa . . . ?" Shalindra blinked, looked into her mother's eyes, and was suddenly awake. "What is it, Mama?"

"Sssh. Keep your voice down."

"Why are you—"

"Up. Get dressed. Quickly."

"Where's Feenya?" A duke's daughter expected assistance of servants.

"Asleep, and I want her to stay that way. If you need help, I'll do it. Now hurry."

She didn't really need help. Just turned eleven years old, she had not yet graduated to the elaborate, laced and boned feminine attire impossible to don unaided. More curious than fearful, she jumped out of bed and dressed herself in the clothes her mother had laid out. Warm, sensible, dark-colored garments, she noted. Suitable for outdoor wear. Traveling clothes? Interesting. A novelty, an adventure. But Mama's tight lips and hard jaw promised no pleasure jaunt.

Shalindra fastened the last button, then looped a ribbon about her unruly mass of black hair. "Ready."

"Good girl. If there are any keepsakes here that you value, small things that will fit in your pocket, then take them now."

"But why—where—?"

"Hurry."

Imperative tone; argument inadvisable. Quickly she selected a few of her choicest treasures; glass paperweight enclosing the tiny golden figurine of a rearing horse: carved ivory fan, her mother's gift; penknife with a mother-of-pearl handle, given by her brother. "Done."

"Then come with me. Quietly."

Repressing a spate of questions, Shalindra obeyed. In silence, she followed her mother from the bedroom, through chambers grown warm with color in the months following the Duke of Otreska's death, to the little marble foyer, where her brother waited. Cerrov, like herself, was plainly dressed; unlike herself, unwontedly grim-faced. His eyes sought his mother's. Wordless signals flew. He knew what was going on, that was obvious. The Duchess had told him something, but she hadn't confided in Shalindra. And it wasn't fair, not fair at all. Cerrov was only thirteen, not that much older than his sister. She was very grown up for her age, and there was no reason she should have been excluded. She wasn't going to stand for it, either.

She bent an insistent gaze upon her brother, willing him to look at her. When he did, her eyes transmitted the silent query, *What's going on?*

He shook his head minutely, and his eyes replied, *Not now.*

Sometimes it was like that with Cerrov. Often she felt

that she could read his mind, and vice versa. Oh, perhaps not literally—it wasn't as if they were telepathically linked, there was nothing magical about it (and come to think of it, even the real magicians, the bona fide necromancers, owned no power to read living minds). It was just that the two of them were so close, knew each other so well, that often they sensed one another's thoughts.

Right now, she sensed huge obstinacy. When he got that way, he was immovable, there was nothing to be done with him. Eventually, however, she'd worm the information out of his head; sooner or later, somehow—for there was in her an unfeminine curiosity that couldn't be trained out of existence, and wouldn't be denied. It was her chief character flaw, which, as her late father had explained, if ineradicable, she must at the very least learn to conceal. That much she could manage, for the moment.

In silence, the two children followed their mother from the ducal apartment, along the chilly corridor, and down the stairs. It was odd to be wandering the House Uloric in the middle of the night. The familiar galleries seemed somehow altered, almost foreign; unwontedly silent and stark, filled with nervous, gliding shadows. A little sinister, more than a little stimulating. One glance at her mother's set face, however, quelled all exhilaration.

The stairwell was dimly inimical. It seemed to descend into nothingness. Noting her qualms, Cerrov took her hand, and the shadows lost a measure of their menace.

Down they went. More corridors; little, dusty, mean ones, normally traversed by servants alone. Cold and silence, and the soft tap of their careful footsteps upon bare flooring. Through an inconspicuous little side exit, and out into the wintry chill of the great central courtyard. Straight across the windswept expanse, to one of the several modest wooden gateways spaced at wide intervals along the Zalkhash wall. Such gates were invariably locked. To Shalindra's amazement, the Duchess produced a key, unlocked the door, and led the children through.

In the street beyond, a sledge awaited—a plain, very ordinary vehicle, little better than a common sledge-for-hire. The Duchess advanced; exchanged a few quiet words with the driver. He nodded, and she turned back to her children.

"Everything's in order. Your route's planned, transports and transfers arranged, fares paid, escorts readied along the way. Your bags are already aboard. Best start now. No good delaying." The Duchess spoke in a businesslike, matter-of-fact tone that rang alarmingly false.

Shalindra looked up into her mother's drawn white face, and composure deserted her. *What are you talking about? What is this?*

"You and your brother travel to Aennorve, there to claim his Majesty Dasune's protection."

"Protection from *what*?"

The Duchess decided not to soften her reply. "From your Uncle Varis. I think he means you harm."

"He— *Why* do you think so?" Shalindra was astonished. "He doesn't even notice us, except maybe on our birthdays."

"He notices far more than you think."

"Why do you say so, Mama?"

"That's hard to explain. There have been certain things . . . Odd circumstances surrounding the death of your father and then the Ulor. The observations of Varis's servants—one of them is paid to report to me—"

"You mean, you've got your own *spies*?"

"A necessity, my darling. My agent has reported things—strange residues found at the bottom of drinking cups—peculiar incidents, abnormal behavior. Then, there's the way I've sometimes seen him looking at you . . ." The Duchess' voice trailed off. Acknowledging the vagueness of her response, she concluded with a shrug, "But mostly it's instinct, just a feeling I have. I want you out of your uncle's reach."

"Oh, but Mama, that's—"

"No argument."

"But *Aennorve*. It's so far away, and they don't speak Rhazaullean, and I've read that they eat their flogae raw. I don't see why we—"

"Shalindra. Enough." The Duchess' tone sharpened. "You'll do as you're told. Now kiss me good-bye, and get in the sledge."

"Good-bye? If we go, you're coming with us!"

"No. At least, not yet." Her daughter's shocked eyes reproached her, and the Duchess explained, "If I go with you, our flight will be noticed at once. Pursuit's possible. If I stay behind, it may be days before they realize you've left. So the two of you will go now, and I promise to join you as soon as I can."

"No, that's not—"

"Shalindra." Cerrov laid a hand on her arm. "You're making it harder. Don't be a baby."

That silenced her. He was right, of course. She was far too old to storm and sulk. She'd show some maturity, if it killed her. She hugged her mother hard. "Come to us soon, Mama," she said in a low voice; bestowed a final kiss, and climbed into the waiting vehicle. Through the open door, she watched and listened.

The Duchess embraced her son, then handed him a sealed letter. "For his Majesty," she explained. "Trust no intermediaries, give it to him yourself. And—" Her fingers fumbled at the back of her neck. A tiny clasp parted, and she removed a circular gold locket set with diamonds that flashed purely even in the low light of the sledge lanterns. The ornament changed hands. "Show him this. He'll remember where we were when he gave it to me, and he'll remember what he said then. I hope."

Cerrov carefully stowed locket and letter in an inside pocket, kissed his mother, and entered the sledge, closing the door behind him. The driver's whip spoke, and the sledge creaked off along the icy street. The Duchess stood watching it go. When the last faint glimmer of its lanterns disappeared, she dashed the tears from her eyes, turned, and went back inside.

Initially it was reported that the children were visiting their mother's kin in Lazimir. Within the week, however, investigation revealed the falsity of this claim, and Varis recognized the ruse. Cerrov and Shalindra had disappeared. The revelation was unsettling, but generous doses of SD-9b maintained his equanimity throughout a trying period. It seemed he had vastly underestimated his middle brother's widow. Almost he could admire the Duchess, even while contemplating her destruction; for so sharp a thorn demanded removal.

A courageous, resolute woman, but she couldn't hope to hide them away for long. His intelligence network was extensive and efficient; he'd discover their whereabouts in a matter of days. Their reprieve was temporary. In the meantime, however, the state of his dreams warned him not to sit idle. The great plan had to go forward, and thus he was forced to turn his attention at last upon the little Ulor and twin ulorinnes.

All three of them were well-guarded, but no more so than their father had been. Still, the task of their removal presented certain strategic challenges. The royal nursery was never clear of attendants. There were bodyguards, servants, a ferociously devoted amazon of a nurse, even a pet dwarf—sort of a miniature jester—forever hanging about. It would not be easy to circumvent so many protectors. There was no question of luring the tots forth, as Hurna had been lured to his death—they would simply not be permitted to go. Moreover, the use of multiple ghosts—so effective in Breziot's disposal—was impracticable in this case. The bedchamber of the twin grand ulorinnes didn't even lock from the inside. Someone would hear something, someone would run to the rescue . . . No good.

Poison was out of the question. The dwarf sampled all

food entering the nursery. Bribery of a guard or two? Perhaps. But impossible to bribe them all. Too many people.

Persuasion, deception, or coercion of one of the servants? Triple infanticide and then an obliging suicide? Infeasible, but the idea suggested a possible method.

Isolation of the targets was essential. Separation from, or elimination of, all witnesses and potential defenders. Not easily achieved, but in this, the very devotion of the children's allies might serve a useful function. Varis considered. Alone in his dim chamber at midnight, he sat, fingers steepled beneath his chin, too-brilliant eyes fixed on the blank wall before him, and he thought. The images floated through his mind. Guards. Servants. Dwarf-jester. Nurse.

Nurse.

The little Ulor Lishna's nurse. A valued family retainer. Nurse to many a Haudrensq heir, including the youthful Hurna XI, as well as Hurna's younger brothers. Mivvi, her name was. She had been Varis's own nurse for a time, decades earlier. She'd had no use for him at all, he recalled; no patience with his physical shortcomings, his timidity, or his daydreaming. "Little Sister." "Weepybooby." "Master Sissydoodle." She'd an endless supply of nicknames for him. Then there had been the incessant unfavorable comparisons with his exuberant older brothers, both of whom she'd adored . . . He had never dared to complain, because he'd been frankly afraid of her. Understandably so. A tall woman, burly and broadshouldered, with big hands and a face of iron, hers was a formidable physical presence. Now, twenty years later, she was elderly, with iron hair to match the iron face, but formidable as ever.

Mivvi. He hadn't really thought of her in years. Her devotion to the little Ulor Lishna was said to border upon the obsessive. Many a time she'd bragged of her willingness to die or to kill for him.

Perhaps.

His plan, once conceived, was simple and straightforward, necessitating another trip to the royal crypt. He had last visited upon the mildest night of summer, there to raise Breziot's unwilling shade. Now it was the bitter dead of winter, and it was the former Ulor, Hurna XI himself, that he sought.

He would rather have spared himself the encounter. A confrontation with his murdered brother would certainly prove taxing; all the more so, when Hurna discovered what was required of him. It would be simple enough to silence the shade's fulminations, if he cared to. But, he was beginning to realize, the simple domination of infinitely manipulable shades was losing its appeal, along with its novelty. He was no Deathmaster Clotl, taking perpetual childlike delight in pranks, petty humiliations, crude little displays of power. Nor was he an Arkhoy, demon-spurred to expand the limits of atrocity. Nor did necromantic revenge lighten the stain of old memory. The ghosts he commanded were helpless to oppose him; he could do anything he chose with them. This established, the exercise was starting to seem . . . rather pointless.

And if so—what else was there?

These were profitless thoughts. His goal. His great project. Best to focus on that, to the exclusion of all else.

Accordingly, he sought the crypt and summoned his brother's ghost.

Predictable outpouring of spectral wrath.

Varis issued his commands, and Hurna convulsed. Presently recognizing the futility of fury, he began to beg, and his abject humility was unexpectedly dreadful. Varis found he couldn't listen. Slightly sickened, he dispatched the ghost about its business; then sought the sanctuary of his own apartment, where there were potions and powders guaranteed to restore lost tranquillity, for a while.

Mivvi, nurse to the royal brood, had no idea what woke her from her dreams. A noise, a cold draught across her

face, an internal vibration? It could have been almost anything, for she slept very lightly, ears unconsciously attuned to the sound of a child's cry. No child cried now.
She listened intently. The nursery was quite silent.

The curtains of her bed were parted, as always, and the
door to the adjoining chamber where the little Ulor slept
was open. Yet she lay in utter darkness; for Lishna, thank
goodness, was none of your sickly whiners, requiring the
reassurance of a nightlight. A robust, pugnacious, rather
unimaginative little boy, very reminiscent of his golden
father at a similar age, Lishna was never troubled with bad
dreams or nighttime terrors.

The tiny twin sisters were different, of course; weaker-
minded, and prone to whimpering. Sometimes, when they
cried immoderately, she was obliged to slap them; for only
thus would they learn the courage and self-control demanded of grand ulorinnes. With Lishna, however, such
measures were never necessary. Lishna owned all the
bright assurance in the world. He was entirely fearless,
healthy as a bear cub, self-willed, a real Haudrensq. He
was the hope of Rhazaulle, and, as an orphan, he was *hers,*
utterly hers, in a way that the others, much as she had
loved some of them, never had been.

Best and most beautiful of them all.

But was he safe and well? Had it been some premonition of danger that woke her? Probably a false alarm, but
she'd best make sure of that. Pushing the covers aside,
Mivvi sat up in bed; and froze, openmouthed, staring eyes
fixed upon a point midway between floor and ceiling,
where a cold light glowed faintly. As she watched, the
glow intensified, thickened, and ordered itself. A human
form took uncertain shape. The outlines sharpened, details
molded themselves, and presently the translucent, palely
luminous figure of Hurna XI floated there, marvelously
distinct, and complete down to the last detail of his elaborate costume.

Poor Hurna. In life, he would scarcely have tolerated

such garments. But thus he had been interred, and now he would wear them for as long as his ghost remained bound to the physical plane.

Mivvi was awestruck, but hardly frightened. How, indeed, could she fear Hurna? But for Lishna, he had been her favorite nurseling. She had fed him, bathed him, watched him take his first step. She had chastised him when he showed signs of weakness, and otherwise cherished him. He, in his careless way, had been fond of her. In life and death, that bond endured.

The ghost, she saw at once, suffered horribly. His look of grief and pain terrified her; in all his years of life, he had never appeared half so piteous. He spoke at length, very fervently, but inaudibly.

Mivvi gaped.

Perceiving her incomprehension, Hurna's shade altered course. Decades earlier, his nurse had given him his first lessons in reading and writing. Her diligence was now to find its reward.

The ghost lifted a pale hand. His index finger looped and swirled. From that finger flowed an ectoplasmic script. The luminous words hung in the air.

Mivvi read aloud, haltingly. "Treachery. Danger. Guards and servants plot murder. Protect children. Defend Lishna." She raised incredulous eyes to the ghost's face.

Hurna underscored the final sentence.

"Defend them how? Shall I carry them away? Hide them?"

Slowly, as if unwillingly, the ghost shook his head.

"What, then? Tell me, trust me. I'll do anything."

Hurna wrote. The words glowed.

Kill Enemies.

"Kill?" She was startled but unafraid.

Hurna nodded. His eyes held hers for a moment, then he faded into nothingness. The message lingered for a few seconds more; then it was gone, and the darkness rushed

in to fill the resulting vacuum. Mivvi sat upright in bed,
eyes wide and blindly staring. The paralysis passed. Jumping from bed, she groped in the dark for a candle, laboriously contrived to light it, then stole soundlessly from her
closet into the adjoining chamber of the little Ulor.

Lishna V slept soundly. A faint rosy flush of good
health stained his cheeks. He was unharmed and untroubled as always. Similarly tranquil were the grand
ulorinnes, sleeping together in their big bed in the neighboring room. Beyond the sleeping quarters lay the nursery
proper, where the servants, potential murderers all, snored
the night away upon pallets scattered about the floor.
Only one guard remained awake and on duty. He sat at a
wooden table beside the door. By the light of a single
candle, he was polishing his brass belt buckle. When the
children's nurse stuck her head into the room, he turned
mild inquiring eyes upon her. Mivvi stared at him pierc-
ingly, as if to read his mind, and the fellow's expression
grew puzzled. Scowling, she withdrew.

Back again to her own closet. Snuffing the candle, she
crawled into bed, pulled up the covers, and lay there wide
awake, the fears and doubts swirling through her head. In
the midst of confusion, however, a single certainty sat
steady as a rock in a windstorm; whatever was necessary to
ensure the young Ulor's safety, she would willingly perform.

Anything.

Sleep found her at last, and in the morning, she woke
wondering if it had all been a dream. The winter sun was
shining. Her three charges romped noisily, the servants
functioned efficiently, normality reigned, and last night's
incident seemed unreal. Surely, she must have dreamed it.

If so, the dream repeated itself. That night, Hurna
came to her again. Aspect tragic, he scribbled his message
upon the air. The words had not changed.

No dream.

And he had come to *her,* to Mivvi, the one he had

known and loved in life, trusting her to save his children, because he remembered her energy, her devotion, and loyalty. He had chosen her, and no other. She would not fail him.

The next day, she sought out the Ulor's personal leech. When she described her insomnia, he did not hesitate to sell her a vial of his strongest soporific.

Still, she hesitated to use it. She believed Hurna's warning, and yet it seemed fantastic. For another day, she watched. Servants, guards, dwarf-jester—they all seemed so harmless, so predictable and trustworthy. Search and sniff though she might, she caught no whiff of conspiracy. They were remarkably clever, or else they were innocent. Confused, Mivvi held back.

He came to her again that night. He wept spectral tears. He was indescribably miserable, and Hurna had never been a dissembler. It was impossible to doubt him. She should never have doubted him. He was depending on her.

No more questions. No more delay. The nursery received its usual delivery from the kitchen in the early evening. That night, she dosed their dinners liberally with the contents of the doctor's vial; taking particular care, however, to spare the plates of the children. Servants and guards ate freely. Much earlier than usual, they were sleeping soundly.

Still, she waited. Waited until the children slept, waited until the rhythms of the House Uloric had slowed almost to a halt, waited as long as her sense of duty permitted her to wait, and beyond. Eventually, of course, the time ran out. Hurna's imperative shade reappeared, and she was forced out into the nursery, there to ply her carving knife upon a collection of undefended necks.

It was easier than she had expected. For one thing, she had her sense of sacred mission to sustain her. For another, she had in childhood witnessed her farmer-father slaughtering swine, and thus the jet of arterial blood, the convulsions of the sizable dying body, were not unknown to her. It was really very like slaughtering hogs, an unappealing necessity. She went for the throat, as her father had. There was some mess, but not a great deal of noise; not enough, it seemed, to draw attention.

Chest heaving, she looked slowly around her. Not a single treacherous nursery attendant remained alive. Corpses lay sprawled about the room. The floor was awash with blood, a shocking mess. It would have to be cleaned up before the children awoke to see it. She herself was splashed with red from head to toe. Nasty. Sticky. But unavoidable, and anyway, what did such trifles matter? She had done her duty. She had rescued the Ulor Lishna V, she had preserved the hope of Rhazaulle. She was a heroine, but she mustn't let it go to her head.

Still, she had a right to Hurna's gratitude—such was no less than her due. She had fulfilled his commission, to the letter; no doubt his ghost was hovering near at hand, eager to bestow praise. If so, however, she didn't see him. She called his name—her voice a startling croak in that blood-drenched silence—but he did not respond.

Perhaps he was in the next room, watching over his son?

She checked the little Ulor's chamber. Lishna V slept in innocence, wholly unaware of the nursery carnage. He was alone. Likewise alone were the slumbering grand ulorinnes. No sign of Hurna's ghost.

She would have enjoyed seeing him, basking a bit in the admiration that she deserved. But that would come later. At the moment, she needed to summon aid. The plot against the Ulor's life had been destroyed, thanks to her, but now an investigation would begin. There were questions to be asked and answered, reports to be filed. More important, the children required immediate transferral to new quarters. The palace guard would assist; they were the ones to notify. Several of them would be awake and on duty, even at this hour.

There was no one to send down to their headquarters on the ground floor. There was nothing for it but to go herself. She didn't like to leave the children alone, even momentarily. What if Lishna, waking, should come wandering out into a nursery transformed to abattoir? But Lishna wouldn't wake; he never did. He and his sisters would be quite safe where they were, for the few brief minutes she meant to be absent; safer yet if she locked them into their respective chambers. This she did, sliding the small bolts soundlessly. The children slept on.

Still clutching the fouled carving knife, she strode from the nursery, carefully locking the door behind her.

Moments following Mivvi's departure, the ghost of Hurna XI reappeared within the locked sleeping compartment of his twin daughters. Hurna's face, a luminous mask of rage and agony, was streaked with glowing tears. Briefly he seemed to struggle against sorcerously induced compulsion, translucent form flickering with intense effort. Resistance was useless, however; ectoplasm was pitiably malleable stuff. Necromantic power effortlessly crushed him, and defiance buckled almost at once. The ceremonial costume in which the dead Ulor's body had been interred included an ornate dagger. Hurna drew the ghost-blade now, and swiftly plied it twice. Like the dagger of Celgi Haudrensq, the weapon penetrated living flesh, and the blood of the grand ulorinnes stained the pillow. The twins died swiftly and in silence. Their father's shade winked out of existence, to resume visibility in the sleeping compartment of the Ulor Lishna.

He had postponed his son's destruction for as long as possible, perhaps in feeble hope of some last-minute miracle rescue. In fact, the delay proved unfortunate, for during that interval, some nameless instinct woke the little boy.

Lishna sat up in bed, wide eyes fixed upon his visitor's luminous face. He smiled. "Father," he said.

The ghost-blade plunged. Blood spouted. Lishna died. And the shade, with a voiceless howl of anguish, vanished.

Alone in his apartment, necromantically linked to his ghostly tool, Varis experienced the moment. A shudder shook him.

Subsequent events, some of them, became a matter of public record. The nurse Mivvi—regicide, infanticide, mass murderess—related a lunatic tale comprising conspiracy, treacherous attendants, even ghostly visitation. Freely she confessed to the drugging and slaying of guards, servants, and harmless dwarf-jester; but for reasons best known to herself, maintained her innocence in the deaths of the three royal children. Never mind the fact that the children had died of knife wounds similar to those found upon the adult victims. Never mind the fact that she'd led the Uloric guards back to a locked slaughterhouse that no one other than herself could have entered or departed. Mivvi swore she'd never touched her charges.

It was naturally assumed that the nurse attempted to pass herself off as a madwoman. Judged mentally incompetent, she might forgo the Funnel in favor of life in the Wrecks. Had she but proved a more talented actress, her chances might have been better. As it was, nobody really believed the stolid, iron-faced culprit deranged. More likely, she was shielding her coconspirators, for it seemed all but impossible that this dull creature could have conceived of such deeds on her own.

Conspiracy. The concept found a receptive audience, for it explained so much, otherwise inexplicable: the appalling succession of royal deaths in recent months, the unlikely accidents, the varied mysterious circumstances, the happenings too improbable to be written off as accident—conspiracy could account for it all.

But who would stand to benefit?

Anarchists, attempting to destroy the entire royal family? Almost unbelievable.

A claimant to the Wolf Throne? Following Hurna's three dead children, the next in the line of succession was the Duke of Otreska's son, Cerrov. The boy was only just thirteen, too young to hatch plots. The same could not be said, however, of his mother—a woman of very questionable character, suspected of vanity and harlotry. Her brazen flirtation with the King of Aennorve had initially seemed a piece of conventional misbehavior, but perhaps it went beyond that—perhaps the Duchess of Otreska was a traitor, conspiring with a foreign power for advancement of her own offspring. Additionally suspect, at such a time, was the disappearance of the boy Cerrov and his younger sister Shalindra. Clearly, the Duchess had hidden them away. Why?

Perhaps, speculated an imaginative minority, the Duchess was less guilty than fearful. Perhaps she simply sought to protect her children. Or maybe the youngsters weren't hidden away at all—maybe the two of them were already dead and buried, murdered long ago. And by whom? Well, directly behind Cerrov and Shalindra in the line of succession stood their Uncle Varis. But this suggestion seemed farfetched. Grave, ascetic, cerebral Varis, with his remote formality, his solitary bookish ways, his unblemished record of faithful service to the Ulor Hurna—Varis, a monster-murderer? Unlikely. Most Rialsquis dismissed the possibility; although a few, notably of Venerator persuasion, continued to wonder.

But there was little profit in speculation. The obvious source of sound information was the literally red-handed nurse. If conspiracy existed, the murderess could surely be prevailed upon to reveal its nature and membership.

Mivvi's interrogation took place behind discreetly closed doors. Her questioners were Varis's agents, whose methods were creative.

The old woman proved unusually resolute, her resistance continuing a full two weeks. In the end, however, she capitulated; signed a full confession acknowledging herself killer of the royal children, and supplied a list of her coconspirators' names—or rather, put her signature to a list supplied by her persuasive examiners.

At the head of the list, to nobody's surprise, was the Duchess of Otreska's name, followed by the names of her closest friends and allies, together with the late Duke's staunchest supporters. Mass arrests promptly followed.

The Duchess and a clutch of her accused henchmen faced a tribunal presided over by a panel of judges quietly appointed by the chief defendant's former brother-in-law. The trial, like the interrogation of the guilty nurse, proceeded behind closed doors; a courtesy ostensibly offered in consideration of the Duchess' gender and rank. In reality, the exclusion of random observers freed the prosecution of virtually all restraint ordinarily imposed by law and custom.

The secrecy of the proceedings heightened already-intense public curiosity. Throughout the three-day duration of the trial, the inquisitive loitered in the gallery outside the Zalkhash council chamber serving as a courtroom. Those entering or leaving were routinely pelted with questions, but no information was forthcoming until the close of the first day. At that time, a bespectacled, plainly clad little man emerging from the courtroom was pounced upon by a trio of prominent Noble Landholders.

Their luck was good. They had bagged the recording clerk of the court, who—clearly awed by the rank of his captors—proved cooperative. Whisking him off to the nearest tavern, they sat him down, plied him with vouvrak, and proceeded to pick his brain.

"How's the Duchess holding up?" demanded the Noble Landholder Stratkha.

"Admirably," replied the clerk. "Such regal dignity. Such composure. Such an air."

"Such a strumpet," opined Stratkha.

"That's as may be, Noble Sir. But she does not appear so."

"She's got you hoodwinked, that's clear," observed the Noble Landholder Pire Zelkiv. "Did she say what she's done with Breziot's brats?"

"Her Grace declines to reveal the whereabouts of her two children—"

"Oh, she *declines*!"

"—But declares them safe and well, beyond reach of their enemies," the clerk concluded.

"And what enemies are those, pray?" inquired the Noble Landholder Deenyi Polchenskoi, a round-faced and rubicund lord.

"Her Grace declines to name them."

"Declines again!"

"Now there's insolence practiced as an art."

"With all due respect, I must disagree, Noble Sirs. If you will pardon my presumption, I will testify to her Grace's perfect courtesy. Barring the matters you have touched upon, her Grace answers all questions put to her most civilly."

"Very good of her. She's confessed, then?"

"No indeed, Noble Sir. Her Grace maintains her innocence. Permit me to observe, gentlemen, that her Grace speaks most movingly and convincingly in her own defense."

"Pah, she's got this fellow bewitched," scoffed Pire Zelkiv.

"If so, Noble Sir, she has similarly bewitched the majority of her listeners," the clerk replied. "I don't believe the judges themselves remain unaffected."

"I may vomit. That incredible slut!" exclaimed Stratkha.

"Her codefendants are similarly plausible," the clerk continued, not without complacence. "Entre nous, Noble Sirs, I think their acquittal not impossible."

His audience groaned.

By the close of the second day, however, the little clerk's optimism had waned. The same group of Noble Landholders set upon him as he exited the courtroom; carried him off to the same tavern, sat him down at yesterday's table, bought him a bottle, and demanded the news.

"Finished." The clerk shook his head. "Noble Sirs, all is finished. It was the nurse."

"Old Mivvi? Turned up in court, did she?"

"Not in person, Noble Sir. It would seem she is presently unfit to testify—evidently prostrate with remorse and guilt—"

"Remorse and guilt will do it, every time," Polchenskoi nodded.

"And so, her signed and witnessed statement was read aloud before the tribunal. Alas, Noble Sirs—the evidence was unequivocal."

"Tell us, fellow."

"The nurse Mivvi freely confesses to the triple murder of the Ulor Lishna and the grand ulorinnes. To this hideous act she was led by avarice and pushed by fear—"

"Fear of what?" Stratkha inquired.

"Threats. Harm to her family members. Vengeance."

"Her Grace's?"

"Exactly so. The Duchess of Otreska, resolved to secure advancement of her own illegitimate offspring at any cost, had expressed her determination to crush every obstacle—"

"Her *illegitimate* offspring?"

"So Mivvi attested, Noble Sir. '. . . nameless product of their mother's notorious promiscuity,' I believe the statement read."

"If only we'd been there to hear. It sounds *glorious*," sighed the Noble Landholder Zelkiv.

"If only Breziot had heard it."

"He'd have foamed at the mouth."

"Poor old Breziot."

"Good man for a revel."

"The best."

"A real loss."

A moment's reflective silence honored the departed Duke of Otreska.

"But the two children—the missing ones." The Noble Landholder Polchenskoi jumped into the conversational breach. "Is it a sure thing they weren't Breziot's? I mean, didn't the boy *look* a good deal like Breziot? And didn't both of 'em have the Haudrensq eyes, with the yellowish ring around the center? Or am I imagining things?"

Frowns about the table.

"I don't remember."

"Neither do I."

"Who notices such things?"

"They were—children."

"Irrelevant," the Noble Landholder Stratkha informed them. "The paternity of the whelps is beside the point. What matters is the guilt of the mother. I've said all along that woman ought to be dealt with."

"Ah, Noble Sir—" the clerk of the court bowed his head in regret. "I think it more than likely that she will be."

The Duchess and her allies were inevitably adjudged guilty. Condemnation swiftly followed. Culprits of the common sort were publicly bled atop the Funnel. Criminals of the Noble Landholder class met the headsman. For the two major actresses in this ugly drama, however, special penalties were ordained. Bloody Mivvi, as the populace now termed her, was consigned to Rialsq's sporting Wolf Den. There, the animals were bred, reared, trained to race and fight. Continual semi-starvation maintained their requisite state of ferocity. And there, under the eyes of a boisterous mob, the nurse's body was slowly carved, and flung bit by bit to the ravenous wolves. Mivvi was obliged to watch as the vital scraps of her substance went flying to eager lupine jaws. Such the vivisectionist skill and care of the executioner, that hours passed before her consciousness lapsed.

The Duchess of Otreska was subjected to no such vulgarity. On a bitter evening in mid-winter, the condemned woman was conveyed by open sledge from the Rialsq House of Correction to the White Level, site of the annual House of Ice; this year, the gleaming facsimile of a Lanthian palace, fully furnished and complete down to the last detail of ice-dishes and goblets, ice-cushions, and delicately etched ice-portraits, enclosed in sculpted ice-frames. The Duchess was ushered into the palace, and all the doorways were sealed behind her. For a few minutes, the curious spectators lingered to gawk at the doomed figure moving about behind imperfectly transparent walls, but a merciless winter wind soon chased them from the Level.

In the morning, when the soldiers came to open the House of Ice, they found the Duchess' frozen body up on the top floor, dead eyes fixed upon a glasslike skylight that must have afforded her a clear view of the night sky and stars for as long as she remained alive to watch them. The interior walls of the palace were unmarred. The prisoner hadn't tried to batter or chew her way out. Quite the contrary, in fact; she had voluntarily stripped down to her linen chemise, allowing the cold every opportunity to finish its work quickly.

She seemed to have died peacefully. Perhaps it was for this reason that her shade cleanly escaped the physical plane, as Varis discovered when an attempt to summon his dead sister-in-law for interrogation failed.

The Duchess' son was next heir to the Wolf Throne.

But Cerrov was missing, and in any case, quite possibly illegitimate. Likewise absent—the daughter, Shalindra. And probably just as well. For at such a time, in the wake of tragedy and scandal, Rhazaulle required a strong ruler. No child-Ulor, but an adult, preferably a male Haudrensq of proven energy, intelligence, and competence.

And there at hand, fulfilling every possible requirement, was Hurna XI's youngest brother.

The installation of the Ulor Varis I was restrained in pomp, the coronation ceremony downright modest. A tasteful and becoming piece of Uloric humility, it was thought. In fact, more than humility accounted for the decision. Personally, the new Ulor disliked excessive display; beyond that, he chose not to supply his enemies with ammunition. For there *were* enemies; secret, cowed, and bitterly whispering critics. Somehow, against all reason, some of them seemed to have guessed the truth. They were calling him murderer, necromancer, usurper. There was no evidence to support such accusations, yet somehow —they knew. False Ulor, they muttered. Fratricide. Monster. Following the recent great purge of his rivals, they had learned some discretion; but they were still there, penning their anonymous accusations, even within the walls of the Zalkhash itself. That fact became too apparent upon the very night of his coronation.

At the close of festivities curiously devoid of genuine gaiety, Varis I returned alone to his apartment—his old apartment, which he had not abandoned, for somehow he couldn't bring himself to appropriate the master suite once occupied by his older brother. Another example, it was thought, of the new Ulor's commendable modesty. The hour was late, the ceremonies had been wearisome, he was heavy-minded with fatigue and a disappointment whose source was not apparent. It had been, after all, a day of triumph. He had singlehandedly made himself Ulor of all Rhazaulle, his coronation marking the completion of metamorphosis from despised nonentity to absolute ruler. He had recreated himself, and yet the alteration seemed almost superficial. And there, he unwillingly realized, was the trouble. Elation, regal assurance, tranquillity—all the expected rewards remained elusive. He was solitary, cold, remote from humanity as always; if anything, more so than ever. Expecting inner transformation, he found himself—absolutely unchanged.

He wanted solitude and sleep. Dismissing the servants, he undressed, and parted the bed curtains. A note lay upon his pillow. Unfolding the paper, he read:

Homicide. Monster.

Monster. That word again. No signature or symbol. *Monster.* Thoughtfully, he set the note aside, snuffed the candle, and lay down.

They were in the House Uloric itself; perhaps among his own personal servants. They taunted, even challenged him. His sorcerous skills would serve to hunt them down, if he chose; to destroy them, or to scare them into silence. Or else—the thought occurred to him for the first time, and it was beautiful as summer's dawn—perhaps he might win them over, instead. Perhaps he might prove so wise and just a ruler that even his enemies would grudgingly grant his worth. His path to the Wolf Throne had been crooked and blood-drenched, but that was all behind him now. He needed a goal, a great ambition. He'd always needed that, and now that he was here, he had one. Time to be Ulor; time to be great.

So heartening and soothing was the thought that he drifted off to sleep without benefit of sedatives.

Clotl came to him again that night, but it didn't matter, for the Deathmaster owned no power to jangle his nerves.

So. You've actually done it. Picked off your rivals, avenged yourself upon your brothers' ghosts, massacred moppets, planted your bum on the throne. Not half bad for a lad of twenty-four.

"Twenty-five."

Whatever. Good work for any age. You've done your old teacher proud, boy. Congratulations.

"Rhazaulle will benefit."

Oh, Rhazaulle. I see. RHAZAULLE. Heh. Patriotism is a beautiful thing. Let's hope the nation is properly appreciative. Feeling pretty bouncy at this point, are we?

"Confident."

CONFIDENT. Now, what exactly do you mean by that? D'you mean you're CONFIDENT in yourself—enough to throw away your pills and powders, including the glop you stole from me? Eh? D'you mean you're CONFIDENT in your intimates— those devoted servants and courtiers who leave notes on your pillow? Are you CONFIDENT in benevolent destiny, maybe because virtue like yours deserves reward? Or did you mean that you're CONFIDENT in the loyalty of your subjects, who'll surely stand by you to a man when your brother's boy turns up to claim the throne? Which sort of CONFIDENCE do you enjoy? All of them? None of them? Eh?

"Unlikely that Breziot's boy will return."

Sure of that, are you? Really sure? The rightful heir is missing, you've no idea where to find him, his very existence reproaches your reign, yet you think it "unlikely" he'll return? Oh, such optimism—such CONFIDENCE! Heh. Heh!

The ghost's high-pitched giggles woke Varis. He opened his eyes and sat up abruptly. He was alone. The faint gray light pushing in under the curtains told him it was dawn. No hope of any more sleep, for now. Unrested, he rose from bed and dragged himself into the next room, where yesterday's unopened correspondence lay in a basket on the desk. There was a great deal of it. Apathetically, he shuffled through the packets, noting the crests upon the wax seals. Ritual congratulations and avowals of loyalty to the new Ulor, for the most part; a petition or two, and several personal requests for favors from ranking Noble

Landholders. Little of real interest. And then the familiar clumsy handwriting upon one of the folded missives arrested his eye, and he broke the seal with eager fingers.

By dawn's faint light, he read a report from one of his far-flung agents, who wrote to disclose the whereabouts of Breziot's missing children. Cerrov and Shalindra had been located in Aennorve. They were both in Feyenne, living quite openly at court under the protection of their late mother's admirer, his Majesty Dasune.

7

"WHY ARE WE here?" Shalindra turned demanding eyes upon her brother. Her black brows arched.

"Here in this universe? Here in Aennorve, here in Feyenne, or here in this particular street at this particular moment?" Cerrov inquired. "Be more specific."

"If you can answer the universe one, go right ahead. But I meant, here in Aennorve," Shalindra returned with dignity.

"Don't you like this place?"

"Oh, it's very nice, and the King's been really good to us, and all that, but we've been here for months now, and nobody tells me why."

"Mama gave you an answer."

"Not the whole answer; she left a lot out. And she hasn't written, she hasn't joined us, and I don't understand it. And I miss her." She couldn't quite suppress a vocal quiver.

"I know, Shalli. Me too." He touched her shoulder; a light, brief consolation.

He understood. Her eyes stung a little. If the tears escaped, she'd look like a crybaby. Anxious to avert that calamity, she inquired with slightly labored pertness, "Well? She told you more than she told me. I could see it. What is it you know that I don't?"

"A very great deal. Enough to fill volumes."

"C'mon."

"You're way too nosy."

"You're way too trap-mouthed. Anyone'd think I'm a baby."

"You are."

"Pig."

"Brat."

"Tell me."

"What a little snoop. Why don't you turn that curiosity to better use? Take a look around you." Cerrov's gesture encompassed the broad Feyennese avenue, with its warbling vendors, its gaudy pushcarts, white stucco architecture, arches, and wrought-iron grillwork. Overhead, the unveiled summer sun blazed in a cloudless blue sky. The shadows underfoot were short, dense ink-splotches spreading over the pale dusty cobbles—altogether unlike Rhazaullean shadows. The smells of warm humanity, bemubit trees, and grilling czenni roll-ups filled the warm air. It was early afternoon, and the merchants were curtaining their booths against the sun in anticipation of a three-hour midday closure—another exotic Aennorvi custom. "What do you see?"

"A hot, white street."

"You can do better than that. Look around you. Everything here is strange and new. Sights, sounds, even the smells—everything. Listen to the song that vendor's singing—it's nothing like Rhazaullean music. And look at the clothes the people wear—so light and bright, so foreign. And look over there at that tiny woman—a midget, I guess she is—doing acrobatics. Nothing like that in Rialsq."

"Not in such a costume. She'd be arrested, if she didn't freeze first. You're trying to change the subject."

"What subject? I'm only suggesting that you make good use of this time. You know—expand your mind."

"Until my head's as swelled as yours?"

"Broaden your outlook. Acquire wisdom. You could use some."

"Nosedrip, you sound just like Master Lunune."

Lunune, the young tutor appointed to instruct the Rhazaullean refugees, strolled several paces ahead of them. Beside him walked the gauze-clad Princess Olisi, still childlike despite her eighteen years and widow's status. Theoretically, the quartet made for the Bellenore Gardens, and an alfresco botany lesson. In fact, their progress was slow and meandering, for this excursion furnished the perfect excuse for a ramble through the color-filled streets of Feyenne—a city so informal and liberal of outlook that the public appearance of his Majesty Dasune's daughter, afoot and all but unattended, scarcely raised an eyebrow.

"Just like Lunune, eh?" Cerrov considered. "Well, you won't mind that, will you? I know how much you like him. In fact, I know you're sweet on him."

"*What?* I am not! That's a lie! That's—that's—it's *stupid*!" Beet-faced, Shalindra sputtered.

"Isn't. You're always going on about him. The way his eyes crinkle when he smiles. The way his pretty brown hair curls. The way his blue jacket makes his shoulders look so *wide*—"

"*I didn't!*"

"His white teeth, his radiant smile, his remarkable nose. What was that word you used so often? 'Cute,' I believe it was."

"Shut up, you fungus-face. He'll hear you!"

"No, he's too far away. He's a lot more likely to hear *you,* if you don't lower your voice. Yes, you're sweet on Lunune, all right."

"I'm not! You're a liar! You're a—oh, I see, you're just trying to change the subject again. I see straight through you, Cerrov. And if you think—"

"And the thing is," Cerrov continued musingly, as if he didn't hear her, "it's just not practical. Even if you were five or six years older, not quite the infant you are now—"

"Beetle-brain!"

"—Even if you were a woman, it wouldn't make any difference, since he's got eyes for Olisi alone."

"Olisi?" She goggled up at him. He was deliberately baiting her, of course. He was doing all he could to divert her mind from Rhazaullean affairs, because he regarded her as a child in need of protection. His manipulations were transparent, but it didn't matter, he could have his way for now, for this latest lure was simply irresistible. "Master Lunune and Olisi? Go on! Don't tell me!"

"See for yourself. Just look at the way he's dripping around, mooning over her. Eyes like a mildly costive spaniel. On an invisible leash, poor mutt."

"He's got beautiful, romantic dark eyes!"

"And all for Olisi. But I don't think she's even noticed."

"I don't believe it." Professed skepticism notwithstanding, Shalindra studied her tutor avidly. Cerrov's descriptive terms, "dripping" and "mooning," were unkind exaggerations, and yet—Master Lunune *was* attentive, very attentive indeed. He never strayed a step from Olisi's side. His stance, and the inclination of his head, bespoke deferential solicitude; quite appropriate in a paid attendant, but perhaps here carried to unnecessary extremes. His face was visible to Shalindra only intermittently, and in profile; but those glimpses informed her that the beautiful, romantic spaniel's eyes anchored immovably upon the Princess' visage. And Olisi? Apparently quite unaware. No perceptible sign of embarrassment, gratification, or self-consciousness. Wholly at ease, she ambled along, chattering brightly and nibbling fried ganzel puffs from a paper cone purchased of a vendor.

Maybe Cerrov was right. Shalindra's interest was edged with jealousy. Olisi just didn't seem to know how lucky she was to be eighteen, and all grown up! But then, sometimes it seemed as if the Princess didn't quite realize herself that she was an adult. Former ulorre-consort of Rhazaulle, presently a widow, she still loved playing Hidden Statues, Eebo-deebo, Poppers, and other such childish games. A sad poem or a harsh word could start her tears flowing; a joke or endearment could just as easily dry them. She seemed more a playmate to Shalindra, perhaps a slightly older sister, than a real *adult*.

But evidently, Master Lunune thought otherwise. Interesting. Sort of unfair, but *most interesting*.

The next best thing to having him herself.

"Well, maybe you're right," Shalindra conceded. "If so, he ought to tell her how he feels. Or write her a letter. Or a sonnet—they're good. Or give her flowers. Or—"

"Ridiculous. He can't do that; he wouldn't dare. He's a tutor, a nobody. The King would have his ears."

"Unfair! He's not nobody."

"Mind your grammar. Fair or no, that's the way it is."

"Well, he shouldn't put up with it. *I* wouldn't, and that's flat. After all, Olisi might be putting on an act. Maybe she returns his feelings, but won't let on. Or maybe she *would* return them, if only she knew. How can he find out if he won't ask? He's got to show some—some initiative, that's what."

"Suppose she does like him. What then?" Cerrov inquired, unmistakably pleased with the success of his diversionary tactic.

"Why, then they get married, of course. That's what people do, isn't it? And the King would come around. He'd have to, after that. Of course, they might have trouble finding an Aennorvi magistrate to marry them. They'd have to run away. Elope, in disguise. She could pretend to be a tradesman's daughter, and wear one of those little short jackets with all the braid—"

"This is all very pretty, but you haven't considered—"

"You haven't considered Destiny. You haven't considered Fate." The voice was feminine, high, and tweetling. Its owner walked at their side. How she had managed to approach unnoticed was difficult to fathom, for she was anything but inconspicuous.

Shalindra recognized the acrobatic midget they had passed moments earlier; an odd figure seen at a distance, more startling yet, close at hand. She was not taller than an average child of three or four, but she was no child. The body barely clothed in a brief scrap of purple-sequinned costume was mature, well-proportioned, and hard with muscle. The face was shrewd and sharp-featured beneath its layer of paint. The hair, a frizzy explosion, was dyed an improbable shade of red.

"You have questions. I know where to find the answers," announced the polychrome stranger.

Too intriguing to ignore, of course. Shalindra was instantly hooked. Cerrov, cool would-be sophisticate that he was, actually meant to walk on, but she wasn't about to let him get away with that. She tugged hard on his arm, and her brother reluctantly halted. The midget did likewise.

"What sort of answers?" Shalindra demanded.

"The best sort. The right ones."

"How can you be sure of that, when you don't even know our questions?"

"Every question lights the path from our imperfect world to the ideal plane of absolute truth."

"Ummm. Oh." Shalindra digested. "And who are you?"

"A messenger. A guide, if you will. Ordained to lead you to the font of truth and wisdom." The midget curtsied, turned an expert backflip, curtsied again.

Cerrov's smile was skeptical, but Shalindra laughed and clapped her hands delightedly. Feyenne, she decided, was a *lot* more fun than Rialsq.

"Will you follow me, young sir, and young Rhazaullean maiden? You see, I know a thing or two."

"Yes, you know a Rhazaullean accent when you hear

one," Cerrov remarked, and felt his sister's elbow dig into his ribs.

"Follow you where?" Shalindra could barely contain her giggles.

"Not far. A few paces to the sanctum of my hierophant—"

"The what of your which?"

"The house of my master. There, all questions will be answered, all doubts resolved, all knowledge revealed."

"Oh, that can't be." Shalindra's denial lacked real conviction. She couldn't resist asking, "Who's your master?"

"Wise men revere the name of Queluro the Bloodflamer."

"Queluro *who*?"

"Bloodflamer. That's an Aennorvi term for a certain kind of diviner," Cerrov told his sister. "She means, she's the shill of some fortune-teller. Give her a coin, if you like, and let's go. Master Lununé will be missing us."

"Fortune-teller!" Shalindra's eyes caught fire. Yes, Feyenne was entertaining, all right.

"Swindlers," Cerrov announced. "Crooks. Charlatans, all of them."

"Cerrov, that's *rude*."

"Oh, your poor brother's ignorance cannot offend me, young noble lady." The midget's quick eyes gleamed. "He means well."

"How did you—what makes you think he's my brother?"

"Perhaps my master Queluro has trained my eye to read auras. Perhaps the silent, invisible emanations speak to me." The midget's serene gaze sought far horizons.

"Perhaps you've noticed that her eyes and mine are just the same color," Cerrov suggested.

"Oh, wise young Rhazaullean gentleman, there is often a mundane explanation to still the terrors of those faint hearts unwilling to confront the fantastical truth."

"Faint hearts! Ha, she got you that time." This time,

Shalindra couldn't repress the giggles. Cerrov scowled at her.

"But if you are not afraid," the midget continued, "if you dare to brave the unknown, then follow me to my master's house, and hear the prophecies of Queluro."

"Oh, yes, let's!" Shalindra exclaimed.

"What nonsense."

"I want to. It'd be fun."

"Complete waste of time. A silly fraud. Anyway, we'd better catch up with Lunune and Olisi, or we're in trouble."

"No, they're coming back for us. Look there." Shalindra pointed.

Tutor and princess arrived an instant later. The midget curtsied and turned a cartwheel. Lunune's brow wrinkled, Olisi's eyes rounded.

"We're going to have our fortunes told!" Shalindra proclaimed, and Olisi's confused expression gave way to smiles.

"Our botany lesson!" Cerrov protested.

"Lessons, pooh! Some other time!" Olisi's airy gesture abolished the obstacle. "This is much better. Show us the way," she instructed the midget, and proffered a copper coin.

And the midget, ignoring the money, tweetled back, "Impossible."

"What did you say?"

"Impossible, royal lady. Today, my master—an artist in media intangible—has sent me in search of fresh-hued, pure, transparent auras. That is to say, the auras of children. The noble young Rhazaullean lady is possessed of a perfect aura; her brother's is more or less acceptable. You other two are—alas—too old."

"Well! So my aura's too used—too *soiled*!" Olisi's face puckered.

"Too deeply colored with knowledge and experience to

fulfill great Queluro's needs of the moment," the midget concluded. "Another day, perhaps, royal lady."

Olisi appeared somewhat mollified, but Shalindra's face fell. For this was certainly the end. Master Lunune would never allow his two students to wander off alone. And Cerrov wasn't really interested, and it wasn't working out at all—

But Lunune surprised her. Beautiful, romantic spaniel's eyes fixed devotedly upon the Princess's face, he remarked, "Diligent scholars deserve a reward, now and again." Turning to his charges, he told them, "Go along, you two, and enjoy the show. Join us in the arboretum at Bellenore Gardens for your lesson when you're done. I suppose the bemubit trees will wait for you." He smiled dismissively, and then the dark eyes jumped back to Olisi's face.

For a moment, Shalindra was astonished, and then she understood. Of course. Master Lunune wanted to be alone with Olisi in the park. Walk down the shady paths with her, talk with her, perhaps even try to flirt with her, unobserved for once. No wonder he was so obliging about the fortune-teller. And the Princess never thought to remonstrate, for, characteristically, she failed to view her Rhazaullean friends as mere *children,* requiring adult supervision. Bless her. What good luck! Barely able to contain her triumph, Shalindra pulled at her brother's arm. "Well, what are we waiting for? Let's go!"

Gusting a resigned sigh, Cerrov allowed himself to be dragged off.

The midget's purple-sequinned figure bobbed and danced before them. They followed her along the dusty, crowded thoroughfare for a time, then turned off into an avenue far less populous and prosperous. Another couple of turns, and they found themselves in a narrow tunnel of an alley, where the projecting upper stories of the ancient tenements almost met overhead. The sun was nearly excluded, but the twilight dimness that seemed to offer relief from the noonday heat was in fact ovenlike. The air was motionless, dead, lead-heavy, and sewage-stinking.

Loathsome. Shalindra's enthusiasm was fading fast. Maybe this had been a mistake. Of course, she'd been the one determined to come, and she'd look an absolute fool if she tried to back out now, but even so—

She was on the verge of suggesting retreat when the midget paused at the door of a tumbledown tenement. The stucco facade was filthy and cracked, the paint on the shutters was blistered and peeling. There was no sign or carved emblem, nothing at all to distinguish this particular hovel as the abode of a genuine bloodflamer.

The midget knocked, and the door opened. Within, all was darkness. Turning to her companions, she wiggled a tiny beckoning finger and slipped inside. The gaping door invited.

Brother and sister traded glances.

"Boring," Cerrov said. "I'd just as soon go straight on to Bellenore Gardens."

If only he had really meant it. But Shalindra knew him too well to believe that. Perceiving her uneasiness, he offered her a dignified way out. If she took it, he'd never reproach her, never laugh at her, for that wasn't Cerrov's way. He teased her continually, but never said anything that *really* stung. Nonetheless, they'd both know she'd proved herself a timorous infant, what Rhazaullean children called a "posy-breech," and anything was better than that.

"I want to go in." *Liar.* Too late to take it back. Squaring her shoulders, she advanced. Cerrov shrugged and followed. Together they entered the tenement and found themselves in a cramped, bare foyer. Before them rose a short flight of steps, with a closed, featureless door at the top. To the left, an unpainted wooden stairway sloped down into darkness. The midget was nowhere to be seen, but the light tap of descending footsteps was audible. At once, Shalindra started down the stairs. If she paused to think, she'd lose her nerve, she'd disgrace herself, and also, she'd never see the fortune-teller. Down she went, with Cerrov close behind her, both of them feeling their way along in the dark.

The stairway took a right-angled turn, and then things got easier, for a faint, wavering light struggled up out of the cellar. At the bottom of the stairs, another turn, and they stepped through a low doorway into the subterranean lair of Queluro the Bloodflamer; a murky, incense-reeking, low-ceilinged chamber, all tricked out in billowy wall hangings of cheap purple cloth. The floor was gaudy with fringed rugs and mounds of embroidered cushions. On one such mound reclined the sequin-glittering midget. Beside her, a tripod supported a tray laden with worked-brass vessels and cups, stoppered carafes, and covered bowls. A small lantern with a colored glass globe glowed redly overhead. The only other source of light was a coal fire smoldering in the brazier that stood at the center of the room. Behind the brazier, upon a rug, sat Queluro himself—a skeletal but powerful-looking figure swathed in voluminous black robes. A swarthy, hollow-cheeked, somber visage; lusterless black eyes, lank white hair and beard. He might have been anywhere from fifty years old to one hundred fifty.

He looked exactly as a fortune-teller should—dramatic, exotic, a little sinister. Just right. Shalindra's spirits began to revive. Perhaps this was going to be fun after all.

Queluro raised his head. His eyes probed. Silent seconds passed, and Shalindra began to fidget. Even her brother, possessed of an almost adult composure, could not sustain that depthless stare. To deflect it, he spoke.

"We've come to hear your prophecies." Cerrov successfully masked all outward sign of uneasiness. "What is your price?"

"That is not spoken of." Queluro gestured. "Come."

They advanced.

"Sit."

Both visitors sank to the floor. The cushion beneath Shalindra was soiled and split along one seam. The brazier was tarnished. No matter. The Bloodflamer himself fulfilled all expectations. He was magnificent.

"You are in exile."

The voice was suitably sepulchral. Queluro spoke Aennorvish with a guttural foreign accent. There was something in the rhythm of his words, the exaggerated sibilants, that seemed familiar. Shalindra considered the voice, the dark complexion and features; then she had it. Turo. Obviously. The Turos traveled everywhere in their boat-shaped caravans, infiltrating all lands despite sometimes brutal laws of exclusion, and there were many self-styled seers among them. Some were charlatans; others, undoubtedly gifted.

"We are visitors," Cerrov replied, and their host smiled, closed-lipped, at the careful wording.

"You are in peril," said Queluro.

"Why do you think so?" Cerrov asked.

"I do not speculate. I observe the aura. Its message is clear."

"What exactly do you mean by 'aura'?"

"A common term, describing an occult phenomenon incomprehensible to the uninitiated."

Cerrov appeared unimpressed, but Shalindra was fascinated. "What else do you see?" she asked.

"I see high rank, wealth, promise. A dangerous greatness, a great danger. Flight. Ease and comfort in a foreign land, yet strangeness and a longing for home."

All true. Shalindra turned excited eyes upon her brother, but Cerrov's expression did not alter.

"Nothing that you couldn't have guessed. Or been told," observed the boy.

"Who would tell me such things, young Rhazaullean?"

"You must have your sources." Cerrov shrugged. "Paid informers."

Why was Cerrov *baiting* the man? Shalindra wondered. It seemed so unnecessary and disagreeable.

Queluro, however, was not offended. He smiled a little, and the fleeting expression afforded a brief glimpse of sound teeth disconcertingly edged with black at the gumline. "So young, and already so cynical. How shall I convince you? Shall I speak of the old palace, in the great royal enclosure that once was your home? Shall I speak of your dead father and his legacy? Or shall I speak of your mother, and her fears for you?"

Magic. Astonishing, and a little scary. This, surely, would convince Cerrov. Now, he would have to believe. Shalindra searched her brother's face, and found, for once, that she couldn't read it. His eyes reflected a certain distilled attentiveness; beyond that, he was expressionless, impenetrable. For the moment, she was quite shut out.

Cerrov was silent and motionless, eyes steady upon the fortune-teller's face, so Shalindra spoke up for him; or rather, for herself. "You see all that in our auras? What else do you see?"

"Much." The fathomless black gaze held her. "But all that the aura tells me is of the past or the present. Have you not come seeking intelligence of your future?"

She nodded vigorously. Cerrov made no sign.

"Then we must perform a bloodflaming," Queluro decreed. "For it is within the physical substance of your being that the key to your destiny lies hidden."

Splendid phrases. A bit vague, but gorgeous nevertheless. Just the way a real fortune-teller *ought* to talk. Half doubting, half awed, Shalindra nodded.

"A trifling sacrifice of blood is required. Zyffia will assist."

Queluro snapped his fingers, and the midget flowed to her feet. From the tray beside her she took up two small brass cups. A moment later she was across the room, proffering refreshment to the guests.

"No." Cerrov's tone was barely polite. "Shalli, you don't want that."

He really wasn't entering into the spirit of things at all. Well, let him be that way if he chose. She wasn't going to let him spoil *her* fun.

Shalindra accepted a cup, and examined it curiously. The tarnished little vessel brimmed with thick liquid. In the low reddish light of Queluro's lair, the stuff appeared almost black. "What is it?" she asked.

"A potion to soothe and solace you, to ease the small discomfort of a tiny blood-letting," Zyffia murmured.

"Leave it alone," Cerrov commanded.

Who did he think he was?

Shalindra sniffed. She detected no odor.

"Harmless and consoling. No need to fear, noble young lady." The hint of a smirk hovered about the midget's lips.

The creature was all but calling her a posy-breech. Shalindra scowled and drained the cup at a gulp. Her brother's protesting exclamation came too late to stop her. She caught a sharp vocal note of genuine feeling—anger, alarm, or something of the sort—and deliberately ignored it. He was simply peeved that she wasn't letting him tell her what to do. He'd have to get used to it—she was growing up.

The potion was too sweet, too slow and heavy on her tongue, but its effects were agreeable. No sooner had she swallowed, than a warm luxury suffused her mind. Her muscles slackened. She lolled back on the cushions, and the world went soft.

Something had hold of her right hand. There was a sudden pain that somehow seemed blunted and distant. There was some sort of protesting noise from Cerrov. She looked up, almost dreamily. The sequinned midget had jabbed her middle finger with a bright steel bodkin. Now Zyffia was squeezing the injured digit, methodically milking droplets of blood into the emptied brass cup. Shalindra watched wonderingly. There was very little discomfort; the dripping blood seemed hardly her own.

Satisfied, the midget released the captive hand. Shalindra sucked her punctured finger. The bleeding ceased, almost at once. Now what?

Zyffia presented the brass cup to her master, who set the vessel on the floor before him. A glass vial materialized in Queluro's hand; he seemed to have plucked it from the air. The fortune-teller poured, diluting the blood in the cup with the nameless contents of the vial. The vial vanished as mysteriously as it had appeared. Queluro stirred the cup, bent his white head, and began to intone.

To Shalindra, the invocation seemed endlessly protracted, but perhaps her perceptions were skewed.

Mumble-mumble-mumble. Mutter. Croak. Mumble.

Mice gnawing in the wall, it sounded like, but Shalindra didn't mind. She was comfortable, warmly relaxed, and content. She let her eyes wander around the room. Colors and edges were melting, blurring; the place was really quite beautiful. She could look at it all day. Queluro was welcome to drone on forever.

But he did not. The invocation ended, and Queluro, with a superb flourish, sprinkled the contents of the cup over the coals glowing in the brazier before him. Instantly, a swirling column of smoke and steam ascended, struck the low ceiling, and broke like a wave, seething and billowing in all directions. Those turbulent red-tinged vapors were hypnotic as leaping flames, and like flames, seemed full of teasing, fugitive images.

Pictures of her future?

"See." Queluro's voice was quiet and slow, slow, slow. It seemed immensely distant. "The essence of life holds the secret of destiny. Blood is the book of the future, flame illuminates the text. Behold your fate."

Shalindra gazed up at the sanguinary clouds. And they moved slowly, so very slowly, seemed to pause in midair, somehow suspending themselves in time and space.

"Shadows and darkness about the clouds. Your future is uncertain, balanced finely upon the razor edge of your choices. Eminence, and a kind of tranquillity await you, yet the path to these things bridges an abyss. The bridge is no wider than a handspan. It is veiled in mist and buffeted by gales. A voice calls to you from mists. You are allured, and your vision is clouded. You may be persuaded to step from the bridge."

The words seemed to come so terribly slowly that Shalindra was in danger of losing their sense. And she wanted so much to understand, she was struggling hard to focus her attention upon the Turo-accented voice, but it was very difficult—the blood-clouds floating overhead were so distracting. There were faces in the clouds, faces that hovered upon the verge of recognizability; the suggestion of architecture, of towers and turrets; hint of a boat, swell-sailed in the wind; the jagged intimation of mountains. Faces again, and growing clearer now. Cerrov was up there—yes, it was certainly her brother, but older, all grown up, with mature grim mouth and jaw. And another, a man, still indistinct, deliberately anonymous.

"The voice calls from the mists," Queluro continued tonelessly, as if reading dry text. "It is not your own voice, and yet it is as if you spoke to yourself. Each word sings in your veins. At that moment, the memories of childhood furnish the light to guide you through the mists. It will be—"

Shalindra, drugged mind struggling to sort slow syllables, was utterly unprepared for what happened next. Beside her, Cerrov shifted weight. The next instant, his right leg straightened and thrust hard. The heel of his boot clanged upon the lip of the brazier. The metal pan overturned, and the radiant coals went flying.

Now she'd never hear the rest of that prophecy.

The coals seemed to creep through the air. Shalindra's gaze followed one of the multiple luminous trajectories. The flying ember described an elegant arc, struck a wall, and dropped to the floor, coming to rest upon the trailing edge of a purple wall hanging. The fabric beneath the coal began to blacken. The dark area spread. The flimsy cloth ignited, and a tongue of flame jumped. At least half a dozen similar fires were kindling at irregular intervals along the wall.

Incredible. Cerrov had done it on purpose. Absolutely unbelievable.

A hoarse cry drew Shalindra's attention from the fiery hanging. She turned her head to behold Queluro beating the flames that licked the edge of his hugely voluminous sleeve. The man's expression was frantic, yet his flailing movements seemed so slow, almost leisurely, like ritual gestures in some mad pantomime. Likewise languid—the graceful, rippling undulations of the flames. Remarkable spectacle. Hard to believe that any of it was real.

Queluro flung himself to the floor—seemed to take weeks to get there—and rolled. Orange flames snailed their way up the purple hangings. Smoke curled indolently.

Shalindra sat watching in glazed fascination. She would have remained there indefinitely had not Cerrov hauled her to her feet. She frowned. Why was he pulling on her arm that way? Why was he so rough and rude? Why didn't he just leave her alone, to enjoy the show in comfort?

No such luck, however. He was dragging her toward the exit, and he was terribly determined, there was no resisting him. She'd certainly let him know what she thought of such behavior, but not now. For now, best to concentrate on remaining upright. She was unaccountably dizzy and sluggish. Her vision was blurred, her eyes full of smoke. The fiery chamber was wheeling about her, and she didn't want to walk, she wanted only to sit and rest, but her lunatic big brother wouldn't let her.

Relentless tug on her arm. Limbs heavy, clumsy, as if weighted with lead. Hard to walk, much too hard. She

looked down. Through the haze of smoke she descried a
small, malevolent face, haloed in flame. An imp, a malig-
nant sprite? No, a scarlet-haired midget. Zyffia clung to
her leg like a monstrous tick. Full weight of that dense,
muscular little body impeding progress. Shalindra jerked
and pulled, without success. She slapped clumsily at the
midget's head and shoulders. Useless. Trapped. Frightened
now, she tried to run, and a small, cunningly placed bare
leg tripped her. Shalindra tumbled to the carpeted floor,
wrist sliding from her brother's grasp, and then the
midget was crouched on her chest, solid weight suffocating in that smoke-filled place, furious grinning face but
inches from her own, quick little hands flying, and one of
them armed with a steel bodkin.

Frightened, almost panicky now, and the midget ferociously strong, impossible to dislodge—

Unreal. Nightmare confusion, weight on her chest,
smoke in her lungs, no air—

The toe of Cerrov's boot caught Zyffia square in the
ribs. The midget squawked and loosed her hold. A fierce
shove sent her sprawling. Once again, Shalindra felt her
brother's grasp close on her wrist. No time to think, back
up on her feet, blind progress. There were stairs beneath
her feet, and she was climbing toward the gray light. Confused glimpse of a shadowy little foyer, then through the
door and out into the alley. Close, malodorous air, yet
fresh by comparison to the atmosphere of the fortune-
teller's den. Shalindra coughed and hacked. The world fell
into sharper focus, but remained somehow distant.

Fire? Pursuit? What of Queluro and Zyffia? Shalindra
turned her head, trying to look back, but Cerrov was pulling her along; there could be no lingering.

They were out of the alley, she hardly knew how. Another couple of turns—a couple of minutes, a couple of
hours?—and they were back on the crowded street, where
the midget had first accosted them. The shadows were
longer, now. A few streets away, a black plume of smoke

was visible above the rooftops. Otherwise, nothing had changed. The entire fantastic incident might well have been a dream. Shalindra blinked in the strong sunlight. Vision and mind began to clear, but she remained a little groggy. Perhaps it *had* been a dream, a nightmare reaction to Queluro's potion? But no. Her throat and lungs were scratchy; she'd breathed smoke. The sleeve of her gauzy summer blouse was ripped, and there were scratches on her arm. The midget had wielded a steel bodkin . . .

Bewildered, she looked up at Cerrov. His jaw was set, and his hazel eyes were hard. He looked far older than his thirteen years. At that moment, he seemed very like the grown-up image she had spied in Queluro's blood-clouds. He was steering her firmly along the street, and just then it didn't occur to her to question his authority. She merely asked, "Where're we going?"

"Genevreen."

His Majesty Dasune's Feyennese palace.

"What about—?" It was hard to order and express her thoughts, but Shalindra vaguely recalled an appointment in the Bellenore Gardens. Master Lunune. Botany lesson. That was it.

"Doesn't matter. We'll have a doctor clean those scratches of yours."

"No. Can't."

"Can't?"

"No. They'd ask questions." Mind still dragging, but she managed to point out, "They'd find out. What you did."

"I'm going to tell his Majesty the whole story."

"No! You'll get in trouble—you'll be punished—"

Cerrov halted and turned to face her. Pedestrian traffic neatly split to skirt the new obstacle at the side of the road. "You've no idea what happened, do you?" he asked.

"You went mad and set the place on fire. They mustn't ever know. You're old enough to go to gaol. But don't

worry, if anyone says it was you, I'll lie, I'll swear we were
somewhere else—"

"You don't need to lie, not ever. And I won't be punished. Listen to me. This is important, wake up and listen.
Our meeting with the fortune-teller was no accident. His
assistant sought us out and lured us back to that house. If
all had gone according to plan, we'd probably both be
dead by now."

You're cracked. The words almost slipped out, but one
look into his eyes stilled her tongue. He was quite in
earnest. Suddenly far clearer in mind, she awaited enlightenment.

"We've enemies in Rhazaulle," Cerrov continued dispassionately. "Queluro is a felon, and he's come from a
Rhazaullean House of Correction—either Rialsqui or
Lazimiri. Did you see the black tattoos on his gums?
That's the emblem of the *Moyansq*—a correction-house
brotherhood of the worst criminals. The first entrance requirement of the Moyansq is the murder of a gaol guard or
turnkey; then, the removal of the heart and the—but you
don't want to hear about that. These men have nothing to
lose, you see—they're for the Funnel upon the next assizes,
and they know it—so little remains to them in those last
weeks between capture and trial, but the domination of
their fellow-prisoners, and they rule like Noble Landholders over the peasantry. I've no idea how Queluro avoided
execution, but I knew him for a Moyansq the moment I
saw him smile. In view of our situation, that was all I
needed to know."

In view of our situation. He sounded so—adult. He
sounded so certain, but he couldn't be right; it was too
fantastic. Instinctively, she sought to deny.

"Why should anyone want to harm us?"

"There are things that have been kept from you too
long. You're not a baby, and for your own safety you'd
best know. For example—in Rialsq, Varis has been
crowned Ulor."

Impaired as she still was, it took a moment for the meaning to sink in, and when it did, the implications were appalling. "Cousin Lishna, and the little twins?"

"Dead. Among others."

And no word for weeks from Mama. But that thought, too dreadful to confront, expressed itself as a cold mental ripple; somehow her mind found a way of cutting it off a whisper below the level of consciousness. Aloud, she asked blankly, "Dead how?"

"I don't know. There could be little news from Rialsq until the roads summer-hardened, of course. Lately, there's been some communication, but I haven't learned much. I think some information's being kept from me on purpose."

Something deep in her brain warned her not to wonder why that should be. Fortunately, there were other matters to claim her attention.

"Cerrov—if all three of our cousins are gone, then you're next. You're Ulor." Her tone was wondering, almost awed. "Not Uncle Varis. You."

"Now do you understand, Shalli?"

Never had she imagined that this could happen. Too many heirs between her brother and the Wolf Throne; Cerrov as Ulor had never seemed an actual possibility. But now, amazingly, it was here, very real, and the immediate consequences were horrendous.

"Uncle Varis—sending an assassin for us—?" Her heart was thumping, and the rush of blood through her veins seemed to sweep the lingering cobwebs from her mind. "But it doesn't make sense. If Queluro wanted to kill us, why didn't he just do it, the moment he got us down into that cellar? Why waste time telling my fortune?"

"I don't know." Taking her arm, Cerrov resumed progress. "All I can think is, he didn't plan to kill us then and there. Maybe he meant to drug us, then take us off somewhere else and do it."

"Why? Why go to that trouble?"

"Or maybe he didn't intend to kill us at all. Perhaps someone commissioned him to kidnap us, to lock us up somewhere."

"What would be the point of that? If someone wants us gone, wouldn't it make more sense just to—?" The edge of her hand chopped air suggestively.

"You'd think so. But maybe it was Queluro's own private game. Perhaps he intended to squeeze his client—hold us alive somewhere, and sell us at a huge price."

"As if we were just—things. Horrid." Shalindra considered. "But, even then—why would he keep us alive? After all, we might always have escaped. Wouldn't it have been easier and safer for him to kill us, and then just *say* he had us locked up somewhere?"

"What a mind you've got, behind that girlish face. I can't answer your questions, Shalli. I don't know what he planned. I only know it was a lucky thing for us he was so intent on the bloodflaming—for I think he was a real Turo, believing in his own prophecies. If I hadn't taken him off guard, we'd never have gotten away. He was big enough to have broken me in two."

"D'you think he burned to death?"

"No. He'd be all right."

"Then he might come after us again?"

"Not he, now that we know him. Next time, it'll be someone else."

"Next time?" Shalindra glanced back over her shoulder, half expecting pursuit. The implications sank in. "You mean, it could be—anybody? Anybody at all? We can't trust people anymore? We can't even walk around *outdoors*? Cerrov, what'll we do?"

"Tell King Dasune what's happened, for a start. He's looking out for us; he'll see we're protected."

"Protected how? He'll coop us up in the Genevreen, that's what. We'll be *prisoners*."

"Guests."

"We'll never see the light of day again. We'll turn into human mushrooms."

"That should attract attention."

"He'll set servants to watching us."

"You'll get used to it."

"I don't want to get used to it! How long would we have to go on living like that—never feeling safe?"

"For a long time, I hope. People of our rank should never feel safe, Shalli. It's time you learned that."

"Stop talking down to me. You know what I meant."

"Yes. You meant, how long before there's a change? Only as long as it takes for me to return to Rhazaulle and claim what's rightfully mine."

Shalindra threw him an astonished glance. There was that dauntingly adult look about him again, the grim expression that somehow set a distance between them. And the cool, deliberate way he spoke! So assured, as if he could do whatever he wanted. She didn't know how to treat him when he looked like that; he hardly seemed the brother she knew. Not quite sure what to say, she prompted uneasily, "The Wolf Throne—?"

"Is mine."

"Maybe so, but Uncle Varis—"

"Can be dealt with."

"You know, Uncle Varis might have nothing to do with any of this."

"Mother thought otherwise."

"She could've been wrong."

"That remains to be seen. Why are you taking up for him?"

"I'm not taking up. I'm only trying to be—what d'you call it—*objective*. After all, Uncle was always decent to us."

"How, 'decent'? He didn't know we existed. Except to wish us each happy birthday every year, he scarcely spoke to us."

"But when he did," Shalindra pointed out, "at least he

didn't treat us like babies. You know that icky-sweet, smiley-bouncy, disgusting voice that grown-ups use when they talk to children? Uncle Varis never did that, even when we were really little."

"Oh, that proves his good character. I didn't know he was one of your favorites."

"He wasn't. He was sort of interesting, the way he always looked as if he saw everything, but said almost nothing. Really different—"

"He was that."

"But really—distant. So he wasn't exactly one of my *favorites*. I'm just trying to be fair, and I think you should do the same."

"Oh, I'm ready to be fair, all right," Cerrov assured her. "If he hands over the throne that's mine, and proves he's got nothing to do with anyone's death, then I'm quite prepared to be fair."

"And if he doesn't?"

"Then he's a traitor, a usurper, a murderer, and he'll be punished as such."

"How, Cerrov? How will you punish Uncle Varis, or take the throne from him, or do any of these great things you talk of? Exactly how?"

For the first time since the conversation began, Cerrov's assurance faded, and he looked more his real age. Following a brief pause, he answered, "I'd need troops. Weapons. Ships. Supplies. But," he continued more confidently, as if striving to reclaim elusive maturity, "I think that King Dasune might help."

"You mean, he'd just give you all of that stuff?"

"He might. If he thought I could win, and if he thought it would be good for Aennorve if I did."

"But will he?"

"I have to persuade him. Offer him something—make promises—say anything that'll convince him."

"You're thirteen!"

"I'm Ulor of Rhazaulle."

Shalindra was speechless. Her brother, the big brother she thought she knew so well, was once again spouting incredibilities. Suddenly he seemed very far away, and she was frightened; for without Cerrov, what should she do here in this colorful, alien land of Aennorve? Without Cerrov, she would be alone, a foreigner and a child, isolated here. One instant suddenly clarified the totality of her dependence. She needed him, he was all she had. Her grip upon his arm automatically tightened. Unwilling to cling, she forced herself to let go. Cerrov appeared unaware.

They had reached the Genevreen. Behind a fanciful gate of gilded wrought-iron curlicues rose the Aennorvi royal palace—a lofty, delicate, intricate structure, green-coiffed with rooftop gardens, spiked with slender towers, and crowned with a cat's-cradle of crisscrossing aerial walkways. The sentries at the gate admitted the Rhazaullean children without demur. Cerrov conducted his sister to the apartment of the court physician, Dr. Treluna, at whose door he left her.

Before her brother made good his escape, Shalindra bombarded him with questions. Cerrov dodged most of them, but when she asked him where he was off to, he told her he sought the King.

"Maybe you'd better think some more about what you're going to say—" she attempted.

"I've got to persuade him," Cerrov returned, and was gone.

Nighttime. Skinny new moon, spangled velvet sky. Genevreen windows standing wide open, to admit the sultry breezes.

His Majesty Dasune's private study was decorated in muted tones of lavender and gray—a combination recalling but not duplicating the sacrosanct violet and black of Aennorve's flag. The King himself—comfortably attired in a light summer dressing gown of dove-colored silk—was seated at his desk. In the privacy of his retreat, he had set aside his peruke, and the candlelight glinted upon his balding head. That head was bent over a parchment sheet imposingly stamped, ribboned, and sealed with the wolf emblem of the Rhazaullean Ulor. For perhaps the tenth time, Dasune's eyes scanned the beautifully penned lines. The Ulor's communication was characteristically clear and concise. It contained an invitation to reopen last year's inconclusive discussions concerning the formation of a Rhazaullean-Aennorvi mutual defense alliance. Prompt negotiation of such a treaty, the Ulor pointed out, would doubtless put an immediate halt to foreign encroachments upon the valuable fishing rights in the Sea of Silence, to the equal advantage of each signatory.

Quite true. But it would accomplish rather more than that for Aennorve, as the Rhazaullean ruler was certainly aware. Aennorve's vast debt to the Dhrevate of Immeen had now fallen due, and present payment proved predictably inconvenient. Default of the loan would precipitate an assortment of ruinous penalties, not the least of which involved forfeiture of the Aennorvi colony at Jumo; a condition agreed upon some twenty years earlier, prior to the discovery of the Jumoese diamond deposits, and the excavation of the mines. A mistake; such loss was unthinkable. And all but unavoidable—until now. Alone, the nearly bankrupt state of Aennorve was in no position to resist Immeen's enforcement of the loan's original terms. Allied with militarily vigorous Rhazaulle, however, Aennorve might request and obtain an extension of indefinite duration, at a nominal rate of interest.

The young Ulor's offer, useful and obliging beyond belief, could hardly have come at a better moment. Salvation presented itself upon a silver salver. It remained only to accept the offering, and yet Dasune was not quite easy in mind. His eye fell to the final, gracious paragraph of the letter, wherein a single suggestion stood out like a nettle in a bouquet of roses:

The renewal of Aennorvi-Rhazaullean diplomatic exchanges surely indicates the date of the return to their native soil of the deceased Duke of Otreska's natural son and daughter, currently enjoying your Majesty's protection. Subsequent to the date of our last correspondence, the illegality of Otreska's supposed union with the condemned felon wrongly accorded title of Duchess has been conclusively demonstrated. This so, the woman's haste in banishing her offspring is explained. Investigation suggests, however, that the two children may indeed be illegitimate offshoots of the Haudrensq line. If so, it behooves us as Ulor to protect and preserve our own. With joy, we anticipate the return of our niece and nephew. We intend to accord them all respect and easeful condition commensurate with their exalted connections . . .

So the present Ulor wanted those two children back. Interesting.

King Dasune leaned back in his chair, applied a corner of the parchment to a corner of his lips, and considered.

Ulor Varis.

Impressions. Recollections of Hurna XI's youngest brother.

A long, lean, quiet figure; pale of face, dark of hair and garb. Almost deliberately self-effacing, yet impossible to overlook. Formidably intelligent, cerebral, composed—too composed; odd things going on beneath the still surface, but impossible to say just what. Hidden shoals. In terms of education, breeding, and natural dignity, several cuts above his oafish Rhazaullean brethren; almost, the Ulor could have been taken for an Aennorvi. Dasune had not parleyed with the young Minister of Diplomacy, as Varis had been then. He had not deemed it necessary, and Varis's manner had not invited intimacy. There had been no way of guessing that this reserved, formal, apparently negligible character should end as Ulor of Rhazaulle.

It had happened, however. Against all probability.

But Varis wouldn't last, Dasune reflected. His hold upon the Wolf Throne was shaky, legally questionable, unstrengthened by the love of the populace. If he'd been born Ulor, things might have been different, but as it was—? He'd never rest secure upon the throne, there were too many problems, too many impediments. Two of which resided in the persons of his exiled nephew and niece, the children whose lives he indirectly demanded as a condition of his consent to a highly advantageous Aennorvi-Rhazaullean alliance.

Two royal Rhazaullean brats. That was all. A small price to pay for domestic tranquillity, and yet—

Dasune reflected. The children's current value was high, yet how much higher their potential future price? The longer he kept them, the greater the threat their existence posed to the Ulor of Rhazaulle, and thus, the greater their worth. He did not wish to commit the blunder of selling too early.

Moreover—and here the King deplored his own weak sentimentality—there were certain additional factors, intangible, but impossible to ignore. The Duchess of Otreska he recalled as a rather charming woman. His liaison with her had lightened the tedium of last year's otherwise dreary sojourn in the chilly land of Rhazaulle. The affair had run to its natural conclusion, yet pleasant recollection persisted. He found he could not altogether rid himself of a certain sense of obligation, and therefore he had consented to accept her children, the two juvenile refugees whose lives now proved so unexpectedly significant. She had sent them to him because she had been afraid, and because she had believed—as females generous with their favors were unrealistically wont to believe— that she possessed some sort of hold upon him. She had seen him as her best hope, poor creature. In short, she had trusted him. Her naïveté in no wise indebted him, and yet—

The news of her execution, arriving mere days earlier, had saddened him for the space of an afternoon. He had not as yet decided how best to inform the children of their orphaned state. Of course, should he choose to comply with the Ulor's request, the question more or less lost significance; beyond doubt, the two would promptly follow their mother.

Their late-discovered illegitimacy was probably sheer fabrication. Their existence was more than embarrassing to the present Ulor. Their fate, upon return to Rhazaulle, was quite predictable.

Very unfortunate. No real concern of King Dasune's, yet sad nevertheless. And distasteful. Child murder. Something that, despite his assiduously cultivated pragmatism, he wanted no part of.

His ready compliance would not look well.

Then, there were the children themselves to consider. They'd been hanging about the Feyennese court for months now. He'd seen them at their lessons, at their games, at their meals alongside his own daughter. He'd chatted with them, joked with them, and it was now impossible to regard these luckless little political pawns as altogether faceless. That young girl, Shalindra—so full of life, spirit, and curiosity. So much charm, and as yet not fully aware of it, but give her a few years. And then the boy, Cerrov—an impressive youngster indeed, determined and precocious, as he had demonstrated that very afternoon, when he'd come seeking an audience of the King.

The sentries had stopped him at the entrance to the royal apartment; but, impressed by the lad's demeanor, one of the guards had relayed the request. His Majesty—primarily through curiosity—had consented to a brief meeting.

Young Cerrov had made excellent use of his time, Dasune recalled. He had related a fantastic tale of attempted murder and/or abduction (Sequinned midget? Turo bloodflamer? Very colorful); blamed the attempt

upon his usurping uncle (He was probably right about
that); requested a special bodyguard for his sister (but
none for himself); sought his Majesty's financial and military assistance in recovery of the Wolf Throne, in justifica-
tion whereof he presented a commendably cogent
argument supporting the legitimacy of his claim (unaware, at age thirteen, of this last point's irrelevance); and
finally, in exchange for said assistance, vowed future repay-
ment, together with immediate treaties of alliance between the states of Rhazaulle and Aennorve (An offer
amusingly reminiscent of his uncle's, of which the lad
knew nothing).

Dasune had gravely promised to think about it.

Yes, a remarkably promising boy. A few years hence,
and Cerrov might be causing his Uncle Varis some sleepless nights; if he survived.

If . . .

A real pity to consign the attractive young pair to
death in Rhazaulle. All in all, he would prefer to avoid it.
Dasune's lips turned down at the corners. He realized then
that he had broken one of his own cardinal rules. Without
intending it, he had developed a fondness for the two children. Ridiculous. He was losing his politic detachment,
along with his hair.

And yet—effective use of two such valuable commodities didn't necessarily dictate acceptance of the Ulor
Varis's initial, admittedly tempting proposal. The Ulor
surely had more to offer. A skilled trader—and Dasune
was skilled indeed—might even effect the suggested alliance, without relinquishing control of both children.

Cerrov or Shalindra; equally appealing, equally useful
potential weapons.

Which to sacrifice? One? Both? Neither?

Absently fingering the Ulor's missive, King Dasune
pondered the question.

8

FOLLOWING THE QUELURO incident, things changed, and not for the better. Thereafter, brother and sister were confined to the Genevreen grounds, with servants or tutor hovering always within earshot. No more rambles through Feyenne. No more adventures. Not much privacy, either. Exactly as predicted. And yet, Shalindra reflected, it wasn't all bad. There was still plenty to see and do. There were lessons, books, games. There was a wonderfully labyrinthine palace to explore. The Genevreen sky-walks, with their glass walls and spectacular city views, were a world unto themselves. The rooftop gardens were a perfect picnic site. The frequent companionship of Master Lunune wasn't hard to take, either—even if he did persist in treating her as a child. And it wasn't so bad to feel comparatively *safe*.

Courtiers and servants, for the most part, were friendly. Perhaps they guessed how much she still missed her mother, for many of them went out of their way to be kind, particularly the women. Probably, they were sorry for her. Not that they were so tactless as to express open pity; rather, their sympathy took the highly acceptable form of treats—bonbons, sugar biscuits, petit fours—and a constant trickle of small gifts. So far, Shalindra had amassed a pleasing collection of perfumes, lacy handkerchiefs, silk scarves, wax flowers, stationery, carved combs, rings, seashells, and even a little pot of lip rouge that she dared experiment with only in the privacy of her own bedchamber. Yes, Genevreen confinement had its compensations.

Fortunate indeed that King Dasune was so hospitable. She often had a feeling that she didn't really know or understand the King very well, but it didn't seem to matter much. A monarch so charming, so amusing and cordial, was unmistakably trustworthy. Cerrov didn't share her confidence—even went so far as to label their host a "slippery codger"—but he was probably just trying to demonstrate maturity with a display of stylish cynicism. Cerrov was very concerned with maturity these days. She supposed it was inevitable, all things considered. But still, some of it had to be a pose, and an annoying one, at that. Cerrov, she decided, was putting it on a bit.

Even Cerrov, however, had no complaints about his Majesty's daughter. Princess Olisi, Shalindra and her brother agreed, was lovely; gentle and affectionate, generous and sympathetic, very like a not-much-older sister. Perhaps, to be honest, the princess was not quite the cleverest of girls; but so sweet-natured that cleverness didn't much matter. And it wasn't that she was actually *slow*—Olisi possessed sound intellect enough, only slightly offset by juvenile tastes.

Her passion for children's games, for example.

Shalindra smiled to herself. She and Olisi presently played at Hidden Statues. The boundaries of their game included the third story of the Genevreen, west of the central corridor, and no more. At that very moment, Olisi sat, theoretically petrified, somewhere within the warren of private apartments, shared baths, service cubbies, closets, and cubicles composing the designated area. The goal of the game was to hunt the princess down. Predict-

ably Cerrov had refused to join in; he was now far too
grand for such foolery. Shalindra herself would have hesitated to suggest such an infantile pastime to other
children of her own age. Grown-up Olisi's whims, however, could be indulged without fear of ridicule. And in
truth, childish or no, Hidden Statues was still fun.

Shalindra searched with a will. Closets, cubicles,
baths. No sign of the princess. The private apartments, she
avoided. Their tenants would hardly countenance intrusion; not Olisi's, and most certainly not her own. This so,
what remained?

Shalindra's own room, or else Cerrov's. Of course. The
last place that would occur to her, and the first that should
have. Probably the hunter's private chamber, for the sake
of dramatic effect. Very likely, Olisi was now curled up
under Shalindra's bed, laughing to herself. But not for
long.

Still smiling, Shalindra reversed course and sped back
along the marble corridor. A quick trot carried her to her
own door. Unlocked, for the servants required free access.

In she went. The pretty rose-ivory-gilt room appeared
deserted, but following months of residence, she was an
old hand at this game. She checked beneath the bed first.
Nothing there, not so much as a speck of dust. Good maid
service in this place.

Behind the window curtains of rose-colored brocade?
Nothing. Tufted window seat? No.

Lacquer-gleaming wardrobe? She flung wide the doors,
and there was Olisi, red-faced and cross-legged, spouting
excuses.

"I'm sorry! I never MEANT to do it!"

"Do what?"

"I couldn't help myself! I LOST CONTROL!"

"What happened?"

"I was weak! Can you forgive me?" Olisi proffered a
pasteboard box, lined and padded in blue satin. A few
smears of chocolate sullied the interior. There were also

several sugary blue morsels that looked like remnants of candied flowers. "I only meant to eat one or two! He'd never have noticed! But they were so good, things got out of hand, and I'm so sorry!"

"What are you talking about?" Shalindra was genuinely confused.

"Cerrov's birthday present. I could kill myself."

"Present?"

"Well, that's what these were for, weren't they? I came in here for Hidden Statues, planning to petrify in your clothespress. Brilliant me. I climbed in, and here was this beautiful box of candy, just waiting. For your brother's birthday, I thought. At first I ignored it, or tried to. But I sat here, time passed, and the chocolate smell kept getting stronger and stronger, until finally I couldn't stand it any longer. I took a look, and they were so beautiful, each piece with its own candied flower on top, that I couldn't resist eating just one. You can guess what happened then. I ate another. And another. Oh, I was so greedy! I gobbled up the whole box! But I'll replace them, I promise! Shalli, you're not angry at me?"

"No, just confused. I don't know anything about this stuff."

"Wasn't it for Cerrov?"

"Not from me."

"Sure?"

"Sure."

"Why's it here, then?"

"No idea."

"You're probably just being nice."

"I'm not that nice, not when it comes to candy. Maybe it was meant for me. Maybe Cerrov left it here for me."

"I'M SORRY! I'LL MAKE IT UP TO YOU!"

"Oh, calm down. I don't know where it came from. Maybe it belonged to one of the chambermaids. Don't worry about it." Magnanimity required some effort. Shalindra loved chocolate—it was one of her favorite

things, and Olisi hadn't left her a single piece. Such gluttony! But then, the princess was extraordinarily generous
with her own belongings and money. Only last week,
she'd given Shalindra a beautiful silver brooch that she
claimed she was tired of, together with a bagful of lemon
drops. She was certainly entitled to an occasional chocolate
binge, and more. Shalindra mentally shrugged and dismissed the incident.

That evening, when the Princess Olisi failed to appear
for dinner, there seemed little cause for concern. Olisi,
surfeited on illicit candy, had probably lost herself in a
book. The next day, however, the princess kept to her
room, and early in the afternoon, it was given out that her
royal highness was indisposed.

Indigestion, most likely. Too much chocolate.

But afternoon lengthened into evening. The princess
did not appear, and Shalindra began to worry. At last she
climbed to the third story and rapped on the door of
Olisi's suite. A harried-looking waiting-woman answered.
The princess, it seemed, was receiving no visitors. Frown-
ing, Shalindra departed.

The next day, it was the same. Olisi continued seques-
tered. Three times Shalindra visited—once on her own,
twice in Cerrov's company—only to be turned away at the
door. Dr. Treluna was tending the princess now, and there
could be no doubt that her Highness' illness was serious.
Notes, cards, and small drawings began to fill the silver
bowl left out in the corridor beside Olisi's door. The bowl
was emptied several times daily, but such was the princess' popularity that it always refilled quickly.

No visitors were allowed in, however, and the affair
began to take on the aspect of a mystery.

Reliable information was not available, but rumors
were flying about the court. It was said that the princess—
pregnant by a handsome officer of the guards—had attempted amateur abortion, with dire results.

Few familiar with Olisi's character believed this.

The princess, it was suggested, had contracted a new and highly lethal variety of plague. Her flesh was covered with greenish eruptions, and her body had swollen to monstrous dimensions.

The princess—despondent, suffering unrequited love for a handsome officer of the guards—had attempted suicide.

The princess—having spurned the advances of a handsome officer of the guards—was victim of an attempted homicide. The despised suitor, driven to amorous despair, had fed her poison.

All equally unlikely, but the poison theory set off alarms in Shalindra's head. Could poor Olisi's body have developed some peculiar antipathy to chocolate? That *did* happen to people sometimes, she'd heard. For no apparent reason, they'd wax violently intolerant of certain foods, insect stings, cat hair—anything and everything—reacting to these hitherto harmless substances as if to poison. Usually they just vomited, or sneezed and itched. But sometimes it was worse than that.

The doctor should know of his patient's recent chocolate-flavored excesses. Perhaps the information would assist him. Possible that he already knew, but best to make certain.

Shalindra went to her wardrobe. The blue satin box still lay in there where Olisi had left it. She snatched it up, exited her room, and set off down the corridor at a trot. Moments later, she reached the princess' suite. Discreetly, she tried the door; locked from within, as expected.

She knocked, and a waiting-woman answered the summons. The woman frowned; drew an irate breath. This time, Shalindra didn't pause to argue. Ducking beneath the other's outstretched arm, she scooted on into the princess' little sitting room. Angry exclamation behind her. *You'reintrouble* noises.

A couple of women sat near the window, heads bent

over embroidery hoops. The heads jerked up. Eyes and mouths popped open. Shalindra ignored them. Fortunately, the princess' suite was familiar territory. Across the sitting room she streaked, before anyone could move to stop her. Through an arched doorway and into the bedchamber beyond, where she halted, staring.

The curtains were closed against the sunlight; the chamber was dim and quiet. A heavy sickroom stench soured the air. Dr. Treluna, white-haired and fatigued, sat beside a canopied bed. In the bed reposed the motionless and apparently unconscious Princess Olisi, sheet drawn up to her chin. The low light could not disguise the changes in her face—the grayish pallor, the charcoal smudges beneath closed eyes. Nor could it begin to disguise a far more startling alteration—the loss of hair. Olisi's straight, fine brown locks must have fallen out in clumps. Only a few thin strands yet clung to a shockingly white scalp. Shalindra felt the color draining from her own face. She'd no firsthand experience of real illness, and she hadn't expected anything so ugly. For the first time, it occurred to her that Olisi might be dying. The gooseflesh prickled along her forearms.

"Doctor—" she heard herself begin.

The waiting-women caught up with her. A hand clamped down on her shoulder; shook her hard.

"Let go!" Shalindra wriggled uselessly.

"Little, beggarly, Rhazaullean savage!" Furious female voice. "Who do you think you are?"

"Let *go*!" Shalindra aimed a futile kick.

"Stop that! You unmannerly little—"

"Enough." Dr. Treluna waved a tired hand. "Let her alone. Please go."

"But this barbarian dwarf—"

"Please."

Glaring, the women withdrew. The doctor turned to the visitor. "What is it, child?" he inquired.

Suddenly, she felt a perfect fool; a clumsy, blundering,

intrusive fool. She should never have forced her way in here, caused such a stir. *Rhazaullean savage.* Why was she always doing such silly, impulsive things? Mistake, idiotic mistake; but she had to go through with it now.

She took a deep breath. "Doctor, I—"

"Who's there?" Tiny whisper from the bed. The voices and commotion had roused the princess from her slumber.

"Olisi, I'm sorry, I didn't mean to disturb you."

"Who is it?"

"It's Shalli. I—"

"Where?"

She was standing directly in the princess' line of sight. Olisi's eyes were wide open, and aimed straight at her. Shalindra's mind froze over for a moment. She glanced questioningly at the doctor. Treluna lifted a hand to his own eyes; shook his head.

She couldn't see, he meant to tell her. She was blind.

Shalindra wanted to turn and run away. She found herself scared, clammy-fleshed, and ashamed of her own revulsion. It was not the way she was supposed to feel. She must be, she realized, a mean and shabby character. But this was infinitely worse than anything she had ever expected to find here.

"Shalli? Where?" Olisi stretched forth a hand.

She was expected to grasp it. She didn't want to touch the sick girl, didn't want to be in the room at all. But the doctor was watching her, willing her, while Olisi—Olisi was *groping,* so hopefully and helplessly—

Shalindra took the other's hand in both her own. It was ice cold and strangely limp. She squeezed gently, but felt no answering pressure.

"Shalli? You here?"

"Right here. I've got your hand."

"Can't feel it. Sorry."

Shalindra had no idea what to say.

"Cerrov?" Olisi asked.

Voice so faint, so nearly extinct that she had to bend

near to hear it. The princess didn't smell right. Not an
unwashed stink, no foulness of breath, nothing so obvious;
only an indefinable, deeply frightening wrongness.

She isn't going to get better.

"Later. He'll come later. He really wants to see you,"
Shalindra heard herself babbling.

Olisi smiled faintly.

She was supposed to think of more to say. "Everybody
misses you." She tried hard to make her voice smile. It
came out sounding not too bad. "Everyone's been asking
after you. When you're feeling better, you're going to have
more visitors than you know what to do with. Of course,
they won't let anyone see you yet. I only got in by *pushing*
past your women—" She broke off, aware that she was
prattling like an idiot.

"Naughty."

"But everyone else'll be here soon." Cheery, lying
voice.

"Oh—good . . ."

"Olisi, please get well soon." She couldn't smile any
longer; her face would crack. "Please, please try. You will,
won't you? Olisi?"

No answer. The princess had relapsed into sleep or
swoon. Shalindra carefully released the chill hand; turned
frightened eyes upon the doctor. "Can't you *do* anything?"

"I've done what I can," Treluna told her. "I've kept
her cool and dry, burnt aromatics, fed her liquid sootheries
to still the spasms—"

Spasms? Shalindra looked away.

"Permitted your visit, in hope of raising her spirits.
No leeches—I didn't see their value in this case—"

"But what's the matter with her?"

"Inner upheavals, an excess of melancholy humors—
perhaps occasioned by her widowhood—a derangement of
glandular balance—hemal confusion—possible clandestine
incursion of the Invisible Poacher."

"Could she have got it from eating too much choco-late?"

"My dear child—"

"I mean *way* too much. Look, Doctor—" Shalindra extended the candy box. "This thing was full of choco-lates, and she ate all of them at one go. That'd be enough to make anyone sick. But what if she'd got one of those—what d'you call it—one of those special troubles? I've heard it can happen all of a sudden. That could make her *really* sick, couldn't it? But then, if that were it, maybe there's something you could do—"

"Possibly." The doctor's tone was patient. He accepted the box; politely glanced into it.

He took her for an idiotic child. Maybe he was right. Maybe not, however.

Dr. Treluna seemed suddenly interested. He was peer-ing closely into the box, prodding the scanty contents with the tip of one finger. Selecting a single blue petal, he crushed the sugared morsel, sniffed the released fragrance, and tasted cautiously. At last he turned back to Shalindra, and there was nothing remotely patronizing in his manner as he inquired, "These candied flowers—have you any idea how many of them there were?"

"No, but she said there was one on every chocolate piece. Why? What are they?"

"I'll need to check my book to be certain."

"All right, what do you *think* they are? Did they make Olisi sick?" He looked at her, and suddenly Shalindra wondered how she could have been so dense. "Are they poison?"

Why had it taken her so long to think of that? She ought to have been quicker. *People of our rank should never feel safe, Shalli.* Cerrov's words rang in her mind. He'd been right, so right. From now on, she'd remember.

"Time for you to leave, child."

"That's not fair! I brought you that box. You wouldn't have it if it weren't for me, so I've a right to know. Tell me if it's poison." *He needn't. You already know. What's more* —the thought struck like an ax—*that candy was left in your room, and it was meant for you.*

"Little girl, you did the right thing in coming here, and I thank you for it. But I've no time to answer your questions now, there's work to be done, and you are in the way. Now, bid your friend good-bye—"

Good-bye?

"And let me do my job," the doctor concluded.

He was right, of course, and she stifled her urge to argue. She went to the bedside, stooped, and planted a light kiss upon Olisi's forehead. It wasn't as difficult as she'd expected. The princess didn't stir. Shalindra straightened, turned, and walked out, past the glaring women. She didn't look back, but Olisi's pitifully altered image was fixed in her mind.

If she dies, it's because of you. She didn't want to think about it.

Impossible not to think about it.

King Dasune received the news of his daughter's death with genuine regret. He had planned on offering the princess in marriage to the eldest son of the Talgh of Strell, and such a match would at the very least have guaranteed an abatement of the crushing tolls currently imposed upon Aennorvi vessels navigating the Strellian-held Nizi Channels. Now that chance was gone. Unfortunate. His Majesty was disappointed; beyond that, he was mildly surprised. Insofar as he had taken note, he'd thought Olisi healthy enough. Her sudden demise was unexpected, and most earnestly did he pray that the incident did not herald an outbreak of lethal intestinal gripes, necessitating temporary relocation of the entire court.

Interment was prompt, obligatory obsequies well-orchestrated, grieving expressions extravagant even by royal standards. It would seem that the sweet, harmless, and short-lived Olisi had actually been quite well-liked.

Nevertheless, the matter of the princess' death might promptly have fled his Majesty's thoughts, but for the revelations of the physician Treluna.

The doctor's observations were uninvited and unwelcome, but impossible to overlook. It seemed that the little Rhazaullean refugee Shalindra had presented Treluna with a candy box whose contents the princess had unwisely devoured just prior to the onset of illness. A few scraps of candied floral decoration remained in the box, enough to identify as blossoms of the jhanivianus plant. In and of itself, jhanivianus was harmless, serving as a potent laxative and nothing more. For some as yet unexplained reason, however, when combined with the juice of native thonz berries and the essence of bitter blifilnuts, the blue blossoms turned deadly; producing all the symptoms observed in the recently deceased princess. Dr. Treluna could not vouch for the presence of berry juice, but the odor of blifilnuts clinging to the satin box was unmistakable.

This intelligence struck his Majesty as abstruse, and the implied possibility, decidedly farfetched. Who, beyond a qualified physician, would possess such knowledge? An accomplished professional assassin, perhaps; of which there were none at court. An apothecary. Perhaps a Turo. An herbalist, a botanist.

A botanist?

Unlikely, and yet—Dasune at once summoned Master Lunune to his presence, only to learn that the tutor had departed the Genevreen within two hours of the princess Olisi's first complaints. Subsequent investigation revealed that Lunune had traveled by stage from Feyenne to the port city of Theunn, and thence embarked for Rhazaulle.

A clean escape.

Inconclusive, but highly suggestive.

Once again, King Dasune sat at the desk in his lamp-lit study. Before him lay the latest of the young Ulor Varis's communications; this one dangling the lure of a

Rhazaullean-Aennorvi trade agreement. The tenor of the
Rhazaullean ruler's correspondence waxed increasingly urgent, Dasune noted. The children's price was rising. If
pushed to the limit, what might not the Ulor be moved to
offer? Temporization thus seemed the obvious canny
choice. On the other hand, the entire game might be lost
at a single stroke, should a random assassination attempt
like the last succeed in eliminating either or both of the
prizes.

Even within the confines of the Genevreen, the brother
and sister were dangerously vulnerable. Perhaps best to
sell them at once, before the opportunity vanished, and
before their disruptive presence wreaked courtly havoc.

However—and here his Majesty's brows contracted—
there existed certain considerations beyond the politically
expedient. The children themselves, for example. He
found both of them distinctly likeable. Then, of course,
there was the matter of his daughter.

He had not cherished any particular affection for Olisi.
Marriageability had been the most significant of her attri-
butes. Still, she was his, and the Rhazaullean Ulor had
swatted her like an insect—not intentionally, of course;
the poor girl had simply been unlucky—but the accident
smacked of disregard, even disrespect. Dasune could swallow an insult with a smile, as necessity dictated, but he
never failed to store such incidents away in the archives of
his mind. Time passed, circumstances altered, and sooner
or later, the opportunity to avenge himself would inevitably arise.

This time, however, there was no need to wait. He had
decided upon the proper means of dealing with young
Ulor Varis. The two children were about to vanish. Suddenly. Completely. Mysteriously. His Majesty Dasune,
quite bewildered, would disclaim all knowledge of their
whereabouts.

Ulor Varis, of course, would not believe him.

Ulor Varis was going to stew.

He should have thought twice before crossing the
King of Aennorve.

There were commands to issue, authorizations to sign
and seal. Drawing a sheet of parchment to him, Dasune
dipped his quill in ink and began to write.

It reminded Shalindra of the night she'd fled the
Zalkhash; familiar hand shaking her awake at an odd hour,
familiar face inches from her own. This time, however, it
wasn't night, but dawn; and this time, the hand and face
belonged not to her mother, but to Cerrov. Her brother,
fully dressed, knelt beside her bed. The moment she
opened her eyes, he applied a cautionary finger to his lips.
Very well, she'd be quiet; but not silent.

"What?" she asked. Wide awake, composed, even
businesslike. She was no longer quite the same child she'd
been prior to Olisi's death.

"We've only a moment or two. I gave 'em the slip, but
it won't take them long to catch up."

"Who? Gave who the slip?"

"Retainers—guards—whatever. They wouldn't let me
talk to anyone, but I couldn't leave without saying good-
bye."

He was badly upset. He was trying hard to appear
calm, but he couldn't hide his agitation from her. Cerrov
was rarely upset. She felt the fear stirring to life inside her.

"Good-bye?" she asked.

"They're sending us away. Now."

"You mean, right *now*?"

He nodded.

"Well—well—" she tried to find the right words to
reassure him, to reassure herself. "Maybe that's not such a
bad idea. We'll be safer. Where are we going?"

"I don't know. You don't understand. We're to be separated."

"You mean, travel separately? Meet up someplace
later?" She didn't really need to ask. His face, his posture,

his tension told her more than she wanted to know. The sick fluttering at the pit of her stomach told her.

"No. Really separated."

"No." She didn't even realize that she'd caught hold of his arm. "They can't do that. Why should they want to? What for?"

"They won't talk. I suppose the King thinks it'll be easier to hide us that way."

"Well, he's wrong! And he can't do that." The fear was alive and active now. She heard her own voice, shrill and squeaky and maddeningly ineffectual. "We're family. They can't divide a family!"

"I'm afraid they can do anything they want."

"Not to me, they can't! Not to *us*. I won't let them, that's all. Look, we'll tell 'em we won't be parted. We'll just dig in our heels, that's all."

"Shalli, this won't do any good and you know it—"

"I *don't* know it!" Her grip on his arm tightened.

"We've very little time; let's not waste it. Here, I want you to have this." Cerrov gently freed his arm, then fished in his pocket to bring forth something small and glittering. Faceted brilliants shot hard sparks. A single midnight diamond seemed to radiate black light. "See, it's Mother's locket, the one she liked so much. Look here." He touched the clasp, and the locket opened. Each half contained a miniature painted on ivory; tiny portraits of Shalindra and her brother, done the previous year.

Shalindra studied the images. She'd grown taller over the course of the year, but otherwise changed little—on the outside. Cerrov, on the other hand—he wasn't just taller, his entire face had lately taken on a new look; squarer of jaw, stronger, altogether older. Already the portrait was obsolete, a remembrance of something lost.

"I'm going to keep your picture with me." Cerrov pried his sister's miniature out of its setting and slid the ivory tablet into his pocket. "The rest belongs to you. It'll remind you—" He looked embarrassed. "Here."

I don't need a reminder! Silently, almost with reluctance, she took the locket. A beautiful thing. Very valuable, very adult. The great black diamond was almost mesmerizing. Under other circumstances, she'd have been thrilled. Just now, she could hardly bring herself to look at it.

"Better keep it out of sight."

Obediently she slipped the chain about her neck and fastened the clasp, allowing the pendant to slip down inside her nightgown. The gold warmed quickly against her skin.

Footsteps in the hall. Low voices. The door opened, and into her bedroom came four men; nondescript figures, plainly attired. Strangers all. Unrevealing faces. Servants —guards—hired thugs? Impossible to tell. Shalindra felt the panic rising to choke her. For a moment, her throat seemed to close. Instinctively, she turned to her brother, and saw that *he* was wonderful—calm and dignified far beyond his years. He was rightful Ulor of Rhazaulle, after all—and she was his sister. She'd act the part. She sat up straight in bed; took a deep breath. Staring straight into the face of the leading intruder, she somehow managed to demand, "How dare you set foot in my room?"

The men paused, half startled, half amused.

"Leave," Shalindra commanded. They didn't move, and she added evenly, with a creditable air of detachment, "The King will hear of this."

The four traded glances, and one of them—a stocky character with a very flat face—replied, "The King already knows."

As expected. She began to wilt inside. She hoped her despair didn't show.

Flat-face looked at Cerrov and remarked, not unkindly, "Time to go, lad."

"Go where?" Shalindra demanded. No answer, and she turned to her brother. "Tell 'em to go hang themselves."

He didn't, though. He rose, faced his captors, and inquired courteously, "How shall I send word to my sister?"

They shuffled. They actually looked uncomfortable.

"That's as pleases the King," Flat-face finally told him.

Not good enough! Shalindra wanted to shout, but she said nothing, for Cerrov wasn't arguing. He knew it was useless; he wasn't even wasting his breath. He was going, she was about to lose him, it was happening *now,* and it couldn't be happening. Almost, she clutched at him, but restrained herself. Clutching wouldn't do any good. And she mustn't make him ashamed of her.

He walked to the door, turned, and told her, "I'll find a way of getting a letter to you."

"Cerrov, don't let them do this. *Fight* them."

"There's my fire-breathing little sister." He manufactured a smile. "Try not to worry; this won't be forever. Be a good girl, and do what they tell you. I'll write, as soon as I can. Take care, Shalli."

"Take care." She had trouble getting the words out, but they were less intolerable than the more genuinely appropriate "good-bye." There seemed to have been so many good-byes in recent months, too many, coming too swiftly upon one another. This latest was perhaps the worst of them all, and she wasn't sure she could stand it.

Cerrov exited between a couple of guards. The door closed behind him. Heedless of her appearance in a thin muslin nightgown, Shalindra sprang from the bed. She had some dim notion of chasing after him, but that was impossible—a pair of the guards remained to block her way. She took a few steps forward, then stopped, glaring at them.

The men exchanged embarrassed glances, and one of them said, "Nothing to fear, lass. We mean you no harm."

"I'm not afraid." She was pleased to find that this was true. Somehow, fear and grief transmuted to anger; stimulating and far less painful.

"That's right, that's good. Now, you go along and get dressed, or whatever you got to do. Then we'll go."

"Where?"

"Can't say."

She opened her mouth and shut it again. No use questioning these dutiful automata, no use even trying; she'd get nothing out of them. More to the point to take her complaints elsewhere; to King Dasune, for example. If only she could get to him, she could persuade him to revise his orders. He'd been Mama's friend, after all. And then, his Majesty was so unfailingly affable, so pleasant and smiling and delightful. Surely, Shalindra reasoned, such amiability proceeded from the warmest of hearts. Yes, the King would certainly help her—if only she could get to him . . .

Dawn. His Majesty would be in his own apartment, probably still asleep. Under the circumstances, he'd forgive her intrusion; she knew he would. If only she could elude her guards for just a few moments. Cerrov had managed it—she could do the same.

Shalindra went to the wardrobe. Quick flash of recollection; Olisi, sitting in there cross-legged, blue satin box in her hand . . . Gone. Wardrobe empty again. Grabbing a few comfortable garments, she hurried to her dressing room, closing the door behind her. Alone, and unobserved for at least a couple of minutes. Much good it would do her, though. The dressing room was windowless, three of its four walls lined with mirrors. The sole source of natural illumination was the skylight, some twelve feet above the floor. She'd never reach it—no good . . .

Resentfully, she pulled her clothes on; light and bright in the Aennorvi style, but simple juvenile garments still, appropriate to her slight, flat, child's body. Finger-combing her hair, she plaited the dark mass into a single long braid, inspected herself briefly in the mirror, and noted the gleam of gold at her throat. A section of fine gold chain was visible above her collar. Carefully, she tucked it away out of sight, then emerged into the bedroom to discover one of the guards stuffing the contents of her wardrobe into a large valise. While he was thus occupied, she went to the washstand, splashed a little water onto her flushed face, and thought about escape. No chance of that as yet, however. The second guard had planted himself squarely before the door.

The valise closed with a snap. The guard straightened. "Let's go," he said.

There were plenty of trinkets in the room that she didn't want to part with; most notably, those she'd carried with her from Rhazaulle. But she'd no intention of begging for time to collect them, and in any case, there was no real need; once she'd caught his Majesty's ear, such issues could be dealt with at leisure.

Out the door and down the hall. A guard on either side of her, a light but firm hand on her shoulder, no chance to run. Perhaps when they reached the stairs? She'd be ready.

Click-click of heels on marble flooring, and, to her surprise, they bypassed the broad red-carpeted central stairway and made for the little servants' flight at the end of the corridor. Very inconspicuous. The servants' stairway, she recalled, descended to the lower levels of the Genevreen, where a maze of passageways and storage chambers offered concealment and a variety of potential escape routes.

She marched along smartly. Anyone might have thought her compliance voluntary. When they reached the door at the end of the hall, and she stepped through first, the action seemed quite natural. The next instant, she gave the nearest man a violent shove, turned and leaped for the stairs—

Only to find herself brought up short, head yanked backward by the force of a guard's firm grip upon the flying black braid of her hair. She sat down hard, and the breath oofed out of her. Her tailbone hurt; her pride hurt worse.

Her captor relaxed his hold, permitting her to rise. "Now, now," he admonished mildly.

She wouldn't look at him. Color heated her face. He was sharper and quicker than she'd expected. Perhaps Cerrov's momentary escape had alerted the guards; they weren't about to let *her* fool them. Still, she meant to do it. Somewhere along the way, their vigilance was bound to relax.

But it did not. Down the stairs, through the narrow passageways, up a couple of wooden steps, and the smallest break in the rhythm of her stride produced a simultaneous tightening of the guard's grip upon her shoulder. Not that his large hand hurt her in the least; it was simply, indubitably, *there.*

Through a doorway, out onto one of the little graveled drives permitting tradesmen and deliverymen access to the back entrances of the Genevreen. But the roomy, substantial carriage waiting there belonged to no tradesman. Carriages were to Aennorvis as sledges were to Rhazaulleans; necessary conveyances, but often expressions of opulent personal fantasy. This one, however, while costly, was clearly utilitarian.

Crunch of footsteps on gravel. They were hurrying her toward the waiting vehicle, and once they got her into it, that would be the end. She had to get away from them now, if ever.

The same thought evidently struck her guards, for when she turned on the nearest—intending to kick his kneecap, intending to wrench herself free and make a run for it—he was fully prepared. Before she could launch a single kick, he scooped her up in his arms like a baby or a lapdog, bore her forward a few paces, deposited her upon the seat in the carriage, and climbed in to sit beside her. Shalindra squirmed, twisted, and wiggled, to no avail. With one hand, he pressed her firmly back against the leather upholstery.

"Behave," he advised.

Having placed her valise atop the carriage roof, the second guard descended to climb in on the opposite side. She now sat trapped between the two of them. The door closed. The driver plied his whip, the horses snorted and strained, the carriage moved. Shalindra slumped in her seat. The tears of defeat burned her eyes. She did not think to look up to one of the dark third-story windows, where King Dasune stood observing the entire scene.

Thereafter, the days blurred; each one long, tiresome, uncomfortable, and indistinguishable from its predecessors. Each one filled with heat and dust, cramped limbs and achey muscles, flies and unutterable boredom. There was an initially exotic changing panorama of summer-seared Aennorvi scenery, but scenery swiftly palled. There was a carriage devoid of books, games, puzzles, diversion of any kind; and all but devoid of conversation. There were, however, creaks, rattles, groans, and metallic screeches from the vehicle itself. There was teeth-rattling, spine-jolting progress over rutted roads—progress that Shalindra could not help but compare to the rushing glide of a Rhazaullean sledge along a frozen river; a sensation akin to flying . . .

The nights were spent in a succession of inns, all of them comfortable and respectable. Unlike Rhazaulle, Aennorve abounded in such conveniences. In this land, there were no warmstops, yet it was possible to travel almost anywhere and never spend a night out of doors (assuming solvency).

Solvency. Money. Shalindra thought about it for the first time in her life. At every stop, some sort of payment was required, and somehow or other, her guards always provided. Again and again, she watched silver coins changing hands. King Dasune's money? It certainly wasn't her own. *Little, beggarly, Rhazaullean savage!* The snarls of Olisi's waiting-woman rasped in her memory. She'd hardly heard the taunts at the time, but she considered them now. Beggarly. She was the daughter of a duke, the

niece of an Ulor; as of now, the sister of an Ulor. She was
Haudrensq, a member of the royal family, one of the natural rulers of the world. Ease, plenty, pleasure, security,
deference—all these were her natural due. Or so she had
thought, so she'd been taught. Even her own father, criti-
cal though he'd been, had acknowledged as much. Vulgar
financial concerns could hardly apply to *her*.

   Little, beggarly, Rhazaullean savage!

   Beggarly or not, she always got a room to herself.
Every evening, she ate well at some inn, then retired to a
spotless bed in a private chamber, where she rested undisturbed until morning. She wasn't locked in, and the exit
was never guarded, but she made no attempt to escape, for
that seemed hopeless, now. She was a child, penniless, lost
—if she ran away, where would she go? Back to the
Genevreen? Where was it? How would she get there? And
what would be the use, if Cerrov was no longer there?
They didn't need to watch her, and they knew it.

   Her guards had somehow become guardians. They
worked in relays, like the horses. There were always two of
them, looming up on either side of her, shepherding her
along the way for a day or two, from one inn to another; at
which point, another pair would take over. All of them
were solid, stolid, competent characters. All were uncom-
municative, but courteous enough. One of them, equipped
with an Obranese deck of cards, relieved the tedium by
teaching her the game of Antislez, which kept her entertained for hours. Another scarcely spoke to her at all. Most
fell somewhere in between those two extremes. Their faces
blurred and melded, their voices were all but indistinguishable. None of them consented to answer questions
concerning her ultimate destination. None of them ever
volunteered his name or asked hers.

   They were traveling south. The roads grew dustier, the
hills yellower as they went. By morning of the seventh
day, however, the land began to green itself, luxuriance of
vegetation suggesting irrigation. Shalindra's schoolroom

recollections furnished explanation. Chief river of southern Aennorve was the Meste, flowing north from Lake Eev, a body of fresh water so vast as to suggest an inland sea. The old city of Foneev occupied an ever-lengthening arc of lakeshore. This, presumably, was their destination.

The next evening, they reached Foneev. They spent the night at an inn on the outskirts of town, and early the next morning, clattered through the already teeming streets, down to the great waterfront, where the guards, whose pockets seemed bottomless, chartered a boat. Shalindra watched curiously. She could only assume that they meant to carry her to one of the countless towns and villages dotting the vast circumference of the lake.

They boarded and embarked. The shoreline receded and presently faded from view. Shalindra stood watching the sky, the birds, the rushing water beneath the bow. She was proud to discover herself a natural sailor, not seasick in the least. When the sun reached its zenith, and one of the crewmen produced a coarse lunch of black bread, sausage, and pickled vegetables, she ate heartily. The hours passed. The voyage continued. She had never dreamed that a lake could be so huge. Eev's gray-green expanse, she discovered, was studded with islands—some sizable and populated, some apparently uninhabited; some cultivated, others forested; some bare of vegetation. Amending her original theory, she now supposed one of the populated islands to be their destination.

The boat sped on. Her curiosity grew. When the sun was sinking below the horizon, the long-repressed question could no longer be contained. "Where are we going?" she inquired, not really expecting reply. To her surprise, one of the crewmen answered.

"There." He pointed.

Straight ahead, not more than a couple of hundred yards distant, rose a great dark outcropping of granite, supporting a stone edifice grim and massive as a fortress.

She went cold at the sight of it. "What's that?"

"It's Fruce, girl."

"Prison? You're taking me to prison?"

"That's Fruce."

"What d'you mean?"

The sailor shrugged.

He didn't have the heart to tell her. But she didn't need confirmation—that vast heap of granite couldn't possibly be anything but a prison. The King had betrayed her, she realized, and now they were going to lock her away from the sun and sky, when she had done nothing, nothing at all to deserve it—

Her stomach churned, there was a sour taste in her mouth, and she heard herself speak, with a ludicrous air of command, "Turn this boat around at once, and take me back to shore. I order you to turn it!"

The sailor gave her a bored look and walked away.

Trapped. No rescue. No Cerrov to save her. Iron bars, locked doors.

No!

For a moment, she considered jumping overboard. The impulse was powerful. She'd learned to swim since she'd come to Aennorve; no telling how far she might get. She clutched the deck railing with both hands and stared down at the water.

Ridiculous. Nowhere to go.

Trapped.

Her eyes rose again to the fortress. The boat bore her inexorably toward it.

9

SHE'D BEEN WRONG, of course. It wasn't actually a prison. In name, anyway.

Dawn. Faint gray light seeping in through the window of her cubicle, and Shalindra woke. At the Genevreen, whose atmosphere was permissive, she'd loved to sit up late at night, then sleep far into the morning; but recently her habits had changed. Understandably so. Not much use sitting up with no light to see by. And not much light, and not for long, when *one* skinny candle had to last the entire week. For that was the niggardly rule, one candle a week, and the resident prematurely consuming his or her waxen allowance was consigned to darkness at sundown. Then, of course, there was the matter of food. Simple, nutritious, boring communal breakfast was served at sunrise. Thereafter, nourishment was virtually unobtainable until midday. Nobody forced her to retire or to rise early. Nobody forced her to do much of anything. But three months of residence had taught her the power of the Fruce Library's various unwritten rules. The consequences of noncompliance included no actual punishment; just minor discomfort, inconvenience, or embarrassment. Very effective.

Shalindra sat up in bed, scowling. Unobtrusive coercion. It was one of the aspects of Fruce that she disliked most. But then, there weren't many aspects of Fruce that she didn't dislike. Starting with her room—closet, really —which was tiny, colorless, and austere; equipped only with a cot, washstand, and a small chest of drawers. No rug to cover the floor, no curtains at the single window; no cushions, hangings, pictures, ornaments, or knickknacks. When she recalled her rose-ivory-gilt jewel-casket of a room in the Genevreen—or even the luxury of her starkly black-and-white Zalkhash quarters—dissatisfaction sharpened to a knife edge.

Well, she didn't have to spend much time in her own room; wasn't expected to, in fact. Fruce was huge, and there were countless chambers to explore. All of them lined floor to ceiling with books; innumerable books, a universe of them. Books on every conceivable topic, on every *inconceivable* topic. Books of all nations, all languages, all epochs, hoarded like dragon's gold over the course of the centuries, gathered together under one roof to form a collection vast and swollen beyond compare— the greatest collection that ever was. And she, who'd always loved to read and learn, found herself imprisoned in this place like a mouse immured in a giant wheel of cheese; already surfeited to the point of nausea upon the erstwhile delicacy.

She was supposed to study, to expand her mind and improve herself. She was supposed to be grateful for the opportunity. The other students in this place—some two dozen of them, all years older than she—were certainly grateful. They were always maundering on about the great privilege they enjoyed in living and working at Fruce; that is, when they weren't maundering on about their research, their scholarly minutiae, their interminable theses, bibliographies, and footnotes. Perhaps that was because their attendance was voluntary; indeed, they'd competed fiercely for the few available places. While Shalindra, on the other hand, considered herself a prisoner—a prisoner of *state,* she privately consoled herself—and was rapidly coming to loathe the sight of a printed page. Whatever accounted for the difference, she had nothing in common with them, and thus far had failed to forge a single real friendship.

Nothing in common with the other students, who cared nothing for the world beyond the grim granite walls of Fruce. And certainly nothing in common with the staff —the assistant librarians, under librarians, visiting librarians, trainees, apprentices, visiting scholars, and the like. They were all book-crazed as the students. Amiable enough, some of them, in an otherworldly sort of way; but distant, incomprehensibly erudite, and old, so terribly *old.* No companion of her own age to be found among the Frucians, as staff and students termed themselves. Certainly no one to talk to, as she'd used to talk to her brother.

Cerrov. Automatically, her fingers sought the hard curve of the locket that she wore always hidden beneath clothing or nightgown. After a moment, she drew the ornament forth, snapped it open, and studied her brother's painted image. This was an action she performed at least a dozen times a day, for he was always in her thoughts, and the sight of his likeness seemed to bring him somehow nearer. Sometimes she addressed the portrait, most often silently; but when no one was near, she spoke aloud.

"Miss you," she told him for at least the thousandth time. "A lot. Hope you're safe, and well, and happy. Hope you're in a nicer place than I am. But where? Where are you?"

She couldn't stop wondering about that. Obviously, nobody at Fruce Library could satisfy her curiosity, but there was at least one person in the world who might. Within days of her arrival, she had written a letter to King Dasune, expressing her gratitude for all of his kindnesses, and requesting news of her brother's whereabouts.

This letter had been entrusted to the captain of one of the boats that brought supplies and post from the mainland out to Fruce Isle every two weeks. The missive was well-sealed and clearly addressed. Barring theft or natural disaster, there was nothing to prevent its eventual delivery. The weeks had passed, however, and the boats docking at Fruce Isle carried no response from Feyenne. Shalindra had written a second letter—to be followed by another and another and another, all increasingly urgent in tone—but King Dasune had never replied.

It was as if she had ceased to exist.

"Where are you?" Shalindra repeated. Sometimes she imagined that if she concentrated hard enough, she might send her thoughts questing over land and water to touch *his* thoughts, wherever he was. She'd tried it two or three times—squeezing her eyes shut, tensing her muscles, working her brain until her head throbbed and concentration faltered—but failure never quite convinced her that it couldn't be done. Somehow. Some day.

But not this morning.

The tears of frustration were starting up in her eyes—another commonplace occurrence, these days—and she didn't have time for them now. Better get up and dressed if she didn't want to miss breakfast. And after breakfast, there was a meeting scheduled with her appointed advisor, Assistant Librarian Jevuni, who'd want to discuss her progress in the study of the Proto-Strellian dialect. Once she'd mastered Proto-Strellian, she'd be able to read *The Lay of Warrior Grylgh* in the original. Thrilling prospect.

Still, no point sitting around sniveling. Shalindra closed the locket, allowing the pendant to drop back to its usual place. Jumping from bed, she washed up, then rummaged in the wooden chest for something to wear. It was mid-autumn, yet the south of Aennorve continued sunny and mild. In Rhazaulle, the bitter winds would already be sweeping down from the Bruzhois. Here, she was still wearing her gauzy summer clothing, insubstantial garments never designed to withstand prolonged usage. The bright, fragile skirts and blouses were starting to look a little shabby. And, she realized for the first time, there was no lady's maid or seamstress to refurbish them or to make her new ones. And no money to pay for fabric and labor. Money again. Amazing how often that formerly disregarded issue seemed to arise.

Little, beggarly, Rhazaullean savage!

She dressed hurriedly, started for the door, and paused to look back at her bed. Unmade. And so it would remain, if she didn't fix it herself, for there was no servant to do it for her. Lips sullenly adroop, she pulled the covers into place and exited.

The halls she traversed were stone-floored, barrel-vaulted, ancient, and cheerless. They were lined on both sides with the inevitable shelves of books. Row after row stretched on into the shadowy distance. All color-coded and neatly numbered, all arranged according to the Fruce system of classification, the finicking intricacies of which librarians and scholars alike were required to learn by heart. Personally, Shalindra saw little point in memorizing a great long list that could so easily be written down. Her protests went unheeded, however. All residents learned the system; that was the Fruce way.

Down the narrow stairs she went, to plod dispiritedly along another book-lined hall until she came to the refectory, where breakfast was already in progress. The big, high-ceilinged chamber contained three tables—two long, one short and slightly elevated—placed to form an open-ended rectangle. Senior librarians and favored guests sat at the high table. Lesser staff members, trainees, students, and ordinary visitors occupied the benches of raw planking that ran the length of the two long tables. Scores of residents sat there eating, but the level of noise was low. Conversation buzzed, lively but muted; this restraint characteristic of Fruce gatherings. It made Shalindra long to shout, stomp, bang pots and pans together.

Inadvisable.

She found a place without difficulty, seating herself between Under Librarian Oruno and Visiting Scholar vo Trevierre. The two men, looming up on either side of her, were easily able to talk across the top of her head. This they proceeded to do, soon embroiling themselves in debate over the proper form and placement of footnotes in monographs intended for publication. Under Librarian Oruno, a conservative, favored the traditional method of Nine-Line Squaring; while the radical vo Trevierre supported the newfangled Noom's Indented—an ugly and abhorrent perversion, in the Under Librarian's opinion. The dispute waxed intense.

Thoroughly bored, Shalindra transferred her attention to the food before her. Plentiful helpings of porridge. Well-boiled water, a couple of herbal teas. Dark bread, drippings. Stewed apples, unsweetened. Raisins and nuts. Nutritious, inoffensive, plain fare, exactly the same every day. Dull, dull, dull. She couldn't help but think back to the breakfasts she'd shared in Feyenne with Cerrov and Olisi; the rainbow array of juices, the braided breads flecked with poppy seeds, the butter-layered crescent rolls, brioches, jewel-hued fruit preserves and honey, eggs cooked a hundred different ways, sausages and bacon and kippers, waffles and crepes, fresh fruit glowing with color, and the pastries, oh, the *pastries.* Sighing a little, she scattered raisins across the surface of her porridge, where they lay like lumps of coal half-sunk in grimed Rhazaullean slush.

Shalindra ate without talking, without tasting, and without listening to the verbal volleys passing inches over her head. She might have chosen another seat, but it wouldn't have made much difference. Conversation throughout the refectory tended to depressing consistency. All through the meal, her eyes remained fixed on the nearest window, which opened onto the big central courtyard wherein Frucians took their daily exercise. The courtyard was empty at the moment. But after breakfast, they'd be out there, devotedly performing their calisthenics, heedless of the punishing granite pavement underfoot. Many years earlier, one of the Assistant Librarians had once informed her, a group of students had imported hundreds of sacks of loam from the mainland; enough to cover the entire courtyard to a depth of half a foot. This done, they'd planted grass, shrubbery, and flowers. For two or three years, the garden had flourished, and then, despite all efforts at irrigation, fertilization, and cultivation, the flora mysteriously died. This did not surprise Shalindra in the least.

Above the courtyard wall, an expanse of deep blue sky was visible. Clouds hovered there, and birds swooped. She watched the birds, and daydreamed of flying with them.

Breakfast concluded, but Shalindra was not yet free to depart, for today came her turn to assist in the washing and drying of dishes. Students and junior staff members drudged upon a rotating basis; there were no exceptions. The luckless might be required to scrub pots and pans; to scrub floors, walls, windows, or even privies; to chop vegetables, wash linen, rake ashes, make soap. There was no end of horrid alternatives. All in all, washing dishes was by no means the worst of possible indignities.

She worked in the kitchen for the next couple of hours. Thereafter, she was free to meet with Assistant Librarian Jevuni for another lesson in Proto-Strellian. Jevuni's office was perched at the top of Hoojun's Tower, in the oldest section of the building. Shalindra hurried along the ground floor central corridor (booksbooksbooks), through a couple of big square rooms (stackstackstacks, naturalphilosophy, geographymapsmapsmaps), and through a skinny passage (quartosquartosquartos) that brought her to the foot of the tower. She stood upon a tiny landing. Before her, the narrow staircase spiraled toward the summit. At her back, the stairs continued, presumably twisting their way down to some deep chamber carved into the granite substance of Fruce Isle. But this was only surmise, for the descent was blocked by an ancient, iron-strapped oaken door sporting a modern steel lock and a printed warning: NO ADMITTANCE.

Shalindra wasn't particularly interested. What could be down there, after all? (Booksbooksbooks.) She hurried up the stairs to Jevuni's office. The sooner she got there, the sooner her lesson in Proto-Strellian would be over, and the sooner she'd have some time to herself, to watch the sunlight dancing on the waters of Lake Eev, to dream, perhaps to compose another pleading letter to his Majesty Dasune.

The door at the top of the stairs stood open.

Assistant Librarian Jevuni's office was circular, with a steep, high, conical ceiling crisscrossed with age-blackened beams. Unlike the majority of Fruce chambers, this office possessed potential charm; a potential that its tenant predictably failed to realize. A desk and chair stood in the middle of the floor. A second chair stood before the desk. Ranged about the room's circumference were several unfinished wooden bookcases, their straight edges warring with the curved stone walls. No color, no ornament, not a single personal belonging. At the desk, balding head bent over a manuscript, sat Jevuni himself; a middle-aged, middle-sized man, clad in a suit of the olive drab hue the Frucians had adopted as their own. He looked up as his advisee entered. His face was round, bespectacled, beard-fringed, and expressionless.

"Good morning, Miss Vezhevska," he droned in his customary monotone.

"Good morning, Assistant Librarian Jevuni," she returned dutifully, while privately wondering, as she always wondered, whether he knew her real name. At Fruce, she was "Miss Vezhevska." A commonplace Rhazaullean surname, and whoever chose it had been wise; for despite her fluency in Aennorvi, Shalindra's accent still betrayed her. Thus she became Vezhevska, a foreign student, the sole

Rhazaullean among the Frucians. (First name? None. An inessential, in this place.) And yet, some of the staff had to know who she really was. Certainly The Librarian, (THE Librarian) chief of this entire bibliomaniacal establishment, must have received instructions directly from his Majesty Dasune. Very likely, several of the assistant librarians were in on the secret as well. She always wondered which ones. Jevuni? His bland face told her nothing.

"Have you prepared your lesson, Miss Vezhevska?"

"Yessir." She wondered what would happen if she said, "Nosir." She wondered if he'd frown—blink—anything.

"Proceed."

His empty automaton eyes were turned toward her, but she wasn't certain that he actually saw. Sometimes she was tempted to gesture obscenely—she'd picked up a few good ones during last summer's Feyennese street rambles —just to find out what he'd do. Someday, she promised herself, she'd work up the courage to try it.

Producing her textbook and notebook, Shalindra began to read, tongue kinking upon the clearly inhuman gurgles and snufflings of the ancient dialect. Still, she'd studied hard, if unenthusiastically, and her progress was good. For a while she translated, occasionally glancing up from the page to discover Assistant Librarian Jevuni's blank gaze fixed on the window, and the sky beyond. Did he *hear* her? If she paused, would he notice?

Presently, she found out. Stumbling upon a villainous passage, she faltered to a halt.

Strained silence.

Assistant Librarian Jevuni's eyes never turned from the window. "Problem, Miss Vezhevska?" he inquired.

"Stuck," she confessed.

No response. She'd expected guidance. He offered none. The silence stretched. She began to fidget. Assistant Librarian Jevuni stared out the window. The silence grew unbearable.

"Well?" she demanded.

"Well?"

"What next?"

"Indeed. Possibilities?"

Possibility, that you're a worm's hind end.

Awful, unbearable silence. She couldn't stand it. She couldn't stand *him,* with his impenetrable omniscience. "Possibility," she suggested aloud, "that I flash you the Four Feyennese Fingers. Sir."

Had she actually *said* that? For a moment, she wasn't sure. His eyes were now aimed at her, but there was no change at all in his nonexpression. Perhaps she'd only imagined it.

The pudding-face rippled. Words issued. "That is indeed one of your options, Miss Vezhevska."

Ruination. She *had* said it. Now she was dead.

Assistant Librarian Jevuni displayed no hint of rancor; no hint of anything, in fact. "But is it the best one? What are some others?" he inquired.

"Others?" Tremulous, squeaky, stupid voice. *Nitwit!*

"Options, Miss Vezhevska."

Her mind went blank. She sat dumbly red-faced.

He permitted the silence to continue a full five minutes, before prompting, "What method does your training suggest, Miss Vezhevska?"

"Uh—" Recollection began to trickle into the mental void. "Uh—you analyze a problem—"

"And?"

"You reduce it to its—its components." She was imprecisely parroting the method set forth in the *Introduction to Fruce Library* pamphlet presented to new students. She'd been required to learn certain passages, and fortunately, her memory was retentive. Good thing, too. The Frucians set inordinate store by their precious method, made no end of worshipful fuss over it. "You consider your options. You formulate—uh—alternate strategies. If you can."

"And?"

"You list possible solutions or methods in order of apparent plausibility. The one at the top of the list is the one you try first. If it doesn't work, you go to the others, in order."

"And in this case?"

"The problem is that I don't understand two of the words in the tenth verse of this poem I'm translating. I could ask you what they mean, but you wouldn't tell me. I could find someone who *would* tell me, but that would take a lot of time. I could go to the dictionary in the Reading Room, but that would also eat time. I could chuck the whole lesson, but that would get me in trouble. Or I could look at what the poem is actually saying, and use that to figure out what the missing words must mean. That is to say, I take a guess. The good thing about that is, it's fast. And I'd know right away if it's worked, because if I'm right, you'll just let me keep reading. If I translate wrong, you'll stop me." She glanced at him questioningly.

"Is your analysis completed, Miss Vezhevska?" His eyes were fixed on the wall, somewhere above her head.

"Umm—I guess so." Did he expect more? What else did he want? As usual, his face told her nothing. Deadpan ogre probably enjoyed watching her squirm. Of course, she'd asked for it.

Silence again. She suspected he'd let it continue indefinitely this time.

The one at the top of the list is the one you try first.

The words in question most probably meant—

Taking a deep breath, she resumed translation, and read through to the end without interruption. She looked up from the page to find her advisor studying the overhead beams.

"Adequate, Miss Vezhevska," Assistant Librarian Jevuni conceded, without turning his eyes.

He meant she'd made no mistakes. Far be it from the Assistant Librarian to offer praise. Shalindra sat listening as her advisor spoke of accent, inflection, verbal anomalies, idiomatic expressions. She supposed she ought to be interested. In reality, it took a fearful effort to keep her mind from wandering.

It ended at last. He assigned her a new passage to translate—a long one, this time—and then she was free to go. Finally. Courtesy alone kept her from dashing for the door. She rose decorously and performed the abbreviated bow from the waist that Frucian etiquette demanded of students. The gesture was wasted on Jevuni, of course. His head was once again bent over the manuscript on his desk. Eager to escape, Shalindra headed for the exit; but, almost without volition, paused on the threshold and turned back to ask, "Assistant Librarian—?"

"Miss Vezhevska?"

"What's behind that door at the bottom of the stairs, with the NO ADMITTANCE sign on it?"

"The crypt of the librarians." He looked up from the manuscript. For once, he was actually looking straight at her. Expressionless as ever. "And certain rare books."

"Oh." More books. And dead librarians. So much for the mystery. "Who gets to look at them?"

"Authorized staff members enjoy free access. Others submit applications."

"Do *you* have free access, Assistant Librarian?"

"A full list of authorized staff may be obtained from The Librarian. Your request for such information must be presented in written form, and must contain a strongly reasoned argument demonstrating the legitimacy of your needs and intentions. Should your explanation favorably impress The Librarian, you will be granted an interview, following which, at the conclusion of the thirty-day waiting period, you will be informed of the final decision. In view of your recent linguistic accomplishments, I would urge you to compose your initial written request in the Proto-Strellian dialect. In fact, I should insist upon it. Such exercise is likely to strengthen your skills."

"I see. Thank you, Assistant Librarian Jevuni. Good morning."

"Good morning, Miss Vezhevska."

Departing without a backward glance, she hurried down the stairs. Compose a lengthy inquiry, in Proto-Strellian? Not likely. As he well knew. Once again, she'd been politely out-maneuvered. Well, no matter. They could keep their precious, pointless secrets, and welcome. She'd better things to think about.

Nevertheless, she paused on the landing at the foot of Hoojun's Tower to eye the forbidden door. Behind it—more books. And some old crypt. Not interesting. She shrugged and passed on along the narrow corridor, through the hushed chambers and galleries, across the small rear foyer and straight on out of the building, for she was free, now—quite free until her next scheduled meeting with an under librarian, two hours hence, for a review of the Chorkan Variations. Theoretically, she'd spend that time in one of the reading rooms, gorging her brain upon luscious text. In reality, she had other plans.

No one stopped her at the back exit. The clerk on duty didn't hinder or even question her, for that wasn't standard Frucian procedure. The portal stood open. Shalindra stepped forth into sunlight so brilliant that her eyes closed involuntarily. One hand went up to ward off the glare, and for a few seconds she stood blinking. Familiar. Blinking, watery eyes . . . Reminiscent of something . . . someone. *Uncle Varis.* Of course. Varis's eyes used to water painfully, all the time, even indoors—and then he'd gone away—and when he came back, he'd changed, and his eyes were all right. Strange.

Uncle Varis, sitting on Cerrov's Wolf Throne . . . Cerrov, sitting—where? Unconsciously, she fingered the locket.

Her eyes adjusted. She looked about her. The library's spreading bulk occupied nearly the whole of the artificially leveled summit of the great rock known as Fruce Isle. A broad, flagged esplanade, edged with a low stone wall, girdled the building. Beyond the barrier, the cliffs plunged straight and sheer to the silvery waters of Lake Eev. Shalindra approached the wall; gazed out over glinting water to a clear, featureless horizon. No sign of the mainland. Nor were any of the numerous lake islands visible from her present vantage point. Off in the distance, she descried a single boat, frivolously pink-sailed, obviously someone's pleasure craft. Nothing else visible but water, intense blue sky, lazy clouds, more water . . .

She walked along the esplanade, and as she rounded an angle of the building, the view altered, and she could make out the sister-islands, Fenellina and Fenelletta; dark, distant masses marring the smooth expanse of Lake Eev. Not much to see. When she'd first come to Fruce, she used to watch Fenellina and Fenelletta for hours on end; making up stories about the warm, generous residents, who loved and valued children, who'd welcome her with open arms, if only she could find a way of reaching them . . . Then she'd learned that the sister-islands were uninhabited, barren, and her interest had withered.

On she went, around to the front of the library, and on this side, the descent from island summit to lake was steep, but not precipitous. Here, a gap in the wall marked the head of a very long flight of stone steps leading down to a lakeside quay too small to accommodate more than a handful of modest vessels. Even so, Fruce Isle quay was never filled to capacity. Often, it was completely empty. Not today, however. Today, the packet *Lakelily* floated there, pennants asnap in the autumn breeze. The crewmen were unloading crates of foodstuffs onto the quay. And there on deck directing their efforts was stocky, curly-bearded Captain Brunule, in his usual billed cap and blue coat with silver buttons. Shalindra's face brightened, and her pulse quickened. Emissaries from the real world out there beyond the water. Perhaps this time—?

Black braid bouncing, she ran down the steps. Reaching the quay, she skirted the growing mound of crates, bestowed a perfunctory smile or two upon the laboring sailors, and scurried straight up the gangplank. Nobody objected. The crew of the *Lakelily* was accustomed to these visitations.

Captain Brunule greeted her with a smile. "Ah, the perilous Dark Lady," he remarked. "Fortune favors me today."

Shalindra returned the smile. She liked the Captain. No matter how busy he might be, he always found a little time to spare for her. And the way he talked to her was irresistible. *Dark Lady.* It sounded so glamorous, so mysterious. It made her feel wicked, dangerous, and—pretty, definitely pretty.

Pretty. But was she? When pressed to the wall, Mama had used to tell her that she showed "promise," that she possessed "tremendous potential." His Grace her father, on the other hand, had not scrupled to voice his opinion that she resembled a floor mop dipped in coal dust, then inverted. Not encouraging at all. But to Captain Brunule she was—the Dark Lady.

"Hello, Captain."

"And what intrigues has my lady fomented lately, eh? What hapless wretch have you lured to his doom since breakfast?"

"Nobody today." Shalindra giggled. This sort of conversation required effort, but it was fun, and she suspected it would become easier with practice. "I've got plans for my advisor, though."

"Poor fellow. Poor fellow. Doesn't stand a chance."

"Doesn't deserve one." Shalindra tossed her head.

"Ah, the merciless fair. Are you cruel to your lovers as you are to your victims?"

"My lovers *are* my victims."

"Hmm, advanced for your age. Oh, you're a fatal, coldhearted villainess, you are."

"Well—" She lowered her eyes modestly. "I try."

"Witch. Pity the luckless librarians, with you in their midst to wreak havoc. But how comes a dazzling young bird of paradise to such a grim rock as Fruce Isle? Fleeing your enemies, no doubt? I assume my lady is incognita."

"Something like that," Shalindra mumbled. Playful invention failed her, and she was suddenly nervous. Incognita? Fleeing her enemies? How had he guessed that? How much did he actually know? She darted a searching look up at him. He looked absolutely normal—casual, amiable, amused—just as he always looked when speaking to her. He was a friend, it was absurd to suspect him, she ought to be ashamed . . . But into her mind sprang the image of Princess Olisi, bald and blind, lying upon her deathbed in a darkened chamber. And suddenly it didn't seem absurd in the least to suspect him—to suspect anybody and everybody. Captain Brunule was probably all right, and yet—

She drew back from him a little. "Do you have anything for me this time, Captain?" she inquired unsmilingly. "A letter?"

"Not today, Dark Lady." His own smile faded.

He must have sensed the change in her mood. Maybe he'd wonder about it, maybe he'd even recall his own remarks, make the connection, and realize—

She'd have to be more careful. She'd have to learn to control her face. At least, in this case, her sudden sobering could easily be mistaken for ordinary disappointment—recurring disappointment. No letter from Cerrov. No response from King Dasune. Not today. Not any day. She'd lost count of the times this scene had repeated itself over the course of recent months. Same question, same answer, again and again, and always the same sense of aching desolation, perennially fresh and sharp.

"I see." Shalindra spoke very calmly. "In that case, Captain, I wonder if you'd carry something to Foneev for me?" She produced a missive, sealed and (illicitly) stamped with the Fruce insignia, addressed: *To His Majesty Dasune, at the Genevreen, in Feyenne.*

"Gladly." Accepting the letter, he stowed it carefully and respectfully in his wallet, for all the world as if he imagined the document significant. Thus he accepted every letter—every disregarded, unacknowledged, unanswered letter—as if each were the first.

The man had tact. And kindness, too, it seemed; for now he was digging in his pocket to bring forth a wad of cheap yellowish paper covered with printing. "Here, Dark Lady. I brought these for you. Turo peddler in Foneev was wrapping trinkets in 'em. Thought you might be interested."

"Why, thank you, Captain." Curious, Shalindra accepted the offering. "What are they?"

"No idea. They're printed in Rhazaullean, and I can't make out a syllable to save my life. No offense, but you northerners squiggle out a barbarous alphabet. I go cross-eyed at the sight of it."

"Really? Show me." Shalindra held up a printed sheet, and Captain Brunule obligingly crossed his eyes. She laughed, good humor partially restored. His disquieting remarks moments earlier must have been coincidental. As for her disappointment—well, she should be used to it, by now.

Captain Brunule's eyes, properly uncrossed, sought the workers on the quay. Shalindra took the hint. "Well, I'll be going now," she told him. "Thanks for the papers. It'll be nice to read in Rhazaullean."

He nodded. "You take care of yourself, little Dark Lady. And try not to ruin too many librarians. We need a few left up there to look after all those books."

"The women," Shalindra told him firmly. "The Fruciannes are safe from me." Departing the *Lakelily,* she made her way along the quay, then up the steep stone stairway. The long climb back to the esplanade scarcely quickened her breathing. She looked about her. The shadow upon the sundial set into the wall above the library's front entrance told her that an hour or more of freedom remained to her. How to fill it? The sunshine was glorious; she didn't feel like going back inside.

Tomb. It's like some giant, silent tomb in there. The crypt of all books.

For a moment, the sunshine seemed to lose its warmth. She walked on. Presently reaching a low stone bench built into a jog in the wall, she seated herself. For a few moments she gazed idly out over the scintillant surface of Lake Eev, and then, recalling Captain Brunule's gift, drew the papers from her pocket.

It was an odd little assortment that she held. There were a couple of handbills for a play performed at the Duke's Theater in Lazimir the previous year. There was one issue of *Beyond,* a pamphlet published at irregular intervals by the Venerators of Rialsq. A couple of broadsides advertising the healing skills of a certain mountebank calling himself "The Miraculous Dr. Redodo." And several copies of a circular, months old, titled *The Great Regicide Punish'd; Being a True and Authentic Account of the recent Execution, in Rialsq.*

That last looked interesting. Shalindra read:

> For the Benefit of the good Folk of Rialsq, Lazimir, Truvisq, and all the several Cities and Provinces of Rhazaulle, let it be known that Justice has triumphed. The notorious Harlot and Murderess falsely styling herself Duchess of Otreska has suffered the extreme Penalty; which, if greatly less in severity than this Regicide and Infanticide deserves, is yet as severe as the gentle Law will allow.
>
> This Day, around Sunset, the Criminal was carried through the Streets of Rialsq, as far as the White Level, and the House of Ice. The mean Nature of her Conveyance exposed her fully to the

Eyes of the Multitude, and it was noted by All that the Criminal's Demeanor was haughty, unflinching, and to the last Degree insolent. There were Some so misguided as to laud this Creature's calm Resolution, and to These I say, let such Fools but note the Condition to which her Greed and Vanity have brought her at the Last!

The Populace assembled upon the Level greeted the Condemned with well-deserved Scorn and Jeerings. This just Opprobrium she disregarded, as if she did not hear it; an Affectation that could but wake the Contempt of the Judicious. Upon the very Threshold of the House of Ice, she handed a gold Brazzle to the Captain of Guards conducting her thither, as if she mistook him for a Footman or Lackey; another Impertinence much deserving of Censure.

She entered the House as if by her own Choice, and they sealed the Ice-Portal behind her. Thereafter, she sought to hide herself from View within the hidden Recesses of the House; for such the monstrous Pride of this high Harlot, that she could not abide public Observation of her just Doom. The Majority of Spectators then abandoned the White Level. But the wisest among Observers remained for a Time to muse upon the Aptness of the Sentence condemning the counterfeit Duchess of Otreska—whose Heat of Appetite and Ambition occasioned the Murder of an infant Ulor—to Death by freezing . . .

There was more, but Shalindra's eyes were already blurred with tears. Curious. She was quite numb, as if some anesthesia blocked full knowledge from her mind. But her body comprehended well enough; her tears, tremors, and racing heart bespoke her body's awareness. She stuffed the printed sheets into her pocket. Her hand flew by instinct to the locket, which she drew from beneath her blouse. Her mother's locket. Her dead mother, her frozen mother, her tortured and libeled mother . . . She stared at the ornament. Flash of gold, glitter of gems, sinister luster of the dark central diamond—Mother's locket, Mother's favorite, Mother handing the jewel to Cerrov as a remembrance—Cerrov's portrait inside, but Cerrov himself gone now—remembrance—everyone gone—

The gemmed gold casing was wet now, and her face was wet, and her breath was all but stopped in her throat. Unable to sit still any longer, she rose, but there was nowhere to go but on around the esplanade, or else back into the library, *Crypt of all books,* or else back down to the quay where the *Lakelily* rested . . . *The boat, free to leave this rock, free.* No good, any of them—

She stumbled on, head bent and shoulders hunched, pressure crushing her heart; seat of sympathetic humors, someone (Dr. Treluna?) had once told her. He must have been right. The pain in her chest was real as a knife wound.

She didn't know how long she continued to walk, how many times she circled the library. Eventually, her feet started to ache, and the shadow on the sundial told her that the hour of her appointment with the under librarian (authority on Chorkan Variations) had come and gone long ago. Ridiculous thing to think of now.

Her face was tight and salt-crusted, her eyes swollen, but dry. The first storm of grief had exhausted itself, and what was left now, but to go back inside, into the library, (Crypt of all books) back to the reading room, her advisor's office, her own bleak chamber? She should tell someone in authority what had happened, she supposed. She should tell Jevuni, or one of the under librarians.

But what use? What could any of them do?

They're grown-ups, they're supposed to do something.

Almost blindly she turned, feet carrying her toward the entrance, and disgust verging on nausea swamped her, and her muscles stiffened in refusal, and the thought came, *Not this, I don't want to be in this place. Not this, not this, not this.*

The tears had started up again. She didn't want to be out here in the open. She didn't want to see anyone, talk to anyone. Best go hide in her own little room. Lock the door, and never come out; petrify in there like Olisi playing Hidden Statues. Hide somewhere, anywhere away from people. Away from the *Lakelily* crewmen, who, burdened with crates, now toiled their way up the stairs from the quay; away, even, from Captain Brunule, who led them.

Flattening herself against the building, Shalindra peeked around the corner to watch Brunule and his subordinates file through the main entrance. They'd be in there for several minutes. It would take them at least that much time to tote the crates all the way to the kitchen. Then they'd have to return to the quay and repeat the entire procedure. It would require three such trips to dispose of the entire delivery. During that time, the boat—*free to leave this rock, free*—remained unmanned and unwatched.

Her feet took on a life of their own. In an instant, she found herself running for the gap in the low wall, then rushing down the long flight of stairs. Once below the first few steps, she could no longer be seen from the library, but still her pace did not slacken. A couple of minutes later, she reached the quay, then the gangplank, then the deck of the *Lakelily.* She glanced around hurriedly. Nowhere to hide on deck, but the cabin stood open. She descended to the crew's quarters, then climbed down another ladder into the hold.

A dark, dank, cramped place, dead-aired and illsmelling. It took eyes and nose a few seconds to adjust. Weak light filtering down from above played upon crates, barrels, sacks, and bales; cargo en route to any of half a hundred islands, lakeshore towns or villages.

She didn't care where it was going, so long as the *Lakelily* carried her away from Fruce Isle. Preferably to the mainland; ideally, to Foneev. And then? A child, and penniless, what would she do?

Make my way back to Feyenne. Somehow. Find the King. MAKE him tell me where Cerrov is.

Cerrov—had he known what had happened to their mother? No. He would never have kept it from her. Her face tingled. The tears welled.

Don't think of it now.

There was a little space between a stack of crates and the curving wall of the hull, space enough to accommodate her slight self. She backed in on her hands and knees, then reached out from her tiny cave to grab the nearest movable sack, with which she blocked the entrance.

She lay in near-total darkness. The slap of water against the hull, the creaking of spars and timbers filled her ears. The raw boards beneath her were hard and splintery. The mild rocking of the moored boat bounced her painfully between crates and wall. When the *Lakelily* embarked, she'd be pulverized. No matter, she could stand it.

All very well, but just when would the *Lakelily* embark? Before too long, she'd be missed at the library. There'd be inquiries, and then they'd start looking for her. And if the packet lingered at the quay—? Probably no real need to worry, though. Captain Brunule wouldn't choose to spend the night at Fruce Isle; he never did. He could make it to the nearest neighboring island before sunset, provided he set sail by midafternoon at the latest. This he was certain to do. Another few minutes, at most, and she might bid the library and its dour stewards farewell. Not a moment too soon, either. Gruesome place.

But a short hop to another island wouldn't do her much good. She needed to reach the mainland, and there was no way of knowing exactly how long it would take to get there. It might be days. And in the meantime, it finally occurred to her to wonder, what would she do about food and water? She frowned. She'd fled the library on sudden impulse, her misery and desperation precluding rational thought. But now, lying alone in malodorous darkness, she'd leisure to consider her less-than-enviable position. Impossible to avoid considering it, in fact. Her mouth was a little dry. Already she was mildly thirsty. Without water, how would she be feeling by this time tomorrow? No denying—once again, she'd been an idiot.

Shalindra's frown deepened. No point wasting time in self-blame. She should be thinking, planning; better late than never, and besides, mental activity helped to stave off grief. She should—

Analyze a problem, reduce it to its components. Consider options, formulate alternate strategies.

Just so. Assistant Librarian Jevuni would approve. With any luck, she'd never see the four-eyed fart again.

Presumably most of the provisions were stored in the galley. The *Lakelily,* touching at least one port every day, wouldn't need to carry much food for her small crew, but there'd surely be emergency rations, and plenty of fresh water. From time to time, when the crew was ashore, she'd have a chance to reach them. Perhaps somewhere she might find an empty bottle, fill it with water, and bring it down to her hiding place. She could hoard food down here as well. One way or another, she'd make do.

Thus reassured, she relaxed a little and found herself unwontedly drowsy. Her nose was stuffed, and her head ached. The passionate weeping must have exhausted her. It would be good to sleep, good to forget things—

Shalindra drifted off, but woke minutes later to the thud of footsteps on the deck above. The crew was back aboard. Brisk voices overhead. Hurryings to and fro, unidentifiable noises, flurried activity, and the *Lakelily* cast off. The wind caught her sails, and she came alive in the water. The stowaway caught her breath. She was under way. Fruce Isle was receding. She was actually *doing it.*

Elation and excitement buoyed her for the next hour or more. Eventually, however, excitement subsided, and physical discomfort manifested itself. She lay in a cramped and stuffy space. The motion of the boat pitched her to and fro, and her attempts to wedge herself into place were successful only so long as she maintained strenuous effort. It was dark and close in her little cave. She could see nothing, and the stale air was heavy in her lungs.

She was starting to ache; and worse, the fearful, sorrowing thoughts were creeping back into her brain. It seemed that the darkness fostered such thoughts. But she could do something about that.

For a few moments, she listened intently. She heard voices and movement overhead, but the hold, she sensed, was empty. Shifting the sack an inch or so, she peeked from her refuge. She saw bales, crates, barrels; nothing more. Shoving the sack aside, she emerged cautiously. It felt fine to stand upright, to stretch her muscles a little, to cat-foot back and forth. A little risky, with the crew aboard, but all right as an occasional indulgence. For a couple of minutes she snooped around the hold, poking at bags and bundles, strongly tempted to open one or two. No. Dangerous. Time to return to her hiding place.

She took a step in the right direction, then halted, reminded by sudden internal pressure of another matter that, in her haste to escape Fruce Isle, she'd neglected to consider. She needed to relieve herself, and she needed to do it *now*.

Bad. Very bad.

Analyze the problem—consider your options—strategies— NO TIME!

Could she just sneak behind the nearest stack of crates? No, the first time anyone set foot down here, it would be noticed. In this unventilated space—the smell—

Pile sacks and bundles on top of the spot?

Ick.

But there had to be a pot or slop bucket in the crew's quarters, which were surely unoccupied now. Shalindra crept up the ladder; listened, then raised her head to peek into the compact little cabin hardly large enough to contain a half dozen bunks. Deserted, as she'd surmised. The lidded wooden box, bolted to the floor in the corner, almost certainly housed the slop bucket. Good. She'd have to be quick.

She was up through the hatch in a flash. At the same instant, a sailor descended from the deck. They saw each other, and simultaneously froze; she in horror, he in amazement. He was young, with large muscles, carrot hair, countless freckles. She didn't know his name, but she'd seen him about Fruce Isle quay often enough. He likewise recognized her.

"You're that kid from Fruce!" exclaimed the sailor.

"Sssshhh! Please, don't tell!"

"What are you doing here?"

"Running away from the library."

"Captain'll fry your liver."

"You're not going to tell on me?"

"Sure I am. What did you think?"

"Please don't! Listen—if you help me, I can pay you. Lots."

"Oh, right. You got money, of course."

"Well—not with me, but my family is rich, really, really rich—"

"Royalty, most like."

"And if you help me, you won't be sorry."

"Aaah." He flashed her the Four Feyennese Fingers. "Come on, kid. Up on deck with you. Game's over."

"No, *please!*" A spate of pleas, arguments, and wheedles followed, but the sailor proved immovable.

"On deck," he insisted.

Resistance was useless. Shalindra's shoulders slumped. "All right. Before we go up, though, there's just one thing—" She saw refusal in his face, and added quickly, "May I use the pot?"

After that, things got unpleasant. Horrible, in fact. The carrot-topped sailor herded her up to the deck, there to confront Captain Brunule, with whom she blundered badly.

Brunule listened closely to his subordinate's accurate explanation, then turned on Shalindra to ask, like a magistrate, "What have you to say?"

He was eyeing her expressionlessly, as if he'd never even seen her before, and she had never dreamed that he could look so—cold. Her mouth dried up. This hardly seemed the old friend who teased and flattered her; she found herself facing an irate stranger. But still, if only she could make him laugh, he might come around. If only she could coax so much as a small smile—

Her head came up. "Not at liberty to speak, Captain," she returned, essaying an impish grin. "I'm incognita, as you know, and my enemies are everywhere. I trust I may rely on your discretion."

Mistake. Serious mistake. He didn't smile. His expression, if anything, grew colder. "Answer the question," he said.

She sobered at once. "I'm sorry. I didn't mean to cause trouble. It's only that I had to get away from that island—I had to—I was so unhappy there, so—so very—" Her voice cracked, her throat tightened, and the tears rose to her eyes; perhaps not such a bad thing. If she couldn't make him smile, maybe she could enlist his sympathies—?

Captain Brunule appeared unmoved. "Were you mistreated?" he asked.

"I was unhappy. I—"

"Were you beaten or whipped?"

"No, I—"

"Starved?"

"No, but—"

"Deprived of sleep, shelter, comfort, or dignity? Abused in any way?"

Red-faced, she shook her head.

"Then what exactly is your complaint? Do you *have* a

complaint?" No reply was forthcoming, and Brunule inquired, "Would you like to know what's going to happen now?"

She wouldn't, really.

But he continued almost without pause. "We're going to carry you back to Fruce. We'll arrive near sunset, and we'll spend the night moored at Fruce quay. That throws *Lakelily*'s schedule off for the next week, and folk all through the islands and along the shore will have to wait an extra day for their packages and post. They won't know why. Some will be put out, others will be worried. There's a big loss of time and money. That's what you've accomplished with your little prank. Hope you're proud of yourself."

"Captain, it wasn't a prank. I only—"

"As for you, I plan to charge the librarians the full price of your transport. Baggage rate, I think. That'll cost 'em something, and I don't think they'll be too pleased with you. But that's not my worry."

"Do you really have to tell them about this? Couldn't you just—" The look on his face froze her tongue.

"Now, you take yourself below, and stay there. Until we dock, I don't want to see your face." He turned away from her.

For a moment she studied his broad back, trying to find the words to explain, to apologize; words to restore friendship.

"I'm sorry. I never meant to cause so much trouble. I'm—"

He walked away. Miserably, she dragged herself back to the cabin, where she sat huddled and sobbing on one of the bunks for the next two hours or so. As Brunule had predicted, the sun was dipping below the horizon by the time the *Lakelily* reached Fruce Isle quay.

If only they had just released her there, things would have been all right. Her disappearance from the library had very probably been noted, but left to her own devices,

she could have explained it away. She'd fallen asleep on
the floor somewhere deep in the stacks, she would have
claimed, and slept the afternoon away. Somehow, she'd
have managed . . . This opportunity, however, was denied her. Captain Brunule himself marched her all the way
up the long stone steps, across the esplanade, and straight
through the front door. At the clerk's desk he paused to
request a meeting with The Librarian.

THE Librarian. Autocrat of Fruce. Shalindra's eyes
rounded. This was even worse than she'd expected. Her
feet itched to run. But the Captain's hand rested firmly on
her shoulder; she wasn't going anywhere. In any case,
there was nowhere to go.

The clerk consulted a schedule. Yes, The Librarian was
presently in her office. Yes, she was available for consulta-
tion. Her office was located—he provided directions. Captain and captive marched.

Shalindra had never before ventured upon the sacred
precincts, and never before seen The Librarian save across
the length of a crowded refectory. She'd just as soon have
kept it that way. The office itself was soberly ascetic; so
too was its owner. Observed at close range, The Librarian
was remarkably imposing, with chiseled features, severely
upswept gray-streaked brown hair, penetrating eyes, and
regal carriage to emphasize unusual height. She was, in
fact, the tallest woman Shalindra had ever seen; nearly as
tall as Uncle Hurna himself. When she looked at her visitors, she looked *down*.

While Shalindra stood silent and pale with humiliation, Captain Brunule related the entire story, omitting no
shameful detail. Narration concluded, he received immediate remuneration, together with The Librarian's apology. Somewhat mollified, Brunule departed, without a
word to spare for the culprit. He'd probably never speak to
her again. She felt like running after him. She even took a
step toward the door, but a chill voice stopped her in her
tracks.

"Stay where you are, Miss Vezhevska."

Reluctantly, Shalindra turned back. The Librarian was standing. Oh, but she was tall; positively immense. Her eyes were cold as Rhazaullean winter. Captain Brunule had looked downright cordial by comparison. But something in the measured voice and the brumal eyes reminded Shalindra, *This one knows who I really am.* And might, perhaps, therefore let her off lightly.

Wrong again.

"It would seem you have failed to consider, Miss Vezhevska, the degree to which your follies may discredit our entire community," The Librarian commenced, and there followed a tongue-lashing of awesome duration and severity. Never in all her life had Shalindra experienced so merciless a flaying. Not that The Librarian ever yelled, ranted, vituperated, or even raised her voice. She was guilty of no such human failing. Her manner was detached, her tone analytical, as she spoke of the runaway's immaturity, irrationality, inconsiderateness. She mentioned ingratitude and untrustworthiness in passing, talked much of juvenile self-absorption and irresponsibility. Concluding the dissection long minutes later, she imposed—almost as an afterthought, it seemed—an array of punishments that ranged from temporary loss of Reading Room privileges, to extra hours of drudgery in the kitchen and the privies.

Throughout the protracted tirade, Shalindra stood erect and flint-eyed. Presumably she'd cried herself dry aboard the *Lakelily.* Her tears were now exhausted; her emotions, mercifully deadened. When at last The Librarian gave her leave to depart, she inclined her head briefly, and exited the office without a word.

It was well past sunset. Lamp light gilded the book-lined chambers and corridors. In the refectory, the Frucians were sitting at supper. She could join them if she chose. Likewise, she might return to her own chamber, there to contemplate her mother's death; or to the esplanade, there to look down on the *Lakelily,* moored at the quay below; or else to the stacks, there to resume her study of the Proto-Strellian dialect. She considered. The options were uniformly unappealing. It didn't seem to make much difference where she went, or what she did. Within the confines of the library, she was free to wander where she pleased. (Only one NO ADMITTANCE sign that she knew of.) There were neither bars on the windows, nor armed guards at the doors, but the absence of these things didn't make Fruce any less of a prison.

10

SHE BARRICADED HERSELF in her own room for the next thirty-six hours. During that time, nobody came to disturb her. Expecting anxious or angry visitations, she found herself ignored.

Eventually, hunger drove her forth. She emerged to confront the faces in the refectory, the curling lips and disapproving eyes. They knew, she could tell. Or did they? Imagination?

She couldn't stand the silent reproaches, real or fancied. Better, and easier, to perform the dreary penance ordained by The Librarian. She could pay her debts—drudge in the kitchen, the laundry, even the privies—and then she would be square, her slate clean.

This she did, and thereafter found herself back where she began, an alien condemned to perpetual scholarship. For a joyless stretch of time, she immersed herself in her studies. Proto-Strellian dialect. Chorkan Variations. Frunuuv's Rhetoric. Structure of Logic. Aennorvi Dramatic Verse. Patterns in Philosophy. Not uninteresting, some of it. Never consuming, but often absorbing enough. She was not happy, but constant mental activity blunted the razor edge of misery.

The months were passing. Autumn gave way to a short, dank Aennorvi winter. The skies were leaden, and great quantities of rain pelted the gray surface of Lake Eev. Then the mists descended, thick white vapors wrapping Fruce Isle in a milky cocoon. The world vanished. Reality seemed to begin and end at the stone wall edging the esplanade, and all that remained to confirm the existence of a world beyond was the sound of the fog horns hooting mournfully across the water. Mists notwithstanding, the boats were still out there on the lake. Presumably the packet *Lakelily* touched Fruce Isle quay every two weeks or so, as always. But Shalindra couldn't swear to it, for she'd never again dared approach Captain Brunule. Perhaps he would have pardoned her, perhaps not. In any event, she couldn't bring herself to face him; which meant, no more letters dispatched to King Dasune. Not that it mattered much. His Majesty had never answered any of them, and certainly never would.

One day, weeks later, the rains abruptly ceased. Within hours, the fog began to thin. A weak sun glowed through the clouds, and a freshening breeze swept Eev's surface. The mists dispersed, and, with an abruptness verging on the supernatural, it was spring. The sky took on a deep, soft color never seen in Rhazaulle, the lake dyed itself to match, and the air softened. Preoccupied with an analysis of Dinuve's Twelve Principles of Communication, Shalindra scarcely noted the change of seasons.

She noticed, however, when summer came. When the atmosphere pressed, so heavy and sultry that she found herself homesick for the hard purity of Rhazaullean air, she searched her dresser drawers for the lightest of last year's garments. These she found threadbare, worn almost transparent in spots, and much too small. Obviously, she'd grown in the last year or so; started to change shape a bit as well, and high time. Cerrov wouldn't dare call her an infant *now*. He'd eat that word, the next time they met.

But when will that be?

Automatically, her fingers sought the locket containing her brother's likeness.

What if it's never? What if he's cooped up somewhere, as I am, and neither of us ever gets out? What if he's dead?

But these last possibilities didn't bear contemplation. Better—essential, in fact—to think of something else, anything else. Clothes, for example. Yes, that would do. She'd have to make her own, but that shouldn't be too hard. There were books around this place that would tell her how to cut, fit, and assemble a garment. There were books around this place to tell her everything. Everything, perhaps, except where to get hold of the necessary materials.

As it happened, Under Librarian Kufune, chief of Household Allotments, was able to help her. Ordinarily, the Under Librarian explained, a written request for supplies would be submitted in triplicate, at least sixty days prior to the proposed date of disbursement. In this particular case, however, a possible budgetary loophole existed. A small, fluctuating account labeled "Household Sundries," considered an almost negligible subsidiary of Household Allotments, might perhaps be used to—

While Kufune droned on and on, Shalindra thought of other things. Finally, the flow of words ceased, and she got what she wanted: fabric, thread, needle, pins, scissors. The cloth was pleasantly soft and thin. Its color, however, was the library's official olive-drab; a highly democratic hue, equally unflattering to all complexions. There was enough for a swirling skirt, and a yoked blouse with puffed elbow-length sleeves. Prettily cut garments; but when they were finished and she tried them on for the first time, she saw that the skin of her forearm looked sallow, almost greenish, against the olive-drab background. As for her face—she couldn't see it. She'd no access to a looking-glass, and probably just as well. No doubt she resembled a perambulating corpse.

Sartorial needs satisfied for the moment, she returned

to her studies, while the seasons marched on. Autumn again, and a survey of Bomian Renaissance literature. Some of the faces she knew among the Visiting Scholars gone, to be replaced by new ones. A change or two among the librarians, but it hardly seemed important. Winter, steady rain again, and the personal physical alterations that—if inevitable, and not unwelcome—yet called to mind the passage of time. Winter, and another visit to Under Librarian Kufune, another withdrawal from the Household Sundries account, this time for a length of olive-drab wool, from which to fashion a couple of substantial, unbecoming cool-weather garments.

She was less unhappy, these days. Her emotions, both painful and pleasurable, had dulled. Some part of her mind seemed to have developed a protective carapace, and now she followed her daily routines of work and study, feeling little of grief, frustration, or satisfaction. Sometimes she was aware of loneliness, but solitude was beginning to seem her destined state, perpetual and immutable as the granite of Fruce Isle. Her shell was not altogether impervious, however. Recollections of the past, of mother and brother, produced disturbing cracks. The trick was to avoid such thoughts; not an easy thing to do, when the locket—memento of Mother and of Cerrov both—hung upon her throat night and day.

Consider your options. Formulate alternate strategies—

The solution to this problem appeared obvious. She hid the ornament deep inside her mattress. Burying the memento, however, failed to banish memories. In the time that followed, she found her fingers continually seeking the small, familiar weight no longer there. Again and again, she lifted a hand to her unadorned neck, always to experience the same recurrent flash of startled uneasiness. Over the course of another week, the sensation intensified. She was restless as never before, and fear of burglary began to obsess her. A dozen times a day, she was back in her room to check the mattress.

In this case, the obvious solution proved ineffective. Defeated, she retrieved the locket, hung it again around her neck, and felt much better. She wouldn't willingly set it aside again.

Back to her studies, and the search for effective diversion. An analysis of Hormiform Structural Theory wouldn't do the trick, but something else might. Recently, she'd noticed unusual activity centering about the forbidden door at the foot of Hoojun's Tower. It had begun—or she'd become aware of it—some two weeks earlier; at which time, en route to Assistant Librarian Jevuni's office, she'd come upon her advisor emerging from the crypt. He'd stopped dead at sight of her, his face expressionless as always, but she'd sensed his surprised displeasure. He'd said nothing, however. Nodding briefly in her direction, he'd relocked the door and calmly ascended the tower stairs.

She'd stood gawking after him. So Jevuni was one of the authorized staff members with access to the crypt. Not surprising, but why hadn't he just said so when she'd asked him? Why make such a *mystery* of it?

Probably made the dreary old bookworm feel important. Let him keep his piddling secrets. Nothing of interest there.

She'd probably have dismissed the incident if she hadn't been so bored with incessant scholarship, so hungry for novelty, so in need of a project to occupy her mind; and if, two days later, she hadn't spotted Under Librarian Oruno exiting the crypt so very unobtrusively. Oruno's eyes had been shifty, his air furtive. And when he'd noticed her watching him, his face had reddened, he'd ducked his head, and positively scuttled off down the corridor.

Most peculiar. Quite mysterious, in fact. She thought about it, and her attention, up to that time aimlessly unfocused, began to fix on the locked door.

She took to hanging about Hoojun's Tower. Excuses

were easy to manufacture. The little corridor leading to
the entrance was lined with thousands of small quarto
volumes, most of them copies of plays from the preceding
century. One of the shelves, strategically located, contained about fifty verse dramas by some forgotten hack
calling himself Groje Pizune. Master Pizune's numerous
works, so deservedly obscure, were about due for resurrec-
tion. A proposed *Survey of Recurring Themes in the Plays of
Groje Pizune* would explain Miss Vezhevska's frequent visits.

For the first several days, she saw nothing. Nobody
entered or exited the crypt, and at last it occurred to her
that her own hitherto insignificant presence might be in-
fluencing events. Accordingly she sought concealment in
the shallow space between the top of the bookcase and the
ceiling. A row of volumes masked her hiding place. A
couple of biographies kept her occupied as she lay up there
on her stomach for hours at a time.

Prolonged surveillance was uncomfortable, boring, and
unrewarding. A full two days of observation yielded little
profit. She saw Assistant Librarian Jevuni going into the
crypt late one afternoon. About an hour later, he emerged,
blank-faced as ever. That was all. Very disappointing,
hardly worth her investment of time. And she was all but
ready to abandon both her observation post and the entire
disappointing project, when she spied The Librarian, regal
in archaic dark robes of office, sweeping down the quarto-
lined corridor.

Shalindra froze behind her barricade of books. The Librarian; she of the queenly mien and whiplash tongue.

Here? At this hour?

Pausing only a moment to deal with the lock, The
Librarian sailed majestically on into the forbidden crypt,
closing the door behind her.

She didn't emerge for another two hours.

Shalindra's interest quickened. The matter was worthy
of attention after all. She watched. She listened.

Days passed, and nothing happened.

Days. But what about the nights? She began to wonder. At last, she planned an experiment.

Enforced kitchen duty had its uses. Her dishwashing labors had long since taught her the recalcitrance of dried and hardened egg. The stuff set like cement; the bane of scullery drudges, but a boon to a would-be spy. Just a tiny dab of runny yolk, carried from the refectory at breakfast time, sufficed to glue a couple of Shalindra's long black hairs between door and jamb. She placed them unobtrusively, one at floor level, the other near the ceiling. This done, late one evening, she retired to her own chamber.

Early the next morning, she returned to find both hairs displaced.

Tantalizing. She wanted more. To get it, she'd have to camp out atop that bookshelf—until dawn, if necessary.

She did so, and her efforts were rewarded. Around the middle of a clouded night in autumn, Shalindra watched a group of librarians filing quietly into the crypt. Two or three of them carried lanterns. Low orange light lent exoticism to several familiar faces; including Master Jevuni's, including The Librarian's. The door closed behind them. Darkness and silence smothered Fruce Library.

It was quietly miserable. Shalindra lay on the shelf for as long as she could stand it. No sight, no sound, nothing. Her limbs were aching. Her scalp itched. She needed to move. As quietly as possible, she climbed down from her perch, and groped her way forward to press her ear against the door.

Small mumbling of voices down below. She couldn't make out individual words. It was all so much gibberish, but she found herself strangely cold and shaky.

Instinct counseled retreat. But she stayed where she was, senses straining. She heard the voices, and they were approaching. Hastily, she scrambled back up the shelves. A book slipped under her heel. The volume fell to the floor. No time to retrieve it, and if they spotted it lying there—

Heart thumping, she flattened rigidly into place. No sooner had she done so than the door opened, and the librarians—perhaps ten or twelve of them—emerged.

She wondered if some of them were drunk. Several looked so white, so wobbly and slack-jawed, that alcohol seemed the likeliest explanation. But no. They might be pallid and shaky, but their eyes were sharply luminescent, their aspect quietly elated. Master Jevuni was last out, and he locked the door behind him. The librarians retreated, conversing in low tones. A few words floated up as they passed her hiding place:

. . . *Progress* . . . *Encouraging* . . . *Achievement* . . . *Unquestionably* . . .

Nobody noticed the fallen quarto; a piece of negligence uncharacteristic of these fanatical bibliophiles.

Yes, the matter was worthy of investigation, all right. Here was diversion indeed.

For the moment, however, she was thwarted, and would remain so until she got into that crypt. Presumably every key was guarded by its owner as jealously as she herself guarded Mother's locket. She'd never lay hands on one.

Consider your options—

Perhaps she could manufacture her own key? Impractical.

Perhaps she could pick the lock. How? She wasn't a thief; she'd no idea how to do such a thing.

But she could learn. She was an excellent student when she wanted to be. And there was no shortage of books to teach her; it was only a question of tracking down the right ones.

Next day, the hunt began.

It took a while to locate the information she needed. Having explored several blind alleys, she finally found what she sought in, of all things, *A True Account of the*

Amatory Adventures and Daring Exploits of the Gallant Lodovunio, Famous Captain of the Watch in Feyenne, as Penned by his Own Hand. It seemed that the gallant and famous Captain—enamored of, as he put it, "a titled Lady whose Honor is Preserv'd by Anonymity"—had broken into the locked and guarded mansion of his target. Foiling the vigilance of the lady's rabidly jealous husband, he had—but that was beside the point. What really mattered was Lodovunio's method of lock-picking, which was set forth in boastful detail, complete with diagrams.

She needed a few tools; most notably, a selection of slim steel lengths, which she managed to pick up here and there, about the kitchen, the book bindery, and the utility closets.

The gallant Lodovunio would have been proud of her. She practiced for a time on padlocked tool chests. Armed with the proper instruments, she achieved good results. Insertion, sensitive maneuvering, pressure, *click,* and the lock fell open. Astonishing. Satisfying, too. But so unexpectedly easy; did people ever guess how easy?

Thereafter, she graduated to locked sheds, locked trunks in the storage rooms, even the locked kitchen cold-cabinet, for bacon and buttered bread at midnight. The food was good; the sense of illicit power even better. She was Mistress of Locks. She could go where she pleased, when she pleased. She might be a child, a foreigner and orphan, a *little, beggarly, Rhazaullean savage,* trapped on Fruce Isle, but she wasn't altogether helpless.

But was she ready to tackle the crypt? Shalindra believed that she was. Unfortunately, the nocturnal sortie would cost her her week's candle—

Ridiculous. The library candles were kept in a locked storage room on the second floor. And she was Mistress of Locks. She didn't need to worry about candles ever again.

Autumn midnight—or very likely later, for she'd lost all track of time—and excitement kept her wide awake. They weren't coming tonight, she finally decided. Otherwise, they'd have appeared by now. Beyond doubt, she was free to move.

She climbed down from the shelf without a sound and without disturbing a single book, then paused a moment to light a stolen candle, with the aid of a purloined flint, steel, and tinderbox. These last three items she meant to return to the storage room before the end of the night; otherwise, they could be missed, and the ensuing investigation was likely to prove inconvenient. For the first time, it occurred to her that the candle itself might be missed. True, the box in the storage room contained hundreds. But Under Librarian Kufune was precise in his accounting of inventory, and might very well keep count, in which case—Shalindra shook her head. She wasn't, she decided, really cut out for a life of crime.

Candle in hand, she stole along the corridor, through the arch and onto the landing, then down a few steps to crouch beneath the NO ADMITTANCE sign. Out came her steel instruments. She tried one in the keyhole, tried another; poked, prodded, jiggled; heard the telltale metallic snap, and felt the lock yield. *Good old Lodovunio.*

The door swung soundlessly on its well-oiled hinges. She stood. Skin prickling, she stepped through, pulling the door shut behind her, and started at the sharp sudden click of the bolt thrusting home. The spring-lock had automatically refastened itself, and if her illicit skills should somehow fail her, then she was trapped in this place.

Not the time to think of it.

The stairs descended another few feet, and after that—

Shalindra halted, eyes popping. She'd expected a modest chamber, hollowed out of the rock; a few old tombs, a few old books, nothing more. But the catacombs she now beheld were immense, a triumph of engineering, no doubt the work of many lifetimes. Before her stretched a broad, barrel-vaulted tunnel, its recesses lost in distant shadows untouched by the light of her single candle. Cut into the walls of the tunnel at regular intervals were recesses large and deep enough to qualify as small chambers. She gazed into the nearest, and her jaw dropped. The little room was filled with human bones, presumably the remains of deceased librarians. Scores of skulls lining half the height of the walls on three sides were fitted neatly as stones in a well-constructed hearth. Above these rounded ramparts, elaborate designs of bone adorned the granite walls. There were bleached starbursts of tibiae and fibulae, each radiating from a central core of massed metatarsals and metacarpals; pelvises like great white butterflies hovering above delicate spiky flowers of phalanges; pale cold branches of radii and ulnae; serpentine vertebrae coiling about the branches; and overhead, depending from the curved ceiling, a chandelier of patellae, with graceful projecting ribs to support the candles. At the center of the recess loomed an imposing upright figure; a complete human skeleton, draped in a hooded woolen robe of black. This figure occupied an obvious place of honor. The bones accorded such respect must have belonged to a person of importance, most likely The Librarian's predecessor. Perhaps The Librarian herself might one day occupy a similar niche.

On she went along the tunnel, and the bones were innumerable, and the variety of their arrangement upon the walls awesome. The initial shock soon wore off, and she began to appreciate the artistry. The designs were wonderfully executed, really quite beautiful in their own macabre way.

But did the librarians of Fruce—a small group of them, at least—assemble in this place by night to admire artistry? Not likely. She hadn't found an answer yet.

On further, and as she went, the still air seemed to die around her. The darkness pressed hard upon her small bubble of light, and her lungs began to labor. The deep interior portions of the crypt, she soon divined, were the oldest. The upright skeletons were clothed in ancient rags, and the air was almost unbreathable. In ages past, the Frucian builders must have hewed a passage hundreds of feet straight through solid rock to the very heart of their island, to create—?

On along the tunnel, through a region of eccentric osseous mobiles, where the bones—exquisitely balanced upon their invisible wires—hovered swaying in midair, and the tiny breeze of her passing set them clacking like deathly windchimes. On toward the center, the oldest and earliest section of the crypt, and here the air was so foul that she feared suffocation. Then, blessedly, a distinct stirring of the atmosphere, a faint current of relatively fresh air, and she could breathe again.

She had reached the end of the tunnel, the center of Fruce Isle, and she found herself in a great chamber whose far walls and lofty ceiling were lost in darkness. But somewhere, invisible overhead, there had to be ventilation shafts piercing the entire vast thickness of the granite.

Shalindra paused, striving to sense the place.

Old, old, old. Goes back forever, and beyond. I don't think Fruce was always a library . . . Something else before . . .

Half eager, half fearful, she advanced, trying to look in all directions at once. No good; the place was too large, and the light too low. She could see sarcophagi, a lot of them, crusted with crudely powerful bas-relief figures; carvings and bones upon the walls; niches housing upright skeletons, so old that their robes had rotted away; shallow charred basin hollowed out of the floor, at the center of the room, and looming above the basin, a hugely monstrous stone carving rampant upon its tall granite base.

Hesitantly, she approached the statue. The weak, jumpy light of her candle seemed to animate a figure large of horned head, long of tooth and neck, armed with a double-bladed stone dagger—

Horrid. What IS that thing? Some old god or demon? Some old librarian?

No time to theorize, for vibration trembled the sluggish air, and a low humming of voices approached.

I thought they weren't coming tonight!

Wrong. Again.

She couldn't begin to guess what they'd do if they caught her.

Hiding place. FAST.

The nearest wall niche housed a skeleton still clothed in trailing tatters. Shalindra jumped for the niche, ducked behind the bony occupant, and hunkered down, back pressed hard to the granite. Just in time, she remembered to snuff her candle. The black void swallowed her alive.

Footsteps, voices, golden glow of lamplight, and a dozen Fruce librarians entered.

Shalindra's breath all but stopped. They would spot her, of course. Or else they would hear the pounding of her heart.

But they did not. They came in quietly. Their lamplight filled the entire chamber, but they scarcely glanced at their surroundings. Their eyes fastened upon the monstrous statue—

No. Upon its base.

The group halted, and its leader advanced alone. Kneeling, The Librarian ran her hand along the decorative border carved into the foot of the base, found what she wanted, and pressed. Echoes magnified the slight scraping of stone. A panel swung open.

Lips parted, Shalindra peered from her hiding place. Ancient bones, musty rags, and living bodies obscured her view, but she glimpsed a large compartment in the base of the statue. Within the compartment lay books, scrolls, and some sort of vessel—a vase?

The Librarian reached in to withdraw a large urn of lustrous, translucent stone; alabaster, perhaps. Rising, she turned to face her colleagues, and somehow her straight-spined stance, strong features, and sweeping dark robes suited the grimly fantastic setting. When she spoke, her voice rang through the great chamber.

"Librarians of Fruce, and members of the Conclave. Tonight marks the culmination of our efforts. For the first time, we test the procedure we have all struggled so long and so hard to perfect. Should we achieve success, our accomplishment extends new hope to the countless wretched ghosts, chained throughout the ages to this physical plane, prisoners and slaves to the will of necromancers.

"We of the Conclave can scarcely diminish, much less control, the pernicious prevalence of necromancy. Our development of the FSD107-N formula, however, appears to present a practical means of assisting the necromantic victims. Tonight, we finally attempt a mass spectral liberation. Should our method prove effective, then generations of captive ghosts may expect eventual deliverance—but enough of that. We are all aware of our labor's significance.

"And now, my colleagues, to work. It is time to prepare our minds, to link our thoughts, to merge our hearts, to think and respond for this short span as a single entity. Come, let us begin."

Thus concluding her brief address, The Librarian reached into the urn to withdraw something small—perhaps a pinch of powder, or a pill—which she conveyed to her lips. She swallowed, then passed the vessel to her nearest colleague, who likewise dipped, swallowed, and handed it on. The final librarian to sample the contents restored the urn to its place in the compartment beneath the statue.

Thereafter, things grew more confusing. As Shalindra watched in fascination, the Conclave membership linked arms—they had, she noted, formed a circle about the shallow basin at the foot of the statue—and then they began to declaim rhythmically. Or perhaps they were chanting, or maybe ranting. Whatever they were doing, she couldn't make any sense of it, for the words were unintelligible, and the voices overlapped, cutting into and across one another chaotically. Almost it hurt to listen, but that did not last long. The chanting continued, and gradually the jumbled, warring voices began to harmonize, then synchronize. Presently the Conclave members stood chanting in perfect unison, incomprehensible syllables emerging simultaneously and identically from a dozen throats.

They must, Shalindra decided, be following The Librarian's orders to link themselves. Just how they were actually accomplishing this wasn't clear, but it probably had something to do with the contents of that urn they'd just been dipping into. And maybe the actual words they were sing-speaking were part of it, and maybe some other things as well—magical mental things, of which she could know nothing.

The voices swelled—moaning manic gibberish somehow resolving itself to something akin to an alien music; plaintive, insistent, hovering upon the verge of intelligibility. And when it seemed that she could all but understand the words, the import of which loomed increasingly vital—when she sensed the imminence of a vast revelation —the sound broke off. At that instant, fire leapt from the shallow pit at the circle's center. Shalindra stiffened. She had seen no one set flame to fuel; the roaring combustion seemed spontaneous. The smoke rose to exit through invisible channels.

Silent and motionless now, the Conclave members stood staring into the fire. Their arms remained linked, their circle unbroken. Some of them stood with their backs to the hidden observer. The faces she could see, however, while differing widely in feature, were uncannily alike in expression, or lack thereof. Blank masks, all of them; unaware, almost deathlike. She might have imagined that consciousness had lapsed, but for the sense— distinct and almost tangible—of collective mental activity all but sizzling the air.

They stood there petrified for such a long time that Shalindra's attention began to diffuse, and the questions bubbled in her brain. It was clear their efforts had failed. What were they doing, anyway? And why? How was it

that The Librarian, having roundly condemned the practice of necromancy minutes earlier, now led her colleagues
in magical enterprise? She'd preached a bit, and spoken of
"mass spectral liberation." What exactly did that mean?

A sudden change in the quality of the air snagged
Shalindra's notice. She couldn't account for it. The Conclave stood frozen, and all remained outwardly unaltered,
but there had been a *change*. The gooseflesh rose along her
forearms, and she was afraid again. An instant later, she
knew why.

Ghosts were appearing about the chamber, *all* about
the chamber. The great room held the mortal remains of
hundreds, of whom some score now manifested themselves; that score presumably composed of those expiring
in a state of extreme disquietude. There were men and
women both, although the latter were greatly outnumbered. Their ages ranged from youth to extreme old age.
Judging by their costumes and jewelry, their social status
and epoques likewise varied. And it was possible to judge
by such things, for the ghostly crowd was remarkably
well-defined.

Shalindra had never before witnessed a demonstration
of real magic; her mother had seen to that. But she had
often heard that the ghosts hauled from the grave by necromantic art were wispy, insubstantial things, hovering
upon the smudged verge of visibility. Not these, however.
Every detail of face, figure, and costume was perfectly resolved. She could count the individual stitches upon embroidered sleeves; she could spot the imperfections of
long-vanished complexions. But for their transparency,
their uniformly grayish hue, and their obvious weight-
lessness, the figures would almost have seemed material.

The ghosts appeared alarmed even distraught. This
emotion Shalindra viewed at close range when the skeleton
behind which she crouched suddenly vented a floating figure; male, plump face and body, long lovelocks of an earlier age, clothing of a rich Visiting Scholar—and dark

bloody slashes marking his throat. Most probably suicide, the not-uncommon response of underqualified scholars.

As the ghost ascended, the hem of its robe brushing her face, Shalindra could not repress her small shriek of alarm. The sound echoed through the chamber silent save for the crackling of the fire. The ghosts noticed, and their pale lost eyes turned to the niche. The librarians, however, heard nothing. Faces emptier than the faces of the dead, they stood petrified, unaware of an illicit living presence in their midst. Shalindra automatically followed the collective tranced gaze. Whatever they saw in the fire was invisible to her. There *was* nothing to see. Despite the apparently unorthodox method of ignition, it was just an ordinary blaze—that suddenly went blue and silent. The flames danced vigorously as ever, but their popping crackle ceased. The frozen members of the Conclave stood bathed in eerie cold light, and now the familiar faces were almost unrecognizable, scarcely alive at all. With difficulty, Shalindra repressed her startled exclamation. The ghosts seemed not to do likewise. Their jaws wagged, their transparent lips moved, but no sound emerged; at least, none audible to the uninitiated.

The shades were drifting in restless confusion. Many sought escape. Several made for the passageway, others for the air ducts overhead; but some nameless force bound them to the central chamber. Half a dozen clustered about the exit, tugging upon invisible restraints and voicelessly keening, their struggles and lamentations equally useless.

Shalindra's fears began to subside. These ancient captive remnants were uncanny, but pitiable. She could actually feel sorry for them. The Librarian had expressed similar sentiments. Her eyes jumped to the tall robed figure, erect and motionless before the fire. The Conclave continued frozen and seemingly unaware, yet the sense of intense, almost violent mental energy emanating from the circle was stronger than ever.

Shalindra's attention fixed on the living, and as she

looked on, they concluded their effort. Twelve heads lifted as one, twelve toneless voices spoke as one:

"Be free."

The fire flared, blue flames leaping for the ceiling. Shalindra flinched, but the librarians never stirred. The ghosts, feverishly agitated, rushed about the great chamber like rags of fog driven by psychic winds. For a few moments, the air was dim and seething with them. And then, the weightless forms began to fade—initially an alteration so gradual and subtle as to seem a trick of the flickering light; within moments, unmistakably, a swift and steady lightening.

The ghosts were—astonished. In the eyes of some, as they faded to the very edge of visible reality, Shalindra thought to glimpse a kind of disbelieving hope. But there was little time to analyze spectral reaction. An instant later, they were gone; the room empty of all save human presence. The fire sank, resuming its original color. The crackle of the flames was once more audible. Likewise audible—the deep sigh of expelled breath as the Conclave sank exhausted to its knees. Arms dropped, breaking the links of the circle; individuality reasserted itself.

As the fire within the pit died, several librarians collapsed, sprawling full length upon the stone floor. Others knelt motionless, shoulders sagging and heads adroop. Thus they remained for long minutes, until a measure of strength returned, and they began to drag themselves upright. Some needed assistance. The combined efforts of two colleagues were required to lift Under Librarian Oruno to his feet. When they were all standing, and more or less themselves again, realization of their success began to take hold. Smiling nods and handclasps followed, but all weak and languid. The Conclave members were clearly drained to the point of exhaustion. There was no conversation. A moment more they lingered, then took their plodding leave, carrying the light with them.

The footsteps receded. Shalindra sat alone in the absolute darkness of a chamber unhaunted for the first time in centuries.

What the Venerators might make of that one! she thought. Wonder warred with raging curiosity.

For several minutes longer she sat there, the darkness pressing upon her with an almost tangible weight. Time passed, and the sense of oppression increased. When she could stand it no longer—and when she was quite certain that the librarians had departed the crypt—she relit her candle. The world came back, and her breathing eased. Creeping forth from her hiding place, she ran at once to the great statue. Dreadful face upon that thing. Those fangs, those gaping triple nostrils, those *eyes*—she didn't want to look at them. Kneeling, in imitation of The Librarian, she ran her fingers along the lower edge of the decorative border carved into the granite base. Nothing. She tried again, and this time her middle finger encountered a small hole in the stone. She poked experimentally. Inside, a movable piece, a button or tab worn very smooth. She pressed hard. Stone scraped stone, and the panel opened. Within the compartment—the urn, the books, the scrolls.

Setting her candle aside on the floor, Shalindra withdrew the urn. Polished alabaster, cool and smooth in her hands. She dipped inside to withdraw a few granules of a white, crystalline substance. It could have been common salt, or sugar, but for its distinctive sparkle. She sniffed cautiously. No odor. She certainly wasn't about to taste it. She brushed the granules back into their container, which she restored to its place. Thereafter, her attention turned to the written matter. Not an extensive collection: eight books, three scrolls, half a dozen contemporary-looking notebooks. She chose one of the books at random; an ancient object with cracked leather binding and fading hand-lettered pages. It was difficult to read the eccentric old print by candlelight, but worth the effort. She discovered at once, not to her surprise, that she held a necromantic text. There were descriptions, explanations, instructions, even beautifully colored and gilded illustrations. Mere possession of such material would be accounted a crime in Rhazaulle. She wasn't certain, but thought it similarly illegal here in Aennorve—even for librarians.

When Jevuni told me there were rare books down here, he wasn't exaggerating.

Her eyes were blurring. The crabbed old print swam. The hour was very late. She was deeply tired, worn out with excitement, alarm, and sleeplessness. She was in no condition to batter her brain upon ancient arcana. For now, she needed rest. Shalindra replaced the book, closed the compartment, took up her candle, and stood. For a moment she let her slow gaze wander over granite carvings, blackened firepit, sarcophagi, robed skeletons. Then she turned and walked out, back along the bone-bedecked passage, all the way back to the closed door whose lock she managed to pick. Exiting the crypt, she made her way to her own chamber. Minutes later she lay abed, asleep and wildly dreaming.

Thereafter, life took on new purpose and meaning. It was stimulating—exciting beyond belief, actually—to have set herself a great, yet attainable goal; to be working toward that goal in utter secrecy, by means so thrillingly forbidden. Frucian existence was all at once far more bearable.

She was down in the crypt almost every night. The tunnel, the recesses, and above all the great inner chamber grew familiar as the book-lined corridors of the library above. She soon grew inured to the sight of the bare bones, the robed skeletons, even the fanged statue. Death's assertive presence in this place no longer troubled her, for she was swiftly learning the vincibility of death. The books, scrolls, and notebooks were teaching her all she needed to know of that.

She studied until she thought her head would burst,

but never for one instant grudged the effort. Knowledge did not come easily; she had little natural affinity for magic. And yet, if she studied hard enough, really stretching her mind, it was possible to absorb some of the material. And she didn't need very much, not really; only enough to accomplish her sole aim.

The old volumes and older scrolls were perhaps the most colorful sources, with their quaint language, their polychrome illuminations, their archaic flavor. They were rich in character and historical interest, but often poor in specifics. When she needed definite information—detailed instruction, clarity—it was to the modern notebooks, containing the records of the Conclave's experiments, that she turned. Meticulous and impersonal, they made for dry reading; but they explained. She learned exactly how to perform the rituals. She learned the significance of each spoken word, each gesture. And she learned the infinitely greater significance of the unspoken, the unseen; the rigorous mental exercises, the self-induced controlled psychic convulsions that generated sorcerous strength.

The Conclave, she perceived, primarily concerned itself with the liberation of the dead; with the destruction of threads binding certain shades to the physical plane of reality. Traditionally, such unfortunates might be released upon an individual basis; a time-consuming and inefficient procedure. The Conclave—purely humanitarian in its own detached way—had sought and discovered a swift means of freeing ghostly gangs. In theory, the method might apply to groups of hundreds or even thousands. In theory, the ghosts of the ages might be freed within the space of a few years.

And the Conclave was methodically testing its theory. Shalindra's studies were frequently interrupted. She'd feel the shiver of atmosphere, sense the vocal hum, and know that they were coming. There would be just enough time to thrust the notebooks back into their compartment, close the panel, dive into the niche behind the now-familiar skeleton that she'd nicknamed "Chubby," and snuff her candle, before a couple of them would enter. That was all, of late. Just one or two, come to fetch the urn, while their colleagues waited in one or another of the recesses, somewhere along the corridor. They were freeing the library ghosts, room by room. The account of their activities was set forth, apparently by day, in the most current of their notebooks; perusal of which informed Shalindra that the presence of thick stone barriers between the various recesses impeded mass liberation.

It wasn't pleasant when the Conclave was in session. The central chamber was empty, but Shalindra dared not relight her candle. Sometimes the librarians would linger for hours, and all through that time, she'd have to sit stilly in the fathomless dark, the smell of Chubby's disintegrating robe sharp in her nostrils, the touch of bony fingertips dry upon her cheek. Sometimes, when the darkness squeezed, and her limbs ached with inactivity, and the skeletons seemed to whisper, she longed for escape; regretting the chance that had brought her to the crypt. Then she'd remind herself of her mission, and doubt would subside.

Her mission. It was true that the Conclave concentrated its efforts upon deliverance, but there were other areas of investigation, additional topics touched upon in books and notebooks; including the matter of spectral communication.

It seemed that the ghosts, neither part of nor free of the material world, inhabited a dimension exempt of certain mundane limitations. For this reason, they sometimes addressed one another across the boundaries of time and space.

This suited her purpose. If she but acquired sufficient power to summon and rule a single ghost, then the spectral servant could gather information.

She would finally learn what had happened to Cerrov.

When she knew where he was, she could send him a letter. Eventually, he would come and take her away with him.

But she couldn't afford to delay too much longer, for the Conclave was systematically liberating shades, and soon there would be none left to summon.

Not much time left. The weeks were flying; likewise the ghosts. Thus, on a damp night in early spring, Shalindra prepared to perform her first experiment in necromancy. She did not, some corner of her mind confessed, feel herself truly ready. But that was probably a groundless fear. She'd studied and practiced for months; she'd be fine. Never mind the queasy nervous stomach and the dry mouth. Once she began, her doubts would evaporate, and everything would be all right.

At midnight, she was down in the crypt. She'd little fear of interruption this time. The members of the Conclave had assembled the previous night, predictably exhausting themselves. Full recovery of sorcerous force required some two days of rest. They would not be back tonight.

She sped straight to the central chamber, beelined for the statue, and opened the panel to withdraw the urn. A quantity of the crystalline contents went into the pocket of her skirt. Restoring the urn to its place, she paused a moment for a quick final review of the pertinent passages in one of the notebooks; then replaced the notebook, closed the panel, and left the room.

Back along the passageway she hurried, in search of a recess yet inhabited. Easily located. The librarians, methodical as always, had painted small white marks alongside the entrances of the chambers they'd visited. There were not very many left free of marks, she noted; but one was all she needed.

Selecting one of the few remaining unmarked recesses, she stepped in and looked around her. Scores—no, hundreds—of skulls lining the walls. Upright draped skeleton. Big femurs, humeri, and patellae decorating the walls. Somewhere, in the midst of all these mortal remains, a ghost or two must linger.

She set her candle aside. Now came the scary part—she'd have to ingest a dose of FSD107-N, whose list of ingredients included several poisons. An absolutely essential step in the procedure, however; no way out of it. Shalindra dipped into her pocket. Her hand was shaking a little, and that wouldn't do, as fear would undermine the intense mental control that her task demanded. In any case, there was nothing to be afraid of. She'd watched librarians gobble the stuff dozens of times, and it had never harmed *them*. Quickly, so as not to taste, she dropped a pinch of white grains onto her tongue, and swallowed.

Odd. She felt distinctly odd. There were tinglings along her nerves, and closed doors opening inside her head, and light in her veins, and alien perceptions, and she had no idea if it was right. The notebooks of the Conclave had told her what she should do, but they never told her how she should feel.

She shook her head as if to rouse herself from a trance. To work. She needed to focus her thoughts. The anxiety and confusion were still there, distracting her. The exercises—she needed to remember—

She followed the procedure precisely. Her mind was obedient now, her concentration more than adequate, and the gestures she'd practiced for so many weeks were fluid and sure. But it still wasn't easy, it couldn't be right, because she was starting to feel decidedly sick. She was nauseated, and there was a hot pain searing the back of her skull.

Not the time to think about it.

But it couldn't be right.

Thought, will, vision, total concentration of all that she was, and something was happening. Her mind was *doing* something, struggling with something, but why did her head hurt so much, and why had the light in her veins turned to fire?

She pressed on, and the vibration in her throat told her that the syllables were pouring out of her. But she couldn't hear a thing; her hearing had attuned itself otherwise and elsewhere.

A final brain-crushing effort, and she felt her mind fastening on to something that struggled, dragging it forcibly into the light. Blinking, she opened her eyes.

Nothing there.

But there had to be, she knew it, she felt it. Shalindra squinted into the shadows. And yes, there in the corner—a faint, transparent, nearly invisible shred of vapor; nebulous, but perceptibly human of outline. Its features were invisible; its sex, indeterminate; its existence, pathetically tenuous. But it was there.

No time for triumph. She didn't know if she could hold the ghost for long. The creature was resisting, and she herself was growing sicker by the moment. Best to act quickly, before control broke.

Is my brother Cerrov Haudrensq alive and well? She didn't know if she spoke aloud, or in her mind, or both. She didn't even know if the shade could understand her.

There was no reply in words, but she caught impulses, faint emotion, jumbled impressions, weakly trickling across dimensions. The ghost understood the question. The ghost did not want to be here. There was confused agitation, incomprehension. The ghost knew nothing at all about Cerrov.

Find out. Right now.

She felt that the ghost didn't understand the concept of "now." She sensed miserable reluctance. Too bad. Shalindra exerted her will; it seemed in a way like clenching her fist. There was an impression of retreat, of distance that was not distance, and the wispy form in the corner flickered. She held on with her mind, but there was nothing to hold on to; all was streaming like water through

her fingers. The ghost was going—gone—somewhere
else—

Escaped. And back again. *Got it.* There in the corner
again.

Speechless spectral affirmation.

No words, but no doubt. Cerrov was alive and well.
Where?

But the impressions reaching her were fainter now, or
perhaps the pain in her head was blotting them out. The
ghost was flickering, Shalindra was tottering and clinging
to something elusive, clinging desperately with all the
strength of her mind—

Desperation was fatal. Her focus wavered, and in that
instant, the ghost—was not. She stood alone in the crypt,
and she was sick, so sick she couldn't stay on her feet. She
dropped to her knees. Her stomach heaved. She was about
to vomit, and if she did, she'd have to find a way of clean-
ing it up, or the Conclave members would discover the
mess and guess the truth—she couldn't afford to let it
happen. She collapsed prone upon the stone floor; rolled
over onto her back, and lay still, breathing deeply. Presently the qualm subsided, but the pain was still there,
flaming all through her body, rioting in her skull—

She thought she must be dying. She didn't want to die
here. The Conclave members would discover the mess and
guess the truth—

Shalindra attempted to rise and found that she could
not. The effort set her limbs shaking, her fears swirling.
What's happened to me? But she couldn't just lie there, she
had to get away, back to her room, her bed—

A few minutes later she tried again, this time lifting
herself to her knees. That was as far as she got. Standing
was impossible. If she wanted to move, she'd have to
crawl. This she proceeded to do, dragging along on all
fours, candle gripped in one hand, head hanging, knees
bruising themselves on the granite floor.

The tunnel was endless, and her progress was snaillike; creeping advance interrupted by frequent dizzy spells. Many such attacks she weathered, supine and motionless, but at last a terrible flood of giddiness, overwhelming her in a sick fraction of a second, sent the candle sliding from her hand to the floor. The light went out, and the blackness clamped down on her like the jaws of a trap. She couldn't see, she couldn't breathe. Gasping, mouth and eyes wide open, she felt about her desperately. No candle; it must have rolled. She'd never find it. And she'd never find her way out of this place. She *would* die here.

Terror all but unhinged her then. For a few moments she was mindless, shuddering and whimpering upon the floor. And as she lay there, buried alive, it seemed to her, although she may have been dreaming, that she felt another presence close beside her in the dark. A familiar, uncanny presence, far stronger now that it came of its own accord. The ghost was with her again, and now she thought she could feel its incorporeal touch upon her face, and even hear its formerly human voice whispering inside her head. Female voice; the words faint, but distinguishable:

Leave us alone.

"Go away." No reply. Disembodied touch again upon her throat. She could not rule the creature *now*. Phantom fingers on her face, seeking her eyes in the dark, and no controlling them, no escaping them, and the panic was rising to choke her—

But there was another voice:

Consider options, formulate alternate strategies . . .

Shalindra took a few deep breaths. *Calm*. She lay perfectly still, cheek pressed to the floor, and waited for the frenzied race of her heart to slow. *Calm*. While she waited, she thought. She'd been nearing the end of the tunnel when the light went out. The stairs and the door were straight ahead, only a few yards distant. The wall would

guide her. Presently—still dizzy and sick, but determined
—she raised herself and made her way to the wall, which
she followed on hands and knees. She reached the stairs
and somehow pushed herself up them, to crouch before the
door, fiddling blindly with her purloined pick for an indeterminate period.

Minutes or eons later, the lock yielded, the door
opened, and she was out of the crypt. Faint moonlight
beaming through the library windows seemed almost diurnal by comparison to the unrelieved blackness behind
her. The silent book-lined corridors stretched endlessly
ahead. She couldn't crawl all the way back to her room,
and she had to get there. Call for help? *No.* Leaning her
weight on the nearest bookshelf, she hauled herself to her
feet. Heavily reliant upon the shelf's support, she staggered down the hall. Later, there were other shelves, walls,
doorjambs to help keep her on her feet. The world narrowed to the next ten feet of corridor before her, and then
the ten after that. Mental activity all but ceased. She was
taken almost by surprise when she found she'd reached her
own room.

She entered, closing the door behind her. The atmosphere was suffocating, unbearably hot. Her flesh seemed
to burn, and her thirst was dreadful. Stripping her clothes
off, she fell into bed, and consciousness dwindled, but was
not altogether lost, for somehow she still seemed to feel
immaterial fingers wandering her face, fingers that could
not be evaded, no matter how desperately she thrashed and
flailed; and a ghostly voice that whispered and would not
stop, no matter how loudly she pleaded or screamed.

When Shalindra woke, she found herself lying in bed in
the gloomy ground-floor chamber that served as the library infirmary. She was wearing a nightgown, and a
damp cloth rested cool upon her forehead. Automatically,
her hand rose to her throat. The locket was there, and safe.

She had no idea how long she'd been in this room, or

how she had come. She did not give these matters a great deal of thought, for her mind seemed unfit to deal with puzzles. Dreamily, she regarded the ceiling. It was quiet in the infirmary. There were no ghostly voices here. She slept again.

She was a good deal more clearheaded the next time she opened her eyes. Assistant Librarian Chessuni, the closest thing the library had to a physician, was in the room with her. She was his only patient. Chessuni informed her that she'd lain alternately raving and insensible in the infirmary for the past three days. How long before that she'd fallen ill, he did not know, but the sound of delirious moans issuing from her room had alerted her fellow students to her plight. Now that she was conscious and lucid again, he entertained no doubt of her recovery.

He never questioned the nature of her illness, blithely dismissing the fever as "the blood's heated consumption of polluted humors, a drastic form of self-purification." Certainly, he never suspected the real cause, but then, Assistant Librarian Chessuni was not a member of the Conclave.

She was young, and she mended rapidly. Within hours, she could sit up in bed to accept light nourishment. Shortly thereafter, she was able to stand. Six days later—wobbly but essentially well—she was released from the infirmary. Returning to her own room, she found it just as she had left it—the bed jumbled, and clothes lying on the floor where she had dropped them. Fortunate that they remained untouched, for one of her skirt pockets contained a lockpick, and the other, a quantity of FSD107-N. The pick she hid deep inside her mattress; while the white grains fit neatly into the hollow behind Cerrov's miniature portrait in the locket.

This done, she found herself somewhat at a loss. Dr. Chessuni had warned her against overexertion, but these instructions were redundant. She was still weak, devoid of energy, and curiously devoid of spirit. For want of anything better to do, she returned to her books, immersing herself for the next couple of weeks in the study of Proto-Strellian. She was now reading *The Lay of Warrior Grylgh* in the original. Grylgh's improbable adventures proved more absorbing than expected; enough so to divert her thoughts from uncomfortable topics.

And yet, the recollections haunted her brain. The crypt. The ghost. Her experiment in necromancy, and its results. She'd learned that Cerrov was still alive, but she hadn't discovered his whereabouts. The next logical step was all too obvious. She should return to the crypt for a second attempt; the mere thought of which bathed her in cold sweat. She remembered the blind crawl through the tunnel, the touch of ghostly fingers upon her face, the pain and sickness, the fever that had nearly killed her . . . She wasn't altogether over the effects, even yet. Impossible to face all that again; absolutely impossible.

And equally impossible to dismiss the notion. If her nerve failed her now, she might never see her brother again. She might never escape Fruce Isle.

Certain conclusions were inescapable. Her courage gradually returned with her strength. On a mild spring night, exactly one month following the date of her initial attempt, Shalindra forced herself back to the crypt. The place seemed somehow emptier than she remembered, and that was strange, because it looked the same as ever, quite unchanged.

But no—there was a change, a small one. More of the recesses along the length of the tunnel were marked with white paint. Obviously, the Conclave had continued its work. She hurried along the tunnel, glancing left and right as she went. Every recess bore the telltale mark; the librarians had visited them all. The Conclave's task here was complete. The library crypt was thoroughly cleansed, and the ghosts were gone. All of them were gone.

The weak light was jumping, and skeletal shadows danced on the walls. The hand that held the candle was unsteady. Empty-eyed, Shalindra gazed down the passageway, as if staring down the corridor of the long, lonely years.

PART TWO

The Wings of
the Wolf

11

ON AN IRON-HARD morning late in the thirteenth winter of the Ulor Varis I's reign, the thunder of an explosion rattled shutters in Rialsq. The sound came from the vicinity of the Xana Incline, that gentle grade sloping between the Winter Gate of the Zalkhash and the frozen river. Curious citizens flocking to the spot encountered a colorful spectacle. The blast had gouged a great hole in the ice, and into this hole, a ruined black sledge was rapidly sinking. Shards of ice, slivers of glass, and fragments of wood were scattered everywhere. Mangled horses and uniformed men floundered in the freezing water. Others of the wounded bled and screamed upon the ice. Scorched outriders struggled to control their plunging, panicky mounts. Thick smoke drifted over all. The heat of the explosion had raised great clouds of steam, but these condensed almost instantaneously in the frigid air, to dust the site with fine snow.

Behind the sinking sledge stood an open sleigh, undamaged. Out of the sleigh hopped half a dozen men, attired in the gold-crusted scarlet uniforms of the Uloric Guard. Across the ice dashed the Guardsmen, surefooted upon their spiked Rialsqui boots. Initially ignoring the cries of their drowning, freezing comrades, they looked first to the sledge. One of the men produced a steel-tipped wooden pole, with which he fumbled at the handle of the door. Before he managed to engage it, the door opened from within, and the spectators glimpsed a tall, dark-clad figure, familiar but eternally alien.

Without assistance, the Ulor sprang from the sledge to the unbroken ice. He appeared unhurt. There were no visible marks upon him, and his demeanor was characteristically unruffled. True, his angular face was almost grayly pale; but for him, that was usual.

Once safely free of the sinking sledge, the Ulor personally took command of the rescue operation, which thenceforth proceeded efficiently. Half-frozen guardsmen were plucked from the water. The wounded, the hypothermic, and the dead were placed in the sleigh, which sped at once for the Zalkhash; as it happened, no civilians had been harmed. Horses were calmed and restrained; those damaged beyond repair, and those still in the water, were dispatched with pistol shots. Moments later, the black sledge sank from sight. The icy waters of the Xana roiled briefly, then pacified themselves. The Ulor, on the best horse left intact, and accompanied only by a couple of his men, rode off without addressing the fascinated citizens, and without being addressed or approached by a soul. Two of the uninjured officers remained to guard the place until help should arrive to remove the equine carcasses, and to cordon off the gaping hole in the ice. Two others circulated through the crowd, seeking eyewitnesses to the event itself. In this, they were indifferently successful. At least a dozen citizens had seen the initial fiery flash, beneath the horses' hoofs rather than the sledge's body—an evidence of the poor aim that doubtless accounted for the failure of this latest attempt upon the Ulor's life. No one, however, had noticed who had actually thrown the bomb; or at least, no one was telling.

By the time Varis reached the House Uloric, the entire Zalkhash was buzzing with rumors. Everyone had heard conflicting accounts of the incident, but nobody knew which story, if any, to believe. Nor was their master disposed to enlighten them. Upon his return, he merely stated his intention of busying himself in his own office, upon which no intrusion was permissible prior to midday. He then withdrew, habitual composure fully intact. His face was so still, his demeanor so impenetrable, that the closest of his personal attendants would never have guessed that any unusual care oppressed him. But then, the closest of his attendants was not particularly close.

Varis repaired to his own apartment; still the same old apartment, the younger brother's apartment, even after all these years of sovereignty. Still dim, with heavy dark curtains barring daylight, as if the old ocular weakness plagued him still, even after all these years of unimpaired vision.

He dismissed his servants and his secretary, taking particular care to address them each by name, to disguise the fact that he often had trouble remembering their names. They went without demur and without surprise, being well acquainted with their master's peculiarities. All had heard of the failed assassination attempt, but none offered expressions of outrage, commiseration, or encouragement, for the Ulor's manner invited no such familiarity.

Varis found himself alone. Expelling his breath in a quiet sigh, he allowed his shoulders to sag a little. He stood motionless, head bent, for a moment or two; then went into his office, where the correspondence proliferated relentlessly. The basket on his desk was full, as always.

Application never reduced the volume of paper for more than the space of hours. Sometimes the endless accumulation troubled him, as it had never for one instant troubled Hurna (wont to employ the latest petition from the greatest of Noble Landholders as a spill to light his pipe). But it did not trouble him today.

He had thought, in seeking this retreat, to quiet his nerves with a draught of some illicit sort. Now, he decided that he didn't need it. For years, he'd limited his intake of sorcerous substances to the bare minimum needed to stave off physical and mental horrors. He'd found that was best. His health was good, and his mind was clear. And if he missed the old sense of unbridled power—the exaltation and intensity of it—yet his present life offered compensations. Unwelcome spectral visitations were few; old Clotl's irregular shade had not haunted his dreams within the last decade. Hostile fraternal shades might or might not be near. Sometimes he thought to sense inimical presence, and sometimes the faces of dead children wrecked his slumbers, but these things could be dealt with; just as the tremors that now assailed him could be managed without recourse to artificial aids.

He was fully in control.

Varis seated himself at his desk, but turned the uncomfortable chair to face the wall. Leaning back in the ill-padded seat, he steepled his fingers under his chin, and allowed his thoughts to wander. The morning's explosion echoed in his mind. He could still hear the roar of the blast, the crash of shattering ice, the screams of stricken men and horses. He could still feel the shock, the atmospheric blow, the rush of burning air. What he could not sense, however, was the mind of his would-be assassin.

It had not been the first attempt upon his life. There had been other failures over the years, efforts demonstrating varying degrees of homicidal ineptitude. An Ulor secure in his rightful position—Hurna, for example—would have dismissed such attacks as inconsequential, but Varis possessed no such assurance. Impossible to keep from wondering who hated him so greatly, who sought his death, and why. Illogical that any of his own subjects should do so, for he had proved himself a model Ulor.

Years earlier, he had opted for progressive liberality of rule, and the present state of the nation confirmed the wisdom of his choices. Rhazaulle was a power in the world, as she had never been in the past. Royal subsidy of the Truvisq Trading Company, Voytoff Ltd., the Rialsq Syndicate, and other ventures of similar ilk—resulting in the commercial exploitation of hitherto unenlightened regions overseas—had ushered in a new prosperity. Defense of colonies and shipping lines, necessitating expansion and modernization of the navy, had established Rhazaullean preeminence upon the seas; a source of greater prosperity yet.

The Ulor had seen to it that his subjects of all degree and kind shared in the fruits of the new wealth. The ordinary citizen of Rialsq, Truvisq, or Lazimir was better housed, better fed, and better clothed than ever before. His children were better educated. Thanks to the creation of new public schools, open to all, the sons and even the occasional daughter of such folk as shopkeepers, greengrocers, and cabinet makers were learning to read and to write. And the latitude allowed them in their choices was altogether unprecedented. They could read, write, and speak almost anything, short of outright sedition. Never before had Rhazaulleans enjoyed such freedom—and not only the townsfolk.

Within the last decade, Uloric decree had curtailed many of the old feudal privileges of the Noble Landholders. In consequence, the lot of the rural peasantry was vastly improved. Yes, the recent reforms had benefited nearly every Rhazaullean. The Ulor responsible for it all might reasonably expect in return, if not warm affection, at least wholehearted acceptance.

Which was eternally withheld.

It didn't seem to matter what he did, or what he gave them. They never forgot, and they never forgave. Varis's blind stare focused on nothingness. The good years meant little; likewise the good intentions, and the good deeds. The old suspicions lived on in Rhazaullean brains, and it seemed that suspicion was enough.

Nobody could prove a thing against the Ulor. There was not a shred of solid evidence supporting the muttered charges of regicide, fratricide, infanticide, even necromancy. No matter; proof was not required. The mere suspicion—perhaps exacerbated by the Ulor's marked lack of the common touch—fostered undying hostility. Unskilled as he was in gauging human hearts, still he could not fail to observe the sullen coolness of the Rhazaullean crowds (the unconcern of this morning's spectators a perfect case in point); the deferential hypocrisy of his courtiers, among whom he inspired some awe, but no affection; the dutiful indifference of his own closest servants. Many were no doubt loyal to the Wolf Throne. But there was not a man or woman among them granting personal allegiance to the present Ulor. Never the fervent devotion won so effortlessly by golden Hurna; never the firm loyalty that would have belonged to Hurna's children, or to Breziot, or even to Breziot's young offspring. Who were both possibly still alive, somewhere; their location known to King Dasune alone.

A vein in Varis's temple throbbed. First sign of the old, devastating headaches. His jaw was clenched, his neck and shoulders rigid. Deliberate relaxation of all muscles usually served to stave off catastrophe. But perhaps, this time, he *would* treat himself to one of the wondrous powders or potions. This morning, the perennial longing was uncommonly sharp.

But he didn't move yet. His gaze remained fixed on the wall before him, and his mind projected images. The boy, Cerrov. Rightful Ulor of Rhazaulle, and, if still alive, now grown to manhood. His sister, likewise an adult, if alive. But the probability of their survival was low. So many years had passed, and none of the busy uloric agents had ever succeeded in dredging up the slightest clue as to the whereabouts of the missing siblings subsequent to their disappearance from Feyenne. Which meant, most likely, that there were no clues, because the pair had died long ago. Illness, mishap, assassination—something must have finished them, for such prolonged invisibility was otherwise unlikely.

Of course, he would have preferred certainty; in hope whereof, he'd often resorted to necromancy. Repeatedly, in earlier years of his reign, he'd sent the subservient ghosts ranging far and wide in search of Breziot's children. Such spies, however, had always failed; for the threads binding spectre to mortal remains, while decidedly elastic, were not unlimited in their ability to stretch. The ghosts might hunt the length and breadth of Rhazaulle, but they were hardly capable of carrying the search to foreign lands. Their reports had been inconclusive, but it scarcely mattered. Cerrov and Shalindra were almost certainly dead, even if his Majesty Dasune of Aennorve was sometimes pleased to hint otherwise.

Varis's brows contracted, and his head throbbed a warning. Dasune. A thorn in his side for the past thirteen years. Always shifty, subtle, manipulative. Usually unpredictable. Frequently treacherous. And of late—dangerous, unlikely though it seemed.

The Ulor's headache gathered strength. Even as his temples pounded, his lips assumed an ironic bend. Thirteen years earlier, he hadn't recognized the potential Aennorvi threat. Back then, Dasune had appeared a weak petitioner; debtor-monarch of a decadent nation, in financial thrall to the Dhreve of Immeen, militarily feeble, dependent upon the patronage of vigorous Rhazaulle. And so it had been, at the time. It would have taken a clairvoyant, if such existed, to foresee the Aennorvi recovery. Only a clairvoyant could have predicted the opening of the Brilliance Gallery in the diamond mines at Jumo, the spoils of which had replenished the depleted Aennorvi treasury. Only a clairvoyant could have dreamed that the Jumoese windfall would facilitate activation of the apparently fanciful loophole clause in the Czennivhor Islands lease, a clause permitting penalty-free prepayment and termination of the contract. And surely it would have taken at least two clairvoyants to foresee the historically improbable, culturally unstable Aennorvi-Immeenish alliance that currently posed such a threat to Rhazaullean welfare.

Rhazaulle and Aennorve were rivals now. All but inconceivable, thirteen years ago, but there was nothing ridiculous about it these days. Aennorve's fleet was large, well-equipped, and modern; plenty of strength there to challenge Rhazaullean dominance in the Sea of Immeen, plenty of strength to defend those alluring diamond mines at Jumo, and even strength to establish and protect Aennorvi colonies in remote savage areas all but crying out for Rhazaullean development.

Worse yet—intolerable, in fact—were the recent Aennorvi attacks upon Rhazaullean vessels along the merchant shipping routes; depredations of which King Dasune blandly disclaimed knowledge. Random acts of piracy committed upon the high seas equally outraged all civilized nations, in the King's opinion. The offended citizens of Rhazaulle claimed his Majesty's sincerest sympathies, together with his solemn oath that no Aennorvi effort should be spared in bringing the lawless captains to justice.

Very decent of Dasune, most gracious; but somewhat less than reassuring, in view of the fact that the funds to outfit the pirate vessels had come straight out of his Majesty's Privy purse.

How best to deal with such duplicity? By matching or

exceeding it. Recent, secret negotiations with Queen Xoxibah of the Nine Blessed Oorexi Tribes had, at considerable expense, secured that monarch's promise to rescind
the old Aennorvi right-of-way through the forests of
Oorex. Given the Blessed Tribesmen's legendary expertise
with blowguns and poisoned darts, the exclusion carried
weight. Overland route from Jumo effectively blocked, the
Aennorvis would be compelled to send their diamonds
home by boat; their course inevitably carrying them to the
Rhazaullean-controlled Yome Channel, where the extor-
tionate tolls imposed upon Aennorvi vessels would more
than compensate for recent Rhazaullean losses. The Aennorvi economy would quake.

King Dasune and his Council were shortly in for a
highly unpleasant surprise. Of course, it was quite possible
that his Majesty—whose intelligence network equalled or
even surpassed Varis's own—already recognized his pre-
dicament. In which case, how would an old fox caught in a
trap react? With fury? Desperation? Enough to attempt
assassination of Rhazaulle's Ulor?

Unconsciously, Varis shook his head. His own removal
would scarcely benefit Aennorve. The agreement with
Queen Xoxibah would stand, and the next Ulor—probably one of the distant Haudrensq cousins—would almost
certainly follow his predecessor's lead. Assassination,
changing nothing, would serve no practical purpose; and
King Dasune was above all politically practical. Whatever
the state of his personal passions, he would never pursue a
policy devoid of advantage. No, it was never the will of
Dasune that launched this morning's attack.

Who, then? The Venerators? They were fanatics; and,
somehow divining his necromantic affinities, they'd always
hated him. But the murderous energies of the Venerators
were, these days, largely devoted to the extermination of
that heretical sect arising among them known as the Colloquists. It seemed that the Colloquists, dedicated as their
more conservative brethren to the welfare of the dead, had

hit upon the revolutionary notion of spectral colloquy, wherein ghosts were, for the first time, actually besought to express their own desires and preferences. Such colloquy demanded recourse to necromancy, which was, in Venerator eyes, inherently abominable, notwithstanding the worthiness of intended application. The Colloquists had persevered, but had wisely done so in secret, and now the Venerators were busy hunting their erstwhile colleagues zestfully all through Rhazaulle. Their attention thus engaged, they probably weren't responsible for the bombing.

Who, then? Random lunatic? Personal enemy? Political zealot?

Varis's cogitations were interrupted by a knocking upon his office door. It was not yet midday. His instructions had been clear, and his servants were obedient. Not a one of them would dare disturb him without good cause.

"Come," he said.

A footman entered, bearing a dispatch marked "Highly Urgent." Varis dismissed the servant with a nod. Alone again, he broke the seal and scanned the contents. The communication, penned by the hand of Rear Admiral Tsupalov aboard the flagship *Vindicator,* reported the devastation of the Rhazaullean fleet at Yome. The fast new Aennorvi warships, launching a surprise attack at dawn, had succeeded in sinking half the Rhazaullean vessels and disabling half the remainder. Those still seaworthy had taken flight, leaving the Yome Channel aswarm with Aennorvi men-of-war, and securely in the hands of the enemy.

Varis set the dispatch aside carefully. Once again, his old nemesis proved unpredictable. He had never expected Dasune to go so far or to dare so much; at least, not so soon. For Aennorvi sea power, despite its great expansion in recent years, did not as yet match Rhazaulle's. And Dasune was unlikely to commit his resources to an unequal contest, unless the advantage was his. It did not appear to be so in this case, but perhaps his Majesty possessed hidden strength.

The headache was now impossible to ignore. Circumstances warranting some self-indulgence, Varis permitted himself a dose of grayish concentrate that banished pain and eased taut nerves. Thus fortified, confident, and even optimistic, an hour later he addressed his assembled Council to inform the Noble Landholders that the states of Rhazaulle and Aennorve were at war.

The faces around him reflected mixed emotions. Indignation. Scorn of the knavish enemy launching an attack prior to the formal declaration of war that the jealous honor of the times demanded. Bellicosity. And finally, a surprise to equal the Ulor's own at the recklessness of the Aennorvi King.

But the mystery resolved itself two days later, with the arrival of his Majesty's belated declaration, addressed *To the Usurper Varis Haudrensq, Falsely Styling Himself Ulor of Rhazaulle, at the Zalkhash, in Rialsq.*

Never had royal correspondence assumed a loftier tone. In grandly turned phrases, Dasune expressed the horror and outrage with which all civilized beings must regard the present Rhazaullean regime. Righteously condemning the crimes and debaucheries of the reigning usurper, "upon whom the discerning Eye cannot rest without Disgust and Loathing," his Majesty expressed profound sympathy for the "suffering, downtrodden People of Rhazaulle;" and concluded with a pledge of support to the cause of Cerrov Haudrensq, "true Heir to the Wolf Throne, rightful Ulor of Rhazaulle, miraculously preserved and providentially restored to the Light, Leader and Savior of his oppressed Nation." Never a word about Jumoese diamonds, commercial rivalries, economic woes. Only justice, nothing but justice.

Seated upon the Wolf Throne, Ulor Varis read the document aloud to his Council in tones scrupulously clear and carrying. Upon conclusion, he looked up, allowing his attentive gaze to travel slowly from face to face.

Silence greeted the Aennorvi denunciation; a restless

stirring of seated bodies, a sidewise shifting of uneasy eyes. Comfortless silence continued, until one of the more obsequious of Noble Landholders opined, "Spew of a notorious liar. An insult to Rhazaulle's honor."

Muttering agreement from the Noble Landholders, whose reserve spoke volumes.

King Dasune might be shameless, but never unintelligent. The nature of his hidden resources now revealed itself. He expected Rhazaulleans to flock by the thousands to the cause of this (probably) false Cerrov. His Majesty did not himself seek to overcome the Ulor; he meant the Ulor's own subjects to do the job.

Ensuing weeks witnessed conflict in the Sea of Immeen, the Sea of Ice, and the Gulf of Strell. Exchanges were bloody, but ultimately inconclusive; while control of the vital Yome Channel remained in Aennorvi hands. There was as yet no battle fought on land, however, and would not be for weeks or months to come. It was common knowledge throughout Rhazaulle that the Imposter, as agents of Uloric authority insisted Dasune's young protégé be labeled, methodically readied his Aennorvi-financed troops for invasion. Nature and necessity conspired to delay the attack, however. Winter had ended, and with the spring came thaws transforming all the land into a giant bog across which no army could hope to travel.

King Dasune made good use of the respite. His Majesty's spies were everywhere in Rhazaulle. Their task—to carry the news of Cerrov Haudrensq's return to the populace, and, if possible, to whip up local support. Thus, the illicit pamphlets, broadsides, and circulars flooded every town and hamlet. The eloquent harangued in the taverns, the candlelit cellars, and the secret meeting places. So receptive an audience did these agents find among folk whose notion of a sane universe demanded immutably ordered Uloric succession, that presently the Imposter's partisans were rioting in every major Rhazaullean city.

The Ulor Varis likewise made effective use of his time —conferring with his generals, ordering preparations, personally quelling civil demonstrations, systematically rallying and wooing the citizens. In this last endeavor, the Ulor proved surprisingly effective. His impassible demeanor, his remoteness and ineffably alien quality precluded popular affection, but not popular respect. The Ulor, despite all peculiarities, possessed undeniable force; and his inscrutably authoritative presence calmed the unruliest of crowds. Throughout these weeks of effort, Varis appeared always unmoved, purposeful, immune to doubt or weakness. Only one or two of his few personal servants, passing before the Ulor's closed bedroom door late at night, occasionally caught the droning vocal overflow of uneasy royal dreams.

So, how's our little Ulor these days? Having fun, are we?

In his dream, Varis opened unwilling eyes. Clotl was with him again. Scrawny, slightly transparent frame, plaited beard, smirking lips, familiar and unchanged. Clotl.

"What do you want?" the sleeping Ulor asked.

To check in on my favorite pupil, boy. To see how he's getting on. To chat a bit. To SOCIALIZE.

"It's been years. I'd thought I was rid of you."

I've been remiss. But I'll make it up to you, never fear. I'll not neglect you again.

"What has brought you back?"

Duty, boy. Pure duty. My best and brightest pupil, about to resume his interrupted necromantic career, requires the Deathmaster's guidance.

"No. Necromancy has served its purpose. I want no more of it."

Oh, you WANT no more of it. Heh. Which sort of WANT are you talking about, then? Desire? Or need? Or both? Eh? Ever stop to consider? No? Then let's consider.

Need, now. There's plenty of that; it's downright urgent. You

NEED to identify the traitors. You NEED to know who's plotting against you, maybe out there, maybe right here under your nose. Don't you? Unless maybe you think that your subjects love you, that you've bought their gratitude with all those pretty new laws and reforms of yours. Appreciative, are they? Eh? Not quite? Then you NEED to know when the next bomb's apt to blow up in your face, or at least it might be convenient. It'll take the magic to get you those answers. And by the way—you NEED to know which of your Noble Landholders will throw their support to your brother's son, when he comes calling.

"An imposter."

HEH! Wrong. Dead wrong, I assure you. The genuine article.

"You would not know that."

Don't be impertinent, boy. The Deathmaster knows. He always knows. He's seen with his own two dead eyes.

"Impossible. Breziot's boy is not in Rhazaulle."

Correct. What of it? Is Deathmaster Clotl bound by commonplace ties? Is Clotl just ANYBODY? Think again. The Deathmaster is free—don't you recall? You freed him with your own hand. Blued flame to char the threads, very prettily done. And now, thanks to you, the Deathmaster wanders where he will. He has traveled across the water to inspect this Cerrov—who's unmistakably Haudrensq, with those parti-colored eyes and all. Your very own nephew, and no mistake. Oh, and the sister's still around, and she's authentic too. Thought you'd like to know. Nothing to say, boy? Where's your family feeling?

"If you've the power to travel freely, there is much you could tell me."

There is, isn't there? Clotl giggled. *There really IS. If I chose. But we were talking of your choices, not mine. Weren't we? Your WANTS, as I recall. We'd considered need, but we hadn't yet touched upon desire. So what do you say, boy? Don't you miss the magic? Don't you still think of it, dream of it?*

Varis was silent.

Of course you do. You haven't forgotten; none of us forget.

You remember the power, unrestrained by fear or pity, the totality of power—

"I am Ulor. That is enough."

Ulor—pah! A tiny trumpery title. Tell me, sonny, had much joy of your ulordom? Brought you a lot of satisfaction, has it? Plenty of contentment? Peace of mind?

"I have what I wanted."

But do you have what you expected? HEH. Don't answer that. Only remember what you once had, and what you've given up. And for what? Life as a walking target?

"A hazard of sovereignty."

For you in particular, as you've never secured the succession. How is it that you've never married and gotten yourself an heir, anyway? What's the matter—children make you uncomfortable, somehow? Or maybe begetting the heir's the problem. That it? Heh. Maybe—

"There is no lack of Haudrensq successors."

But not your own. Eh, boy? Haudrensq successors—cold comfort, that. What about—

"Unimportant."

But is it? What's all your effort been for, after all? Is there nothing more than—THIS? Ever stop to consider—

"Leave me."

If you weren't asleep, I'd swear you were PETULANT. Never mind, the Deathmaster takes no offense. No matter how much everyone else may hate you, the Deathmaster's still your friend. Eh? Now, if you want MY advice, you'll get back to doing what you LIKE, what you NEED, what you're really GOOD at—

"Go."

—Before it's too late!

Anger jolted Varis awake. He sat up. Dead of night. He was alone in the darkened chamber. He was bathed in sweat, and his heart was pounding. He sat still, and gradually his pulses slowed. When his ragged breathing eased, he rose and dressed himself.

There were, as dead Clotl had so rightly observed, things that he needed to do. At this point, there was really no choice.

The old hollow space beneath one of the bedroom floorboards was still stocked like a miniature apothecary's shop. From this compartment, Varis removed a small jar half full of opaque gray-brown jelly. He had not tasted this substance of his own compounding in years, for its effect was unpredictable, and its power was formidable; but he had never forgotten it. Now he stood weighing the jar in his hand. Once he moved as if to exchange it for another; checked, opened the container, and, not allowing himself time for further reflection, swallowed a massive dose.

For a few seconds he stood motionless, eyes closed, blood thrilling through his veins, mind aglow within his head. It was more than he remembered, impossibly more.

The Zalkhash attendants were not astonished by their master's quiet nocturnal departure. It was by no means the first such excursion.

Cloaked and hatted against the raw breezes of early spring, vizarded against possible recognition, Varis rode alone through the streets of Rialsq. He encountered no one. The city slept in profound silence; the clop of his horse's hoofs upon thickly mudded cobbles echoed through the night. The sky above the conical city rooftops was a moonless, starless void. There was only the small glow of the single lantern hanging from one stirrup to light his way to the Nightfields.

The old cemetery had scarcely changed since his last visit. There were a few more communal grave markers poking up out of the ground; otherwise, all was the same, grim and desolate as ever.

He left his horse hitched to the iron paling. Taking the lantern, he entered, glanced about quickly, and selected a communal grave. Moments later he was at work, summoning a crew of the ghosts that would henceforth serve as his spies in Rhazaulle. Despite the long hiatus, his powers were perfectly in hand. He had never been stronger or surer, and he was himself again, whole again, fully alive for the first time in years.

12

THE YEARS BROUGHT little change to Fruce
Library. The book collection grew, expanding
into available attic space. Certain assistant librarians and under librarians began taking brief
leaves of absence, six or eight of them simultaneously dis-
appearing for days or sometimes weeks at a time. The
purpose of these excursions was never discussed, but it
might have been noted by the knowledgeable that the
wandering Frucians were all members of the Conclave. It
might also have been noted that reports of hauntings
throughout Aennorve were markedly on the wane. But
these small alterations scarcely affected the pattern of ev-
eryday life at Fruce.

The inhabitants continued book-besotted as ever. Only
one among them found herself forced to change, or else
succumb to despair.

Shalindra, by healthy nature disinclined to melancholia, had adapted to her surroundings as best she could. In
this case, adaptation demanded true involvement in her
studies, and this she had conscientiously cultivated. It
hadn't been easy to work up an interest in Choop's No-
menclature, trade regulations of ancient Dizna, or

Chorkan Variations. Some of the other subjects, however
—Aennorvi literature, history of the Confederated Nations, contemporary philosophy, and the like—were absorbing, and in these she'd deliberately immersed herself.
Slowly, over the course of the months and the years, she'd
come to take a genuine pleasure in her work. This so, she
could participate in the scholarly conversations that
buzzed in the refectory every day. She had no close friends,
but there were several pleasant enough acquaintances. She
could contemplate the prospect of someday taking her
place as an under librarian of Fruce with equanimity, if
not enthusiasm. She had not forgotten the world beyond
the water, and she had not forgotten her brother, but these
memories had gradually receded. And if she sometimes
opened her mother's locket to brood over Cerrov's likeness, she no longer suffered the piercing grief of earlier
years.

"I'm going to use Noom's Indented for the Immeeni Se-
quences article." Visiting Scholar Aeftie's proclamation
broke the silence of hours. "I don't care what anyone
says."

"Oruno won't take it," Shalindra replied.

"I don't care."

"He's a stickler for Nine-Line Squaring."

"I don't care."

"You'll care when he tosses out your monograph for
impropriety of footnotational form."

"There's no impropriety!" The Strellian Visiting
Scholar's plump face lit with passion. "Nobody with an
ounce of sense could think that! Oruno's got his head
stuck back in the last century!"

"Well—" Shalindra shrugged. "But he's got final approval."

"I don't care! I won't be intimidated by a pebble-
brained fossil! I've more integrity than that! It's Noom's

Indented for the footnotes, or else I submit a complaint in writing. I've tried to be nice, but there are limits!"

"Sssshh, Aeftie—this is the reading room."

"I don't care!"

Steam was all but spouting from her ears. Over footnotes. Shalindra shook her head. Twelve years of residence, and she still didn't understand her fellow Frucians. She'd never really understand them. She glanced about her. The reading room was empty but for the two of them. Aeftie was free to rave to her heart's content.

Where was everyone? Shalindra raised her eyes to the window. Outside, it was springtime twilight, and silent. Staff and students would be at dinner now. Absorbed in her studies, she had lost all track of time.

A messenger walked into the reading room, handed a note to Shalindra, and left.

"What is it?" Aeftie was staring. "Read it, read it aloud."

" 'Miss Vezhevska is summoned to The Librarian's office.' " Shalindra frowned, unpleasantly surprised. Only once had she ever set foot in the autocrat's sanctum, an experience so humiliating that the mere recollection still made her squirm.

"What would Old Granite Face want with you at this time of day?" the Strellian scholar inquired.

"I've no idea."

"Have you *done* anything?"

"Not lately." Shalindra rose from her chair. "Do I look all right?"

"Oh—" Aeftie flapped a vague hand. "I suppose. I tell you, Vezhevska, I'm going to stand by my principles. It's my duty to myself."

"Oh, a moral imperative, absolutely." Glancing down at herself, Shalindra brushed a few specks of dust from her sleeve, adjusted a fold of cloth to cover an ineradicable ink stain, raised a hand, and hurriedly smoothed her hair. She still wore the comfortable homemade olive-drab blouses and skirts of her childhood days, but these garments now clothed a slim, long-legged, young woman's body. She still wore her thick crow's-wing hair in the same careless plait down her back; in the absence of mirrors, there had been little incentive to experiment. Rudimentary toilet completed, she departed the reading room.

Behind her, a defiant mutter. "I mean what I say. It's Noom's Indented, or nothing."

Minutes later, she stood knocking upon The Librarian's door. An authoritative contralto bade her enter, and she walked into the lamplit office. The Librarian—austere age-defying visage still almost unwrinkled—sat at her desk. Before the desk stood a young man attired in the silver-laced dark blue uniform of an Aennorvi officer, the smart cut of which emphasized wide shoulders and a trim waist. He had plentiful brown hair, wonderful cleft chin, and blue eyes—very nice blue eyes, Shalindra noticed, that brightened with unmistakable interest as they rested on her.

She wasn't used to that.

The Librarian rose, and once again Shalindra marveled at her stature. She herself, like most members of her family, was tall; but the older woman still towered over her, still looked *down* as if at the erring child of yore.

"This is she," The Librarian told the officer. "Miss Vezhevska, allow me to present Colonel Syun, of his Majesty's Household. Colonel, Frucian Scholar Vezhevska."

Colonel? He didn't look thirty years old. He had to be well-connected. Shalindra thought that Miss Vezhevska might be expected to curtsy. Her Ladyship Shalindra Haudrensq, sister to Rhazaulle's rightful Ulor, would not. She answered with a civil inclination of the head. "Sir."

Advancing several paces, he bowed deeply—such a bow as a duchess might have received. "An honor and a privilege, Madam. I beg leave to inform your La— Miss . . . Vezhevska—that I come as the emissary of his Majesty Dasune. On behalf of his Majesty, I extend a greeting. The King desires to convey his warmest regards. He expresses his respect and deep affection, in token whereof, I am commanded to present this document." With a second bow, Colonel Syun tendered a folded missive, gold-sealed with the royal arms of Aennorve.

Dazedly, Shalindra accepted. It flashed through her mind that the young man's rigidly formal style of address did not seem natural to him, but such thoughts perished quickly; astonishment left no room for them.

A letter from King Dasune. After all these years. How often had she prayed for this, and how often had she been disappointed, until at last she'd given up all hope? She'd thought he'd forgotten all about her long ago. She'd finally managed to reconcile herself to Fruce. She'd finally achieved tranquillity, if not exactly contentment. And now—this.

Could he be writing to inform her of Cerrov's death?

She realized she was standing motionless, staring stupidly at the letter in her hand. She blinked to break the trance, and opened it. It was a fairly long composition, ornate in style, and almost overwhelmingly gracious in tone. Addressing her as "Most Honored Sister of Rhazaulle"—a form reserved for fellow royalty, no more "Vezhevska" fiction—Dasune announced the reappearance of "the Most Royal Cerrov Haudrensq, rightful Heir to the Wolf Throne, true Ruler of all Rhazaulle and her many Dominions." The true heir, it seemed, having grown to valiant manhood, now prepared to reclaim the Wolf Throne, presently "occupied and defiled by the monstrous Usurper, the Bloodiest of Tyrants, Detested and Universally Despised." (Uncle Varis?) Aennorve and its justice-loving monarch pledged unstinting support to the cause of the true Ulor. Said Ulor, currently his Majesty's honored guest, longed for reunion with his beloved sister, and therefore, her Ladyship Shalindra was most earnestly besought "to grace the Genevreen with her fair presence."

His Majesty's trusted aid Syun would escort her from Fruce to Feyenne.

She had to read through twice to be certain she was getting the true sense of it, and even then, she could hardly believe.

Why now? What's happened? Why NOW?

Aloud, she simply said, in wonder, "He invites me to Feyenne."

"So I surmised," The Librarian replied. "Will you accept?"

Shalindra's brows rose.

"You are not constrained," The Librarian observed, correctly interpreting the look. "You may remain here if you wish. Your progress has been good, but you have by no means developed your faculties to the fullest. Certain areas of study remain unexplored, and there is reason to believe you are not without ability."

Shalindra's confusion deepened as The Librarian unlocked a drawer in her desk, removed something small, and extended it upon an open palm. It was the small remnant of an ordinary candle, yellowed and old-looking.

"Perhaps you recognize this?" The Librarian inquired. "It was discovered some years ago—just at the time, as I recall, that you were taken so mysteriously and dangerously ill that we feared for your life. It was lying on the floor in the locked crypt, not far from the entrance. None of the authorized staff members could account for its presence there."

Shalindra remembered only too well. She let nothing show on her face.

"The seclusion of Fruce offers peace and security, two commodities often undervalued until lost," The Librarian suggested. "As it appears possible that you possess certain aptitudes, you may, if you choose, remain to receive special instruction."

It was not a difficult decision. The mere recollection of her experience in the crypt iced her blood. She did not wish to study ghastly necromancy, or indeed, ever to think of it again. "I accept his Majesty's invitation," she said at once.

"Excellent, Madam." Colonel Syun smiled, revealing very white teeth. The conversation, temporarily mystifying to him, was clear again. "His Majesty will be delighted. Your brother, also."

"You've seen Cerrov?"

"Indeed."

"How does he look? How is he? Tell me."

"In excellent health and spirits, Madam. Very anxious to see you again."

"He must be all grown up, now." She tried to imagine.

"The Ulor is ready to assume his rightful place, Madam. And not, I think, ill-suited."

The Ulor. It was one thing to think it, another to hear someone else say it. "I can hardly believe it," Shalindra marveled. "It's been so many years since I've actually thought I'd ever see him again, much less— How are we to travel?"

"The schooner *Bloodflamer* lies at anchor off Fruce quay. She'll carry us to Foneev, where a coach and armed escort await us. You will not, I think, find the journey unduly uncomfortable, Madam."

"When do we leave?"

"Tomorrow morning. Early."

"That soon?"

"Will your preparations require additional time, Madam? Be assured, the *Bloodflamer* crewmen will render all necessary assistance."

"It isn't that," Shalindra told him. "My preparations will hardly take any time at all. It's just that I've been here such a long time, and this seems so—I don't know— so abrupt."

Colonel Syun smiled, appearing at once surprised and a little amused by her naïveté. "His Majesty, eager though he is to welcome you as his guest, will wait upon your leisure, Madam."

She could take some time to get used to it.

But The Librarian observed, remorselessly, "There is little point in delay. In view of Miss Vezhevska's decision, the interests of the library are best served by her prompt departure."

"Interests?" Shalindra inquired.

"Your room. We've other uses for it."

"Oh."

"You will perhaps wish to make your farewells. No doubt you need to gather your belongings. You've permission to withdraw, Miss Vezhevska. If we do not meet again, I wish you a safe journey."

"But, Librarian—"

"Good-bye, Miss Vezhevska."

There wasn't much to do. Her possessions were pathetically scanty, easily packed within moments into the same old valise she'd brought from Feyenne, so many years earlier. The only belonging of value or note hung, as always, about her throat. Her farewells to Aeftie, Oruno, Jevuni, and a few other acquaintances were politely tepid. They wouldn't miss her, any more than she'd really miss them. Her own fault, something lacking in her? Sometimes she wondered.

And then it was darkness, and sleeplessness in her narrow bed, and the last night she would ever spend at Fruce. The memories crowded her brain, despite all effort to exclude them. The doubts, questions, and fears kept her awake for hours. Finally, a short span of unquiet slumber; then up and out of bed at the break of dawn.

They made an early departure. Shalindra, lightly mantled against the gray coolness of the morning, stood on the deck of the *Bloodflamer,* watching Fruce Isle recede. Her eyes rose to the fortress of a library, perched atop its granite pedestal, and a frown creased her brow. So often she had dreamed of this moment; and now that it was here—? She wasn't unreservedly joyous, as she thought she should have been. Instead, she found herself uneasy. Whatever its shortcomings, Fruce had been familiar and safe. "... *peace and security, two commodities often undervalued until lost* ..." And now she was leaving it, for—what?

Colonel Syun stood beside her on the deck. She stole a sidelong glance at him and found that he was watching her with the same expression of interest she'd noted earlier. Her pulses jumped, on instinct, for she'd never before received such attention. There were males aplenty at the library, but they could hardly be counted as men—they were genderless Frucian bookworms. But here was no Frucian, and she found she didn't know where to look. If she kept her eyes fixed on the library, he'd continue studying her profile. If she turned to face him, she'd have to think of something to say. And if she went below, to the private cabin assigned her—for, this trip, she was being treated as a person of consequence—she'd certainly elude him, but that wasn't quite what she wanted.

Colonel Syun solved her problem. "Sorry to go?" he inquired.

"Not sure," she confessed. "It all seems unreal."

"Well, that's understandable. You'll soon get used to things," he returned easily.

"What things?"

"All of them. Don't worry, it'll be easier than you think. You'll do very well."

"How do you know?"

"It's obvious. I can tell."

She noted the relaxation of his formality. It suited him.

"But I've no idea what to expect. Tell me about Feyenne, Colonel," Shalindra asked, and her companion obliged. For the next hour or more they strolled about the deck, while Syun talked of the city, and all the changes occurring there since her last visit; of the court, which he knew well, for it happened that he was one of the King's many nephews; of the recent hostilities between Aennorve and Rhazaulle; and finally, at her urging, of himself—his boyhood in the provinces, his commission, his experiences in the Teurn-of-Zin campaigns. His conversation revealed good humor, good sense, good breeding. Liveliness of mind, but no remarkable scholarly brilliance, and probably just as well, for an excess of literacy could only have unbalanced an admirably level head.

The *Bloodflamer* dropped anchor in Foneev Harbor around sunset, and the schooner's boat carried the passengers to the wharf. Shalindra gazed about her, faintly alarmed. Noise, bustle, and confusion battered her senses. She'd forgotten what the real world was like. Accustomed to the almost enchanted stillness of Fruce Library, the stir of a city now struck her as overwhelming. Instinctively, she clutched Syun's arm. He glanced down at her, surprised; then smiled reassuringly, as if at a child, and led her from the wharf to the street, where a coach awaited—a varnished behemoth of a coach, touched with silver and blazoned with the royal arms of Aennorve. Driver, guard, and a quartet of armed outriders flaunted the ornate blue and silver of his Majesty's Household Guards.

Unprepared for such splendor, Shalindra was suddenly conscious, for the first time in years, of her own shabby appearance; homemade olive-drab cloak, clunky Fruce sandals, childish pigtail down her back. She looked like a peasant girl. On Fruce Isle, it hadn't mattered, but it mattered now. She was happy to conceal herself from view inside the coach. Colonel Syun issued orders to the driver, then climbed in to sit opposite her. Coach and outriders clattered off down the street at a smart clip, pedestrian and vehicular traffic invariably yielding to the royal conveyance.

They went only as far as the *White Raven;* a quiet, spotless, luxurious inn of the sort patronized by the wealthiest of travelers. There they dined upon lakeskimmer bisque, spiced quails, trout fresh out of Lake Eev, stuffed aubergines, a mixed salad of two dozen different greens, chocolate-almond meringues—such food as Shalindra had all but forgotten existed. She hoped she wasn't making a pig of herself. She didn't want Colonel Syun to think her unladylike, and he *was* eyeing her askance as she downed her third meringue, but she couldn't help it. There were years of porridge to make up for.

After dinner, Syun saw her to her room, which was probably the best in the house; large, opulently furnished, with curtains and bed hangings of smoke-colored brocade, glorious thick rug, and a cheval glass in a gilded frame, the first mirror she'd seen in years. No sooner had the door closed behind him than she was standing before the glass, studying herself microscopically. Her figure, as she already knew, was tall, long-legged, too slim for perfection, but lithe and not ungraceful. As for her face, she was startled by the changes. Not that she was at all unrecognizable; there were the same features—narrow nose, large hazel eyes with the Haudrensq corona, startling black brows—that she remembered from childhood. But the contours had altered. The childish softness was gone, and now the clear white skin stretched itself smoothly over prominent, precisely modeled bones. Her expression had changed, too; juvenile eagerness had given way to settled melancholy. All in all, an individual and undeniably arresting face, if a little too chiseled of feature for fashion. Too severe, perhaps? She tried smiling. It helped. Teeth excellent, white and even.

Her hair looked stupid, she decided. Unbraiding the great dark mass, she combed and brushed it until it gleamed, and that was much more becoming, but unacceptable outside the bedchamber. She had no pins, clips, combs, or ribbons to confine the streaming locks. But there were scarves in her valise, silken trifles carried from Feyenne, and still pristine, for there had been no use for such frivolities at Fruce. Choosing a bright red one, she folded the rectangle carefully into a band, which she looped about her head and under her hair. Tying a knot at the back of her neck, she checked the mirror to gauge the effect. Not bad; much better than the pigtail. Would people think her attractive? More to the point—would Colonel Syun think her attractive?

For a while, Shalindra wandered to and fro in her room, enjoying the unaccustomed spaciousness and luxury. Then it was time to sleep, and she climbed into a great canopied bed, with finer linen and softer pillow than any she had known in years.

A discreet tapping upon her door awakened her at dawn. She washed, dressed, and descended, without troubling to bring the valise. One of the guards would see to her luggage. It was wonderful to be an important personage.

Syun was sitting alone at a small table in the dining room. Standing as she entered, he observed, "You should always wear your hair that way. You might be a witch-princess out of one of the old legends."

Success. She could feel the color rise to her cheeks. Her memory itched. The compliment reminded her of someone—someone else who teased and flattered, long ago. Captain Brunule. "I'm no witch," she returned lightly, as she might once have answered the Captain, "but I have been known to turn my hand to sorcery, now and again."

"I don't doubt it," he said, smiling. "You're probably very good at it."

"No, not very. I haven't enough experience."

"In Feyenne, you may acquire some. Or even en route."

"That could be dangerous."

"Not for a real sorceress."

"Especially for a real sorceress. We rely so greatly upon our powers, which sometimes unexpectedly fail us."

"The same might be said of ordinary men. But perhaps a sorceress offers a magical restorative?"

"Some do, no doubt. I don't presume to claim such expertise."

"Possibly you underestimate your own magic."

"It's scarcely been put to the test."

"Time to change all that. Talent thrives on challenge."

"Does yours?"

"Yes. Shall I be called upon to prove it?"

"Oh, I'm only a sorceress, not a fortune-teller."

Syun laughed, conceding the match.

Nice smile, Shalindra thought. *Nice face.*

After breakfast, the journey resumed. They were headed north, retracing the route whereby she had once traveled from Feyenne. Then it had been summer, with dusty dry roads and parched landscape. Now, in the early springtime, the fields were green and dotted with wild-flowers, the trees were newly leafed, and some of them were veiled in pastel blossom. The roads were damp and difficult. At least once a day, and sometimes more, the coach bogged down in mud, and then the passengers were obliged to emerge, and to wait—sometimes for hours—while guards labored and horses strained. These interludes scarcely troubled Shalindra. It seemed she never tired of studying the flowers, the trees, and even the commonest of weeds—there had been no live vegetation upon Fruce Isle. And if the flora had lost its charm, there was always Syun to keep her entertained.

He *was* good company, she soon discovered; attentive, considerate, amusing, unfailingly even-tempered, and easy-humored. He told her stories about the more eccentric of Genevreen courtiers and Household officers. He told her jokes and anecdotes. He told colorful tales of adventure at Teurn-of-Zin. He encouraged her to speak of Fruce library and its inhabitants, and when she hesitantly obliged, he never seemed in the least bored. She didn't mention the haunted crypt or her experiences therein. But she described Assistant Librarian Jevuni, and Under Librarian Oruno, and some of the others, and he laughed as if greatly diverted, while his blue eyes rested upon her face with the peculiar intentness that she recognized upon instinct. Then she was gratified and unbearably self-conscious, excited and apprehensive all at once.

When conversation palled, they played cards, board games, guessing games. He taught her Kalique, currently the rage at Court. She had little aptitude for Kalique, but found that she could beat him at chess every time, and that defeat never marred his good humor.

The long, slow days passed pleasantly. The nights were spent at inns, invariably luxurious. By Fruce standards, the food was sinful. The green land flowed by, and time seemed to stop. Shalindra would have been quite content to continue thus indefinitely.

But they did not. Around noon of the eleventh day, they reached Feyenne, and things changed. Now they were bumping and clattering over cobbled streets clogged with traffic. The buildings rose up on either side, and there were people everywhere. White architecture, arches, and wrought-iron grillwork; pushcart vendors, street singers, bemubit trees in the green public parks. Feyenne, just as Shalindra remembered it. Not much had changed.

Then, the Genevreen rising before her, its fanciful slim towers and glass-enclosed sky-walks the stuff of dreaming recollection. King Dasune. Princess Olisi. Dr. Treluna. Master Lunune. Cerrov. The faces rose before her, and she was filled with trepidation as she had not been since Foneev. Now, as then, she wanted to grab Syun's arm, but this time resisted the impulse. She couldn't possibly do such a thing; somehow—now—it would mean something, say something. Her eyes cut across to his face. He was watching her, and his expression was distinctly regretful.

"End of the journey," Syun observed. "Now I must go back to calling you 'your Ladyship.'"

"It's still Shalli," she said.

"Will you remember that, this time next week?"

"Try me."

"I will."

The coach halted before the great front entry. Liveried servants streamed from the building. Syun handed her from the vehicle, up the broad marble steps, and into the foyer. Before relinquishing her to the care of the chief chamberlain, he bowed, and his lips brushed the back of her hand. The brief touch thrilled along her nerves, and she repressed a start.

"You'll do well. Shalli," he said, and retired.

Suddenly bereft, she watched him go. But there was no time to brood, for the attendants were clustering about her—no doubt about it, she was now a decidedly important personage—and the chamberlain was speechifying, and then a little gang of them were conducting her to her lodgings.

She'd had some idea of returning to the pretty rose-ivory-gilt chamber she remembered from long ago, but soon found she'd graduated to greater things. She now merited a pompous second-story suite, with gleaming onyx foyer, gilded bedroom, dressing room, sitting room, private kitchen, dining room, and superb green marble fantasy of a bathroom; such quarters as were normally reserved for visiting royalty. There were gowns hanging in the dressing-room wardrobes, she quickly discovered; linen in the chest of drawers; even some jewelry in one of the caskets. Certainly the King, or one of his household attendants, had thought of everything. Opening off her kitchen were several small closets designed to house servants. And, amazingly, there *were* servants; cook, factotum, and a sturdy, stolid, competent workhorse of a lady's maid aptly christened Diligence. She'd never, even as a child at the Zalkhash, had attendants of her own. It was dreamlike.

No dream, however, that his Majesty had arranged a special reception in her honor. (She wished The Librarian might have known.) And no dream that her brother, the Ulor Cerrov III, had expressed the intention of greeting

his sister in private, prior to the reception. That would be
best, of course—to meet alone and unobserved, but the
prospect frightened her a little; for it seemed to Shalindra
that she and Cerrov, once so close, might now find themselves strangers. Perhaps there would be nothing to say to
one another. Almost she wished that Syun might be present at the meeting; no trouble with conversation when *he*
was around.

Diligence helped her prepare. First, there was a bath, a
long and sybaritic perfumed soak. Then a fitting. Shalindra chose a low-necked gown of deep forest-green velvet,
rich and dark as moss. It needed some alteration, of course.
For the next hour or more, she waited while the maid
pinned, basted, and stitched. While waiting, she experi-
mented with some of the cosmetics arrayed upon the vanity. Many of them she didn't recognize, and these she set
aside for future study. The function of the blush-colored
powder was obvious enough, however; a light dusting
across her cheeks brought her face to life. Likewise self-
explanatory—the rosy paste that ripened and defined her
lips. Her eyes, with their thick black lashes and strong
black brows, required no artificial enhancement.

The dress was ready, and perfect. Shalindra put it on,
and then sat still while Diligence did her hair—did it
properly, for the first time in her life, with curls piled atop
her head, and a couple of long black switches falling over
one shoulder. Earrings and decorative combs set with am-
ber picked up the golden tones of the Haudrensq Corona;
her mother's locket glittered at her throat.

When her preparations were complete, Shalindra
gazed upon herself, quite astonished; less by the new
splendor than by the unexpected sophistication. She was
so thoroughly adult, and maturity had crept up on her, at
Fruce, so—unobtrusively. It would have been easy to grow
old there, without ever noticing.

An hour or so remained until the reception. She might
expect Cerrov to appear at any moment. And sure enough,

almost too promptly—*Not ready! What'll we say?*—there came a knock at the outer door. The factotum answered. There was a murmuring of voices that resolved itself as Shalindra emerged into the sitting room. Cerrov was there, and he had come alone. She dismissed her servant with a gesture, and the factotum retired. Brother and sister surveyed one another in silence.

Grown-up. Not a trace of childishness left in him. Taller than his father, though nowhere near as huge as Uncle Hurna. Something of Hurna's vitality, though. Powerful, solid build, less elegant than indestructible. Strong featured, square-jawed, intelligent face. Eyes colored like her own. Tawny hair cut militarily short. Clean-shaven, attired in an impeccable uniform that she didn't recognize.

He was inspecting her with equal attention, and then they spoke simultaneously, as if they were linked like the members of the Conclave:

"It's still you."

"All grown-up," said Cerrov, his voice resonant, a man's voice. "And beautiful."

No, it's just the dress, she almost blurted, idiotically. But she said nothing, for her throat had closed up; and needed to say nothing at that moment, for they were in each other's arms, and it was well she'd applied no cosmetics to her eyes, for tears would have smeared them now.

They stepped apart, but he retained her hand. "Where have you been all these years?" Cerrov asked. "Time and again, I've begged the King for news of you, but his communications told me nothing."

"You mean, he *answered* you?"

"Occasionally."

"Well, that's more than he did for me. I thought he'd forgotten my existence. I thought everyone had. That rock was secure as a prison, and even if I'd escaped, there'd have been nowhere to go. I'd just about resigned myself to a life sentence when the word came—"

"What rock? What prison? Where?"

"Fruce Isle. The library."

"Lake Eev?"

"Not the worst place in the world, but lonely. They treated me well enough, though."

"Did they know who you are?"

"I suppose at least a few of them must have, but they never let on. 'Miss Vezhevska,' they've called me for years, and treated me like any other slightly backward Visiting Scholar."

"Backward, never. You were always too clever for comfort."

"Not by Fruce reckoning. To those librarians, I must have seemed a nitwit, no matter how hard I studied."

" 'Visiting Scholar.' Strange rearing for Rhazaullean royalty. What have you studied?"

"Oh, all kinds of things. I'll bore you with the list some other time. What about you? Where have you been? So often, I've tried to imagine. Tried to send thoughts to you."

"Sometimes, I think, they reached me. They haven't always had so far to travel, after all. I spent four years under an assumed name at the Giliune School in Bokunisse—"

"That's right on the lakeshore. So close—!"

"For the first four years. Then I went to the Military Academy of the North Anche, in ChuVray—spent another four years there. Then there was a year in the Teurn-at-Zin, as aide-de-campe to General Hune. Two years as staff officer in Ziquerne. Then back with Hune for the Tenjihk negotiations."

"So many places! You must have seen so much, and done so much!"

"It's been varied. Certainly Dasune has seen to my education."

"Generous."

"Expedient. He has, as he believes, shaped me to his own use."

"What do you mean?"

"Shalli, you understand why we've suddenly been taken out of the box, dusted off, and placed back on the board after all this time?"

"Not entirely," she replied after a moment's thought. "I know that King Dasune supports your claim to the throne of Rhazaulle. I expect he finances your expedition. But I don't know his motives, and I can't account for the timing."

"But my clever little sister can probably figure it out, if she tries."

"Guessing games? Well, I shouldn't like to think it impossible that he supports your claim because it's just—"

"There speaks the innocent recluse of Fruce Isle."

"Not quite as foolish as that. I assume that you and the King have struck some sort of bargain, the terms of which must benefit Aennorve."

"Greatly benefit Aennorve."

"That's to be expected. But I can't guess why it's happening precisely *now*."

"The question wasn't fair. Shut away from the world as you've been, you couldn't know of the friction between Rhazaulle and Aennorve. You see—" He proceeded to explain the situation in terms commendably lucid.

Shalindra listened, astonished. Her brother's grasp of politics and economics was impressive. His observations were keen, his power of analysis admirable even by Fruce standards. He had profited by his experiences, and now he was infinitely more knowledgeable of the real world than she. Compared to Cerrov, she knew herself for a book-learned ignoramus; or perhaps, as he'd more gently put it, an "innocent recluse."

"It seems our good Uncle Varis has done such a masterly job of squeezing the Aennorvi purse that his Majesty, in sheer self-defense, is driven to the unusual recourse of resurrecting a rival claimant to the Wolf Throne—a miracle that Dasune has been dangling before my nose for years," Cerrov summarized in conclusion. "It suits his Majesty very well that I depose our uncle, as he expects to find in me a conveniently malleable successor. Whether his expectations will be fulfilled or not remains to be seen."

Shalindra mulled it over for a few seconds. "Your plans," she inquired at last, "depend heavily on Rhazaullean support?"

He nodded.

"Well, what makes you so certain you'll get it? Judging by everything I've heard, Varis has proved himself a strong and progressive Ulor. He may be a usurper, but give him his due—he's a very able ruler, perhaps even a great one. That being so, how can you be sure that the Noble Landholders, with their money and resources, won't remain loyal to our uncle?"

"Because he isn't rightful Ulor, according to the old rules of dynastic succession. The Noble Landholders see that flouting of law and tradition as a threat to their own security. And the more honorable among them are morally outraged. But more important than that—Varis may expect little loyalty because he isn't liked, and he isn't trusted, at any level of Rhazaullean society. He's inaccessible, incomprehensible, and sometimes thought inhuman. There is nothing he can do to erase the stain of his usurpation. He's thought guilty of murder and worse. Particularly in recent months—apparently he's devised some new means of domestic surveillance, and he's been filling the prisons with suspected conspirators and spies."

"Wrongly suspected?"

"Makes no difference. Right or wrong, he's hated for it."

"Hardly seems fair."

"Well, I shouldn't waste too much sympathy on Uncle Varis." Cerrov's face hardened, momentarily aging.

"When he loses, what happens to him?"

"I'll have him executed." Voice flat.

She could have expected no other reply, but it was curiously shocking nonetheless, and she couldn't forbear observing, "He is Haudrensq."

"Do you know what became of our mother?"

She remembered the cheap printed paper in her hand. Mercilessly brilliant sunlight. The smell of the *Lakelily's* hold.

"I see that you do. Then remember who Varis is, and what he is."

"Does anyone know just what he is?"

How could she have worried about talking to Cerrov? They'd always communicated like two branches of the same mind, and that hadn't changed. Together again for the first time in twelve years, and it was as if they had never been apart. It was that natural, that right. And talk? There was no end to it, and it was dizzying—much of it personal, but some of it such talk as might alter history. Would she wake to find herself in the reading room at Fruce? It seemed they'd barely begun talking when the clock struck, and it was time to proceed to his Majesty's reception.

A very good thing that Cerrov was there to escort her. She'd otherwise have been scared to death, for the quiet of the library still seemed the norm to her, and these glittering, chattering Aennorvi swarms dazzled her vision and bewildered her ears. Her brother, however, was splendid. Dignified and thoroughly assured, he led her into the Presence Chamber through jeweled throngs that parted, bending and dipping in brilliant slow waves, as if for a reigning monarch. Beautiful, but faintly absurd. *But he really IS Ulor!*

She could feel the eyes of a multitude boring into her. Her grip on Cerrov's arm tightened. She kept her gaze fixed on the dais straight ahead, atop which sat three very ornate gilded chairs; two equal in size and ostentation, one slightly smaller and plainer. King Dasune occupied the middle chair. He rose as his two guests of honor approached, and for a moment Shalindra felt herself unsettled in time, for his Majesty had scarcely changed. The mobile face beneath the dark peruke carried slightly deeper lines and grooves than she recalled. The middle encased in an embroidered waistcoat was a little larger. Beyond that, Dasune was much as he had been twelve years earlier.

"Don't let the old humbug fool you," Cerrov advised in a voice that reached her ears alone. Together they mounted the dais.

"Brother of Rhazaulle," Dasune intoned, and the two men embraced ceremoniously. This obligation fulfilled, they separated, and his Majesty turned to Shalindra. "Fairest sister, we bid you welcome!"

He kissed her, once on each cheek. His little dark mustache tickled. His breath smelled of cherry brandy overlaid with peppermint pastilles. She fought the urge to pull away from him. Fortunately, he released her quickly.

"Majesty." Early training had not been forgotten. Her sweeping curtsy was irreproachable.

"Dear sister, the years have been long, but never has your Ladyship been absent from our thoughts."

Really? Then why haven't we ever troubled to answer any of my letters? Shalindra wondered in silence. She smiled sweetly, and maintained the smile for the next five minutes or so, while the King delivered his gracious, practiced little speech of welcome.

He spoke well. It would have been easy to imagine the cordiality genuine.

Dasune concluded and resumed his seat. Cerrov sat in the large chair upon his host's right-hand side; a privilege reserved for the King's few equals. Shalindra's chair, while smaller and plainer, was placed upon the same level as the others; a signal honor.

Thereafter, a seemingly infinite number of Genevreen courtiers queued to approach the dais. Each in turn was announced, titles and all, by the Chief Chamberlain. One after another, they advanced to bow and press their lips to royal hands. Shalindra found it all mildly ridiculous. It was not, after all, as if she and Cerrov could possibly expect to remember all those names and faces. She couldn't imagine the more boisterous Rhazaullean courtiers lining up and patiently awaiting the opportunity to abase themselves to foreigners. Nor could she imagine Rhazaulleans ever affecting the airs and graces, or the exquisite flourishes, of Aennorvi aristocrats. For a time she amused herself studying the variety of faces, forms, and costumes before her. Feyennese women, she noted, were much given to scalloped trains, aigrettes, and jeweled rings incorporated into their coiffures. The colors, knotting, and arrangement of the bunched ribbon loops worn by the young and handsome of both sexes apparently constituted a language; one in which she herself was illiterate.

Eventually the diversion palled, but the parade of courtiers continued. Shalindra smiled, nodded, and controlled her fidgets. She was, after all, being observed, *closely* observed, by multitudinous Aennorvi eyes. For a little while, she wondered what they must think of her. Then, she stopped caring. Her smile remained fixed in place. With an effort, she kept her eyes from wandering. Her head bobbed mechanically, while her thoughts floated off across Lake Eev. She was roused from her reverie by a light touch upon her arm. Her eyes flicked to the right. King Dasune.

"Tedious, is it not? Take courage, my dear. Contrary to popular belief, eternity is not unending."

And his smile was so warmly humorous and charming —his dark eyes so sympathetic and admiring—that she had to remind herself of Cerrov's warning, for it seemed natural to like and trust him.

The queue snaked forward. Smiles, nods, genuflections. The tedium briefly enlivened when Colonel Syun turned up, dashing in his dress uniform. He bowed expertly, and all at once, she was wide awake again. His lips touched her hand, and her pulses jumped. Had he noticed? Could he tell?

Syun straightened. His face was respectfully grave, but his eyes smiled. "Ladyship."

Shalli, she mouthed silently.

He inclined his head, but not before she saw the smile spread out from his eyes. Bowing again, he retired, and her gaze followed him.

The parade continued, with practiced grimaces and exaggerated compliments addressed to, simply, her Ladyship; which, modest though it seemed under the circumstances, was correct. She possessed no title of her own, and would not until such time as her brother chose to grant one. That he should do so at some point or other seemed likely, however. Conferring of title upon the Ulor's siblings was customary, almost automatic; although certain exceptions had occasionally been known. She vaguely remembered, for example, some discreet tongue-wagging over Uncle Hurna's failure to bestow a dukedom upon his youngest brother Varis. Apparently Hurna had been reconsidering, during the final months of his life; his ruminations cut short by an untimely plunge from the House Uloric rooftop.

King Dasune was right. Eternity ended at last, and she was free to descend from her throne. Even then, however, her trials were not ended, for the courtly throngs closed in on her, cutting her off from her brother, and cutting her off from retreat to the adjoining rooms where the orchestra played, where the gaming tables and buffet tables stood. No escape. Aennorvi courtiers, she couldn't help noticing, were partial to perfume. Too partial. They crowded around her, chattering frenetically, and she had to resist the impulse to clap her hands to her ears. She couldn't talk to them, she couldn't even understand them. Didn't they see how hopeless this was?

Irrelevant. The novelty of her presence piqued their curiosity, and they meant to inspect her at close range. Conversation was quite beside the point. Shalindra concentrated; began to catch snatches of speech, florid compliments, witticisms, and questions, silly questions. What did her Ladyship think of Aennorvi morals? How did her Ladyship rate Aennorvi cuisine? Was her Ladyship homesick for Rhazaulle? And some not so silly: Did her Ladyship trust in the Rhazaullean Noble Landholders to support her brother's cause?

She replied as best she could. The frivolous questions were easy. Those touching upon the conflict to come were more difficult. She had little knowledge of war—only so much as she had picked up in studying the conquests of Boru and Hezziki, the campaigns of General Dynoh, and v'Ierre's *Account of the Jurlian-Zenki Wars*. Of strategy, tactics, logistics, and weaponry, she knew next to nothing. Moreover, her brother's specific plans as yet remained unknown to her. She could only smile, manufacture evasions, and pray for rescue; which presently appeared.

A tall form in a silver-laced dress uniform was bending over her hand. Colonel Syun straightened, meeting her gaze to inquire, "Shall I enjoy the privilege of escorting her Ladyship from the Presence Chamber?" He spoke very formally, very correctly; but there was complicity in his eyes.

Shalindra cast a glance about the room. King Dasune had disappeared. Cerrov stood hemmed in by an avid jeweled crowd. No reaching him. She turned back to Syun. "Granted, Colonel," she murmured, with all the composure of the great lady these courtiers expected her to be.

He looked more amused than impressed.

She took his arm. A path opened before them, and he

whisked her from the room, leading her into the adjoining chamber, where the orchestra played, and the couples tripped to the strains of a Linniana. Shalindra did not know the Linniana, or indeed, any of the currently fashionable dances. She knew only a few traditional Rhazaullean favorites acquired at the Zalkhash years earlier.

Syun read her expression. "Like to learn?" he inquired.

It did look like fun. She nodded, inwardly praying she wouldn't disgrace herself. Taking her hand in his, he spun her about to face him and lightly clasped her waist. No one had done that since her childhood. She found herself elated but nearly unable to look him in the face.

Syun appeared not to notice. "Like this," he said, guiding her through the steps.

It was easy and exhilarating. Within moments she was dancing, indifferent to the speculative eyes of the court. After that, he taught her the trierge, the drinnado, and the Feyennese Square. She hadn't enjoyed herself so much in years; perhaps she'd never enjoyed herself so much. Although the pleasure, she discovered, diminished noticeably when she had to change partners. This occurred with flattering frequency. Half the gentlemen at Court, it seemed, were set upon dancing with the Ulor's sister.

A new partner—short, stocky, swarthy, and she hadn't caught his name—she couldn't possibly keep track of the names. Another, blond and wiry, who pelted her with questions. Then, suddenly, she was dancing with her brother, whose entrance she hadn't noticed.

"You've picked up the steps quickly." Cerrov smiled down at her, and once again it was as if the years of separation had never been.

"Colonel Syun taught me," Shalindra said. He didn't answer, and she slanted a quick look up at him. "You know him?"

"For years."

"What do you think of him?" she asked casually.

"Not strong on strategy. Has his royal connections to

thank for his rank, I'd say. Still, a competent logistician—"

"I mean, what do you think of him *personally*?"

"Syun? A good fellow. The best."

"Ah." She was satisfied. "That's the impression I formed. On the way here from Fruce, you understand."

"Hmm. Yes, I quite understand. Well, little sister, enjoy his company while you can. I'm afraid I'll be snatching him away from you in a matter of days."

"Days?"

"The troops are assembling at Denz. Some Aennorvi, but mostly Rhelish mercenaries. Seasoned, disciplined, well-equipped. Expensive, but worth their price. It's spring, and the Rhazaullean ground is nearly dry. The army will probably move out the week after next."

"So soon!"

"No point in delaying. If we're to strike at Rialsq this year, we need to cross the Bruzhois before winter. Once the snows begin, the TransBruzh's gone."

"If that happened, then we'd winter in Lazimir?"

"Possible, but undesirable. We'd lose momentum, discipline would suffer, there'd be the inevitable trouble with the locals—"

"That's true. What about the Ayzin Pass, though? How are we to deal with The Tollbooth?"

"I'd planned on—" Cerrov looked into her face and frowned. "What is this 'we' you keep mentioning?"

"Don't worry, I'll be no burden. I'm in good health, and at Fruce, I learned to live simply."

"Stop." His frown deepened. "Surely you don't imagine you'll travel with the army?"

"Certainly I will."

"Absurd."

"Isn't. I have the right and the obligation. You can hardly pretend this isn't a matter that directly concerns me."

"Immaterial. Too dangerous."

"I'm not worried."

"I am. In any case, it's impossible."

"Because I'm a woman?"

"Because you'd serve no useful function. You'd be dead weight, and, frankly, a burden, despite your good intentions. What did you expect to do with yourself, anyway? Lower your neckline and follow the camp? Pick up a saber and lead a cavalry charge? Now there's a pretty picture."

"Actually, history has several such pretty pictures to offer. Oh, go ahead and laugh all you like, but it's true. What about Ulor Zurin IV, who brought his ulorre-consort along with him to Yolskivo River?"

"Two hundred years ago."

"General Dynoh took his wife along on the Szarish campaign, and several of his officers brought theirs."

"Lost that one, didn't he?"

"Arlieau, sister to Dunulus the Great, went off to the Jurlian-Zenki wars, and v'Ierre wrote, 'The sight of her fair and gracious countenance never failed to cheer the soldiery.' And Dunulas *did* win that one."

"Delighted to find you so well educated, but it changes nothing. You'll remain in Feyenne, Shalli. That's best for you, best for everyone, and there's nothing more to be said."

We'll see, she thought. His obstinate expression harked back to their childhood days. She remembered it well. No point at all in arguing with him when he looked like that. She'd never succeed in changing his mind, but the matter was hardly concluded. There was, after all, a higher authority.

The dance ended, and Cerrov relinquished her to another partner. He withdrew, and she quickly lost sight of him. There was more dancing; wine and edible frivolities at the buffet table; conversation and questions, endlessly repetitive questions. Again and again she rattled off the same answers to the same queries; always smiling politely, always careful to conceal her growing boredom. She might

not have managed to maintain the polite charade had not
Colonel Syun periodically appeared to lead her onto the
dance floor. Certainly no tedium in *his* conversation, but
the truth was, he didn't need to talk at all. She was quite
content to glide speechlessly about the floor with him.
Syun eschewed perfume, she was happy to discover. His
height was perfect. Engaging smile-lines fanned from the
corners of his eyes.

Later, much later that night, when the reception was
over and she lay abed in her gilded apartment, the images
and impressions whirled in her brain. So many faces.
Syun's most vividly recollected; his expression when he
looked at her. But Cerrov's face was there, too; set in absolute refusal. He was her beloved big brother, and rightful
Ulor as well, but she wasn't about to let him bar her
return to Rhazaulle. One way or another, she'd find a way
of circumventing his decree.

King Dasune stood in the Genevreen hothouse, drinking
the fragrance of unseasonable roses. This section of the
great glass enclosure abounded in thorny bushes, and clus-
ters of lush blooms unfurled everywhere. Dasune was fond
of roses. Their unabashed opulence, miraculously free of
vulgarity, appealed to both the artist and the voluptuary
in him. He visited the hothouse often.

"Your Majesty."

He turned at the sound of the low-pitched, faintly
foreign voice to face the Rhazaullean Ulor's sister; a striking figure in her morning gown of deep rose. The color,
contrasting strongly with the glossy mass of her black
hair, echoed the tones of the surrounding flowers; all in
all, a nice composition. Dasune, possessing fine judgment
in all things artistic, fancied himself a connoisseur of
women as well. This one was a little too slim and chiseled
for his taste. Still, the face was arresting, the eyes were
quite extraordinary, and she would certainly age well,
with those bones. She did not much resemble her brother.

In coloring and slender height, she shared more of a general family likeness with her uncle, the usurper.

"I thank your Majesty for allowing me this audience." Shalindra swept a low curtsy.

"A very great pleasure, my dear." Pressing her hand lightly and briefly, he produced his most reassuringly paternal smile. "But come, no formality here. Stroll with me among the roses, and let us talk as friends. Is something troubling you? We cannot have that. Allow me to place myself at your service."

"Your Majesty is generous beyond my desert. I hope I do not presume too greatly upon your patience in seeking your counsel and assistance. My plight is simply this; I wish to accompany my brother to Rhazaulle, and he forbids it."

"Indeed. You surprise me, my dear. I had hoped we should enjoy your company here at Court for some few months to come, at the very least until the Ulor's victory is secured. How shall I tempt you to remain with us?"

"Majesty, I am greatly tempted. You have made me most welcome, and I'm grateful. Duty, however, demands my return to Rhazaulle."

"Ah? Enlighten me."

She promptly obliged, rattling off a string of reasoned arguments with a facility suggesting careful preparation. She spoke much of obligation, patriotism, personal honor, familial loyalties, and the responsibilities of royalty. She spoke eloquently, but King Dasune hardly heard her, for his mind was speeding along its own track. The Rhazaullean girl wanted to go with the invading army, and it might be desirable to second her request. She was obviously young, personable, bright but somewhat naïve, and possessed of considerable charm; in short, a perfect mascot for the soldiers. A pet, a fantasy, an icon, a symbol to stir the imagination of the men; to boost morale, to draw Rhazaullean recruits, to anchor loyalty. In such a capacity, she might well prove useful.

Of course, his Majesty realized, in packing the lass off to war, he'd expose her to some danger; a point that she, in her youthful idealism, seemed scarcely to consider. The young always imagined themselves invulnerable. But what if the worst should happen, and she came to grief? Dasune considered. She'd win fame as a martyr. Her memory would live on, and her name would serve as a rallying cry. A dead heroine was worth even more than a live mascot; not that he would deliberately engineer her death, for he was a civilized man. Either way, however, her Ladyship's presence in Rhazaulle was certain to benefit Aennorve.

The girl appeared to be winding down.

"And so," Shalindra concluded, "I come to you in the hopes that your Majesty will undertake to discuss this matter with my brother. Perhaps your Majesty's wisdom and eloquence may serve to sway the Ulor."

King Dasune repressed a smile. Despite her rather delightful air of unworldliness—souvenir, no doubt, of her long bibliothecal incarceration—the Ulor's little sister was not devoid of shrewdness. She had wit enough to realize that Cerrov was in no position to refuse the request of the Aennorvi monarch whose gold had bought him an army.

"My dear, I yield to your wishes." Plucking a rose that perfectly matched her dress, King Dasune presented the blossom with a bow. "You have quite conquered me. I can refuse you nothing."

13

"YOU WILL VISIT the estate of the Noble Landholder Deenyi Polchenskoi in Urusq," Varis commanded. "Observe Polchenskoi, without making your presence known, then return to inform me of your findings."

No.

"You will take particular note of the Noble Landholder's visitors."

No.

"You will leave for Urusq at once."

No.

"Resistance is pointless."

Perhaps.

Varis studied the ghosts. There were six of them—faint and nebulous apparitions, lacking the sharp clarity usually characteristic of his conjurations. Still, they were visible enough by moonlight, and there could be no doubting his power to control them. Their spokesman was tall and broad of form, with a grimly determined face; in life, no doubt possessing much force.

In silence, Varis exerted his will. The ghosts flickered and wavered. One or two faded to the verge of escape.

Astonishing. His hold on them seemed tenuous tonight. Even as he watched, he could sense the resistance intensifying. They had found some means of working together against him, and holding all six of them at once was proving remarkably difficult—

One of the ghosts vanished. Clean away.

Amazement shook Varis's concentration, and the remaining five spectres faded. Hastily, almost amateurishly, he clamped his mind down on them. Five sets of colorless eyes beamed triumph at him. Misplaced triumph, of course. He could retrieve the escapee if he chose. But then, that was hardly the point. What mattered was that the escape had occurred at all. Such a thing had never happened before.

"Do not try my patience further. Go now to Urusq," he ordered.

No.

It was all wrong. Doubt and something like fear eroded his concentration. His mind was inadequately focused tonight; his command, diffuse. He had practiced necromancy continually of late, perhaps not allowing sufficient intervals between summonings, and overexertion was undermining his strength. Fortunately, the remedy was close at hand.

One of his pockets yielded a small wooden box filled with liver-colored tablets. He had not expected to make use of them, for he had fortified himself with SD-9b prior to this latest Nightfields excursion. He had thought that dose of stimulant liberal, certainly more than sufficient to his needs. By all indications of past experience, it should have been enough.

No matter.

Placing a tablet upon his tongue, Varis swallowed, and the effect was immediate. To make matters sure, he swallowed another. Never before had he ingested stimulants in such quantity. Perhaps the dosage was excessive, but the results seemed to justify the risk. His mind sharpened, glowed, caught fire. Assurance and authority were there again, stronger than ever. He had lost nothing.

The box went back into his pocket. His attention returned to the ghosts, and instantly they were clear, sharp, immediate as any he had ever known. He met the rebellious eyes of their spokesman, and the rage swept through him like wildfire; an unfamiliar, unrestrained, almost lunatic rage, doubtless homicidal, were its object not already dead. His mind attacked.

Ectoplasmic substance twisted and stretched. A mental jerk tore the ghost's right arm from its body. A mental thrust flung the severed limb to the ground, and further, down through layers of soil and rock, deeper and deeper until Varis's necromantic senses finally lost all trace of it. A second such exercise similarly disposed of the left arm.

The ghost's eyes bulged, and his face contorted. Possessing no corporeality, he was presumably incapable of pain. But his mind and responses must have remained more or less as they had been in life; nothing else could have accounted for the look of indescribable horror.

Twist, yank, hurl. The ghost's right leg sailed through the air, slammed into the ground, and was gone. The left leg followed. Head and trunk remained.

Varis took his time ripping the torso vertically in two, allowing his victim ample opportunity to savor the experience. Presently the separate halves, trailing the ragged recollection of organs, went flying in opposite directions. The disembodied head floated, mouth wide open and screaming. Varis willed, and the head went hurtling off across the Nightfields, struck a hillock a hundred yards distant, and plunged down into the ground.

No trace of the refractory shade remained. It could not have been destroyed. The ectoplasmic fragments yet existed, and awareness certainly continued to reside in the head, wherever that was. Quite likely, the assorted pieces would blindly seek one another. Some day, reunification might well occur. But the search would be prolonged and laborious, success elusive for centuries at least.

Varis lifted his gaze to the four remaining ghosts.

"Go now to Urusq," he commanded tonelessly. "Your orders have altered, however. Polchenskoi conspires against me. Further confirmation of his treachery isn't required. Kill him tonight, together with any members of his household catching sight of you. Go."

Without further argument, they departed. Varis stood alone in the Nightfields. His heart was pounding, his temples were bathed in sweat, and the moonlight upon the granite grave markers seemed to him bright as daylight. Abandoning the cemetery, he rode back to the Zalkhash. Along the way, the moon shone like the sun, and the details of the cityscape, preternaturally clear, branded themselves upon his vision.

He went to his own apartment. It was the very dead of night, the silent and intensely solitary span just preceding dawn. The House Uloric was still; it might have been uninhabited. And yet, no point in seeking sleep. He was wide awake, unmercifully conscious. For a time, he tried to read, but his awareness—so strongly focused an hour earlier—was erratic and uncontrollable now. His thoughts sped to Urusq, where his ghostly minions were about their business, their very necessary business, but he didn't want to be there. He wrenched his mind away, and now his tangible surroundings were abhorrent. Perception lapsed, and for a time he was without intellect, although his body continued active.

It must have continued active. So much he inferred by the wreckage of his room, when consciousness returned, late in the morning. The sun was high in the sky, but the curtained chamber remained discreetly dim. Shadows masked the broken glass and furniture.

He had thought all that was over. He had thought that he ruled his powers and himself, but such was not quite the case.

He had slept long, but remained tired to death. His thoughts continued chaotic. Concentration was all but impossible, and the substantial gap in his memory of the preceding night frightened him. He remembered dispatching the ghosts to destroy Deenyi Polchenskoi; a sudden impulse that had somehow seemed a necessity at the time. But the period between his arrival at the House Uloric and the morning's awakening was a blank.

A bad sign.

He needed rest. He needed to recover his strength, else run the risk of losing it altogether. And for the first time in many years, he was forced to consider the dangers of sorcerous excess—and the possible result.

Cerrov had taken defeat with good grace, Shalindra reflected. King Dasune's intervention had proven effective, as she'd expected. Her brother—in no position to flout the will of his ally/host/creditor—had grudgingly granted consent, and now she would accompany him to Rhazaulle. It wasn't what he wanted, and it wasn't what he thought safe, but now that his hand had been forced, at least he wasn't sulking. He was close to her as ever; kept her informed—up to a point—of his plans; and even seemed glad of her company.

The last days passed quickly, in a whirl of dinners, dances, and galas. Then it was time to depart with Cerrov, a clutch of his officers, and a small escort of the Household Guard to join the army at the port of Denz, where the ships waited to ferry them across the Straits of Bitheen.

She was not to travel with her brother. King Dasune had given her a carriage of her own—as befit her status, he explained—and her disappointment at the separation was more than offset by her pleasure in the offering. It was a gleaming jewel of a landau, blazoned with the Haudrensq arms, additionally embellished with a painted birch leaf, to distinguish them from Varis's similar arms; gilded trim, and a roof constructed in two sections for lowering.

("Lower it often, my dear!" the King had advised. "Let the soldiers see your delightful smile. You will charm them as you have charmed me!") She had her own driver, a couple of bodyguards, and the maid Diligence to attend her.

In late springtime, the Aennorvi roads were good. The distance between Feyenne and Denz was not great, and the journey was completed in a mere four days. The approach to the port took Shalindra's breath away, for the troops had gathered on the fields outside the town limits, and the men and beasts, the carts and wagons, the tents and make-shift buildings, darkened a seemingly endless swathe of meadowland. Here and there flew the colored pennons distinguishing the various Rhelish regiments, and the two banners of Aennorve and Rhazaulle, equally honored, floated over all.

Her brother's party passed straight through the encampment, and the cheering was considerable. Shalindra kept the landau's roof lowered, as the King had suggested, and the bright Aennorvi sunshine played upon her face, and the soldiers cheered her, too. Their enthusiasm took her by pleasant surprise, but she didn't let it go to her head, for she guessed its evanescence. A few days' march across boggy Rhazaullean terrain—a good, chill, drenching Rhazaullean spring downpour—might well suffice to literally dampen their ardor. Best to enjoy it while it lasted.

They seemed so vigorous and confident. Not personally loyal to Cerrov, of course, or to anything Cerrov represented; for none were Rhazaullean, and the majority were mercenaries, but that was almost beside the point. There were so many of them, or so it seemed to her unschooled vision; enough, with all their paraphernalia, to fill the meadows, almost as far as the eye could reach. How could Varis hope to stand against such power?

A fleet of gunboats lay at anchor in Denz harbor. It would take days to load equipment, weapons, supplies, animals, and vehicles aboard. Shalindra's landau was one such vehicle, to her delight. She had expected to relinquish the carriage upon embarkation, but the will of King Dasune overruled all mundane considerations of practicality. ("Let the soldiers see your delightful smile!") She was to travel in princessly style; with luck, all the way to Rialsq. The landau, for all its elegance, was sturdy enough to navigate the TransBruzh, assuming the absence of heavy snow.

Hours before the dawn of the final day, Aennorvi troops and hired Rhelish regiments filed aboard their respective vessels. The Rhazaullean Ulor, his sister, aides, and ranking officers boarded the flagship *Exultation,* and the fleet set sail at sunrise.

Until that time, Shalindra had not known exactly where they were bound. Only her brother, his generals, captains, and a handful of officers knew which of the various towns and cities edging the inhospitable Rhazaullean coastline had been chosen to receive them. Once out upon the Straits of Bitheen, however, Cerrov told her. They were bound for Yzhnekh, the old sabling center at the southeastern tip of Rhazaulle, where the sea-sable pelts delivered from the ships were cleaned, processed, and readied for delivery to the farflung furriers waiting to effect fashion's metamorphosis.

"Why Yzhnekh?" Shalindra wanted to know. "What's there? Besides warehouses?"

"Support. The Trenyul clan," Cerrov explained. "Oldest, richest tribe of local Noble Landholders. Relatives of ours."

"Ours? Trenyul?"

"By blood and marriage, through Mother."

"Ah." Shalindra's face didn't change. By tacit consent, she and her brother spoke little of their mother. Some day, that would change, but not yet.

"Yzhnekhi Guild of Merchants speaks for the fatter tradesmen, and they hate Varis for slicing their profits.

Seems our uncle imposed limitations on the killing of sea-sables."

"Doesn't that actually protect their profits, in the end?"

"Yes, but the immediate effects are dissatisfying."

"When you're in Rialsq, will you abolish the limitations?"

"No, but the Yzhnekhis needn't know that just yet. For now, we have their support, and no doubt a warm reception."

Personally, Shalindra wondered. If expected support failed to materialize, she supposed the gunboats would bombard the town, and the army would have to fight its way ashore; else choose another landing site.

She might have spared herself the worry. The fleet dropped anchor in Yzhnekh harbor in the late afternoon. *Exultation*'s boat carried messengers ashore, under a flag of truce. A couple of hours later, the boat returned, bearing replies from the Mayor and Corporation, the Guild of Merchants, and several prominent Noble Landholders. The city of Yzhnekh, united and fervent in its loyalty, welcomed the return of its rightful Ulor Cerrov III.

That simplified matters.

The sun was setting, and it was far too late to begin the giant task of disembarkation. The troops would spend the night aboard the ships. However, the Ulor Cerrov, his esteemed sister, and such attendants as they cared to keep about them, were entreated to honor the house of the Noble Landholder Zyze Trenyul, second cousin to the Ulor's lamented mother.

And she had thought they might have to fight.

In view of the ancient Rhazaullean traditions of kinship and hospitality, there could be no doubting the good faith of the invitation. Cerrov didn't hesitate to accept. Only a handful of attendants accompanied the Ulor and his sister; half a dozen ranking officers, including the captain of the *Exultation;* Shalindra's maid, and six armed guards—any more guards would have impugned the hospitality of their host.

Shalindra wasn't thinking about diplomacy as she stepped onto Rhazaullean soil for the first time in thirteen years. The temperature here, at the southernmost extreme of the land, was not much lower than the temperature of northern Aennorve. But the breezes were different, smells were different, the feel and texture of the atmosphere were different. Familiar, long-lost, never-forgotten—

Home.

A heavy carriage, freighted with ornament in typical Rhazaullean style, waited to convey the Ulor and his sister through the crooked streets to the big gray stone townhouse of the Noble Landholder Trenyul. Officers, servants, and guards followed in lesser vehicles.

Trenyul—burly and bearded, attired in an old-fashioned fur-trimmed caftan—welcomed Cerrov with the duty of a subject and the warmth of a kinsman.

"My house," he intoned in time-honored style, "belongs to the Ulor."

There followed one of those evenings with which Shalindra was to become well acquainted throughout the ensuing weeks. The Noble Landholder's hospitality was ponderously old-fashioned. There was a little ceremony of welcome attended by all the household, complete with elaborate courtesies, speeches, traditional offerings of oat-cakes and knotted straw ghost-wards. There was a leaden reception, attended by many of the local gentry; rough-edged, unlettered provincial nobility, ill-at-ease in society, but eager to display their loyalty to the true Ulor. Then there was a marathon dinner—Rhazaullean cooking of monumental solidity, endless courses, oceans of vouvrak; toasts, speeches, smoky warm air, forthright table manners of the last century—for Yzhnekh was backward, even by Rhazaullean standards. No women in evidence. Following the initial formalities, the ladies of the house had withdrawn to their customary, old-fashioned seclusion. Fortu-

nately, no such humility was expected of the Ulor's sister.
It was, she thought, like traveling backward in time.

Long before the dinner ended, Shalindra's eyes were
itchy from all the smoke, mouth tired of smiling, stomach
full to bursting, and the gigantic courses were still coming. She looked to her brother, seated in the place of honor
at the head of the table. His eyes sought hers at the same
instant, and a glint of amused commiseration flashed
quick as a spark between them; a look too subtle and
fleeting for strangers to catch, but enough to assure her
that the old bond was strong as ever. Her eyes traveled to
Colonel Syun, who commanded no regiment, but whose
kinship to King Dasune purchased special favor. He
wasn't looking at her, and his face was unrevealing, but
she fancied that their host's display might strike Syun as
coarse, even vulgar. An Aennorvi, after all, could have no
real understanding of Rhazaulle's code of unstinting, almost overwhelming hospitality, a direct response to the
dire threat of the winter.

The voices were loud, and sometimes slurred with
vouvrak, but they spoke in Rhazaullean. It was the first
time in thirteen years she'd heard her native language in
general use, and it was undeniably a guttural tongue, but
beautiful all the same. Comfortable, but a little oddly fla-
vored in her mouth; for the long exile had left its vocal
mark, and more than one of the Noble Landholder
Trenyul's guests laughingly remarked upon her acquisition of a slight Aennorvi lilt.

The dinner ended at last. Had the occasion been
purely social in nature, the festivities would have continued with singing, perhaps dancing, and steady drinking;
might easily have continued all night long. The gravity of
the Ulor's mission admitted of no such frivolity, however,
and the guests, including Cerrov's officers, departed at a
mercifully early hour. Shalindra breathed a sigh of relief as
she made her escape. Another half hour would have sunk
her in a stupor. One of the servants conducted her to her

chamber, where Diligence waited. She took particular care to speak kindly to the maid that night, for it occurred to her for the first time that Diligence, despite her air of stolid competence, was a stranger in this land, unable to speak a single word of Rhazaullean.

The next day, Cerrov was out about his business. While the unloading of the ships proceeded, he was busy conferring with his officers, with local dignitaries and Noble Landholders. Shalindra knew there was no sense in trying to join him—she'd only be in the way. Thus she was left very much to her own devices, and available options appeared meager. She could socialize with the ladies of the Noble Landholder's household, but they were a shy and abysmally ignorant lot, stiffly uneasy around strangers, and all but devoid of conversation. She could, in the company of her guards, explore the gray streets of Yzhnekh, but there was little to see; and in the northeastern section of the town, the stench of the tanneries all but poisoned the air. She could read—the books she'd carried with her from Aennorve, for the house of Trenyul contained not a single volume. Fortunate that Fruce had taught her self-sufficiency; she would clearly need it.

So passed the next five days, during which she didn't see her brother. After the first night, Cerrov didn't even sleep at the Trenyul house, but divided his time between the wharves, where unloading proceeded, and the growing encampment just outside the city. He sent her written messages a couple of times, but never found time to visit. Fortunately, the same was not true of Colonel Syun, who managed to call occasionally. When he did, she bombarded him with questions.

"Why are we just sitting here?" she demanded. "Does it take so very long to unload a few ships?"

"Unloading's complete," Syun told her.

"Then why don't we move? I thought you men were supposed to be such fire-eaters!"

"Hard on the digestion. Right now, we're taking ad-

vantage of the favorable local climate to lay in a surplus of
rather more conventional provisions. Who knows when
another such opportunity's likely to arise? More important, we're gathering recruits. There's been a fine turnout
of Yzhnekhi lads, and half the Noble Landholders we met
the other night are culling their peasantry for able-bodied
men."

"Oh, that's excellent. That's all we could possibly
ask."

"Yes, your brother commands impressive loyalty, here
in the south."

"Well, he should—he's in the right."

"But he's also young, inexperienced, a stranger to his
country these thirteen years, and seeking to supplant an
established ruler of proven ability."

"A usurper, and very likely a murderer, or worse."

"But competent."

"You are my uncle's admirer, sir?"

"I give credit where it's due, Madam. Shalli."

"Hmm." She repressed a smile. "Take care, Colonel.
Your King's at war with Varis. Your frankness could land
you in trouble."

"Then I should count upon your Ladyship's intervention to clear my name. Perhaps to save my life, or my
happiness."

"Are you so certain you could count on it?"

"I am certain I'd hope, for hope is limitless and devoid
of humility. Should I find my hopes crushed?"

"I can hardly say, Colonel. I never give answers on
account. But I'll tell you how to gain the strategic advantage of placing me in your debt."

"How shall I do so?"

"By making my brother visit me. Tell him I miss him.
I haven't seen him in days."

"And won't, I'll wager. Even at cost of all potential
strategic advantage, I can't oblige you. The Ulor's up to

the hams in work, and nothing—not even you—will tear him away from it now."

"Which is as it should be, I suppose." Shalindra sighed. She was bored and lonely, and Syun's visits were too few and brief to fill her days. Of course, she'd brought it on herself. *What did you expect to do with yourself, anyway?* Cerrov's impatient query rang in her memory. Never mind, she'd keep herself occupied; she'd show him. "Any idea how much longer we'll be here?"

"A few days, not more."

"And then?"

"Straight north to Rialsq."

"Straight?"

"Depends on what stands in the way."

"Varis?"

"Eventually. But he can do little, as yet. This entire southern region of Rhazaulle, civilian population included, is solidly behind your brother. Lunacy to tire troops with a long march south to attack the enemy in the very heart of his stronghold. Varis will have to wait."

And so will I, Shalindra thought.

But she didn't have to wait for long. Two days later, the army finally moved out. Shalindra, accompanied by her maid and bodyguards, gladly departed the Trenyul household in the early morning. King Dasune's landau bore her through the streets to the north gate of the city, where, to her surprise, a gathering of local notables waited to intercept her. There were a few ceremonious speeches of farewell to sit through (always ceremony; it was something she'd somehow have to get used to), and then a presentation of Yzhnekhi gifts, intended, as the President of the Merchants' Guild explained, for "autumn in Rialsq." For Cerrov, there was a cloak fit for an Ulor, embroidered in gold and fully lined with the incomparable golden pelts of sea-sables. For Shalindra—a carriage-robe, hat, and muff of Smoke Cloud fox; pale gray undercoat, with long steel-gray guard hairs tipped in black. Fur so luxuriant and luxurious that the touch of it bathed her brain in pleasure. These people really *were* behind Cerrov. Eyes misting, she managed to express her appreciation; not discreditably, judging by the gratified expressions of the Yzhnekhis.

It ended, and her landau sped from the city, across the fields to join Cerrov's army, which had swollen startlingly since she'd last beheld it. No telling, at an untrained glance, how much by way of reinforcements her brother had acquired during his stay in Yzhnekh. No telling how many new companies there were now; square-built Rhazaullean peasants, groups of them sashed or cockaded in the colors of their respective Noble Landholders, such groups gathered beneath banners striped and pied in the hues of the district, blazoned with the royal arms of Aennorve, and marked with the green birch leaf of Cerrov Haudrensq.

They recognized her, of course, as the open landau passed through their midst, and they cheered her, but now she was starting to wonder. What, after all, had they to cheer her for? What had she ever done to deserve it? Shared a mother with the Ulor? Smiled and waved at them prettily? That was about the extent of it, but then, what else could she do?

What did you expect to do with yourself, anyway?

A staggering array of men and power, more than she had ever dreamed of. Columns of infantry, armed with everything ranging from antique pikes and halberds, to— in the case of the expensive Rhelish mercenaries—the latest in rifled flintlocks. The musket, however, appeared to be the weapon of necessity, if not choice. Rhelish cavalry upon their perfectly trained mounts, waves of Aennorvis upon their tall Brindle/Blonds, locals upon—according to rank—their hacks, their hunters, or their plough horses. Big guns riding caissons, wagons of cannonballs and barrels of powder, a small collection of outlandish firespitters. Supply carts, loaded with provisions; barrels, sacks, crates, and bales. Blare of trumpets, beating of drums. Glint of the early sun upon buckles, insignia, weapons. Flash on metal, brilliant color, moving glitter, deep vibration of ground and air.

For a time it seemed as if sorcery ruled, for there was no opposition. The human tide flowed on, with only changes upon the horizon to mark its progress. There were long stretches of open countryside, soundly dry in late spring. There were rivers to ford, bogs and marshes to circumvent. Cerrov's army expanded as it advanced, the villages and estates of the region yielding rich crops of recruits.

The towns were uniformly friendly, and Shalindra spent most nights indoors, enjoying the hospitality of assorted Noble Landholders; such occasions, more often than not, almost indistinguishable from that first night at the Trenyul house in Yzhnekh. There were massive dinners, where she learned the art of barely picking at each of innumerable courses; countless introductions, and she found she was acquiring tricks of memory to keep the names and faces straight; and speeches, speeches, interminable speeches—to which she learned to listen with half an ear, while appearing devotedly attentive. She was getting better at being the Ulor's sister, but found it a genuine relief when they made their camp in the green open spaces between the towns, and she could dine in peace with Cerrov, then spend the night in the commodious, cleverly designed tent provided for her use.

"You know, you were right about Arlieau," Cerrov remarked during one such dinner.

"Who?"

"Arlieau, sister to Dunulas the Great, who went off to the Jurlian-Zenki wars, and whose 'fair and gracious countenance never failed to cheer the soldiery.' You remember fair-and-gracious?" Cerrov was in a good humor, as he generally seemed to be these days. Good humor, however, did not camouflage a relentless purposefulness, a mental focus almost intent as a necromancer's.

"Oh, yes. What about her?"

"Well, you're her reincarnation, that's all. I have it on good authority that your fair and gracious countenance cheers the soldiery."

"Excellent. Then I'll have a portrait done in woodcut, and we can sell my likeness at five brazzles the copy. We'll make a fortune."

"Enterprising. But I'm serious. I didn't expect it, but your presence actually seems to boost morale."

"Really?" Shalindra was absurdly pleased. "Then you're glad you brought me along?"

"No. I still think it's folly. But not the disaster I envisioned."

"Very handsome of you. But not good enough, big brother. One of these days, mark my words, I'll get you to admit that bringing me was a good idea."

"Ask me again when we get to Rialsq."

Rialsq. They'd probably be there in a matter of days, for nothing hindered their advance. It appeared to Shalindra that all of Rhazaulle was united in support of Cerrov —at least, that was the view from her landau. Town after town welcomed him with cheering crowds, birch-leaf banners, and joyously pealing bells. New recruits were adding themselves to the army every week, and Cerrov's northward march seemed less a campaign than a triumphal progression.

Grozhunsq—Yersli—Nolatka—all along the old Truvisq Road, the town and city gates stood open, and the citizens cheered the Ulor Cerrov. Spring had given way to summer, before the army encountered resistance, and then it was relatively minor.

Strilki River, marking the boundary of the old union of southern provinces, likewise marked the northern boundary of Cerrov's stronghold. And here at Zynoff Bridge upon the Strilki, "loyalist forces," as they termed themselves, skirmishers from the walled city of Zyn upon the river's far bank, attempted to halt "the Imposter's" advance. They managed to hold Zynoff Bridge for some hours, until at last the concentrated fire of Cerrov's musketry drove them back into the city, which shut itself up like a clam.

Cerrov's army crossed the Strilki. The big guns were trundled over the bridge, and bombardment of the city walls commenced. Twenty-four hours later, its walls crumbling, Zyn surrendered. The gates opened, and the army marched in—marched quietly, and in order, for the terms of surrender prohibited a sack; prohibited retribution or indignity of any sort visited upon unresisting civilians. Such restraint, favorably impressing the relieved citizens, encouraged their swift submission. Before the troops departed, virtually all adult male Zynskis had sworn an oath of allegiance to the Ulor Cerrov.

North flowed the army, to encounter General Ruzeff's loyalist divisions of the Lazimir-based Legions of the South on the plain before the town of Kuulz. There, for the first time, Shalindra viewed a full-scale battle. Seated in her landau upon a wooded ridge overlooking the fields, with her taciturn maid beside her and group of guards about her, she could observe the deployment of the opposing forces. Observing it was one thing; comprehending it, another. From her reading, and from her brother's conversation, she'd formed the impression that an engagement was an orderly affair, calculated and controlled as a chess match. Perhaps to the generals it seemed so.

For hours she watched, marveling at the discipline that sent Ruzeff's columns of cavalry—tiny as toy figures, from her vantage point—repeatedly hurling themselves against the unbreakable bayonet-bristling squares of Cerrov's infantry; marveling at the robotic obedience that sent men marching like automata straight into the face of enemy fire. Incredible that they could do that. They'd undoubtedly march off the face of a cliff, if so ordered. And she was profoundly grateful she had not been born a man, of whom such lunacies were demanded.

Artillery roared, fire-spitters belched, and heavy smoke blanketed the distant field. The wind carried the reek of gunpowder, volleying of gunfire, shouting and thunder. She glimpsed rushing figures, great surges of murderous humanity. But the design of it all, if such existed, was lost in confusion.

Another hour passed, and a charge of Rhelish cavalry cut the Legions of the South in two; whereupon Cerrov threw his force against one of the enemy fragments, and smoke and distance mercifully obscured the ensuing slaughter. When the smoke began to clear, General Ruzeff's forces were in retreat, and the ground was strewn with dead.

Afterward, when the advance resumed, Shalindra's landau passed straight across the field, and the carnage, previously remote to the point of unreality, was now inescapably real. Carrion crows wheeled overhead. The air was loathsome, although the corpses had barely begun to decay. So many of them, lying motionless under the too-brilliant sun. Some of them almost children, years younger than she was. Pathetic, ghastly, and so unjust; for these poor lads were sorry dupes, cheated of their lives—and for what? At least the mercenaries among them had known what they were doing, but these others—? What did it really matter to most of them who ruled Rhazaulle? Unworthy thoughts, perhaps, for the rightful Ulor's sister; but at least, unlike these rotting youngsters, she still had a mind to think with.

Cerrov entered Kuulz, to receive the allegiance of the not-unwilling citizens. Thereafter, the march continued, scarcely hindered by the periodic gnatlike forays of Ruzeff's remnants.

Zena—Chatkho—Nevusq—all submitted without struggle. The chill of early Rhazaullean autumn was sharpening the air, and the peaks of the Bruzhois were drawing nearer by the day. Already, those jagged summits glittered white under the sun, for it was only during the height of summer that the mountaintops were wholly free of ice. A light glazing was hardly cause for concern, however. The vital TransBruzh would continue navigable for weeks to come.

Narshk Fens were behind them. Only the great city of Lazimir lay between Cerrov's army and the Bruzhois. Lazimir, ancient link between northern and southern Rhazaulle, was not a possession to be lightly relinquished. Here, if anywhere, the usurper was certain to make a stand. Thus it came as no surprise when the news arrived that the forces of the Ulor Varis were streaming down out of the Bruzhois, to assemble before the city of Lazimir, upon the Bowl of Lannakh.

14

THE NORTHERNMOST ARC of the foothills
ringing the broad, shallow depression known as
the Bowl of Lannakh was occupied by the forces
of the Ulor Varis. For two days they had rested
there, eating and sleeping in comfort, but now the respite
was all but ended. Tonight, the campfires of the Imposter's
regiments glowed along the hilltops at the opposite curve
of the Bowl. In the morning, the two armies would engage.

Had any member of Varis's force been asked to explain
this particular choice of locale, he would without hesitation have cited the need to protect the city of Lazimir.
Ancient capital and heart of the southern lands, second in
size and significance only to Rialsq itself, Lazimir must
never fall into enemy hands. All true, as far as it went, but
most of the soldiers remained quite ignorant of another,
equally compelling reason.

It was not a matter of common knowledge that the
Bowl of Lannakh had, for the space of a century or more,
been known as the "Bowl of Blood." The great atrocities
of the Nivoystzi Massacre, taking place upon this spot
over five hundred years earlier, had all but faded from

popular recollection. The betrayal and slaughter of three thousand fleeing Bruzhoi tribesmen and their families, though once infamous, was now nearly forgotten. Hardly a man among either of the opposing armies recognized the Bowl of Lannakh for the vast graveyard that it was.

The Ulor Varis, of course, knew history.

Dead of night, and Varis rode alone down into the empty Bowl. No moon in the sky. Clad in black, and mounted upon a black horse, the Ulor was virtually invisible. He carried no lantern, and needed none. When his horse would have faltered, he guided the animal unerringly, for his eyes—pupils preternaturally dilated and filled with greenish sparks—pierced the darkness like knives. To him, each detail of the landscape was almost glaringly distinct; the rocks edged in green light, the occasional low clump of shrubbery sullenly aglow. Such was one effect of the combined stimulants with which he'd fortified himself prior to his quiet solitary departure from the encampment. It was a heavier, more heterogeneous dose than he had ever swallowed before, comprising a quantity of old Clotl's peerless gel. The gel was limited in supply, and he usually hoarded it like a miser. Not tonight, however. Tonight, nearly a quarter of the remaining store had vanished at a gulp. The extravagance was shocking but justifiable, for tonight's feat of necromancy—greater by far than any he had ever attempted—would tax his force to the limit. He was ready, though. His entire mind—consciousness and whatever lay beyond or below—blazed with power.

Drawing rein, Varis dismounted. An army lay behind him, another before him. He could easily discern the hulking distant hills, the small banked fires that—to his eyes—seemed to scream through the night. Yet the utter silence and stillness of the place—the great expanse of bare terrain, the black moonless void overhead—produced the illusion of solitude. Almost, he could have imagined himself alone in an empty world.

Divesting himself of his gloves, the better to free his hands for the requisite gesturing, he set to work. The procedure was one set forth in Yelnyk of Krezniu's notebook. He hadn't thought of it in years. Upon receiving news of his nephew's invasion, however, he'd resurrected the old notebook and commenced refreshing his memory. Variation had followed upon variation, and eventually he'd devised a few twists of his own never dreamt of by Yelnyk; perhaps, never dreamt of by anyone.

Time, place, and physical being lost meaning—were not. Intelligence, intention, and interdimensional comprehension fused into one, chose a direction, abolished metaphysical space. The summons flew, such a summons as had never been issued.

The ghosts obeyed.

A killing field's worth of slaughtered Bruzhoi men, women, and children seeped from the ground. Ancient, murdered, wronged, and unwilling slaves to the will of a necromancer. Confused and wretched, ripped from the peace of the grave into an inimical era. And hundreds of them, maybe thousands—certainly too many to count. More ghosts together than a single summoning had ever gathered in one spot; a reluctant battalion.

This in itself was an accomplishment to place him in the first rank of history's necromancers. But he was not finished yet. Now came the twists of his own devising. The outrages committed upon Breziot's shade long ago, and more recently, upon the refractory ghost at the Nightfields, had taught him the endless ductility of ectoplasm. There was almost nothing that couldn't be done with the stuff, given a strong, guiding vision. This so, Varis exerted his will, and the forms shuddering before him began to change—stretching and warping grotesquely, else softening into amorphousness; some darkening and apparently coalescing almost to solidity, others fading beyond the range of any but magically enhanced vision.

He molded them as he required, shutting his sorcer-ously attuned ears to their pleas, arguments, groans, and shrieks. He colored and shaped them according to his own designs, then sent them winging across the Bowl of Lannakh.

They were gone. In his necromancer-mind's eye, he could follow them all the way to his enemy's camp if he chose, but the effort would drain him, and he chose to conserve his strength. He would need it tomorrow.

Unexpectedly difficult to mount his horse. When he swung himself back into the saddle, the effort left him gasping and dizzy. For a moment, his perception narrowed and dimmed to the verge of extinction. His enhanced vi-sion flickered, and something monstrous seemed to slip along the edge of his sight. He turned his head sharply, but saw nothing, nothing at all, for the darkness crashed down on him, and he was blind and alone, or perhaps not alone, in the night. Struggling for breath, he pressed both hands to his eyes. Head bent and shoulders bowed, he sat motionless for long seconds.

It took an effort of will to lower his hands from his face. He looked around him, studying the ground, the shrubbery, the distant hills. All was as it had been. He breathed a shuddering sigh. Profound exhaustion re-mained, but Varis was himself again.

Time skewed, hopped, and lagged. He did not notice how long it took him to make his way back to the camp, nor did he notice the sentry's startled, uneasy stare into his face. Leaving orders with an attendant to wake him two hours before dawn, he entered his own tent, collapsed face down on his cot, and for a while was free of the world.

On the far side of the Bowl of Lannakh, unperturbed by the prospect of the coming battle, Cerrov Haudrensq slumbered soundly in his tent. Or perhaps less soundly than it appeared, for something woke him. A noise, an instinctive sense of alien presence—something snapped his eyes open. He sensed himself fully awake, yet the scene he beheld was purely dreamlike.

The tent was crowded with human figures, hovering weightless in midair; smaller than life-sized, colorless, and slightly transparent, faintly aglow with their own grayish light. Dozens of them, clad in the uniform of the Ulor Varis's loyalist troops. And two recognizable anomalies—an image of himself, accurate down to the last detail of form and feature; and a young woman's slender figure, Shalindra rendered in tones of gray.

Cerrov sat up. The visitors took no notice, for their attention was otherwise engaged. A pack of soldier-figures hurled themselves like wolves upon the terrified Shalindra-figure. Tearing her clothes away, they flung her down, violated her repeatedly, and finally killed her, hacking her with swords and slitting her body with their bayonets. The Cerrov-figure's efforts to interfere were ineffectual. A gang of loyalist-figures subdued and disarmed him, secured his arms and compelled him to watch. When the Shalindra-figure had been reduced to ragged shreds of vapor, they turned their weapons upon the Cerrov-figure, disemboweling and dismembering the simulacrum at their leisure.

The real Cerrov sprang from his camp bed, thus drawing the intruders' attention. Swords bared, a host of floating figures converged upon him. Despite the seeming insubstantiality of the blades and their owners, the first slash opened a bloody gash in his upraised forearm; a wound burningly cold. A cry escaped him. He struck out, and his hand sliced through chill ghostly substance. A moment later, he jerked the hand back, blood streaming from a cut across the palm. Monstrously unfair, that their weapons marked his solid flesh, while he couldn't touch *their* incorporeity; but no time now to ponder the injustice. Lowering his head and throwing one arm across his face, he sprang for the exit. He must have passed straight

through them. An instant's uncanny chill enveloped him.
Then he was through, and out of the tent, with the fresh
night air on his face.

Cerrov halted, breathing deeply. The glow of the
watch fires illumined the silent camp. He turned back to
regard his tent. Dark, motionless, no sign of disturbance.
Nightmare? His right arm and hand were splotched with
blood. No dream. He supposed he should have the cuts
bandaged, but how would he explain them? The last thing
his troops needed, upon the eve of battle, was an inkling
of supernatural opposition. Best to tell no one of it.

Even as he pondered, some half dozen wild-eyed figures came staggering from their respective tents. Among
them, Cerrov recognized his ranking officers. All were di-
sheveled, confused, and alarmed; all marked with bleeding
cuts. It wasn't difficult to guess the cause.

"Necromancy," Cerrov informed his pallid commanders calmly. "Unnerving, distracting, but not unop-
posable. The power of ghosts lies chiefly in the fears of the
ignorant."

"Snow-Spirits," an officer suggested bleakly.

"Folklore," Cerrov replied.

"Uncertain, Ulor."

Cerrov was silent, for his officer spoke nothing but the
truth. Beyond doubt, most Rhazaulleans more than half-
believed in the Snow-Spirits—those shape-shifting wraiths
of legend, possessed of redoubtable powers, incomprehensible intellects, and wholly capricious tastes. Snow-Spirits,
it was said, might lead a lost traveler to safety, else pitch
him into a glacial crevasse; build incredible fairy-cities of
ice for the amusement of human children, or set an ava-
lanche thundering down on a village; ride the white storm
winds harmlessly out to sea, or drive the blizzards upon
the Bruzhois, to trap luckless caravans in the mountain
passes. Impossible to gauge the affinities and antipathies,
the abilities and limitations of the Snow-Spirits, whose
only constant was inconstancy.

"They were small, sharply drawn, and shaped like the living," an officer recalled. "I saw familiar faces among them—I saw my own. These were not the summoned of necromancy."

"Who among us is fit to judge that?" Cerrov inquired.

"Self-evident, Ulor. It would seem that the Snow-Spirits oppose us."

"Or somebody wishes us to think that they do," said Cerrov.

"And if the troops discover it, they'll balk."

"Rhazaulleans might balk. No local bugaboos about to rattle my boys," declared one of the Rhelish commanders.

"And my Aennorvis are sound."

"You don't know our Snow-Spirits," a Rhazaullean observed dourly.

"You don't know my Rhelish."

"Your Rhelish willing to fight the winds, the snows, the enemy of a thousand shapes?"

"Peasant superstition."

"Is it?"

"Unproved," Cerrov broke in. "Inconclusive. Whatever we saw, no need to flurry the men over it. This won't be spoken of."

Grudging nods of acquiescence.

"How long until sunrise?"

"Less than two hours, Ulor."

"Into my tent, then. A final conference."

Speaking glances flew among the foreign commanders, who—accustomed to nearly independent operation—had little use for this mushrooming Rhazaullean Ulor's insistence upon planning, perfect coordination of polyglot troops, and strongly centralized command residing in his youthful self. *This boy thinks he knows it all,* was the private opinion of many. Yet none of them could deny the consistent soundness of the Ulor's judgment, which had carried them smoothly from Yzhnekh almost to the gates of

Lazimir. There could be no arguing with success. A final conference, then. Resigned, they followed him.

Cerrov did not allow himself to hesitate at the entrance to his tent. Apparently serene, he walked in and lit a lamp. His eyes swept the canvas enclosure, which was empty of uncanny visitants, or seemed so. Rumpled camp bed, a single trunk, one chair, and a table presently covered with an enormous map of the countryside south of Lazimir—all seemed normal and undisturbed. They were gone, and the night was nearly over. His tension eased. Turning, he summoned his followers to the map.

Pins, arrows, markings in multicolored inks. Topography, man-made obstacles, disposition of troops. The Ulor Cerrov's preoccupation with the map by turns annoyed and amused his officers, but they found themselves constrained to listen, and their leader's vision relentlessly impressed itself upon their brains. Overly schooled young fellow, but clever, undeniably clever and forceful. Perhaps his pins and ink-scribbles were worth looking at.

They looked for the next hour and a half or so, until the quiet light of dawn began pushing itself into the tent. The lamp was no longer necessary, and Cerrov moved to extinguish it. The lamp, seemingly imbued with life of its own—else clasped in an invisible fist—jerked away from him, skittered backward, and overturned, loosing a tide of burning oil. Officers cursed as oil streamed across the parchment map, which instantly ignited. Flames jumped, and the men stepped hurriedly back from the table. There was no breeze in the tent, but the blaze leapt and danced. A twisting tongue licked canvas, and fire ran up the wall. A second later, flame sheeted overhead. Ulor and officers dashed from the tent.

Safely clear, they turned to look back. Cerrov's tent blazed like a torch. Flames roared, and torrents of stygian smoke billowed; smoke far thicker and darker than circumstances seemed to warrant. Impossibly black clouds spread like panic. A despairing curse escaped one of the officers. He pointed. Above the burning tent loomed three great figures. Insubstantial, wavering and transparent, half-obscured by smoke though they were, their outlines were unmistakable. Through the flame and roiling vapor, the tall, spiky, icicle-crowns and ruffs, together with the famous elongated icicle-fingers of legend, proclaimed the presence of the Snow-Spirits.

Even as Ulor and officers watched, one of the huge figures bent, almost languidly, to scoop up a handful of fire and toss it. The fireball flew through the still morning air, straight to the nearest tent. Flames spouted, black smoke gushed, and the alarmed occupants emerged, wheezing.

"Order the trumpeter to sound the alarm," Cerrov commanded calmly. "Rouse the camp, extinguish the fires."

Moments later, the clear brazen notes summoned every soldier from sleep. They stumbled forth into the morning to find the camp smothered in the heaviest, blackest smoke ever to assault human eyes and lungs. Gasping, choking, and all but blinded, they beat at the fires with water-soaked bedding, sodden clothing, anything that came to hand. The young Ulor Cerrov—face smoke-blackened, garments charred—fought the blaze alongside his men.

The collective efforts might have succeeded but for the intervention of the Snow-Spirits, if that was what they were. No sooner was one tent extinguished, than the un-hurried flick of a ghostly wrist sent fire upon another. The flames cavorted and spread. Suffocating black smoke pressed like iron upon laboring lungs, burned and blinded streaming eyes. Sparks showered, men ducked and scurried, terrified horses screamed, the poisoned air seethed, and the fathomless eyes of the Snow-Spirits brooded over all.

———

The sting of smoke in her nostrils awakened Shalindra. Night or day? Instinct told her that morning had come, but the tent was darker than it should have been. She sat up, blinking, her vision hazed. She rubbed her eyes, but the haze remained. Her tent was fogged with smoke. And the noises outside—the voices, the stir—they were peculiar, and wrong.

Jumping from bed, she ran to the pallet on the ground in the corner and shook her maid awake. Diligence rose at once. Her nose wrinkled at the acrid scent, and she glanced about uneasily.

"Find out what's going on," Shalindra ordered.

Diligence bobbed her head. Before she had taken a single step, the flap masking the entrance shifted, and one of the Aennorvi bodyguards thrust his head into the tent.

"Dress yourself and come away at once, Madam," the guard instructed. "We are commanded to convey you from the camp."

"We're under attack?" she asked.

"No delay. Move, Madam." The guard withdrew.

For an instant Shalindra stood staring after him, and then she obeyed. Within moments, Diligence had laced her into a plain woolen dress. Pausing only long enough to splash a little water across her face and into her smoke-smarting eyes, she threw a cloak about herself and exited the tent, closely followed by her maid.

The moment she stepped outside, she started to gasp for breath. Out here, the smoke that merely fogged the tent's interior was dense, strangling, blinding. She could hear the crackle of flame, the shouting of men, and the panicked shrilling of horses, but no gunshots, no clash of steel or thunder of cannon, no sound of battle. She could see almost nothing. The smoke clawed at her eyes. Her throat closed, and she coughed spasmodically. Beside her, Diligence did likewise.

Where to go? The world was drowned in swirling blackness, and she was lost. The clamoring all about her told her nothing. She took Diligence's hand in her own, and felt the firm clasp strongly answered; no safety there, but comforting nonetheless. Choosing a direction almost at random, she took a sightless step forward, then jumped as someone's large hand closed on her wrist.

"This way, Madam. Careful."

Aennorvi voice. One of her bodyguards. She followed without demur, and he steered her through the smoke and shouting to her own landau. The horses stood in harness. The half-dozen men assigned to protect her were waiting.

"What's happening? Is my brother safe?" No immediate answer, and Shalindra balked. "I asked you, is my brother safe?"

"Yes, Madam. In. That is, if you please."

She didn't move fast enough, and, placing one hand on the small of her back, he gently but firmly propelled her forward. Curbing her outrage, she climbed in. No doubt the man was simply obeying his orders. Diligence entered and sat down beside her. Snapping of orders, and the vehicle began to move; guards leading the frightened horses. In this manner they made their way through the camp, and as they moved farther from the center, the smoke thinned, and the running forms of agitated soldiery became discernible.

Shalindra heard a gasp beside her, felt strong fingers clutch at her arm. She turned to discover Diligence staring up at the sky, terror transforming her wonted stolidity. Shalindra followed the other's gaze. Directly above, partially obscured but visible through the dark clouds, floated a huge, manlike yet inhuman figure; transparent and colorless, wintry of alien eye, crowned and armed with ghosticicles. Diligence wouldn't know what it was, but Rhazaullean-born Shalindra couldn't fail to recognize the classic image of a Snow-Spirit. And yet, it was commonly held that Snow-Spirits, secretive and jealous of their mysteries, never willingly revealed themselves to men. A favored traveler, alone in the wilderness, might catch a fleeting glimpse, scarcely more. The entity above was virtually flaunting itself. Was it what it seemed?

The landau rolled on. The smoke thinned to gauze. The driver climbed into the box, cracked his whip, and the pace picked up. The camp was behind them, and they were bumping through the wooded hills edging the southern curve of the Bowl. The carriage roof was down, and Shalindra could see again. To the left rose the forested slopes; to the right, hundreds of feet below, the great expanse of shallowly depressed terrain stretched on into the distance. She turned to look back. An ugly smear of black atmosphere marked her brother's position. The smear receded steadily, to her uneasiness. She ought to be with him, helping him somehow. But she knew his opinion, his inflexible opinion—that she'd only be in the way.

On they went, up into the hills, until they came to a high, prominent ridge of rock overlooking Lannakh. Here, where the air was clear of smoke and the view was unobstructed, they halted and waited. It was a perfect vantage point from which to view the impending battle; if there was truly to be a battle. The black clouds stifled Cerrov's camp. Flames leaped, distant toy men scuttled, and clouded humanoid figures, broodingly inscrutable, hovered over all. How could that bedeviled army hope to fight?

Time passed, and the sun climbed. It was an incongruously beautiful day, brilliant and sharp-edged with autumn. The sky was translucent, the atmosphere almost crystalline. All but impossible to credit the imminence of violence. Not long, however, before the exclamations of her bodyguards alerted her to movement at the foot of the opposing hills. Cloud of dust, glitter of sunlight on polished steel, brass, gold braid. Varis's troops were advancing across the Bowl.

Cerrov's demoralized forces were quite unprepared to meet them.

She had never felt so helpless in her life, as she sat

there watching the enemy's unopposed progress. The great
river of men surged on. Individual figures, on horseback
and afoot, became distinguishable through the dust.
Crimson uniforms of the Uloric Guard, banners bearing
the Winged Wolf emblem, Haudrensq arms on a gonfa-
lon, regimental pennants, and even individual insignia
discernible with the aid of a good spyglass. A greater
power than Cerrov had hitherto encountered; much
greater. Her spyglass searched the army in vain for its
commander, however. Varis, prone to peculiar asceticism,
distinguished himself by no particular splendor of uniform
or trappings. If he was down there upon the field, she
couldn't pick him out of the throng.

Shalindra at first imagined they would march the entire diameter of the Bowl, but such was not their immediate intent. The crimson tide halted well short of the
southern boundary. The big guns rolled into place, and
artillery bombardment commenced.

It would have been horrible, no doubt, had she witnessed the actual effects. But all that merciless fire was
trained on a featureless distant cloud. Death and destruction, if such occurred, were discreetly veiled in smoke.
Almost difficult to believe that Cerrov and his men were
actually there in the thick of it. But the answering cannon
confirmed their presence with irregular fire, like the uncertain pulse of the gravely wounded.

Shalindra strained her eyes without success. Impossible
to penetrate that smoky shroud. If only she could send one
of her mounted guards down there for news—but there
was no point in trying it, none of them would go. They'd
been ordered to protect her with their lives, and protect
her they would, whether she liked it or not.

Time crawled, the sun shifted, and with it moved a
couple of the Snow-Spirits. The vast, wavering figures
drifted above the trees along the eastern curve of the Bowl,
eventually attaining a position opposite Varis's right flank,
and there they halted. To Shalindra, the languid migration

was incomprehensible. Its significance was clear, however, to someone in the army below. Artillery wheeled to face the east. Heavy fire blasted the slopes. At last, when broad stretches of forest lay smoking, bombardment ceased, and a scarlet detachment of cavalry swooped for the blackened trees. A battered and broken brigade of Cerrov's light horse, emerging to meet them, was swiftly cut to pieces. The enemy's attempted deception discovered and duly aborted, Varis was free to concentrate his full force upon the smoke-palled southern hills.

The loyalist cavalry advanced; broke into a sweeping gallop. Shalindra watched stilly. Under other circumstances, that scarlet charge across the Bowl of Lannakh would have seemed a grand and glorious spectacle. Just now, the vision possessed a certain fever-dream quality.

A shockingly diminished remnant of Cerrov's army met the onslaught. Musket fire crackled, sabers and bayonets flashed, dust and smoke hazed the field. Once again, Shalindra found her view obscured, but this time, the outcome was all too predictable. Her brother's troops—supernaturally beset, battered, reduced, and now vastly outnumbered—didn't stand a chance. The Aennorvi horsemen, obedient to their own commanders, were already in flight. The Rhelish mercenaries and the Rhazaullean patriots, while more tenacious, were hopelessly overmatched. A stubborn core of them fought on, persisting for some hours until the unnaturally black smoke from the burning camp wafted down to the field like a predator selectively seeking its meat. Cerrov's last two infantry squares were blanketed, blinded, smothered. A final lightning-stroke cavalry charge broke them, and they fled from the Bowl in disorder.

Varis's forces chased them into the hills. Those overtaken were slaughtered on the spot. The mounds of corpses proliferated. Presently, trees and distance hid pursuers and fugitives from sight.

She didn't know what had happened to Cerrov. If he'd

survived that carnage, they'd be hunting him. If they caught him, they wouldn't kill him out of hand—not the young Imposter himself. They'd preserve him for trial and public execution. *As they did Mother.* But her landau, with its fresh horses, could save his life, provided she found him first.

"East. Back toward the camp," she instructed the driver.

"South. Get her out of here," an Aennorvi voice countermanded. The ranking bodyguard, the one who had propelled her so unceremoniously into the carriage.

"I said east." Shalindra took care to keep her voice even. She was hot with quick fury fueled by fear and frustration, but it wouldn't do to show it; bluster would only make her ridiculous. "We will join the Ulor. Go back."

"South," said the guard.

The driver looked from one to the other. No telling which he would have chosen to obey had a party of mounted men not broken just then from the trees bordering the ridge. About a dozen of them; gold-braided scarlet uniforms, formidable weaponry, heavy horses—loyalist dragoons, combing the hills in search of fleeing rebels. Without hesitation, the Aennorvi guards raised their muskets and fired. Had every shot found its mark, they would have evened the odds in a single volley. Only two dragoons toppled, however. One cursed and clutched a bleeding thigh. The others remained untouched.

Aennorvi fire was instantly returned, and four of the bodyguards went down. Bare sabers finished the last two.

A crack of the driver's whip sent the landau clattering south in the wake of the retreating army. Their opponents dispatched, the dragoons gave chase, overtaking the fugitive vehicle within seconds. An adroit shot from horseback killed the driver, who tumbled headlong into the laps of the passengers.

Arresting the carriage without difficulty, the soldiers drew near to inspect their two captives. Drawing the pis-

tol from the dead driver's belt, Diligence leveled the
weapon at the nearest dragoon, their captain, who reacted
with reflexive speed. His own pistol appeared as if by
magic, and he fired. She slumped in her seat, and the
weapon dropped from her hand.

Eyes wide open. Black bullet hole between them.
Shalindra gazed disbelievingly into a void. Nothing there,
any more; nothing there at all. No time for grief or re-
grets, however. Her own turn next.

"Don't touch the gun," the captain advised.

She had not even thought to do so. She turned uncomprehending eyes upon him.

He gestured, and one of his men collected the pistol.

"Good, that's better. Now, who are you?" the captain
inquired equably.

She said nothing. They obviously meant to kill her;
why didn't they just do it? She could only hope they
wouldn't decide to entertain themselves first.

"You've got a name? Speak up."

Silence.

"A shy one. Charming. Well, let's see. Travels with a
servant, a driver, a squad of guards, outstanding horses,
and enough luggage to founder a cargo ship, in a blazoned
carriage fit for a queen." The captain's eyes lingered on the
Haudrensq arms. He smiled. "Gentlemen, I believe we've
caught us a fish."

They neither killed nor abused her. No injury or physical
outrage was inflicted upon so valuable a prize as the Imposter's own sister; only the indignities of iron manacles
and an open carriage exposing her to the view of her captors.

They didn't tell her where they were taking her. Her
urgent questions regarding the fate of her brother went
unanswered. The captain, having sent a messenger to his
own commander, lingered two hours for a reply. His or-

ders arrived at last, and the landau, driven by a soldier, sped north in a cloud of dragoons.

Shalindra first thought herself headed for Lazimir, and a gaudy mock trial like the one accorded her mother. Not so, however. A day's jolting travel brought her within sight of the old city gates. Then the landau swung wide, skirting Lazimir and its satellite villages. Surprising. She'd expected they'd enjoy displaying their trophy to the populace. Evidently some authority had decreed otherwise.

They camped that night on the meadows to the west of the city. Shalindra was given a tent to herself, reasonable comfort and privacy. True, there were guards stationed about her quarters throughout the night, but nobody troubled her. The respect and restraint that should have reassured her actually exerted the opposite effect. There was a design in all this, one that she couldn't fathom. She could only be certain she'd somehow be used to her enemies' advantage. A trial and execution in Lazimir was the obvious sequence, but these were clearly not on the program. She couldn't imagine the alternatives, and the uncertainty racked her.

She took care to conceal her fears. No point in amusing these apes.

Morning, and the journey resumed. West in a wide arc around Lazimir, and then a famous, well-worn track running north to the mountains.

The TransBruzh, in early autumn. Clear, dry, well-marked, snaking over the Bruzhois.

She knew at that point they were taking her back to Rialsq. Largest city, center of government, seat of the Ulor, site of the House of Ice—yes, that was where she was going, all right. If she allowed it. They'd make a public spectacle of her, use her against her own brother—if she let them. Travesty of a trial, false confession, conviction, and nightmare circus of an execution—that's what awaited her in Rialsq.

Consider your options.

Few and poor. Escape, impossible. Rescue, improbable. Suicide? Terrible to contemplate, for she was young, healthy, and unready to die. Capitulation? Confession, public shift of allegiance, acceptance of Uncle's narrow mercy? Survival, and certain banishment to some distant country estate, to which the news of her brother's death would wend its way, weeks or months later? Enforced mean marriage, low enough to bar her offspring from all hope of succession?

Unacceptable.

What else, then?

For now, nothing else.

The hours and miles crawled by. The road ascended, and the temperature dropped. The autumn was well advanced at these higher elevations. The breezes were honed, the scrub vegetation already browning. The wind sliced straight through her light woolen cloak, to set her shivering. She didn't want her guards to see that, they'd think her afraid. They'd be right, too, but she wasn't about to give them the satisfaction of knowing it. All her luggage remained intact, including the wooden box housing the Yzhnekhi gift of Smoke Cloud fox. The chain linking her manacles permitted some freedom of movement. She donned the furs, and the shivering ceased, but the fears remained.

Higher and higher into the Bruzhois, up the taxing grade of the TransBruzh, through the black-green ocean of fir and pine. Frequent stops to rest the horses, and then she was permitted to descend from the landau, to stroll back and forth under the attentive eyes of her guards. No chance to run; they were always careful about that.

The conifers thinned, presently straggling out of existence. The TransBruzh wound its way amidst naked outcroppings of granite. Carriage and escort were approaching the Ayzin Pass. Beyond the pass, the road would commence its long descent, and the rate of doomful progress was sure to increase.

A mile or so short of the rift itself, the landau abandoned the TransBruzh to follow a narrow lane up a slope so grueling that the driver was obliged to descend from the box. Presently they attained the summit of a sheer cliff overlooking the Ayzin Pass. Directly ahead loomed the battlements of Castle Haudrensq, the Tollbooth of Rhazaullean history.

Through the tunnellike archway piercing the outer wall, and into the courtyard clattered dragoons and captive. There they halted. Shalindra caught a quick glimpse of gaunt medieval architecture, of uniformed figures hurrying toward her. The castle was garrisoned, she realized; perhaps for the first time in centuries.

They must have been expecting her arrival. The efficiency with which they plucked her from the carriage and hustled her indoors suggested foreknowledge. Grim stone corridors; narrow, winding stairs; down, down, down. A couple of guards took care to keep her between them. Each had firm hold of one of her arms, as if they expected a resistance; but she wasn't about to waste her strength on anything so useless.

Down another flight of stairs and on along a damp, stale-aired passageway. Quick march, no conversation. At the end of the hall, an iron door. They opened it and pushed her through. The door clanged shut behind her, and she heard the scrape of the bolt.

Shalindra stood blinking. Her eyes adjusted, and she gazed unwillingly about her. The closet—no, dungeon— in which she stood was small, perhaps eight feet square; windowless and dim, but not pitch dark; chill and dank, with moisture beading the walls. Almost certainly subterranean. There was a cot equipped with a small straw pallet, a rickety table, a stool, and a bucket in the corner; no other furniture. Water jug and cup upon the table, but no food, and no lamp. It took her a moment to locate the source of illumination. An iron grill in the ceiling admitted a little light from the corridor above. She walked to the table and examined the jug. It was full. She poured herself a cup of water, and drank. Fresh enough, probably drawn that morning. Removing her furs, she set them carefully aside, then went to the cot. Pallet faintly damp, but apparently free of vermin. Lying down upon it, she studied the ceiling. Nothing to see. She closed her eyes. Thought persisted.

Cerrov. Alive or dead? If alive, presumably in flight with the shattered ruin of his army. If dead, she herself was likely to follow him, soon enough.

In which case, what was she doing here, stashed away in the depths of the Tollbooth? No sense to it. Unless—

Perhaps her initial suppositions had been all wrong. They didn't mean to celebrate her capture and destruction after all. Quite the contrary, they wanted to conceal it. She would be secretly murdered, strangled or knifed right here in this cell; her remains destroyed, probably cremated. One more possible claimant to the Wolf Throne, quietly disposed of.

But there was another, more terrible possibility; that they didn't mean to kill her at all. For reasons best known to himself, Varis wished to preserve her. Here she would sit, mewed underground—buried alive—for the rest of her natural life. Decades. At Fruce Library, she'd thought herself imprisoned. She hadn't known the meaning of the word—until now.

The tears were starting to well, and she didn't want that. Closing her eyes, she deliberately relaxed her muscles, willing her mind to empty itself. Almost instinctively, she was practicing one of the techniques gleaned long ago from the sorcerous notebooks hidden at the heart of Fruce Isle. Her thoughts slowed and blurred. She didn't altogether lose consciousness, but reality distanced itself. How long she lay in this state, she couldn't know. It might have been hours.

The rasp of the bolt brought her back. The door

opened. Shalindra beheld a tall, lean form framed in the entry; a very pale visage, remembered from long ago. He was alone. She rose smoothly to her feet. Kept her face a blank.

"Well, Uncle," she said.

15

HE STEPPED INTO the room without troubling to shut the door. There were probably guards in the corridor outside. Their eyes met, and the thought rose unbidden to her mind, *That man is sick.* There was no obvious reason to think so. He was lean to the point of gauntness, but upright and apparently vigorous. Still fairly youthful, although haggard; hair still thick and black. His face was ashen in the gloom, but firm-lipped, and the hazel eyes shone as if lighted from within. Perhaps the eyes were too brilliant; maybe that was what struck her as wrong, unhealthy. She found herself curiously unafraid. His reality scarcely resembled the monster of her imagining, and it was somehow difficult to believe he would actually harm her; at least, here and now. Because? Because he looked too—too—?

Intelligent. He looked too intelligent for commonplace violence.

A naïve delusion.

Remember who he is, and what he is.

Varis was inspecting her with equal attention. His gaze rested briefly upon her locket, and then returned to her face. "Not difficult to recognize," he said at last. "Shalindra."

She repressed a visible start. There was something startling in his use of her first name. Almost it seemed an invasion. And his voice—so quiet, actually soothing, with the cultivated Zalkhash inflections—brought back memories of her childhood. Did he guess that? Probably yes. He meant to confuse her; he was amusing himself. She wasn't about to cooperate. It wasn't her business to entertain him.

"Come to do the job yourself, Uncle?" she inquired. "You've a strong stomach. A lesser soul would have sent a hireling."

"Job?"

"What is it to be? Knife? Cord? Your bare hands?"

"Prone to hasty conclusions, I see."

"Am I? Perhaps I should seek another opinion. My mother's, for example. My brother's. My father's, or my Uncle Hurna's. How do you think they'd advise me?"

"I cannot speak for the dead. Your brother doesn't fit into that category, however."

"No?" Her heart jumped. "Where is he, then?"

"Somewhere in the Bruzhois. A fugitive, with a price on his head."

"You expect me to believe that?"

"Would you rather believe otherwise?"

Her pulses were racing. He had no reason to lie about this, but she hardly dared accept his word. Too much to hope for. She said nothing.

"We search for him," Varis continued dispassionately, "but he eludes us still. The loyalty of his followers is impressive. But that hardly signifies, for his power, such as it was, is broken now. The Bowl of Lannakh finished him. Hereafter, his resistance amounts to little more than an inconvenience."

"Enough to worry you, though. Else I wouldn't be alive now." Her composure masked intense excitement.

Cerrov live and free. The best. If true, she could bear anything.

"You mistake on both counts," Varis told her. "Whatever the fate of your brother, your own death serves no purpose. You overestimate your own importance. I see by your face that you question this, but take my word—young Cerrov's hopes are finished."

"Then I owe my continuing existence to my own insignificance."

"Not too uncomfortable an existence, I trust. No one's harmed you?"

"Not yet."

"But you fear."

"You'd enjoy that, Uncle?"

"It is not my intention to alarm you. Nor do I wish to injure you."

"Oh? The air of this dungeon is scarcely salubrious."

"I regret the inconvenience. But it lies within your own power to alter your circumstances."

"Always. I could starve myself to death. Or dash out my brains against the stone wall."

"Those are indeed two of your options. There are better ones, however, which I hope you may be persuaded to consider. That is what I am here to talk to you about."

"To talk?"

"Nothing more." Advancing a couple of paces, Varis seated himself at the table.

She'd take on the air of a subordinate awaiting reprimand if she remained on her feet. Shalindra sat down on the very edge of the cot. Her eyes never left his face.

"Your brother's rebellion has been crushed," Varis observed. "He himself is ruined, and his claim to the throne will never be renewed. His forces are broken and dispersed, never to regroup."

"Whom are you trying to convince, Uncle?"

"The land remains divided, however," he went on as if

she had not spoken. "The rivalries, hostilities, dissention, and unrest are apt to continue for years to come."

"The reign of a usurper is often troubled. Strange but true."

"Best for Rhazaulle and all her inhabitants if enemy parties were to resolve their differences."

"Easily accomplished. Ever considered abdication in favor of the rightful Ulor?"

"Rightful. Given the history of our entire family, an indefinite term at best."

"Many consider it quite unforgivingly clear."

"Many likewise consider the rightful Ulor to be the claimant proving himself fittest to rule."

"Proving it via destruction of all rivals?"

"That is the traditional method, I believe. As for the abdication you propose, it is an interesting suggestion, but hardly an effective solution. A simple substitution of ulors will hardly satisfy my own adherents."

"Do you have any, Uncle?"

Something flickered a moment in his eyes, and she resisted the impulse to back away from him. *Wrongness, strangeness. Mad? No. What, then?* She made herself meet his gaze without flinching.

Something familiar.

"A reconciliation of warring factions is essential," Varis remarked, again disregarding her pinpricks. "Together with a reunification of our own Haudrensq line. There is one certain means of achieving this end. You understand me?"

"No."

"A marriage between Rhazaulle's Ulor and the pretender's sister, uniting the divided branches of our House, will end domestic discord. We will then be fit to deal with Aennorve."

"What do you mean?" She assumed that he spoke figuratively; that he was proposing a treaty of some sort between himself and Cerrov's followers. Did he imagine her authorized to enter into any such agreement on her brother's behalf?

"I offer you the title of Ulorre-consort."

"That's the Ulor's wife."

Varis inclined his head.

"You mean, when you spoke of a marriage just now, you meant it—literally?"

"Contract, witnesses, ceremony, and all traditional furbelows, if you wish."

Speechless, she stared at him.

"The idea is new to you," Varis observed. "But you will soon perceive the advantages."

"Marry? You and I? You're not serious. This is your warped idea of a jest."

"I am in earnest."

"Then you must be mad."

"There is always that possibility. Try to overlook it."

"Some matters are difficult to overlook. Murder, for example. Usurpation. Persecution. If these strike you as irrelevant, then perhaps you might consider the disadvantages and illegalities of incest."

She had thought to shake him, or at least to gain an advantage, but his face never changed.

"I have more than considered. I have consulted the Codex Rialsqui. The union of uncle and niece is not regarded as incestuous. Such a marriage, while uncommon, is not, as it happens, specifically prohibited by statute. The law is a mutable thing, of course; for a Rhazaullean monarch, alterable as required. In this particular case, however, no such necessity exists."

"I see." She didn't know the law, but somehow she knew he wasn't lying. Incredible. Unreal. Her father's brother. Regicide, fratricide, infanticide, if the stories were true. But they seemed hard to believe. He appeared so civilized, so intelligent. Controlled. And his eyes— those Haudrensq hazel eyes, with the tawny corona about the pupils—they were like Cerrov's, and even more like her own, save for their disquieting brilliance.

Something about that glow—something she knew . . .

She was so far off balance—so astonished, bewildered, and unsure—that for a moment, the possibility seemed insanely real. Varis and Shalindra—uncle and niece, predator and prey, Ulor and consort, man and wife— united in wedlock and presiding over Cerrov's execution. Never the Funnel for a Haudrensq. The House of Ice, like Mother. Early evening, moonlight glistening the ice. Uloric Guard escorting Cerrov into the frozen mansion. Sealing the door behind him until morning. Boisterous cheer from the watching crowd. Shadowy movement within the House. For a little while. Firm pressure of the husband/uncle/ruler/murderer's hand upon her own. Every possible nuance of family feeling . . . Lunacy.

"I will spare your brother."

He must have been reading her mind.

"He need only give me his parole—swear an oath of allegiance," Varis told her. "I'll pardon him and all his followers. I'll restore him to ducal rank, in his father's name. He may return to the Zalkhash, there to enjoy a favored position, if he desires."

Home. He was saying that Cerrov could go home to ease, safety, wealth, and rank. Freedom. Peace. Home. Varis wanted a reconciliation to heal Rhazaullean wounds. Varis extended generous terms. Varis was doubtless lying in his teeth—

"That is a very handsome offer, Uncle. Improbable, though." She hoped her uncertainty didn't show. "A usurper cannot permit the legitimate Ulor to survive. His existence would always threaten you. You would soon put an end to it. And to mine as well, most likely."

"Thereby prolonging domestic hostilities, perhaps for generations to come. Aennorve stands to benefit; Rhazaulle does not. It is thus a worthwhile gamble to accept your brother's parole. I'm willing to trust that he won't go back on his word."

"And he, I take it, must similarly trust in you. Do you think him such a fool?"

"I think him capable of recognizing necessity. As Ulorre-consort, you yourself might effectively safeguard his interests."

Reassurance, or threat? Something of both.

"Moreover, you would not find cause to regret your choice." His face did not change expression. "In public, you'd enjoy the privilege and preeminence traditionally due the Ulorre-consort—a position that you, gifted with intelligence and beauty, would suit well. In private, you would always be accorded respect and consideration. So much I can promise."

Promise? You? She knew she ought to laugh in his face. He might kill her for it—probably intended to in any event—but at least he'd smart. No laughter in her, however. Nor much by way of healthy hatred, either. Confusion, doubt, alarm; plenty of those. A sense of terrible weakness and disorientation, a potentially disastrous longing for solidity. There seemed a certain grotesque plausibility in his offer. It was almost an effort of will to maintain her skepticism. His eyes were holding hers. She couldn't look away; couldn't answer, couldn't refuse, couldn't act.

Varis stood. "I will leave you now," he said. "Consider the matter at your leisure. Should you wish to communicate, strike the door. There are guards about to hear you."

"And if I don't wish to communicate?" Shalindra heard herself ask.

Varis departed without reply, and the iron door closed behind him.

Shalindra still sat, blind eyes fixed on the wall before her. She had no idea how much time had elapsed since her uncle's departure. The light in the cell told her nothing. In any case, she wasn't paying attention to it.

Varis. His eyes. His words. Madness. Lunatic fantasies. She should have been disgusted or outraged.

She was neither, however. His voice in her mind. No getting rid of it. No dismissing the fantastic promises and proposals, because—at last she consciously recognized the obvious—at least part of her accepted and believed them. Difficult not to, despite the improbability. Why?

They offered a way out. A comfortable, adequately honorable, tempting way out. Good for Cerrov and his supporters, for herself, for everyone. Who could blame her for wanting that?

Wanting, yes. Believing?

What he'd told her had made sense. No ulor, not even Varis I, would desire a reign forever beset with internal strife. Only reasonable that he would want to end it.

Killing Cerrov—and me—is the surest way to end it.

His explanation?

Questionable at best. And yet—something beyond the words was at work. Something in Varis himself, some quality difficult to define, but not unfamiliar. It was in the eyes; an uncanny light, like the glow in the eyes of the Conclave members, as they'd stood linked in magic, at the heart of Fruce Isle, years ago.

Very like that. No wonder she'd sensed familiarity. Only strange that it had taken her so long to make the connection. Uncle Varis had the strange lambent eyes of a necromancer in full transdimensionality; only, for him, the condition was apparently perpetual.

Eyes of a driven necromancer. Spifflicates had eyes of that sort, too.

Well, Varis was certainly no Spifflicate. Quite the contrary. He was thoroughly composed and controlled, deliberate and rational—all that a Spifflicate was not. Or so he appeared.

But a necromancer? Rumors . . . she remembered

old rumors, snatches of conversation overheard in childhood. Whispers . . . suspicions . . . always unproveable. Her father's death . . . Uncle Hurna's . . . questions. Never a definite answer, though. And now, the supernatural assault on Cerrov's forces—not demonstrably necromantic in nature, but assuring Varis's victory.

Never a definite answer.

She hadn't anticipated the burden of choice. She'd expected death, not conundrums. Uncle's suggestion was fantastic, a bizarre impossibility. She knew that. But somehow, here in this place, with Varis's quietly persuasive voice still ringing in her mind, those brilliant eyes of his still burning her memory, it seemed neither impossible, nor even repellent as it ought to have been. Here and now, his arguments possessed a species of logic, and acquiescence seemed oddly possible.

She wasn't quite herself, she suspected. Perhaps Varis had jumbled her mind.

No. Even a necromancer couldn't do that.

But was he a necromancer? Had sorcery won the Wolf Throne years ago? Defeated Cerrov's army days ago? If so, was there any point in even attempting opposition?

She didn't want to think about it. She didn't want to think at all. She would have preferred unconsciousness, but sleep was out of the question. If only she had a book, or a puzzle—anything to occupy her attention. But the cell was bare. Either by accident or design, her captor permitted no diversion.

The hours crawled. Thoughts of the interview with Varis fluttered her innards. To stave off such thoughts, she tried reconstructing old, half-forgotten poems in her head. Poems she'd read at Fruce. The memories came crowding back.

"The seclusion of Fruce offers peace and security, two commodities often undervalued until lost." The Librarian. How right she'd been.

Comfortless ruminations were interrupted by the arrival of a guard bearing a meal upon a covered tray. Placing the tray on the table, he withdrew without acknowledging her urgent queries. The door clanged shut, and the bolt shot home. Shalindra stared at it. After a moment, she lifted the cover to inspect the food; a bowl of stew, half a loaf of dark bread, a couple of apples, a carafe of cold mint-flavored tea. Simple fare, reminiscent of Fruce. She ate with decent appetite, but no enthusiasm, as she had eaten in the library refectory. Why did everything have to remind her of Fruce?

She finished her meal. Setting the tray aside, she rose from the table and started to pace her cell. Each time she approached the iron door, she contained her impulse to pound on it. The guards would come if she summoned, she knew; they'd come expecting an answer to carry back to Varis.

Accept. It kept on presenting itself as the best available option.

There was a certain seductive inevitability about it.

Impossible. She was tired, upset, and confused; else she'd see things more clearly. Sleep would sharpen her mind, if only she could sleep.

The light in the cell was dimming. Outside, the sun must be setting.

Not necessarily. They may just have extinguished lamps in the corridor above. You don't know.

But she did know. Her nerves sensed the waning of the day.

Darker and darker in Shalindra's cell. At last, she stretched herself out on the cot. Her mind was simmering; there was little hope of slumber.

But she drifted off almost at once. Slept, and dreamed of Fruce Isle; the crypt at night, the robed skeletons, horned statue concealing a treasure trove. Blued flames. A roomful of ghosts. A gathering of librarians, eyes luminous, minds linked to generate a sorcerous power far exceeding the sum of its parts. The Conclave.

She woke, her mind full of magic. Dead of night, most likely. Absolute blackness all about her. Bright images behind her eyes. Heart pounding. Her right hand at her throat, firmly clasping her mother's locket. It took her a moment to realize why. Of course—logical enough. The locket still contained a quantity of the magical stimulant FSD107-N, carried from the crypt long ago. She'd all but forgotten its existence, but the dreams had reminded her.

She wondered if the Conclave members ever guessed that she had stolen it. Probably not, else they'd have made her give it back. They were, she recalled, jealous of their secrets, and fiercely opposed to necromantic abuse.

What would they make of Varis I, who, magically murdering his way to the Wolf Throne, now magically maintained himself there? Assuming that's what he'd done. She still wasn't certain.

Those eyes of his. Be certain.

Then why not suspected, years ago?

Always suspected. Never proved.

No more sleep, not a chance. Shalindra lay wide awake in the dark. Thoughts ungovernable. It seemed an eternity, but at last the cell began to lighten.

Dim gray dawn at the bottom of the Tollbooth. As soon as she could discern the outlines of the scanty furnishings, Shalindra rose and recommenced her pacing. When that palled, she performed calisthenics until the pain in her muscles finally diverted her mind. Hours later, one of the guards appeared with breakfast. Placing the meal on the table, he gathered up last night's used dishes and made for the door.

"Wait." Probably no sense even trying to talk to him, but silence, isolation, and strain were fraying her nerves. As they were no doubt meant to do. "Would you please bring me some soap and water, to wash with?"

"No orders about that."

She was surprised that he answered her. It was the first time since Varis's visit that she'd heard a human voice.

"Would you ask? And would you also find out if I might have some paper, a pen, and ink?" Seeing refusal in his face, she added quickly, "I should like to address my uncle in writing."

"I'll see." He went. The iron door clanged.

She did not expect success. But he was back half an hour later with a bucket of warm, soapy water, a sponge, and a towel. More important, she got the writing supplies as well.

She was alone again. She washed thoroughly, then sat at the table to study the blank white sheets. She'd told the guard the simple truth. She wanted to pen her refusal to Varis, for she didn't believe she could face him and get the words out.

But she couldn't get them out on paper, either. The white sheets stared at her. She stared back. Empty, they were so empty. She averted her eyes. Her thoughts strayed. When she looked down again, it was to discover an image taking shape upon the page beneath her unconsciously wandering pen; hulking form, horned head, demon's visage—the statue in the crypt at Fruce. Not a bad likeness, either. Fruce, again.

She set the pen aside. Her hand rose to the locket.

Hours passed, and her tension mounted. The solitude, inactivity, and uncertainty were driving her mad. Apart from all other considerations, she was strongly tempted to accept Uncle's offer, just to get out of this room. Naturally. That was the reason he'd put her here.

Late afternoon, probably, and a meal to break the deadly featurelessness. Stone-faced monolith of a guard, no conversation. Scrape of the bolt, solitude again, and she found she couldn't eat. She'd make herself sick by and by. Best accept Uncle's offer without further delay; some part of her had known all along she'd accept. Anyone in her position would.

Anyone? The Librarian? Implacable, uncrackable Librarian. What would *she* do? How would *she* respond to

Varis? Renegade necromancer, murderer, usurper—how would she deal with him?

Why not ask her?

She could ask, Shalindra realized. At least, she could try.

The environs of the Tollbooth were notoriously haunted. Any member of the Haudrensq family knew that. There were ghosts all about, and she knew how to summon them. The procedure, every well-practiced detail of it, was branded upon her brain; she couldn't have forgotten if she'd tried. She had the requisite stimulant in her locket, and the years would scarcely have altered its character.

How would you know?

Well, it was probably all right. She need only swallow a minute quantity—

To sicken or possibly kill herself. She hadn't forgotten. The pain and delirium in the crypt and afterward—in all these years, she'd never forgotten. One of the truly outstanding memories of childhood. She'd privately vowed never to meddle in sorcery again, and it was a promise she wanted to keep, but circumstances pressed.

Did she dare an immediate attempt? Best to wait for darkness and night.

Delay, and she'd probably lose her nerve. Moreover, interruption was unlikely. With the heavy door between herself and the guards in the corridor, she wouldn't be overheard.

Now. Go.

She allowed herself no time for second thoughts. Everything clear, still immediate, as if the intervening years had never been. Close her eyes, and she was back in the Fruce crypt. Now, as then, chill motionless air all about her; same dead air, carrying her back—

The mental exercises came more easily than she'd expected, and when it was time to swallow half her remain-

ing store of FSD107-N, there was intense focus that left
no room for doubt, fear, or hesitation.

Singing nerves. Light in her veins, sudden clarity of
inner vision—all the remembered sensations. Not as terrifying, this time around. She'd done it once before; moreover, she was older and stronger now. Search. Ignore the
rising nausea, the hot pain at the back of the skull.

Mind seeking, grasping—

Connection. Something to fasten on, something to
overcome—

No struggle necessary, however. No discernible resistance. In an instant, it was present, whole and complete.
Shalindra opened her eyes. She was not alone. She blinked.
She couldn't afford to let astonishment shake her concentration, but the ghostly figure hovering before her was
really extraordinarily sharp and clear, nothing at all like
the tenuous wisp of a reluctant wraith she'd once summoned at Fruce. This one was perfectly realized, every
detail finely etched. She beheld a short, scrawny form; explosive locks, even a pattern of decorative scars marking
the face. The creature evinced neither fear nor distress. His
eyes were sly, and he was actually smirking.

Well. A real amateur, observed the ghost. *You need practice, missy. HEH.*

He giggled, and Shalindra jumped. The laugh skittered to the gleeful verge of hysteria and back again. The
transparent limbs and face twitched convulsively. Strange.
Wrong. Mad? Spifflicated? Still, every word absolutely
clear and audible; piping, derisive tone bridging dimensions intact. She had never thought to accomplish so
much.

*Better close your mouth and mind your concentration, little
girl. You're not very good at this, are you?*

"Good enough to bring you here," she replied, without thinking.

To bring me here. Heh. The smirk widened. *You think
that feeble little mental twitch of yours actually BROUGHT me*

here? Presumptuous chit. I CAME, of my own free will. Clotl Deathmaster knows no constraint. He is not just ANY ghost. He comes and goes as he pleases. And don't you forget it.

"Oh. Sorry." She believed him, up to a point. She knew she could never have conjured such an apparition on her own.

Think nothing of it.

"How is it that you're free, but still here, Clotl Deathmaster? That's not usual, is it?"

The Deathmaster is remarkable, in all respects.

"Umm—why did you choose to come, then?"

Curiosity, girl. The itch of an inquiring dead mind. Your faint, peeping little summons roused my pity, and so I came to investigate. Had to see what that lad Varis had locked up in his cellar. One of my favorite people in all the world, Varis. Talented boy. Trained him myself, taught him his necromancy, made him what he is. He killed me, you know.

"Uncle Varis? He really *does* use nec—"

And what should I find down here, but the long-lost niece herself? Nicely caged, like a songbird awaiting a pastry coffin. BUT the songbird has got hidden resources. She knows a little— a very little—magic. No one would have counted on that. Makes things more interesting, eh? Can't wait to see my boy's face when I tell him.

"No! Don't tell him! Please!" The pain in her head was expanding mercilessly. Her veins burned.

Please. I like that. You've manners, little girl. Manners, but not much competence. You're green-faced, wobbly, about to keel over, and all because you're trying to batter your way straight through interdimensional resistance. Bad approach. Rip yourself to shreds that way. Hasn't anyone ever taught you ANY-THING?

"Actually, I—"

Clotl could teach you. If he chose. If you convinced him of your worthiness. Eh, girl? You worthy? Convince me. Go on, try.

Her head was spinning, she could barely stay on her feet. "I called you here—"

Call. What sort of CALL does she mean? Does she mean—

"Because I want to send a message."

Do you take the Deathmaster for a carrier pigeon?

"Please—I need help—"

That you do, little girl. Clotl could help you. If he chose. Heh. IF.

"Yes. Clotl could help by carrying a message to The Librarian, on Fruce Isle. That's all I ask. That's—"

ALL? That's ALL she asks? Shrill phantom laughter hopped nonspace. *Heh. HEH! Hasn't anyone ever taught you ANYTHING? Don't you even know that ordinary, garden-variety ghosts are BOUND? EH?*

Of course she'd known. The entire intent of the Frucian Conclave had been the liberation of captive shades. Had she not been so frightened, so preoccupied and confused, she would have remembered that. But even so—

"They can move about," she muttered. She was tottering, nauseated, and it was almost impossible to think. "They can—"

Think they can leap the Straits of Bitheen, little girl? Think they can just go SAILING off to the south of Aennorve? Eh? From here, the very best of 'em might get as far as Truvisq. Most, not that far.

Defeat impossible to deny. This grinning, gabbing ghost was right. She'd done her best, sickened herself perhaps to death with necromancy, and all for nothing. Ignorant. Stupid. Pitiful. Useless. Useless. Dizzy, suddenly unable to stand, she slumped to her knees.

Clotl Deathmaster, however, is subject to no such limitations.

So acute her misery that it took a moment for the words to sink in. She looked up slowly.

Clotl could carry your message to the brink of eternity. IF he chose. Eh? The ghost winked. *EH?*

"Would you? Please?"

I like it when you say please. You don't have to kneel, though. Clotl doesn't stand on ceremony.

"Please go to The Librarian at Fruce. Tell her to notify the Conclave. Tell her that the Ulor Varis is a necromancer. Tell her he must have used magic to usurp the throne. Tell her that he compels ghosts to murder for him. Tell her we need help. Tell her—"

Clotl KNOWS what to tell her. Clotl requires no instruction from green little girls.

"No, I'm sure not. But—"

BUT, the question remains, will he choose to help you? Lips pursed, the ghost considered.

A real necromancer might have ruled Clotl, for all his pretensions to autonomy. She couldn't, however. It was taking all her determination simply to stave off collapse. No strength or skill for anything else. No choice but await the creature's pleasure.

Might tell her to seek out those Colloquist people. Train 'em. Join forces. Heh! Clotl grinned. *There's a combination would give my boy a run for his money. The lad's had it too easy, too long. Time for a CHANGE, time for a CHALLENGE, time for a little VARIETY! Be good for him, he's getting STALE. Heh. Heh!* He giggled. *Little girl, I've decided to grant your request. You needn't thank me. If anyone owes gratitude, it's Varis. After all, this is sure to build his character. So farewell for now, songbird. Clotl leaves you with a word of advice. If you must practice necromancy, next time try to get it RIGHT.*

Gone. She was alone again, unable to ponder the interview, for the cell was spinning about her, and the fever-fires were licking at her mind. Bed. She wanted to get to it. When she tried to stand, she failed. Pitching forward on her face, she hit the floor hard and lay still.

The dreams were dreadful, full of loss, confusion, and despair; endless deserted corridors, darkening into blackness; hollow voices, echoing across the interdimensional void— voices of the wretched dead. The dreams were her reality, for a while; no telling how long. Isolation, fear, and icy nothingness were all the universe.

It changed almost imperceptibly. A recollection of warmth insinuated itself, a memory of hope. They charged her sluggish blood, and the horrors receded, leaving a residue of depressed exhaustion. Weakness blotted her intellect, and she existed from meal to spoon-fed meal, from one sponge bath to the next. In the midst of such dependence, she didn't question the source of aid.

Time passed, and her mind quickened. Warm currents of air upon her face, and where were they coming from? Light pressing her eyelids, and how did it reach her dungeon? Shalindra opened her eyes, squinting at the unexpected brightness. She lay in a wide bed decently furnished with linen and coverlets. The manacles were gone. It was morning, or so she inferred from the angle of sunlight streaming in through a pair of big, arched windows. Glazed windows, she noticed—a refinement never dreamt of by the Tollbooth's medieval architect. A small, puzzled frown creased her brow. She looked around her. Spacious room, circular in shape, which meant that it occupied a floor in one of the round corner towers. Rug on the floor, heavy tapestries upon the walls. Washstand, chest of drawers, big polished wardrobe, a couple of upholstered chairs flanking the fireplace. Wooden chair and small table beside the bed. Lamp on the dresser, candles on the mantel. Modern comfort imposed upon the Tollbooth's original starkness. Her own trunks and valises, removed from the landau, stood piled in one corner.

A bar scraped, the door opened, and a woman walked in. She was tall, strapping, square-jawed, and large-handed. She carried a meal on a tray.

"Awake," the stranger observed, setting the tray down on the table. Lazimiri accent. "I'm Zordja. Ulor brought me to do for you. You'll eat now." It was an order.

Shalindra made no comment as the other slipped a muscular arm about her shoulders, effortlessly raised her to a sitting position, and proceeded to spoon-feed her. She found herself unexpectedly hungry. The food—a couple of vegetable purees, some very finely minced chicken, thoroughly stewed sliced fruit, all washed down with a cup of cold milk—was bland, unseasoned stuff, suitable to an invalid's diet. Not particularly appetizing, but the hateful weakness seemed to recede with every mouthful. When she'd consumed about half the meal—feeling stronger, and disliking the oppressive intimacy of the powerful arm about her—she observed, "I can do it myself, now."

Zordja hesitated, weighing the suggestion. Nurse or gaoler? Evidently something of both. She must have decided that the spoon lacked destructive potential, for she finally relinquished the implement. Withdrawing a couple of paces to the nearest chair, she sat and watched unblinkingly.

Shalindra ate, trying to ignore the expressionless gaze that rested on her with almost tangible weight. When she was done, she set the spoon aside.

"Finish the carrots," Zordja said.

Shalindra obeyed.

"And the milk."

She drained the last drops.

"Good. You'll sleep now."

"How long have I been in this room?"

"Four days."

"How did I get here?"

"I toted you up. It was easy; you're not much."

"Is the Ulor here in the castle?"

A shrug. "He comes and goes."

"Any news of my brother?"

"No more talk. You'll sleep now."

"But—"

"Sleep." Gathering up the tray and dishes, Zordja departed. The door closed behind her, and the bar outside slid into place.

Shalindra did sleep, drifting off almost immediately.

The conversation must have drained her, for she didn't open her eyes again until the late afternoon. The chamber was dim, but pleasantly lit with the low glow of the banked fire. This time she was wide awake, clear head filled with questions and worries. Had Clotl Deathmaster, as the spifflicated spectre styled himself, fulfilled his commission? Pleaded Cerrov's cause before The Librarian? And if so, would the Conclave choose to involve itself? She might gain answers by summoning the Deathmaster, but this she was not about to attempt. She'd never meddle in necromancy again. The results were consistently appalling, and she probably wouldn't survive a third attempt. In any case, there were other matters to consider. Uncle's perverse proposal, for example.

Still there, still waiting.

She would have to think about that before long, but she wasn't quite up to it yet. There were books in one of her valises. A good dose of poetry or history might crowd the horrors from her brain for a little while.

She was weak and giddy when she rose to her feet. The journey from bed to valise and back again exhausted her. But the prize, a Neraunci history, kept her diverted for the next two hours, until Zordja brought in the evening meal. At that time, all the banished concerns came flooding back, stronger than ever; but her queries regarding Cerrov went unanswered. Evidently repenting her former expansiveness, Zordja now maintained monolithic silence.

Eventually, Shalindra gave up asking. Under the gimlet gaze of her nurse/gaoler, she consumed every scrap of a plain, bland meal. When she put her spoon down, the other finally spoke.

"You will sleep now."

Zordja departed, barring the door behind her. Unwontedly compliant, Shalindra slumbered.

The next day was much the same. She lay in bed, alternately reading and sleeping, her solitude broken only by the periodic laconic intrusions of her gaoler. Thereafter, her strength built quickly. Vitality returned. She was herself again, and further procrastination was impossible.

Uncle's offer. Her own situation. Cerrov's fate. Time to think about them. Now, while she was alone, lucid, and calm.

Consider your options . . .

She glanced about her. The contrast between this chamber and her former dungeon was striking. Likewise significant—the absence of fetters, and the presence of her own belongings. Varis's unspoken message was clear. Comfort and comparatively decent treatment were available; cooperation would purchase both. She'd be treated with respect and consideration, he'd promised, and would most likely keep his word, so far as the outward manifestations were concerned. The disagreeable alternative, of course, was self-evident.

And the promise to pardon Cerrov? Almost certainly specious.

Possibilities? Escape from Castle Haudrensq? Difficult at best. Under the present circumstances, impossible.

Await rescue? That would be a lifelong wait. She'd rot in the Tollbooth's dungeon, unless Uncle thought of a better use for her . . .

Kill Varis? Could she actually kill anyone? And if so, with what? Where would she find weapon and opportunity, locked up here alone as she was?

Perhaps—and now she confronted the one option that some part of her had known from the first moment was the best available—perhaps she should simply submit. Agree to marry him. Of course, the actuality of such a union was unthinkable; but actuality was an issue that she wouldn't need to deal with for some time to come. The wedding of a reigning Ulor was a state occasion, demanding display of the greatest magnificence. Uncle was noted for an eccentric asceticism, but even Varis would bow to custom in this. He'd promised as much, with his offer of "traditional furbelows." The elaborate preparations would require months to complete. And she, no doubt, would find some means of exploiting the respite to advantage. Her liberties and privileges were bound to increase, provided her acquiescence appeared convincingly sincere. Perhaps the chance to escape would present itself. An opportunity of contacting Cerrov might somehow arise. Or maybe, just maybe, if Uncle Varis could be taken off guard, only once—

But that last possibility was one she preferred not to contemplate.

She slept little that night. In the morning, when Zordja came, Shalindra asked, "Is the Ulor presently in residence?"

Wordless shrug.

"If he is here, would you please convey my request for a meeting?"

Zordja departed in silence; her cooperation, problematic. The bar scraped.

An hour passed. Shalindra paced.

A knock on the door, and her breath caught. Her mouth was dry. She swallowed with difficulty. The door opened, and Varis entered. Alone, mercifully. He looked at her, and something registered in his eyes; perhaps faint surprise at the extent of her recovery. She spoke before he could.

"I have considered your offer with care, Ulor," Shalindra said. "And I accept it."

16

DUSK CAME EARLY to the wooded hills over-looking the town of Zena. Here in Zenskoy Forest crouched the battered remnant of Cerrov Haudrensq's once-proud army. Here the rebel forces had withdrawn following the Lannakh debacle, and here they were comparatively safe. Twice within the space of a week, invading detachments of Uloric guardsmen had encountered murderous sniper fire from the trees. After the second such incident, organized intrusion ceased, and the fugitive soldiers were left to lick their wounds in peace —those of them that remained. In the wake of Lannakh, almost half of the discouraged Aennorvi troops had with-drawn, amidst the jeers of their erstwhile allies. Rhazaul-lean supporters continued staunch, as did the Rhelish mercenaries.

The army, forced in flight to abandon many of its supply wagons, was ill-fed, ill-sheltered, and increasingly ill-tempered. Fraying nerves were taxed by enforced prox-imity; during the chill rainy nights, the men were crammed by the score into tents fit for half their number. Even the officers were not exempted, but rubbed elbows by the half-dozen. The young Ulor alone had a tent to himself, and this a somewhat mean affair. Cramped though his quarters were, Cerrov had offered to share with at least a couple of officers. In deference to his rank, the favored men refused, leaving their commander-in-chief no choice but to enjoy the luxury of privacy.

He was enjoying it now, insofar as he could enjoy anything. Alone in his tent, Cerrov read by the light of a single candle. Absorbed in v'Ierre's *Account of the Jurlian-Zenki Wars,* he could for a few moments forget the wretched pass to which he'd brought his followers. Not to mention his sister, who was, it had been reported days earlier, presently a captive in the Tollbooth. Shalindra was evidently unharmed—so far—but quite beyond the reach of any aid. It was with some reluctance that he raised his head at the sound of a familiar voice outside.

"News, Ulor. Permission to approach?"

"Granted."

The canvas flap shifted, and Colonel Syun stepped into the tent. He was rumpled, shag-haired, and stubble-chinned, his formerly elegant self transformed. He bore a paper broadside. Once inside, his formality of manner vanished. Presenting the broadside, he observed, "This tears it."

Cerrov accepted and quickly scanned an official Uloric decree. It seemed that the Ulor Varis, at this juncture desirous of healing Rhazaulle's wounds, promised amnesty and full pardon to those rebels willing to lay down their arms. The Ulor's mercy embraced all, not excluding the arch-renegade Cerrov Haudrensq; who was earnestly besought to surrender himself at once, under the Ulor's guarantee of personal safety. Divisions within the House of Haudrensq afflicted all the nation; patriotism no less than familial duty demanded a reconciliation. The Ulor Varis extended the hand of friendship to his erring kinsman. The Ulor offered peace to all of Rhazaulle.

"Clever." Cerrov set the paper aside. A sour smile bent his lips. "Clever Uncle."

"Cunning bastard's going to steal the troops right out from under us with this," Syun observed. "The men are glum and prickly. There'll be plenty wanting a way out, will snap at this. They'll desert in droves. Couldn't have come at a worse moment."

"Neatly timed, indeed. Where did this come from?"

"Market square in Zena. I'm told the town is solidly papered. They're even tacked up on the trees at the edge of the forest. They're probably floating all through Rhazaulle."

"In other words, no possibility of keeping this from the men."

"None."

"We'll have to convince them that he's lying, and we'll have to do it fast."

"*Is* he lying?"

"Not about the general amnesty. For him, that's a sound move. Perhaps, after all, it's best that the men accept pardon," Cerrov mused. "I've little hope of anything better to offer them now. We've taken a death-stroke. Maybe they should save themselves while they can."

"Rhelish will stick as long as you pay them," Syun pointed out matter-of-factly. "And the amnesty doesn't affect us Aennorvi. As for the Rhazaulleans, they came because they're set on crowning the rightful heir, and plenty are certain to stand by you even yet. Don't be too quick to give up on them—unless you want the amnesty for yourself, of course. And for your sister. There's that to consider."

"That part of the offer smells. He could hardly afford to let me live. Should I take him at his word, no doubt there'd follow a spectacularly public absolution and reinstatement. And then, some time within the next couple of years or so, a discreet dram of poison or an accident of some sort; first for me, and then for Shalindra."

"Do you think he's already—?"

"I don't believe he'd have harmed her as yet. Most likely, she's safe as long as I breathe."

"You know I've great regard for her Ladyship." Syun's tone was studiously neutral. "Great regard. If you contemplate an assault on Castle Haudrensq—a rescue mission of any sort—I'd be honored to lead such an expedition."

"You're a good fellow, Syun." Cerrov smiled briefly. "But attack the Tollbooth, half-crippled as we are? Suicidally useless. For now, we can't help her."

"In that case, would you—"

A new voice broke into the conversation:

"News, Ulor. Permission to approach?"

"Granted." Cerrov braced for fresh disaster.

An orderly entered, saluted smartly as if he still fancied himself part of a real army, and announced, "Ulor, a woman has come, requesting an audience of you."

Cerrov's overtaxed patience wobbled. "Tell her to ply her trade elsewhere."

"Ulor, she presents herself as leader of a band of thirteen refugees fleeing the Nidroonish pogroms. She is clearly a woman of some character."

"Has anyone seen these so-called refugees?"

"They're waiting at the edge of the camp."

"How do they look?"

"Harmless, Ulor. Unarmed, that's certain. A couple of women among them."

"Nidroonish refugees. What do they want here? We've no food or blankets to spare. Best tell them to try their luck in Zena."

"Their leader offers new information regarding the enemy's strength."

"She's a humbug, or else addle-pated."

"She appears neither. She declares herself willing to divulge her information to Cerrov Haudrensq alone. She is very insistent, Ulor."

"Ridiculous. All right, I suppose I'll talk to her. Trot her in."

The orderly retired. A few moments later, he was back to usher in a pair of strangers. One of them, a woman, was remarkably tall, an inch or so taller than Cerrov himself. When she pushed the hood of her cloak back, candlelight fell upon a strong, coldly intellectual visage, surrounded by graying hair. Her male companion was bony and tense, with the heated eyes and white robe of a Venerator.

"Cerrov Haudrensq?" the woman inquired without ceremony, without discourtesy, and without the slightest trace of deference.

"Yes."

"Send—the other ones—away." She spoke careful, heavily accented Rhazaullean.

Cerrov gestured, and the orderly exited. "The officer remains," he said. "Now, who are you, and what have you to say?"

"I am, first, not Nidroonish, not a refugee. I am—" she seemed to struggle through foreign syntax, "high—leader—that is, administrator of the Fruce Library, in Aennorve. This man I bring is Layo Burik, the Colloquist. He is—talk—for my bad Rhazaullean."

Cerrov recalled that a Colloquist was some arcane sub-species of a Venerator. These days, the fanatics waged internecine war. Fortunately, he was not obliged to concern himself. "I speak Aennorvi," he told her.

"That simplifies matters." She switched to the familiar language, and her force, already formidable, seemed to double. "This Aennorvi colonel is in your confidence?"

"Yes."

"Very well. Here is the matter in brief, then. Your uncle, the usurper, is a necromancer, employing supernatural means to win and retain the Wolf Throne."

"That is a common accusation, never proven," Cerrov said.

"Regard it as proven now."

"How so?"

"That you will shortly judge for yourself. Consider the Bowl of Lannakh."

"I consider it almost continually."

"Your forces were defeated by supernatural means."

"So much was obvious. Less obvious—the source, the kind, the strength, the meaning."

"The source—your uncle. The kind—Bruzhoi ghosts. The strength—formidable enough, but less than it must have seemed. The meaning—none, beyond your uncle's triumph."

"And the degradation of the dead," put in Layo Burik, whose services as an interpreter appeared redundant. "An abomination."

"What's your source of information?" Cerrov asked.

"I was apprised of your plight by spectral agency."

"Spectral agency. I see. A ghost appeared to you—in your dreams, perhaps?"

"Not at all. He appeared in my office, at midday. Introducing himself as 'the Deathmaster,' he declared himself a messenger, and boasted rather insistently that he came of his own free will. As a favor, he claimed."

"A favor to whom?"

"That is uncertain. He referred repeatedly to 'the little green-faced girl,' but refused elaboration."

"Little green-faced girl. A nice touch," Cerrov approved. "All in all, an entertaining tale, filled with colorful fancies—"

"These are facts," The Librarian informed him levelly, "with which you have shown yourself unfit to cope. That is not a reproach. How could you, entirely lacking in adequate fortification, hope to deal with the realities of the supernatural?"

"And what is adequate fortification?"

"Knowledge. Training. Preparation. You've none. Your opponent is better equipped. I and my colleagues are here to even the odds."

"Colleagues?"

"We are the Conclave of Fruce, opposed upon principle to the necromantic exploitation of the dead. Our convictions express themselves in practical terms. We have devised and perfected certain means of assisting the victims of sorcerous abuse. To do so, we have often found ourselves obliged to resort to our enemies' methods. It is no exaggeration, then, to assure you that the combined power of the Conclave membership equals or exceeds the force of the greatest of necromancers. This power the Conclave proposes to employ upon your behalf, provided our objectives prove compatible."

"Objectives?" Cerrov inquired.

"We should require assurance of your continuing sympathy to our cause," The Librarian told him. "This man accompanying me tonight, Burik the Colloquist, is your countryman. These Rhazaullean Colloquists, much in sympathy with Conclave convictions, desire freedom to pursue their aims of service and assistance to the dead."

"We will liberate them," Burik stated. His hot eyes glowed. "We will free them all, in time. We owe no less."

A typical Venerator zealot, paired with a curiously impressive madwoman, neither of whom should have been admitted to his presence. Cerrov wondered how best to conclude the interview promptly.

"Should our intervention assist you to the Wolf Throne, will the Colloquists enjoy Uloric sanction?" inquired The Librarian.

"The Colloquists may certainly believe and practice as they please, so long as they do no harm."

"Acceptable. And you, as Ulor, would consistently oppose necromantic abuse?"

"Such has always been my policy. We are clearly in accord, and I trust you are reassured."

"That is satisfactory. Provided you prove constant, you shall have our support."

"I am greatly indebted. And now, Madam, having concluded—"

"It will be necessary, you must understand, to employ necromancy," The Librarian continued, blandly ignoring the attempted dismissal. "We shall summon such ghosts as haunt this vicinity, and when they appear, inform them of our needs, requesting the favor of their aid."

"We will colloquize," said Layo Burik. "We will implore their favor."

"Implore?" Impatience notwithstanding, Cerrov was mildly intrigued.

"To be more specific, we will endeavor to bribe them," The Librarian explained.

"With what does one bribe a ghost?"

"Its freedom. We shall offer liberation in exchange for cooperation. Such an arrangement offers advantages both moral and practical. Ghosts lending aid voluntarily will exert far greater force than those serving under compulsion. Your uncle's domination of the spectral legions is unparalleled. They obey most unwillingly, however, and will beyond question yield to the power and initiative of your own freely assenting ghostly soldiers."

Cerrov glanced over at Syun, and saw excitement in the officer's eyes. It would seem that Syun believed. But the tale was absurd, far too good to be true. A pity.

"Should we succeed in locating the burial sites of those spectres serving the Ulor Varis, there is nothing to impede mass liberation," The Librarian suggested. "Thus may your uncle discover his ghostly strength progressively undermined."

Better and better. The woman knew how to paint pretty pictures. She deserved credit for inventiveness, if nothing more.

"It is clear you do not believe me."

He hadn't realized he was letting it show on his face. Belatedly he tried to amend his expression. No point in crossing a lunatic. She'd want to quarrel, and he had better things to do. Fortunately, however, she seemed not to have taken offense. Her companion was glaring, but the woman herself was unaffected.

"That is hardly surprising," she continued imperturbably. "No doubt you require proof. That is easily provided."

"Indeed."

"I presume Cerrov Haudrensq retains an open mind. My colleagues and I are prepared to demonstrate our powers."

"How?"

"We shall summon a ghost. There must be several tied to this spot—you've lost a number of your men to their wounds, have you not?"

"Too many."

"Lead us to their cemetery."

A waste of time, no doubt. Still, he wasn't otherwise occupied at the moment. Time passed slowly in the depths of Zenskoy Forest, and perhaps the useless exercise might furnish some diversion. These refugees—librarians, magicians, or whatever they were—carried no weapons and offered no threat. Moreover, Syun believed; and would no doubt retain his delusions until the tale was conclusively disproved.

"If you wish," Cerrov returned neutrally.

"The officer here may accompany us. There will be no other spectators."

"Agreed."

At the edge of the camp awaited her cohorts. Eleven Aennorvi librarians, two of them female; cloaked and hooded figures, features all but lost in the deepening twilight. They had been searched upon arrival, and it was certain they carried no weapons. Cerrov and his subordinate were both armed. It was without the slightest trepidation that he led the party through the trees to the little clearing wherein mounds of freshly turned soil marked the graves of the Rhazaullean dead.

Here he looked on in mild curiosity as the Conclave

formed its circle and commenced its arcane chanting. Beside him, Syun watched in extreme interest; but Syun was Aennorvi, unaccustomed to the pretensions of the sorcerous charlatans abounding in Rhazaulle. A few yards distant, Layo Burik stood solitary and transfixed.

The rhythmic voices merged and synchronized, built to an eery crescendo, and then abruptly ceased. At that moment, fire leapt at the circle's center, and Cerrov's brows rose. He had seen nobody set splint or coal to any sort of fuel. The sudden blaze seemed inexplicable. Presumably a trick of some kind.

The hooded figures were silent and motionless now. Ruddy light flickered upon twelve faces identically still and empty. No movement, but for the dance of the flames.

And then the ghosts came.

Cerrov drew in his breath sharply. There were some twenty spectral figures hovering there, about a quarter of the population of the new little burial ground, and he knew them—he knew them all.

There were the recently dead soldiers, the Rhazaullean recruits, a couple of Aennorvi infantrymen, one of the Rhelish mercenaries. The sergeant who'd lingered so stubbornly, after the gangrene set in; the delirious Lazimiri apprentice; the others, equally memorable. All sharply focused, transparent but almost tangible; all attired as they had been in life, forms and faces intact, and marked with the blood of their wounds. All shockingly recognizable.

No sound, other than the crackle of the flames, and the rustle of the wind through the trees. The Conclave frozen, seemingly unconscious. Spectral faces aware, lips moving as if in speech, but no sound emerging; at least, none audible to the uninitiated. Cerrov was almost as still as the necromancers themselves. He'd never witnessed such a demonstration, nor anything remotely approaching it.

Some agreement or understanding achieved between ghosts and necromancers. A nodding of spectral heads.

And then a shuddering of red firelight, a clearing empty of visitants, and a band of necromancers, suddenly bereft of contact, spent and sagging to the ground.

Their leader—the woman calling herself The Librarian —remained upright. Advancing without a hint of un-steadiness, she halted before Cerrov to announce, "They have agreed to assist us. There will be others, soon enough."

He wasted no time upon praise or apology, as her manner encouraged neither. "What, specifically, can they do?" Cerrov asked.

"I suggest that you put it to the test."

Thirty-six hours later, Cerrov Haudrensq's forces emerged from Zenskoy Forest to attack the town of Zena. A transparent company of ghosts attended the rebel army, throwing loyalist forces into such disarray that Zena fell almost without resistance. In the aftermath of the victory, partisans flocked to Cerrov's cause, and the interrupted march north resumed.

"Madam, the Ulor invites your Ladyship to join him upon the walkway below in half an hour's time," announced the soldier.

"I will be there," Shalindra said, noting the faint re-laxation of Zordja's watchful attitude; almost as if the Lazimiri woman had fancied that her charge might treat the invitation as something other than the command that it was.

The soldier saluted and withdrew. Shalindra seated herself beside the window, and her blind gaze fastened on the distant peaks. Join the Ulor for another stroll about the battlements? The fourth such summons in as many days. It seemed he meant to make a habit of it. Following her acceptance of his proposal, over two weeks earlier, he had abruptly departed the Tollbooth, leaving her to uneasy solitude. Now he was back again, without explanation, and disconcertingly sociable. Not exactly difficult to di-

vine his motives, though. The daily, highly visible promenade proclaimed to the world her presence beneath his
roof. Anyone equipped with a half-decent spyglass could
see at a glance that she was there, alive, and well. For the
present.

Cerrov must know where she was by now. He'd be full
of fear for her. As Uncle intended.

And what else did Uncle intend? Their meetings had
afforded her little insight, as yet.

"Better bundle up. Ladyship."

Zordja's voice broke in on her thoughts. Shalindra
looked up. Her erstwhile nurse-gaoler, now metamor-
phosed into lady's maid-gaoler, waited to wrap her in the
Smoke Cloud furs—a sensible safeguard against the au-
tumnal chill of the mountain air. Standing, she submitted
in silence; then surreptitiously rearranged the clumsy angle of the hat, the unflattering drape of the robe, inflicted
upon her by her prodigiously untalented attendant.

"I'll see you safe to the battlements, Ladyship."

"That isn't necessary, Zordja. I know the way."

"I'll see you safe."

Shalindra sighed inaudibly. On the whole, the pre-
tense of Zordja's servile status was a very thin fiction indeed. Argument was useless; the other possessed both a
will and a skull of iron. She shrugged and exited her
chamber. There were no guards at the door, no one to keep
the Ulor's honored betrothed from wandering where she
would—only huge Zordja, tirelessly dogging her footsteps.

Down the corner tower's steep spiral staircase she
made her way, to the low, arched door opening onto the
castle ramparts. The sentry stationed there saluted and
ushered her through, closing the portal behind her.
Zordja, for once, found no need to follow, for the Ulor
himself was out there upon the parapet.

The hard Bruzhoi chill slapped her face, and Shalindra
shivered a little beneath her furs. She'd been far from

Rhazaulle for so many years, she'd almost forgotten the razor edge of her native air; likewise its extraordinary clarity and purity. She'd have to reaccustom herself to the cold that had once seemed so natural, and that clearly was natural yet to Varis, who waited bareheaded and gloveless, thin gray coat unbuttoned, facing straight into the wind. He stood with his back to her; lean charcoal-clad figure sharply etched against gray skies, gray stone ramparts, and gray peaks. The whistle of the wind muted her light footsteps, and it suddenly crossed her mind that a single, decided shove might send him toppling from the battlements, as Uncle Hurna had once toppled from the House Uloric rooftop.

Cerrov's path would be clear.

It was an idle thought, merely. She had no clear intentions, but her advance was silent, or so she imagined. She was still ten feet behind him when he spoke, without turning his head:

"Ladyship."

She couldn't keep her eyes from widening, or her hands from jerking. Fortunately, these reactions were under control before he moved, and she had to look into his face.

"Ulor." She curtsied smoothly, and forced herself to raise her eyes to his.

Like mine, but on fire.

"You'd best do something about your eyes," he observed, as if his thoughts ran on a parallel track to her own. "They reveal more than you intend."

She wasn't about to ask him what he meant, or how he had known she was there behind him. "What shall I do about them, Ulor?" she inquired politely.

"Dark glasses can be useful. I speak from experience."

She stretched a faint smile. She supposed he was somehow mocking her, but she wasn't quite certain. "You wore such glasses long ago, I remember," she said. "But you don't use them now."

"Not for years. I have kept them, though."

"Why, if you don't need them?"

"A sense of unbreakable attachment. Inevitability."

"Inevitability? I don't follow—"

"All the better for you. Come, let us walk. You've forgotten this climate. You'll suffer if you don't keep moving."

Considerate, Uncle.

They walked in silence, perhaps a quarter of the circuit of the wall. Shalindra had feared that he might insist upon touching her; taking her arm, perhaps. But the daylight was clear between them, and slowly, her immediate fears subsided. He'd been right, she noticed; the chill was receding. The sharp breeze whipped the blood to her cheeks, and the quickness to her brain. She felt herself safe for the moment. Her eyes shifted to the surrounding peaks. Cerrov was out there, somewhere.

"You are thinking of your brother," Varis said.

She didn't let herself react. He'd needed no magic to figure that out. He was no mind reader, appearances notwithstanding. "You are thinking of him, as well," she replied. "Else you wouldn't be parading me around these battlements of yours."

"Only partially true. I assume you wish to serve him. I am willing to give you an opportunity to do so."

"Yes?"

"You may perhaps be unaware that your brother's aggression has resumed."

This time, she wasn't able to conceal her surprise. "You said he was ruined—his forces crushed."

"So I believed. It would appear that I underestimated my nephew's resiliency. Two weeks ago, his marauders emerged from their Zenskoy Forest refuge to retake the town of Zena. Since then, they've gathered fresh recruits at Khrov, seized the contents of the armories, and rampaged north."

"That is unexpected." She lowered her eyes. Her mind

spun. *How did Cerrov manage so much, so quickly? Did that—creature—actually carry my message to Fruce? Has the Conclave done something?*

"You appear pleased, but your satisfaction is premature."

He'd caught it. He was infernally acute, as several days' worth of conversation should have taught her. She'd have to do better. She was supposed to be his betrothed, after all.

"I am concerned," she murmured.

"You have cause. The rebel resurgence is noteworthy, but futile—its inevitable result, the wholly avoidable death of thousands."

Sure about that? she wondered silently. But then, what if he was right?

"Your brother's courage and determination are laudable in themselves, but ultimately destructive."

An odd sentiment—coming from you. She said nothing.

"You'd do your brother and all his followers a great service in persuading them to accept the pardon that I offer. Be assured they would find no cause to complain of their treatment."

They'll hardly complain if they're dead. She chanced a quick glance up into his eyes, half expecting to surprise a look of open malice or menace, but she should have known he wouldn't be so easily read. His expression was convincingly somber. Even that preternatural fire in his eyes appeared comparatively subdued, probably quelled by the daylight. Was it possible he spoke sincerely? If she weren't careful, she'd find herself starting to believe him. She looked away quickly.

"It is in your power to preserve lives, should you choose to do so."

Flattery. He must think her a vain, credulous fool. An acid reply rose to her lips, but she managed to suppress it. Eyes fixed studiously upon the jagged horizon, she inquired, "What could I possibly do, Ulor?"

"Write to your brother, encouraging him to lay down his arms. Urge the advantages of this course. Tell him it's your hope and desire that he make his peace. It won't be impossible to place such a communication in his hands."

"I understand." She wondered what he'd do if she refused outright. She wasn't particularly eager to find out. "I fear the Ulor greatly overestimates my poor influence. My recommendation will carry little weight."

"That remains to be seen."

"Particularly in view of the fact," Shalindra continued pensively, "that Cerrov would no doubt suspect, despite all protestations to the contrary, that I wrote under duress. Not even the announcement of our betrothal would convince him otherwise. In fact, I fear the news will produce the opposite effect. He is of a deeply distrustful nature—the result, perhaps, of varied childhood misfortunes—and will beyond question assume the very worst."

"I see." Varis's lips bent down at the corners. "In that case, we must find another means of persuasion."

Why had she thought his eyes even slightly dimmed by daylight? They were brilliant as ever, and she didn't like to gaze straight into them for very long.

They walked on in silence. Shalindra's eyes drank the grimly glorious mountain scenery for a time, then shifted to the uniformed figures patrolling the courtyard below. As far as she could judge, the Tollbooth's garrison was very small; and no wonder. Uncle never expected the rebel forces to reach the Bruzhois. In any case, the defenses were such that a minuscule force might successfully hold the castle.

"Tell me more of the life you led after leaving Feyenne."

Varis's inappropriately pleasing voice startled her from her reverie. He was determined, it seemed, to maintain some sort of civilized facade necessitating polite conversation. A farce, but the alternatives were infinitely worse. "As you wish, Ulor," she replied.

"The air of docility doesn't suit you. It's unconvincing."

"What would you like me to speak of, Ulor?"

"Fruce Isle. Describe the library."

He does know. The magic—he guesses— Alarm flared for a moment. *He IS a mind reader!* But no. That was impossible, even for a necromancer. He was interested in books, that was all. Her closely attended but nearly unrestrained ramblings through the Tollbooth had verified that taste. Varis's own library was large and eclectic. If he'd read even half the volumes, then his learning must be immense. *Not "must be." Is. He knows about everything.* Years ago, she recalled, he always used to carry books with him everywhere about the Zalkhash. Her father had laughed uproariously at him for it.

No, nothing significant in Uncle's request. Polite empty chitchat. Her fears dwindled. She would oblige him, of course, and she'd see to it that he suspected nothing.

"It's a granite fortress, standing atop a rock where nothing grows, rising out of the waters of Lake Eev—" Shalindra commenced, and the memories came flooding back. She was careful to avoid all mention of the Conclave, the crypt, the library ghosts; but there was a great deal else to talk about. Since he had asked of her life after Feyenne, she began at the beginning and found herself speaking of the earliest days at Fruce, the dark desperate time of grief and rage.

She hadn't dusted those recollections in years, but they still seemed newly minted, and the words were pouring out of her as if of their own accord. She spoke of things her mind had buried for years. She even heard herself describing the wretched escape attempt aboard the *Lakelily,* and the subsequent humiliations. Strange that she should speak of that to Varis, of all people. He was inexplicably easy to talk to; she could hardly account for her own loquacity. But then, she reminded herself, the role she was playing demanded an appearance of amiability. And perhaps the performance was convincing, or at least diverting —they were halfway through their second circuit of the battlements, and he hadn't interrupted her once. Maybe he wasn't listening. She slanted a quick wary look at him, and spied in the daylight what would have been invisible indoors—the glint of a few silver threads at his black temples. His gaze was aimed at the horizon. She imagined his thoughts elsewhere, until he spoke.

"What would you have done had you managed to escape Fruce Isle?"

"Searched for my brother," she answered at once.

"Did you really imagine you could find him?"

"Don't know. Perhaps not." *After all, you couldn't.* "I'd have done my best."

"As it was, you remained at the library, presumably confiding your disappointment in some companion or mentor."

"There was no one to tell."

"You plotted other attempts, however."

"No, not after that. After the *Lakelily,* I knew I couldn't get away. It seemed useless to try."

"You found yourself isolated and helpless."

Then? Or now? "Yes."

"No. Not altogether helpless. There was something—knowledge of some sort, a resource. What was it?"

How did he do that? He wasn't even looking at her. Lucky guess?

"You sound as if you knew," she observed.

"So I do, thanks to Breziot."

"Father?"

"Always inventive. By his good graces, I once spent a night caged in the Wrecks of Rialsq."

"The Wrecks? I don't understand. Was it a wager of some kind?"

"A practical joke. One of many. The last, however."

"I see." She saw only too well. "Father's sense of humor was—distinctive."

"Almost unique, I believe."

He used to beat Cerrov, you know. The words almost slipped out, but she stopped her tongue in time. Foolish beyond belief to confide in this man. A blunder to hand him information he might somehow turn to advantage. Aloud, she remarked, "A night in the Wrecks sounds disagreeable, but surely you knew you'd be out within hours."

"For all I knew at the time, I was there to stay."

"Impossible. In any case, Father couldn't have known you'd take it that way." Quite bizarre to find herself defending her sire. *"A practical joke. One of many."* She could imagine.

"No. My point is only this. I've experience enough—"

Enough to warp you. What a waste. Profound sadness filled her. *What a criminal waste.*

"—to know that you had something of your own," Varis concluded.

Useless to deny. He knew as if he'd been there; but perhaps a part of the truth would serve. Something—small.

"I learned to pick locks," Shalindra confessed.

This time, he did turn to look at her.

"Yes," she insisted. "I searched until I found the right books, and I taught myself, in secret."

"Taught yourself, in secret. And then?"

"And then, I could go where I pleased, when I pleased —within the confines of Fruce Isle, that is. I could take what I wanted or needed, and no one would know, and no one could stop me. I still couldn't get away, but it wasn't as bad as it had been at first, for I no longer felt myself quite so—so—" She groped.

"Powerless?"

"Something like that." She couldn't read his expression at all, but she sensed no disbelief, and she knew she'd probably said enough, but something impelled her to speak on. "I never used it much, except at the very beginning. It wasn't important to steal extra food from the kitchen, or to rummage through locked storage closets, or to play practical jokes on people I didn't like. I didn't care about doing those things, so long as I knew that I could if I wanted. If I had that—ability—then actually using it seemed almost—"

"Beside the point."

"Yes."

"And yet, you did use it, from time to time, as the need arose?"

"From time to time."

"And enjoyed it?"

"Yes," she recollected, or recognized. "It was so—real."

"Your accomplishments went unsuspected?"

"I think always suspected—never proved."

"Yes." They walked in silence for a time, until Varis inquired, "Do you still remember how to pick locks?"

"Probably. Not that it does much good here. One needs the right tools." Perfectly true, as far as it went. But she didn't mention that a couple of her old lock picks still lay camouflaged among the hairpins at the bottom of her jewelry box. "And my bedchamber door is barred from the outside at night."

"What if you acquired the right tools?"

"There's still that bar."

"True. The obstacles have increased in magnitude. But they are not insurmountable."

She waited.

"There are finer skills, better tools, and greater knowledge to be won." Varis was studying the distance again. He might have been talking to himself. "There are larger and more important locks to pick, if you dare attempt them. There is triumph, of which your childhood satisfactions were but a weak reflection, or perhaps a premonition.

There is a power, an autonomy, of which you have scarcely dreamed, as yet."

Then it was finally clear to her what he was talking about. The gooseflesh prickled along her arms. *I've more than dreamed, Uncle. I've seen it. I've even tasted it.*

"You've an appetite, I suspect," he said.

"You confuse me, Ulor."

"I think not. You are startled. Wary and uncertain, perhaps, but neither confused nor uncomprehending."

She was silent.

"An Ulorre-consort's position is enviable," Varis observed. "She is free to pursue her own interests, whatever their nature, almost without hindrance. The restrictions governing lesser mortals do not bind her. There's no lore so secret, no art so forbidden, that she may not fathom its mysteries, should she choose. Such a woman will discover, however, that certain endeavors yield highest returns of success and satisfaction when shared. This lesson learned, her potential power is all but limitless."

Impersonal and detached as a Fruce librarian analyzing Chorkan Variations. He hardly seemed to expect reply; which was fortunate, for she had none.

The whistle of the wind filled the silence.

"Why are you telling me all this, Ulor?" Shalindra inquired, minutes later.

"Because you are fit to hear it. Look about you, Ladyship. What do you see?"

"Mountains and valleys. Trees and rock. Sky and clouds." *Freedom,* she added silently.

"Freedom, no doubt you imagine."

She couldn't control the startled tightening of her jaw, but it didn't matter; he wasn't looking at her.

"That freedom is illusory," Varis continued. "In truth, you perceive simply a larger prison of the senses. Liberty and reality lie beyond the externals, beyond the boundaries imposed by human sight and hearing. The walls hem us closely, and the doors are usually locked. It is sometimes possible, however, to pick the locks and open the doors. To do so, three things are required—education, aptitude, and willingness. The first is obtainable. The second, I sense in you. As for the third—only you yourself may judge."

Her own confusion took her by surprise. She wasn't supposed to be confused. At this juncture, she was supposed to be strong, and brave, and very clever. She was prepared to withstand fear and suffering in all their aspects. But she wasn't prepared for Varis's voice insinuating itself deep into her mind, and speaking from that place as if it lived there; sounding chords undreamt-of, and yet familiar.

And only moments earlier, she'd actually come near pitying him.

The wind was cold on her face. Shalindra shivered.

"You are beginning to feel the chill. You'd best go inside." He walked her back to the arched doorway, where they paused. "You will, perhaps, regard the possibilities I've touched upon as worthy of consideration."

"Ulor, I will."

"Ladyship."

She curtsied once, and left him.

That evening, she dined alone. Contrary to his lately established custom, Varis neither joined her nor sent word. The next day, she spent solely in the taciturn company of Zordja. Time limped. No written or spoken invitation summoned her to the battlements, nor did her uncle show himself at mealtime. Shalindra found herself oddly torn between relief and disappointment. His unnerving presence charged the air with electricity; without him, the Tollbooth was dull as a vault. When another day passed, and he failed to appear, her curiosity sharpened. She began asking questions, eventually extracting a few answers from one of the sentries.

It seemed that rebel forces under the command of Cerrov Haudrensq, engaging the remnant of General Ruzeff's Legions of the South on the stony slopes outside the town of Chatkho, had decimated the loyalist troops. There was some talk that supernatural entities attended the victors, but these rumors were unverifiable. Unquestionable fact, however, that Ruzeff was dead, his men dispersed, and Cerrov Haudrensq's army—continually accumulating new recruits—was marching swiftly north. The bulk of the loyalist forces, presently camped at Narshk Fens, would intercept the rebels within the next couple of days; and the Ulor himself would be there to command them.

17

A YELLOW AUTUMN moon glowed above Narshk Cemetery. The air was still, and the night was silent. In the midst of that silence, Varis completed his mental contortions, bringing himself to transdimensionality.

"Appear," he commanded.

Nothing happened. He repeated the summons, which went unanswered. A vertical crease dented his brow, and he sent his sorcerously enhanced mind hunting.

He searched through a consciousless void.

Nothing. Nobody. They were not resisting him. They simply were not there. The cemetery was devoid of ghosts.

Impossible. The burial ground was centuries old. Moreover, Narshk Fens had witnessed countless suicides over the years, as well as multiple murders. The place ought to be teeming.

Vacancy mocked him.

Varis's eyes opened, and the fire in their depths dimmed slowly. He was alone, more completely alone than he had been since the night he'd first tasted of necromancy.

Why?

He blinked, and physical reality reasserted itself. He stood solitary amidst the moss-blurred tombstones. Distant pinpoints of light marked the position of the enemy army. A large enemy army, stronger by far than he might have expected in the wake of Lannakh. Despite the apparent finality of that defeat, the southern Rhazaulleans had managed to regroup, flocking by the thousands to the cause of Cerrov Haudrensq. Irrational. Cerrov had grown up abroad; he was almost more Aennorvi than Rhazaullean. What claim had he upon his countrymen's loyalties and affections? What reason had they to fight and to die for him?

But reason, it seemed, had little to do with it; any more than reason appeared to account for the strange quietude of Narshk Cemetery.

The fault, he was certain, was not in his necromancy. His power, of late sometimes erratic, was strong in him tonight. Had spectres haunted the graveyard, his summons would have drawn them. The place was truly empty.

Unnaturally so.

Somebody had emptied it, liberating all the ghosts.

Explanation: Cerrov Haudrensq employed an anonymous necromancer. An unusually strong and accomplished one, by all indications. Where had he discovered such an ally?

Varis considered. The source of his enemy's sorcerous support was ultimately irrelevant. And the unknown's power, formidable though it was, probably did not equal his own.

It couldn't.

Of more immediate concern was the strength of Cerrov's mundane, flesh-and-blood army. The force had expanded of late, its numbers swelled by desertions from the Ulor's own ranks. The surviving Legions of the South, dismayed by General Ruzeff's death, had lost courage, confidence, and loyalty as well. Now they fled in droves to the enemy. For the first time since the war began, the

rebel army possessed numerical superiority. This in itself
was no catastrophe, so long as ghostly agents remained
available; but such support had become essential.

And Narshk Cemetery was untenanted.

The alien necromancer was probably congratulating
himself—prematurely. The Ulor's resources were greater
than the interloper knew. The notoriously restless graveyards of Lazimir lay miles north. To summon spectral aid
across such distance would be difficult—but not beyond
his power.

The warmth of the latest powdered ingestion still
glowed along his nerves, but it was not enough. Varis
drew a small box from his pocket, lifted the lid, hesitated
briefly, then swallowed all the contents. The dose was very
large, but the task before him was remarkably demanding.

The brilliance flared at the base of his brain, turning
the night into day. His will winged through space and
time and more. A score of reluctant spectres answered the
call, and he ruled them effortlessly, quelling their visibility until such time as he judged ripe to reveal their uncanny presence. His mind blazed like the sun. He had
never owned greater power.

He needed no sleep that night, and wanted none.

The two armies engaged in the morning. Varis, his
awareness attuned to spectral activity, perceived Cerrov's
host attended by two dozen or more phantoms, veiled
from sight like his own, each displaying uncommon enthusiasm, almost as if there voluntarily. But for the necromantic force buoying him, he would have been
thunderstruck. Even as it was, perilous perturbations
quaked his concentration. The unknown necromancer's
power rivaled his own; perhaps even surpassed it. He had
never before admitted that possibility.

He would not admit it now. There was another, more
acceptable explanation. The power at work upon the bat-
tlefield that morning belonged to no individual. Years earlier, he had watched the Spifflicates of the Wrecks pool

their resources to heighten power. Today, he witnessed a similar but far greater combination of powers.

Whose?

The human armies traded fire, and Varis scarcely noticed. His attention anchored on the subtler conflict raging between spectral forces; the contest whose outcome would shape events upon the physical plane, for the victorious ghosts would be free to turn their strength upon the living men below. The clash overhead went unnoticed by all save sorcerously enhanced human eyes; and even if visible, might well have escaped recognition. For they fought not as mortals, but rather as the ectoplasmic entities they were, in rushing transparent tides, with a motionless intensity marking the greatest violence, a waxing and waning of illusory solidity to signal the shifting of strength and advantage.

Cerrov's ghostly minions were numerous and vigorous, powered by their summoners' collective will, reinforced by their own inexplicable volition.

How many necromancers out there? How many trained intellects united?

Evidently, too many to resist. As Varis looked on, his Lazimiri ghosts began to fade. Simultaneously, the enemy phantoms coalesced to the verge of ordinary human visibility, even appearing to wax in volume. Their presence went as yet unnoted below, but that could not continue for long.

Varis sensed his own mind darkening under the onslaught. Beneath the iron necromantic composure, black emotion stirred. He stood in danger of breaking concentration, of losing control like the greenest of amateurs. For one moment, the mocking image of a sly-eyed, smirking, decoratively scarred face arose before him, and his startled will faltered, and his servant-ghosts flickered almost out of existence. A moment to recover, and he had them again. Clotl's face was gone, but it might return, and he could not afford such dangerous lapses.

Focus reinforced, concentration restored intact; and a detached recognition of extreme emergency.

With him he carried a small corked vial, to which he had never expected to resort. Drawing the cork, he drank off the liquid contents. Lightning blasted his mind. His waning force instantly renewed and exceeded itself. His vision took on a new and matchless penetration. For this moment, he could see beneath surfaces—to the rock beneath the soil, the bones and organs beneath the flesh of the soldiers—and the world was suffused with greenish luminosity. His skin had acquired inordinate sensitivity, and the touch of his garments rasped. His heart raced, and his blood seemed to boil.

The lash of a mental whip marshaled his fading ghosts. They were dutifully present and potent once more. His will drove them like storm clouds upon their adversaries, and Cerrov's spectres gave way before them. There was a tremulous alternation of dark and light, substance and nothingness; a final calculated convulsion of controlling intellect; a responsive ectoplasmic frenzy. Then Varis sensed a distant collective shuddering of battered sorcerous minds, and the enemy ghosts began to fade.

They yielded abruptly. Their ties to the physical plane snapped, and suddenly they were not.

Varis's victorious shades, much depleted, hovered upon the edge of nonexistence. Their subsequent descent upon the rebel troops went all but unnoticed. Only a handful of soldiers sensed inimical presence; fewer yet glimpsed faint, fleeting wraith faces and forms. Thus, the battle proceeded all but free of supernatural influence, and the two armies fought each other with conventional weapons alone.

Throughout the hours of mayhem that followed, the Ulor's outnumbered troops held their own. Slaughter was large and mutual. At the end of the day, when the armies withdrew from the field, the fenny ground was thick with rebel and loyalist dead. Each side had sustained great loss; but the final outcome was unclear.

The rebel army, claiming victory, drew back to Nevusq, there to lick its wounds. The loyalist forces, also claiming victory, remained encamped at Narshk; their inactivity dictated less by strategic consideration than by the Ulor's severe indisposition.

At the end of the day, Varis's heightened vitality ebbed with the light. Strength failed in an instant, and he toppled to the ground. The canvas walls of his tent shielded him from observation as he crawled on hands and knees toward his bed. Long before he reached it, recollection of his destination fled. His mind contracted, and darkness pressed hard on his thoughts.

All consciousness was not lost, however, and the twilight sentience left to him was filled with monsters; nightmare beings with distorted bestial forms, and human faces that he'd recognize if he made the mistake of looking too closely. But he had to look, for there was one he sought, one that he actually wanted. Young, fine-boned, with clear hazel eyes, intelligent and uncontaminated. There was a voice to match the face, low and soothing, inexpressibly soothing to lightning-blasted nerves and intellect. If only he could hear it again, the whirling chaos might resolve itself. But she wasn't here, some lucid shred of his mind recalled. She was far away, locked up in the Tollbooth, and she couldn't help him now. And why indeed should she want to, when he'd persecuted her and hers and his own? But somehow he sensed that she didn't hate him, that she'd lull the monsters, if only he found her. He wouldn't find her here, however, *Because she isn't dead, yet,* and the other ones, the dreadful ones, were converging upon him. So he closed his eyes to shut them out, but that only drew them nearer, sharpening their clarity, and their voices were coming at him—eager, chattering, gibbering little voices, somehow terrifying. Impossible to still those voices, they never ceased, but at least he could drown them out—they couldn't be heard above his own cries. But his throat was parched and increasingly sore, and the creatures were growing bolder, and soon, he knew, they were going to touch him . . .

The Ulor's unidentifiable illness, accompanied by fever and violent delirium, confounded a brace of attending physicians. Traditional methods of treatment—bleeding, purging, tonic decoctions, and all such normally reliable remedies—proved ineffective here, and the doctors confessed themselves baffled; confessed to one another alone, for news of the Ulor's condition was carefully suppressed. At the end of the second day, however, the fever broke, and he slept, awakening twenty-four hours later, weak in body, depressed in spirits, but for the most part rational.

He rested at Narshk another day, after which it was clear that immediate resumption of activity was impractical. Leaving the army under command of the competent General Gryshynkho, Varis retired to complete his recovery at Castle Haudrensq.

"Ladyship, the Ulor invites you to join him upon the walkway," said the guard.

So he was back again, his arrival as unheralded as his departure had been. She had thought to sense his unseen presence for the past day or two, but this was the first definite confirmation. Something midway between dread and excitement fluttered her thoughts.

"Tell him I will attend him presently," Shalindra replied.

"He wants you now," said Zordja.

"It will take but a couple of minutes to change my dress—"

"Now," Zordja repeated.

Inadvisable to resist. Zordja was perfectly capable of dragging her off to the battlements by force, if necessary. Capable and quite willing.

"Tell the Ulor I'll be there directly," Shalindra

amended, allowing no resentment to touch her face or voice. Probably her gaoler thought her a meek little thing. Let her think so.

The guard saluted and withdrew. Shalindra donned her furs, and then, closely attended, hurried from her room, down the stairs, past the sentry, and out onto the ramparts. Nearly three weeks had passed since her last stroll along these walls. She had spent nearly all of that time indoors, engaged in futile cogitation. Now, as she stepped through the arched doorway, the cold smote her, and she recognized the advance of the season. Autumn was swiftly deepening into winter. It wouldn't be much longer before the howling storm winds swept the Bruzhois, cloaking the mountains in snow, obliterating the Trans-Bruzh, and sealing the Ayzin Pass for months to come.

And that could stop Cerrov cold, literally.

Varis stood with his back to her. He wore the same thin gray coat he had worn upon their last meeting, but this time, it was buttoned—his sole concession to the falling temperatures. Her pulse quickened a little. She advanced quietly. Last time, he'd somehow sensed her approach before she'd come within ten feet of him. Today, the wind was much louder, and he was unlikely to do so well.

He did better.

"Ladyship."

She was at least fifteen feet behind him. She wondered if he enjoyed this game. He turned, and she stiffened. Varis's face, always pallid, was now positively cadaverous. The cheeks were sunken, the shadows beneath the eyes smudged in charcoal, and the eyes themselves were impossibly luminescent, their expression disquieting and somehow inhuman. Shalindra resisted the impulse to look away, but could not repress the question that rose spontaneously to her lips:

"What has happened to you?"

"I've been ill," Varis said. "But that is finished."

Is it?

"Will you walk?"

"As you wish, Ulor." Shalindra advanced to his side. They progressed in silence for a time. She noted that his step was firm and sure as ever. As always, he didn't offer to touch her. The silence lengthened, until she began to wonder why he had summoned her. The need to advertise her captivity had long since passed. He neither looked at her nor spoke to her. He seemed, in fact, to have forgotten her existence.

Just as well. She stole a sidelong glance at him. Haggard. Drawn. Grayly unwell. Mind probably elsewhere.

"You are very silent," he observed suddenly, turning the disquieting brilliance of his gaze full upon her.

She forced herself to meet his alien eyes. The mind behind them was palpably active.

"You will oblige me by speaking."

"What shall I speak of, Ulor?" She didn't let her surprise show.

"Anything you please. Recite poetry or a laundry list if you wish, but use your voice."

No perilous puzzles today, no veiled suggestions. He only wanted her to fill up silence. Very well, she'd cooperate. Subject matter? Something innocuous, not too interesting. Shalindra began speaking of the latest book she'd picked out of the castle library; a dog-eared copy of Omee Nofid's philosophical *Refutations.*

It really didn't matter what she chattered on about; he clearly wasn't listening. They completed an entire circuit of the walls, and Varis never spoke. He seemed worlds away, lost in his own thoughts, quite unaware. And it crossed her mind then, as it had weeks earlier, that a sudden, fierce shove, to send him plunging from the battlements, was not the worst of possible options. She was unprepared for the rush of revulsion, almost horror, accompanying this thought.

He stopped abruptly and wheeled to face her. Shalindra shrank away from him. He knew. For one moment, she'd forgotten his preternatural acuity, and he'd caught that unguarded thought, and he knew. His eyes were unendurable, and they held her.

"He has found sorcerous support," Varis said.

"What?"

"He has enlisted the aid of a necromantic conclave, and now the legions of ghosts attend his army."

Cerrov. He was talking about Cerrov, she realized, and why he should share his knowledge with her was unclear. She was starting to suspect that his mind wasn't right. Perhaps the incandescence of his eyes denoted fever—or madness.

"I sensed a large group, perhaps a dozen. Not Rhazaullean, or I should have known of them long ago."

They came. The message reached Fruce, and they actually came.

"Powerfully united. Practiced."

She couldn't imagine why he was telling her all this. Perhaps he didn't know what he was saying. He was looking straight at her, but she wasn't sure that he actually saw her. He might have been talking to himself, or to the air, or the stones of the castle.

"I do not know where they came from, or how he found them. Perhaps Dasune sent them."

She didn't let her thoughts approach the truth. Somehow he'd catch the mental vibrations, he'd pick up the scent of old sorcery on her—

If he realized what she was capable of, no predicting his reaction.

"I overcame them at Narshk. The effort was considerable. Success was—costly."

"I see that." So he had sickened himself with necromancy, as she had twice in her life sickened herself. She remembered too well how it felt; the ghastly weakness, melancholia, and disorientation. He was over the worst of it, but no doubt still suffered. She wasn't as pleased about that as she should have been. "Perhaps," she suggested noncommittally, "you should rest."

Silence. He was abstracted, or else his mind wandered. He didn't hear her, didn't even know she was there.

"No time," Varis answered.

She blinked, then prompted cautiously, "No time—?"

"I must rejoin the army. Gryshynkho commands. He is capable enough, but he cannot fight ghosts. Following Narshk, my sorcerous antagonists will find themselves incapacitated for a while. They will soon resume activity, however. I must be there to oppose them."

Still feeling the effects of his latest magical enterprise, and already planning others? Shalindra shook her head.

"Too soon. You'll damage yourself beyond repair," she said, to her own surprise. She wasn't supposed to be worrying about his health. Of course, she reminded herself, she needed to maintain the fiction of a betrothal. She wanted him to think her acquiescent, and she was only speaking the lines her role demanded.

"As they reinforce one another's strength, their recovery is sure to be swift." Varis pursued his own train of thought. "There's a great power in that union of forces, a very great power. It has always eluded me." He studied the horizon a moment, then rounded on her so suddenly that she jumped. "And you? Have you considered the matters we discussed at our last meeting?"

"Ulor?" It came out high and thin. His unpredictability unnerved her. "Matters?"

"Picking locks," he said dryly. "Opening forbidden doors."

She had thought of little else for weeks. His suggestions possessed surprisingly potent allure; a fact she would hardly admit to herself, much less to him. She shrugged. "Some locks are best left intact, some doors are best left unopened."

"Which ones?"

"Those that protect us."

"You protect an infant or an idiot by locking it in, or out. For its own good."

"It's not always children or idiots requiring protection."

"From what? Knowledge?"

"Sometimes. Knowledge can be dangerous, or harmful."

"You are half right. It can be dangerous. Harmful if misused. Never injurious in and of itself, however."

"A fine distinction, Ulor, and perhaps academic."

"By no means. Entirely practical in its application. Consider, for example, the blossom of the jhanivianus plant—a commonplace, reliably benevolent medicinal. When combined with the juice of Aennorvi thonz berries, together with the essence of bitter blifilnuts, however, the flowers assume lethal properties. Would you then outlaw cultivation of jhanivianus—perhaps prohibit study and analysis of the plant—in short, deprive the world of a tangible benefit, through fear of potential harm?"

The dichotomy between his manner and his expression was alarming. The words were rational, the voice even and deliberate, but the eyes seemed to wander through nightmares.

He had paused, as if expecting reply. She gathered her wits quickly, and heard herself start, "I shouldn't wish to suppress study. I'd only hope to keep people from harming one another, if not themselves—"

"You will not do so by limiting their knowledge. Knowledge is amoral. You'll come to see that, presently. I will prove it to you."

"Ulor, I need no proof."

"You will have it, nevertheless. Your own education, while impressive for your age, is far from complete."

"I never claimed otherwise."

"There's much that escapes you now. You do not even know your own heritage. You are Haudrensq, and you do not know the realities of this castle."

"Yes I do. Granite, cold, locked doors, silence, isola-tion, desolation, frustration—"

"Good, but there's more," he told her. "Listen to me, you may profit. All knowledge offers potential advantage. I will increase your store, if you'll hear me."

"Why should you?" she could not forbear asking.

"You are Haudrensq. You are also future Ulorre-con-sort, should the fiction of your consent transmute to real-ity. There is much you should know. If the Tollbooth were to fall—"

"There's a chance of that?"

"None. But use your imagination. Think of flight."

"From this place? Impossible."

"Wrong. Should you find yourself trapped—"

By whom or what, other than you?

"There is a way out," Varis concluded.

He's mad, and he wants me to be mad along with him.

"Are you afraid?"

"Not of you." Uncertain whether she'd spoken aloud. A lie, in any case.

"I will show you."

You are a lunatic.

"Come with me now." Varis extended his hand.

Scared and exhilarated, she flinched away. His hand dropped back to his side.

He didn't intend to force her, she saw. She didn't have to go with him.

"There is something that you should see." Without awaiting reply, he moved away. For a moment she vacil-lated, then followed.

At first, she wasn't convinced he knew where he was going. There was a subtle unsureness to his step, almost as if he were lost. He seemed slow in locating the door he wanted, and that uncertainty frightened her more than anything that had gone before. Then he was through, and off the ramparts, and she could follow or not, as she chose.

She went after him. He was a few feet ahead of her,

hurrying down the dimly lit stone stairway that hugged the southwest face of the donjon tower. His pace was swift; all confusion seemed to have left him.

At the foot of the tower, an oaken door, unlocked. Through the door, and down another flight of stairs. And now there were no windows, and no light, at least none perceptible to Shalindra's senses. Cautiously, she felt her way down step by step, but at the bottom she stumbled, and would have fallen had not Varis's steadying hand closed on her arm. She gasped, and pulled back, for it flashed through her mind that he had lured her down to this black and silent cellar to kill her.

He released her at once. Wordlessly, he resumed progress, and she trailed the steady tap of his footsteps. He never slowed or hesitated, and it occurred to her that those uncanny eyes of his could penetrate the dark. Somehow or other, Varis could actually see.

His footsteps ceased. Somewhere ahead, she heard a metallic snap, followed by a soft creak. A puff of stagnant air touched her face. Then, silence.

"Where are you?" Her voice was small in the midst of that blackness.

"Here."

She blundered toward him; bumped against an obstacle of some sort; changed directions, and lost her bearings.

"Give me your hand." Varis's voice was very near again.

She hesitated only a moment, then obeyed. She extended her hand. He took it, and her blood leaped. His clasp was dry and hot. *Fever,* she thought. He led her forward, and she had the impression of passing through a door; and then, she sensed constricted space.

"Where are we?" Shalindra asked.

"Tunnel. Take care, the ceiling's low."

"Where are you taking me?"

No answer.

Breathless and extraordinarily silent in the tunnel; no

sound of the world above. Dark beyond comprehension; surely even Varis couldn't see through it. He must be feeling his way along, but his pace never slackened. She followed unresistingly. The passage descended at a sharp grade. He was drawing her down into unutterable blackness; she wondered if dying felt the same.

The tunnel leveled. Presently Varis halted. There was another metallic snap, and suddenly—faint light. Shalindra drew a sharp breath. She could now see the outline of an irregularly shaped portal, swiveling on its central pivot. The light came from the other side. He led her through, and she looked about her.

She stood at the rear of a fairly sizable cave. Rows of niches cut into the walls contained scores of carven wooden coffins. Three great sarcophagi topped with reclining effigies evidently housed consequential remains. Light angled in through an arched opening at the front. A gate of heavy iron bars secured this entrance.

She glanced up at Varis. His fever-glittering eyes were fixed on the gate.

"You see. There is the exit. You are Haudrensq. It is fitting that you know."

The exit was locked, she noted. She said nothing.

"I hope one day to give you the key. Beyond that gate rise the forests of the Bruzhois. Here, we are well without the castle walls."

"Who lies in this crypt?"

"Our ancestors. The old man, as well. He's none of ours, but surely deserves no less."

"Old man?"

"He had the pyre and urn he desired. See, the urn's here still."

Mad, he must be mad, she thought. *Or else delirious.*

"There he is, among the Haudrensq dead, forever." He still had her hand, and his touch burned. He drew her forward to one of the wall niches. The compartment contained an urn of traditional design. "After his death, he divulged all his secrets—save one alone. That one, perhaps the greatest of all, he preserves even yet."

"What secret, Ulor?"

"Locked doors, again. See—" He turned her from the wall. "There is Celgi Stoneheart's tomb. That is where it all began."

"Began?"

"Celgi's long gone, but the old man remains. Had I never met him, that evening—had I never followed him here—"

"What, then?"

"Another life. Another universe."

"Better?"

"Smaller. Probably no warmer."

"Ulor, I don't understand you."

"No. May you remain uncomprehending."

"That's not what you said to me a short time ago."

"You are perceptive, but inexperienced. You don't know—" His eyes riveted hers. "But perhaps all might change, even now. It must change. A joining of forces— all the power of that—there's the key, there's the vital difference. The old man would smirk and ask, 'Does he mean *vital* as in important, essential? Or does he mean *vital* as in life?' Both. Both. Winter ends at last, or the world dies. It's time for that change. Late, but not too late. Do you hear me—Shalindra?"

The force of his grip was crushing her hand, but she didn't feel it. He was lost; he was raving. The worst of it was that she found every word so imbued with significance. "I hear you," she said.

His offer. The magnitude. The price.

His eyes still held her motionless. Her mind struggled in a frozen prison. He had seen something in her that she hadn't known was there.

No, I'm not what he thinks.

She realized then that she was very frightened—of herself, and of what she'd discover inside, if she looked. She didn't want to look; she wanted it more than anything.

"Please take me out of here," she said, and they were the hardest words she'd ever spoken.

For a moment longer he stared down into her eyes, then nodded abruptly and conducted her from the crypt. Back along the stygian tunnel he led her, through the cellar and up the stairs to ground level. As they stepped forth into the light, he relinquished her hand, and the severance was oddly chilling.

"Ladyship," he said, and left her.

She stood staring after him. Slowly, her mind resumed functioning. Any belated hope of wandering the castle, unaccompanied for once, was destroyed by Zordja's prompt arrival. Shalindra returned to her own chamber, where she sat thinking of many things, not the least of which was that barred door at the crypt entrance, beyond which lay the forest, and freedom.

Under the watchful eye of her gaoler, she rearranged her hair, anchoring the long strands with an ornate silver clip. In place of the silver skewer ordinarily securing the clip, she quietly substituted one of the steel lock picks still lying at the bottom of her jewelry box. Perhaps she'd never have the chance to use it; should opportunity arise, however, she'd be ready.

Twenty-four hours later—the earliest she judged it safe to attempt reconnaissance—Shalindra approached the cellar stairway. Her gaoler, sometimes costive, was presently occupied with a chamber pot. For this little while, she could come and go unobserved. As it happened, however, Zordja's presence or absence proved immaterial.

When she reached the foot of the donjon tower, Shalindra discovered a sentry stationed at the head of the cellar stairs. The fellow willingly answered questions. In accordance with the Ulor's new commands, he told her, this post was henceforth to be guarded day and night.

"We are ready to resume," announced The Librarian. Lamplight lent her white face artificial color. Outside the tent, the cold autumn stars shone down on the rebel camp outside the town of Nevusq.

Cerrov studied her. She still showed the signs of her recent illness. She was gaunt and hollow-eyed, but at least she was back on her feet; and he needed her. "Your companions?" he asked.

"Quite recovered."

"All of them?"

"Oruno still suffers the occasional syncope. No doubt a temporary inconvenience. Otherwise, all is well."

"What likelihood of relapse or recurrence, would you say?"

"That is difficult to judge. Much depends on the state of your uncle's mind and health. To be frank, his powers are greater than I foresaw. Never, before Narshk, would I have credited an individual's ability to overcome the united Conclave. The quiescence following our defeat is suggestive, however. He has failed to exploit his advantage, presumably because he's found himself unable to do so. It's reasonable to assume, therefore, that victory cost him dearly. He has doubtless sickened and weakened, as we have, or perhaps more. It remains to determine whether our collective recuperative power surpasses his own."

"I see." Once again, Cerrov wondered at the Conclave's willingness to aid his cause. Proprietorship of Rhazaulle's Wolf Throne hardly concerned them, nor did they pretend otherwise; their motives were personal, and rarely alluded to. "No delay, then. If your people are ready, we'll move against Gryshynkho tomorrow."

She inclined her head. "We are ready. Let us hope that the same cannot be said of the Ulor Varis."

The Conclave retired in silence from the camp. No one knew where they went to perform their rites, no one knew the source of their spectral aid. At dawn, the troops found themselves supernaturally reinforced. Gryshynkho's loyalist force, lacking such resources, was easily conquered; and Cerrov's army marched north to enter the city of Lazimir unopposed.

18

THE ROOM WAS dark. Most occupants would have found themselves blind. For Varis, however, the stray moonbeam filtering through a chink in the shutters sufficed. Effortlessly, he descried the outlines of bed, wardrobe, and other furnishings. Confidently, he walked to and fro. He shouldn't have been able to do so, not without the sorcerous stimulation that he had eschewed since Narshk; but in fact, it was easy.

It was the deserted dead of night, and Varis was wide awake. Often, in the past, insomnia had plagued him; but never so persistently. Four nights now without sleep. He should have been exhausted. He *was* exhausted, some part of his mind recognized. The curious sense of detachment from his own body told him as much. Fatigue notwithstanding, he was unremittingly wakeful; as he had been since receiving the news of Cerrov Haudrensq's advance from Lazimir. The rebel forces—swollen with new recruits, (many of them deserters from Gryshynkho's broken army) and backed by the magic of the nameless foreign necromancers—streamed north along the TransBruzh. Another day's march would carry them to the castle gates.

He could have stopped them long ago. He could stop them even yet, if he chose. A visit to the Haudrensq crypt, or to the burial sites in the mountain forests; a summoning and dispatching of ghost-slaves; and within the space of hours, Cerrov's troops would be flying.

So far, he'd resisted the temptation. His powers were strong as ever; strong enough, as he had demonstrated, to overcome the combined necromantic forces of his enemy's allies. But how high the cost of their use? The last great effort had bought victory at the price of health and repose. The days had passed, the fevers had subsided, and the weakness had passed. Sleeplessness remained, however, together with recurrent periods of confusion, and occasional lapses in memory. He knew well enough what these symptoms portended. The signs were clear, the warning unequivocal.

He hovered upon the edge of mental breakdown complete and irrevocable. In short, he approached spifflication. During the daylight hours, he didn't allow himself to recognize, much less contemplate, that prospect. But now, alone with himself in the dark and the silence, there could be no evasions. For months, he'd prodigalized his energy, taxing his magical powers beyond endurance, allowing inadequate recuperative intervals. Always, at any given time, recourse to necromancy had appeared as the best, if not the sole available choice. And now at last, the debt was falling due.

Spifflication—idiocy, degeneracy, unspeakable degradation. The old memories crowded his brain. Professional handlers and their performing spifflicated troupes, in Rialsq, long ago. The faces in the Wrecks, pressed against the iron bars of his cage, hands reaching in through the bars. Drooling goblin-children in a ruined cottage in the frozen forest. A scarred visage, smirking lips, knowing eyes—Clotl. All of them still haunting and hunting him, still clutching at him.

They had trailed him all through his life, and now they were closer than ever before. Very close indeed; all but breathing down the back of his neck, if only they breathed at all. He could almost feel them in the air around him—those dead Spifflicates, and the others—the sane ones, the brothers, the children, the ones whose faces he didn't want to see.

On the other hand, if he did see them, at least he'd know how many were with him, *who* they were, *where* they were. A single swallow of stimulant, a controlled mental paroxysm. Easily accomplished. But exactly what he couldn't afford now, any more than he could afford to send ghosts against his nephew's army. It was just such squandering of sorcerous force that would ruin him once and for all.

He needed rest. Above all things, he needed a respite from necromancy. In time, he would recover. He might resume activity, in relative safety; but only if he rested now.

Fortunately, he had the leisure. He sat safely ensconced in the Tollbooth. The castle, perched atop its cliffs, required no magical defense. Only a small but reliable garrison was needed, and that the Ulor had.

But did he?

Varis paused in his midnight pacing. He possessed no sense whatever of his men's morale. So far, they'd proved consistently obedient. They were decently treated, so far as he knew, and he had no particular reason to question their loyalty. No reason, that was, beyond the general disaffection so unaccountably prevalent among Rhazaulleans of every degree; from the traitorous Noble Landholders of the southern provinces, to the urbanites throwing wide their city gates, to the farmers and craftsmen flocking by the thousands to the pretender's cause, to the deserters fleeing the loyalist army to swell the rebel ranks.

Impossible to disregard these things. Impossible not to wonder sometimes, in the silent dead of night.

The Tollbooth garrison—unsound at center, infected with the popular madness, riddled with secret weakness?

No way of knowing. No point in dwelling on it. In any event, quite possible that the so-called loyalists' loyalty would never be put to the proof.

Cerrov would shortly arrive. But would he launch an attack on the castle, with his sister immured within? Another commander, faced with such a decision, would probably account the girl's sacrifice a minor price; at most, a regrettable necessity. Every available source of intelligence, however, indicated that the bond existing between Cerrov Haudrensq and his sister was exceptionally strong. Conversation with Shalindra tended to confirm this report. When she mentioned her brother, her face and voice spoke volumes; if Cerrov valued her half so highly, she was a precious hostage indeed.

Assuming the Tollbooth continued inviolate, the Ayzin Pass was blocked. The rebels' road north to Rialsq ended here in the Bruzhois; ended for the present, ended for months to come, and possibly ended forever.

Winter was imminent. The long nights were achingly cold, and dustings of snow already filmed the peaks and valleys. Within days, the first of the blizzards would come howling. That first would shortly be followed by others, and soon the TransBruzh would vanish under the drifts. Cerrov's army, thousands strong and needing provisions, would perforce winter in Lazimir; where inactivity, boredom, and frustration would work their respective wonders. Discouragement and resentment would simmer. Presently, the ill-matched Rhazaullean, Aennorvi, and Rhelish partners would fall to quarreling. There would be mortal insults, ethnic slurs, treachery and sudden death, new blood feuds. Toward the end of winter, around the time of the Rift, there would be a rash of desertions, as a host of southern Rhazaullean peasants returned home for the spring sowing. And spring itself, the mild season transforming Rhazaulle into a giant bog, would lengthen the term of the rebels' captivity, perhaps by months. Not at all unlikely that the delay might extend to the early days of summer.

Over the course of so many idle months, it wouldn't be easy to continue meeting the high rates of the Rhelish mercenaries. Upon the first default of contract, the Rhelish would decamp.

Far off in Aennorve, King Dasune—dissatisfied with the progress of the war—might choose to order his countrymen home.

And throughout this interim, the Ulor could rest at Castle Haudrensq, regaining health and sorcerous strength. While the adequately trustworthy Council of Noble Landholders governed in Rialsq, the Ulor might renew vitality, make plans, commune with his niece and future consort—for she would become Ulorre-consort, she'd keep her own expedient promise, although she didn't yet know it. There were a number of sound reasons for holding her to her word, but the strongest among them had only recently become apparent—his own inclination.

More to consider than mere inclination, however.

Essential to success that Cerrov Haudrensq fear for his sister's life. An assault upon the Tollbooth would signal her execution. There must be no doubt whatever upon that point. Already, messengers carrying word of this decree were hurrying to intercept the rebel army. Conveyance of the prisoner's severed ear or finger might have underscored the Ulor's seriousness of intent; such was, in fact, a time-honored Rhazaullean form of emphasis. Fortunately superfluous in this case, though; thus sparing the Ulor the unpleasant necessity of ordering some nameless, luckless, substitute female's mutilation.

Preferably, no need to harm Shalindra herself.

When her brother's rebellion was finally crushed, Varis mused, he would make her Ulorre-consort, in Rialsq. And then he would teach her—there was a great deal he could teach her. She'd prove an apt scholar of sorcery. She had the mind and strength for it, and more important, some latent appetite for it. She'd learn quickly, and when she had knowledge, the totality of their combined powers would far exceed the sum of its parts, and their lives would merge indissolubly.

Or perhaps—and it was the first time, in all the weeks since her arrival, that the thought had entered his mind— perhaps he wouldn't teach her, after all. Perhaps he himself would abjure necromancy. The last great threat to his reign eliminated, there would be little further need of magic. He could afford to give it up, and that would be the cleanest, safest course, both for himself and for her. He could renew his life, start afresh, rule in peace.

Change.

He could do that. He would do it, one way or the other. There remained only to choose the direction, and that choice could be made at leisure. Shalindra's presence forestalled a rebel attack; and more important, prevented the foreign sorcerous offensive that might have forced self-destructive recourse to his own necromantic powers. Because of Shalindra, there was time.

But if Cerrov deemed the price of her safety too high —what then?

Having so clearly stated terms, the Ulor would hence-forth lose stature and credibility should he fail to abide by his own conditions. In the event of attack, the hostage died.

That would be difficult.

Varis glimpsed himself in the small mirror above the washstand. A feeble green luminosity seemed to edge the reflected angles and planes of his face. His eyes glowed like greenish embers. And he hadn't touched a sorcerous

stimulant since Narshk. For a long time he stood motionless and staring.

"I am going to walk on the battlements," Shalindra announced.

"Ulor didn't send for you," Zordja said.

That was true enough. He hadn't requested her presence today, or yesterday, or the day before that. He had
not, in fact, asked her to join him since the day the rebel
army had made its camp on the Bruzhoi slopes below the
Ayzin Pass, in plain sight of Castle Haudrensq. Presumably Varis now considered the display of his hostage redundant. She supposed she ought to be glad of the respite.

In actual fact, she missed the meetings.

No matter. All she wanted was fresh air, and she
didn't need company for that.

"I'll go alone," she said.

Zordja eyed her levelly. "Not alone," she decreed at
last.

The gaoler dogged her down the stairs, past the sentry, and out onto the ramparts themselves—for this time,
the Ulor wasn't present to oversee the prisoner. There
were, these past few days, sentinels stationed at regular
intervals along the entire circuit, but Zordja evidently
reckoned such supervision inadequate. Shalindra forgot the
other's presence, however, the moment she set foot out of
doors, for the skies were dramatically threatening, and the
cold was intense. She was warmly dressed beneath her furs,
but she shivered. It looked and it felt like winter.

Too early.

Her eyes roamed the ramparts. She realized she was
searching for a lean, upright figure, motionlessly outfacing
the wind. She would approach in silence, but long before
she reached him, she'd hear his voice:

"Ladyship."

Not today, however. No sign of him. He might be
resting. *He ought to sleep more, or he'll never really recover,* she

found herself thinking. More likely, however, he was holed up in his workroom again, and whatever he did in there was never discussed.

She started moving, with Zordja trudging half a dozen heavy steps behind. Straight into the whiplash of the wind she walked, and her teeth were chattering, her fingers chilling inside her fur-lined gloves, but she didn't pause until she reached the southern arc of the Tollbooth ramparts. From this vantage point, she could spy the tents of the rebel encampment, here and there visible amidst the firs below. The smoke of hidden cooking fires curled skyward. Occasional movement flashed briefly through the trees.

Her brother's army. If Cerrov happened to be watching the castle, he could probably see her. She was certainly conspicuous enough.

Perhaps that was all the trouble. Perhaps that explained his prolonged inactivity. He thought her life in danger.

Isn't it?

No. Yes. Not sure.

Idiot, how can you doubt it?

Cerrov was sitting down there, day after day, because he feared for her. The stalemate might continue indefinitely.

But a cold, light kiss upon her cheek informed her otherwise. Shalindra started a little. A gloved finger pressed to her face came away wet. A few tiny snowflakes rode the wind through the Ayzin Pass. A few more. She blinked, and the air was full of them, countless specks of white floating down to meet the rising smoke of the rebel campfires.

It was only a flurry, and it wouldn't amount to much. In her mind's eye, however, she watched the snows thicken, watched the storm winds heap white oblivion upon the mountains, watched the TransBruzh fade from existence. It wouldn't happen today. But it wouldn't be long.

No passage through the mountains, for months to come. Cerrov would have to withdraw. By the time the winter snows melted, his polyglot army would probably do likewise.

Varis didn't have to fight at all. He need only sit in the Tollbooth and wait.

Because of me.

The wind veered slightly, driving the snowflakes into her eyes. She turned her face away. Not much to see down there, anyway. The vista was bleak.

She resumed progress, moving as if in a daze, with Zordja ever close upon her trail. When she'd completed a circuit, she went back inside, to her room. Stretching herself fully dressed upon her bed, she shut her eyes and feigned slumber. Presently Zordja's interest waned, and her attention wandered. Relieved of the gaoler's unwinking scrutiny, Shalindra managed to gather her wits. She lay as if unconscious, but her mind whirred.

Consider your options . . .

Words from long ago. Still good.

Now, if ever, was the time to kill Varis. That single death would end the war, ensuring Cerrov's victory. And she was in a perfect position to perform the task, or so it appeared. As they walked side by side on the battlements —all guards and sentries maintaining a respectful distance —a quick thrust with—? *With what?* The pointed steel lock pick securing her hair ornament would certainly serve, if she caught him in a vulnerable spot.

Neck? Eyeball?

Shalindra shuddered. The mental image was horrifying. She could never do such a thing. And fortunately, she wouldn't be called upon to try, for the opportunity would never arise. The Ulor might promenade the battlements with his future consort in seeming confidence; in truth,

however, he was always alert, guarded, all but impossible
to take unaware. She could legitimately dismiss such a
scheme as impractical; and her sense of relief was profound.

What else?

In her mind, she stood once more on the walls, with
the snowflakes dancing about her. *If Cerrov happened to be
watching the castle, he could probably see her.* Well, someone in
her brother's army was undoubtedly watching. Her own
suicidal leap from the ramparts would not go unnoticed.
Neither gaoler nor guards would be able to stop her, and
the great impediment delaying Cerrov's advance would be
eliminated. Probably effective, but there had to be another
way.

Her options, were few; almost nonexistent.

Escape from the Tollbooth? With indefatigable Zordja
watching her every minute of every day? Sentries posted
all over the place? Her chamber door barred from the outside at night? It would take a miracle.

Or else magic, of which she yet retained a very little.

She lay still as a stone. Her breathing was slow and
even. No one, seeing her thus, could have guessed the
tumult of her thoughts.

Magic. Should she achieve full transdimensionality—
questionable at best—a ghost's aid might serve to win her
freedom. She'd elude vigilance, flee by way of the tunnel,
escaping the Tollbooth without recourse to a spectacularly
final plunge from the battlements.

So much she might accomplish, if her luck held. If it
did not, she might simply succeed in killing herself. She'd
come close to doing so upon two separate occasions. A
third such attempt could easily be the last. She'd inwardly
vowed never more to meddle in necromancy—

*Then why have you saved the last of the FSD107-N all
these years?*

One last sorcerous endeavor. Painful, and potentially
lethal. She could feel the fear tightening her muscles.

Not just fear.

No. Excitement, unmistakably.

Understandable. The prospect of freedom—

Or of sorcery? One last time. Remember the ghost in the crypt, at Fruce. The few moments that you actually ruled—remember? One last time in my life.

It might not work. Perhaps she wasn't strong enough, or skilled enough. She'd probably just sicken herself, to no avail. Not hard convincing herself to try, however. In fact, she required no convincing at all.

She'd have to do it during the daylight hours; a regrettable necessity, but she knew that the heavy bar securing her bedroom door every night would defy her best efforts.

What time of day?

Very early. Around dawn. A sluggish hour, nobody wide awake. Few guards posted about the old passageways. The Ulor, largely nocturnal, was all but invisible most mornings. Whether he slept or simply savored solitude behind locked doors, no one knew; but he rarely showed himself before the sun was well above the horizon.

Dawn, then; or thereabouts. As early as Zordja got around to unbarring the bedroom door. And Zordja herself? The first, and perhaps the worst of obstacles? If the necromantic summoning succeeded, she'd be able to deal with Zordja . . .

And after that? Hurry down to ground level, there to confront the sentry guarding the cellar stairs. Different tactics required there, but she'd manage—provided the necromancy worked.

Equipment. Mentally she listed the articles she would need. They were few and easily obtainable.

The plan, very spare and simple, was fixed in her mind. No need to review it again. And nothing left to do but kill time through the rest of the endless afternoon, evening, and night that stretched before her. She could stand it, she supposed; she could simulate an interest in

reading, fancy needlework, or whatever. She'd do well
enough, provided she didn't have to face Varis across the
dinner table. Those eyes of his would see through her.
He'd look into her face, and he'd *know*.

Sometimes he appeared in the great hall to dine with
her; sometimes he didn't. She was taking no chances. In
the midafternoon, she began complaining of vapors and
megrims. Around sunset, she took to her bed, and when
the Ulor summoned her to join him at dinner, she de-
clined. After that, there was no choice but to stay in bed,
feigning illness. She lay there for hours, wide awake; a
span of miserable tedium enlivened only by the unexpected visit of Varis himself, come to observe his betrothed's state.

She heard his unmistakable tones at the door; then,
Zordja's answering drone. She shut her eyes at once. Her
breathing was carefully even. Let him find her asleep, for
she couldn't talk to him, she'd never manage to deceive
him—

His footsteps advanced inexorably. She didn't dare risk
even a quick glance through her lashes, but some sixth
sense registered the pressure of his eyes upon her face.

Torture. She lay still.

Eons later, it ended.

The footsteps receded. The door creaked and closed.

He knew.

Ridiculous. Almost superstitious.

He knew.

She kept her eyes shut for a very long time. When she
finally opened them again, it was early evening. The shutters were closed over the windows, and the bedroom
glowed with lamplight. Zordja sat in the corner. Her
hands were empty. No small task diverted her attention
from her charge.

"Food," the gaoler said.

"No." She couldn't have swallowed a bite.

The gaoler did not speak again. Presently Shalindra rose, chose a book, and pretended to read. When Zordja grew bored watching, she stood and plodded wordlessly from the room, barring the door behind her. She was unlikely to return before morning.

Sleep was out of the question. Likewise reading, for her mind wandered uncontrollably. The night stretched endlessly before her. She'd never get through it.

A deck of cards helped a little. Solitaire, Solo-Kalique, and then more solitaire ate a couple of mindless hours. When cards palled, she paced; opened the shutters to gaze out at the stars; leafed nervously through a volume of poetry; paced some more. Millennia expired, and the clock on the mantel informed her that she was justified in commencing preparations; not that there were many to be made.

Working slowly, stretching the task, she chose the belongings she would carry away; mostly jewelry, and such small keepsakes as might fit conveniently into her pockets. This done, she gathered up the old colored scarves she'd kept for so long, heaping them within easy reach. After considering and comparing a variety of articles scattered about the room, she finally settled on an old silver candlestick, which she carefully set aside atop the scarves. At last, slipping her mother's locket from her neck, she sat clutching the ornament tightly.

She remembered every detail of the procedure; couldn't forget them if she tried. Still too early to begin, however. Hours until dawn, forever until dawn. She was gripping the locket so hard that it hurt. Carefully she unclenched her fist. Gold and diamonds glinted on her open palm; great heart of black fire. Almost idly, she opened the locket to study Cerrov's image. A strong face, even in childhood. Now, he'd fulfilled the promise of his youth—or would fulfill it, provided his sister didn't ruin his chances. She pried the portrait out of its setting, to uncover the remaining store of FSD107-N. Not much left, only enough for one strong, toxic dose. Still too early to use it.

She waited. Eternity revolved. Outside the tower window, darkness ebbed from the sky. Zordja would unbar the bedroom door around sunrise. It was time.

Shalindra took a deep breath and swallowed the white granules, without letting herself taste or think. For a moment she sat unmoving in her chair, eyes closed and muscles tense. A few moments of nothingness, and then the extraordinary dawning light within.

Not exactly as she remembered it, however. This time, something was different.

If pressed to explain the difference, she might have described a sense of heightened strength, control, precision. She couldn't have analyzed or defined it, but for these few minutes, she could use it. The locket slid unnoticed from her hand. Unseeing eyes fixed on the lightening window, she began to speak.

Initially, she'd almost expected to fail. The best she'd hoped for was to catch the crack-brained notice of Clotl Deathmaster, who might or might not answer her summons. Reality, however, exceeded expectation.

Her questing mind brushed ghostly consciousness; touched and clamped like a trap. The shock of that mental violence reverberated all through her. The ghost, terrified, struggled frantically but uselessly. She had it, and she held fast. No telling exactly where the creature was—near, she thought; body probably immured somewhere within the castle itself—or what it was, male or female, serf or Noble Landholder.

Irrelevant. Whatever its nature, that ghost was *hers*.

The intensity of triumph shook her focus. She took a moment to compose herself, then proceeded to draw the captured shade to her presence.

Tricky. But somehow, all at once, the words she'd read

so long ago in the crypt at Fruce made sense, as never before. TransFornian attraction; relevant notebook passages dutifully memorized years earlier, but never truly comprehended.

She comprehended now.

I can do this.

Pride, excitement, and pleasure surged against the mental barriers.

Later.

Shalindra distilled her intentions, excluding distractions, ruling the ghost and pulling it to her. She opened her eyes, and it was there—not so distinct and substantial as Clotl Deathmaster, who had come of his own accord—but clear and sharp, all the same.

Male, bearded, middle-aged. Nondescript appearance, simply clad, probably a servant. His name, his history, the circumstances of his death, forever lost.

Wordless communication ensued.

The ghost was disoriented, agitated, and fearful. Shalindra found that she didn't care. There was something indescribably satisfying in the absolute subjugation of the remnant entity. Odd. She wasn't cruel by nature, and yet this elemental assertion of will was somehow exhilarating. Perhaps it had something to do with the stimulant in her blood, or perhaps transdimensionality itself altered attitude.

Not the time to think about it.

Voicelessly, Shalindra made her requirements known.

The ghost, wafting reluctance, acquiesced.

And then, the last few minutes before sunrise; long minutes spent struggling to maintain equilibrium. No easy task, for her technical improvement didn't save her from sorcerous sickness. The familiar nausea, pain, and dizziness were all there. Intense mental focus blunted their effect, but only temporarily.

Her mind was curiously split—one half conscious of the physical world about her, the bedroom and its contents; the other half, impinging upon unknown dimensions, holding and dominating the captive shade.

Color blushed the dawn sky. Part of Shalindra heard heavy footsteps, a fumbling at the door, a small scrape as the bar was lifted. Then, as if from a great distance, she heard her own voice, clear and cold.

"Zordja. Please come in here."

Silent, surprised pause. A moment later, the door opened and Zordja entered to confront a hovering, wavering, but perfectly distinct phantom. She halted, eyes popping. Transparent teeth bared, the ghost flew at her throat. The gaoler flailed wildly. While her attention was thus engaged, Shalindra stepped up quietly behind, raised the silver candlestick, and brought it down hard. Zordja fell.

Shalindra looked down at her. Zordja lay prone and ominously still. Such a blow to the skull might easily have killed her. Ordinarily, a dreadful possibility; but right now, unimportant. Even uninteresting. An insect swatted. Nevertheless, Shalindra knelt and touched her fingers to the other's neck, where the pulse still throbbed, strong and steady.

Rising, she fetched the silk scarves, returned, and swiftly tied Zordja's wrists behind her back, lashed the ankles together, and gagged the slack mouth. Her hands were deft, her knots secure. Her mind remained preternaturally cleft, each half splendidly efficient. But the pains were lancing through her head, her vision swam, and the dizziness rocked her in waves.

Finished. Zordja momentarily neutralized. Shalindra stood. Wrapping herself in Smoke Cloud fur, she took up one of the lamps, then turned briefly to the ghost.

"Come," she said, and walked out of the room. The ghost followed.

"Go before me. Watch for guards."

Wordless, wretched obedience.

She hurried down the winding stairs. From time to

time she stumbled, and occasionally giddiness forced her to pause, but she stayed on her feet.

I'm getting better at this. I could get better yet.

Down the stairs to the base of the tower, and on along the cramped old passage to the donjon. No sentries posted here. Her eyes were fixed on the faintly luminous wraith floating through the gloom before her. At the passage-way's end, the ghost paused, and Shalindra did likewise, flattening herself to the wall and shading the lamp with her body. A couple of soldiers were passing across the chamber beyond. She waited until they were gone. On the far side of the room, a lone guard stood at the door to the cellar stairs.

Shalindra made her will known, and the ghost advanced.

The guard looked up. His jaw dropped. The ghost beckoned; retreated, paused, and beckoned again. After a moment, the interested guard followed, and the ghost led him away.

Shalindra hurried to the cellar door, or tried to hurry; but her head swam, and her step lagged. She reached the door at last. Providentially unlocked. She was through in an instant, standing at the top of the narrow stairway. Nausea, churning stomach, cold sweat all over. For a moment she rested, leaning heavily against the door, while the dim world wheeled about her. She'd lost track of the ghost. Beyond doubt, it had passed beyond the range of her inexpert control.

Taking a deep breath, she pushed herself away from the door. One hand clasping the lamp, the other pressing the wall for support, she descended. Several times she was forced to rest, but she never lost her footing.

It was worse than this the other times. I'm improving.

Down to the cellar at the bottom of the stairs. And then more stairs down to a deeper place.

She peered about her, lost. The weak light of her small

lamp barely illumined the frigid reaches of the subcellar. But this was the right level, she felt it in her nerves' ends. Somewhere—?

Straight ahead? Somehow that seemed right.

Lamp outthrust like a weapon, she advanced. Floor deadly slick with ice. She faltered, and internal darkness killed the lamplight for a moment. Closing her eyes, she waited; then opened them to behold a low oaken door set into the masonry before her. No attempt at concealment. Varis, like the Tollbooth proprietors before him, deemed this buried level all but invisible.

The door was unlocked. Uncle evidently permitted himself free ingress and egress. Even with an army at his gates? A pointless concern. If enemy forces found their way along the secret tunnel, a locked door at its end would hardly stop them.

She was down on her knees before the door. Her legs must have failed her, but she hadn't noticed when it happened.

Shalindra dragged herself to her feet, tottered through the door and along the tunnel. She remembered this place. She hadn't seen it that other time, but she'd felt it, and smelled it, as he'd no doubt intended. And why had he brought her to it, anyway? Almost as if he'd dared her to use it? Bravado? Derangement?

Cold, cold stone walls on either side, and she needed their support. For a few seconds, reality involuted, and she was back again at Fruce, making her way from the crypt. Sick and shaky, now as then, but this time, not as bad; and the next time she did it, she'd be stronger yet . . .

Faint light trembling on stone. Endless tunnel. On she went, awareness all but suspending itself, until she collided with a mortared barrier. The lamp fell from her hand and went out. Unimaginable darkness crashed down on her. For a few moments, she groped vainly about the floor for the lamp, then transferred her attention to the barrier.

The secret door to the crypt, no doubt, and here she was lucky; on this side, the latch wasn't hidden. She found it easily; pressed, pushed, and the door pivoted.

She stepped through, and then she could see again by the dawn light filtering in through the barred gate at the front of the Haudrensq crypt. She struggled toward the light. Reaching the gate, she clung there, her grip upon the iron bars holding her upright.

The gate was locked, of course, but she could deal with that. Her limbs and senses might fail her, but her mind was clear. Better than it had ever been, in fact. Sharper, stronger, rising to new levels, as if she were finally awakening from lifelong sleep, finally realizing her truest self.

She drew the lock pick from her hair, and the long tresses, suddenly released, tumbled down her back. Inserting pick into padlock, she probed blindly. It had been years, but her fingers retained their knowledge; her fingers, and her gloriously enhanced mind.

The lock gave way, and the gate swung open. Shalindra stumbled out of the crypt. Through the mists she discerned a stand of firs, and toward the trees she made her halting way.

Another sleepless night ended. How many such nights succeeding one another? He'd lost count. Dawn pushed in through the window, and Varis extinguished the lamps. Intense silence shrouded the castle; such silence a harbinger of impending hibernation. Soon, the Tollbooth would be cut off from the world. And then, the stillness would seem almost enchanted; broken intermittently by the shriek of the mountain winds that might continue for hours, but in the end, always gave way again to silence . . .

For now, the TransBruzh remained clear. There was still time to withdraw to Rialsq, leaving the castle garrison under command of its capable officers. And so he might have done, but for the present threat of sorcerous assault. Until the enemy necromancers had been dealt with once and for all, he was bound to this spot.

Not alone, however. Shalindra was here, and her presence altered matters. He had not communicated with her in several days. His thoughts, perhaps affected by sleeplessness, had wandered wildly uncharted regions. For a time, he had all but lost contact with the physical world around him, but now he wished to return, and the way back was harder than he'd foreseen. Much harder.

Shalindra's voice might cool the mental fever. He had often found her company curiously soothing. He realized then that he wanted her company—her voice and words, her gestures and changing expressions. These things had assumed an unexpected importance. He wanted them often, and he wanted them now.

He could summon her to the battlements. They'd walk. The sun was rising, the night was over.

Ordinarily, he would have dispatched a messenger to her room. But an excess of nervous energy—perhaps the same excess that kept him unremittingly wakeful—charged his frame. He needed to move. He'd go to the tower himself.

Through the dim and chilly Tollbooth he hurried, up the spiral stairs to Shalindra's room. The bar on the door had been removed. The Lazimiri maid/gaoler—Zordja, her name was Zordja—was evidently awake and active. Varis knocked; waited; knocked again.

No response. Very likely Shalindra was already up and about somewhere, her watchdog in attendance. He knocked once more, then opened the door to discover Zordja, tightly trussed, face down and motionless on the floor. She was either unconscious or dead. She was twice her charge's size, and she'd come well-recommended for vigilance and caution.

The Ulorre-consort-to-be revealed unexpected talents.

Varis's eyes ranged the chamber, and caught the sparkle of morning light on gems. A piece of jewelry lay on the floor. Advancing a few paces, he knelt and picked it up. Shalindra's locket, that she was never without. Abandoned and forgotten?

He studied the ornament. Unusual and valuable. The central stone was extraordinary. He opened the gold casing. There was an old miniature of her brother inside. A few flecks of white dotted the painted features. The recess behind the portrait contained a few more of the granules. He placed a couple of them on his tongue, and the faint but unmistakable twist of his nerves told him all.

A sorcerous stimulant. She had something of necromancy.

He should have sensed it, long ago. He should have known.

No time now to ponder the implications of his belated discovery. No time to gauge her abilities, or the uses to which she might have applied them since her arrival. Not the moment to consider the most significant of questions: her possible role in the recruitment of Cerrov Haudrensq's sorcerous allies. For now, enough to realize that she was far more dangerous than he had ever imagined.

Her successful escape would trigger the rebel attack he'd hoped to postpone.

Best and wisest to kill her, without delay. The rebels, of course, would remain ignorant of her death. Kill her. Varis hesitated. He'd prefer to spare her—he'd known that from the start. He had never fully recognized the strength of that preference, however—until now. Compunction took him by surprise; but now, as always, he'd rise above such weakness.

And afterward? His throne secure, a healthful abatement of necromancy—he could do that, he'd done it before—tranquillity, an enlightened reign.

Empty years, sterile years, long and cold as endless winter.

Perhaps he needn't kill her. Perhaps he should follow his earlier plan—teach her the high secrets of necromancy, show her Arkhoy's *Memoirs,* introduce her to Clotl's gel, the best of the best. Once she'd tasted of that knowledge and power, she'd never willingly give them up. She'd stay with him of her own accord, forever. Or, at least, until she spifflicated.

No. Spifflication was avoidable. Quite avoidable.

He could think about it later. After he'd brought her back. No question, of course, where she'd gone.

Varis stood. Locket in hand, he set out to track her down.

It was dark in the shadow of the firs. A boreal breeze stirred the boughs, but Shalindra didn't feel the cold. Her flesh burned, and her lips were parched. The ground underfoot was lightly whitened. From time to time she paused to rub a handful of snow across her face, but she didn't dare linger.

On into the silent woods, and she had to keep reminding herself, lest it slip from her mental grasp, that Cerrov's force lay to the south. Very near, no distance at all. South. She glanced about her. Pale shafts of early sunlight slanting low through the trees. Sun to her left, where it should be. Good.

On she lurched drunkenly, and the woods seemed deserted. No visible sign of humanity. Audible sign? No telling. A curious roaring filled her ears, and that was all she heard.

Brief pause. Shaky, confused. Which way? Sun to the left. Yes.

Presently she emerged from the trees to find herself in a small clearing, where the sudden dazzle of sunlight made her blink. The glade was roughly circular, not more than twenty feet across, thickly bordered with conifers. For a moment she stood squinting. Too bright. Too harsh.

She felt intolerably exposed. The shadows called her, and she pushed on toward their shelter.

She reached the trees; paused on instinct to look back. And then she froze into utter stillness.

At the far edge of the clearing, Varis stood watching her. He was motionless and expressionless.

Somehow, she wasn't surprised. Some obscure part of her had expected to see him there.

Shalindra gazed into eyes that were greenish, shading to yellow about the pupils—eyes not unlike her own. Eyes that spoke, eyes that she felt she knew.

"Ulor," she whispered. "Ulor."

No change in his face. Perhaps she had only spoken in her mind. For a moment she fought a confused impulse to cross the clearing to him.

She didn't think of trying to run away. Her mind was as paralyzed as the rest of her. She only wondered, detachedly, whether he would take her back to the castle or kill her where she stood. His face told her nothing; it never did. She waited.

Varis's arm moved. Something flew from his hand to arc through the air. Swift, hard brilliance, with a heart of cold black flame.

It struck the ground before her. Shalindra looked down. Her mother's locket lay half-sunk in the snow at her feet. For a moment she stared at it, then raised her eyes slowly to find herself alone in the glade.

Varis was gone.

She had no idea how long she stood staring stupidly at the spot where he had been. No idea how long before her limbs unfroze and she could move again. She stooped clumsily, picked up the locket, and slipped it into a pocket. Rising, she stumbled away.

Trees about her again, and it was so dark in their shade—or else her sight was failing—and she didn't know where she was. Staggering along now, hard to stay on her feet. And then, a couple of indistinct figures emerging from the shadows—stopping dead at sight of her—

Real? Fever dream? Ghosts?

Her clouded vision failed altogether, and the darkness engulfed her.

19

WHEN CONSCIOUSNESS RETURNED, she opened her eyes reluctantly, afraid of what she might see. She lay on a cot, with a low canvas ceiling slanting overhead. A tent. Coal fire in a small brazier with a perforated cover. Daylight beyond the entrance. A few feet from the cot, a small table and chair. Seated in the chair, a straight-spined, square-shouldered figure, its back to the light. Shalindra frowned, puzzled. Her companion's face was shadowed, but there was something familiar in the set of the head, and the shape of the hands. Then the other spoke, and there could be no further doubt.

"I trust you are yourself again, Miss Vezhevska?"

"Yes, Librarian."

"I would advise you to avoid exertion, for a time."

"Yes, Librarian." She was sounding about twelve years old, Shalindra realized. She raised herself on one elbow. "Where am I?"

"In your brother's camp, below Castle Haudrensq. A couple of scouts met you in the woods, recognized you, and brought you here. I assume you escaped the castle?"

"Yes."

"Remarkable accomplishment for an unarmed woman."

"Umm."

"Quite amazing."

"How long have I been here?"

"Since yesterday morning. You have slept for twenty-four hours. You do not appear surprised to see me, Miss Vezhevska."

"Twenty-four hours! Does Cerrov know I'm here?"

"He does. I persuaded him to entrust you to my care, as I am not unfamiliar with the nature of your malady. It is not your first such attack, as I recall."

"Where's my brother now?"

"At present, overseeing the transport of ordnance to the top of the eastern cliff above the pass. The assault upon the castle is about to begin."

"He certainly wastes no time."

"He has already lost more time than he can afford."

I suppose you think that's my fault.

Actually, there was no telling what she thought, now or ever. Aloud, Shalindra merely observed, "He'll have his work cut out for him. He knows that the Tollbooth's defenses have been modernized?"

"Irrelevant. It is neither the quality of the guns, nor the nature of the castle's physical defenses that will shape the outcome of the battle. But you already know that, Miss Vezhevska."

"Librarian?"

"A number of my colleagues have accompanied me from Fruce," The Librarian observed, as if inconsequently. "Perhaps you would recall one or two."

"I'd remember them all." Shalindra met the other's eyes. "Thank you for coming. Thank you all."

"Thanks are unnecessary." The Librarian rose to look down at Shalindra, from vast height, as always. "We act in accordance with our principles, that is all. Had your uncle's aims coincided with our own, be assured we should have served his interests with all the energy that we now devote to your brother's."

"I can't believe that, Librarian."

"It is unfortunate that your sojourn at Fruce failed to purge you of sentimentality. Perhaps time's passage will remedy the defect. Unfortunately, I've no leisure now to provide instruction. Your condition no longer requires close observation, and I must rejoin my colleagues. There is much to do. Good day, Miss Vezhevska." She turned and made for the exit.

"Good day, Librarian." Shalindra sat up. "Please tell Jevuni and the others that I thank—"

Too late. The Librarian was gone, without a backward glance. Shalindra swung her feet to the ground and carefully rose. She was tired and listless, but clear-eyed and clearheaded.

From the east, not far away, came the first thunder of cannonfire.

Cerrov's artillery pounded the eastern face of Castle Haudrensq for the next four days and nights. By sundown of the fourth day, the upper levels of two towers had been blasted away, and a great fissure rent the outer wall.

And the rebels? Those manning the cannon, scarcely inconvenienced by firing from the castle. The others, the majority of them, invisible among the trees below, but doubtless prepared to protect the eastern heights.

Unwise, in any case, to consider dispatching a detachment from the Tollbooth; the designated men would very likely desert to the enemy. For in recent weeks, Cerrov Haudrensq had somehow managed to resume his golden aura of the early campaign. Many of his followers believed him marked by Destiny, but they would shortly recognize their error.

It was time. No further delay was possible.

In the final dying hours of the night, Varis made his way to the Haudrensq crypt. So impenetrable the darkness of its recesses by moonless night, that for once he brought a candle. Shivering light cast distorted shadows on the walls.

Transdimensionality was easily achieved. Following weeks of abstinence, even a moderate dose of one of the better stimulants kindled the inner radiance.

He called, and they came at once. Celgi Stoneheart was long gone, but there were others, many others. His own dead kinsmen, his ancestors. Perhaps, given a choice, they'd have served him willingly. He would have liked to think so.

But then, they were kin to Cerrov, as well.

He made his will known. They grumbled, but inevitably submitted. He reshaped their substance according to his needs, and this alteration drew anguished spectral outcry. Because they were Haudrensq, he went so far as to explain the transience of their distortions. Most of them disbelieved, and he left the crypt with their dismal curses buzzing in his brain.

Back along the passageway, no need of a light now, for the walls and floor seemed bathed in that sickly viridescence visible to him alone. And no ill effects from the necromancy this time. He was strong and mentally ablaze. He had never been better.

Another hour or so before dawn. No need to rest; he was charged with energy. Fortunately so, for how could he possibly rest with all those sullen, fearful, dead voices whispering inside his head? Somehow or other, the voices had followed him from the crypt, where the captive Haudrensq shades awaited their master's commands. The pleas, complaints, and reproaches had pursued him back along the tunnel, up the stairs, and out onto the ramparts. There, the soldiers on duty regarded him with a certain furtive wonder. For the bitter night breezes of early winter scoured the Bruzhois, and men huddled about their braziers; but the Ulor went overcoatless, ungloved, bareheaded, eyes glowing like a nocturnal predator's.

Varis conferred a moment or two with his officers, then moved off to stand alone, gazing east across the Ayzin Pass. No lights shone on the opposite cliff—the enemy had banked all fires—but his vision pierced the night, and he discerned uniformed figures moving to and fro. The rebel guns were still; the castle artillery likewise momentarily quiet.

The night dwindled to its close. The stars expired, and the skies paled. A light snow feathered the brittle air. The Tollbooth cannon spoke, and brilliant red flashes heralded the enemy's thundering reply.

Varis ignored the exchange, which was, in terms of the impending contest, all but meaningless. His gaze swept the glazed landscape; arrested and anchored. Far below him, down in the woods where Cerrov's magical allies skulked, a pale mist was rising, flowing skyward like snowfall reversing itself. Even at that distance, he could make out individual figures—men and women, old and young, clad in the garments of bygone centuries. The haunted woods had yielded a fine harvest of ghosts, but here were greater numbers than the forest alone could have furnished. Among them he beheld Bruzhoi tribesmen, probably summoned from the Bowl of Lannakh, and Stilthousers from the Narshk Fens—spectres he himself had once conjured, and used, and forgotten. But they were back again now, serving his enemies; far more willingly, he divined at once, than they had ever served *him*.

No matter. Their allegiance was not required.

For a few seconds he stood watching the wraiths ascend. But for his sorcerously enhanced senses, he would have perceived nothing more than a rising mist. Certainly the soldiers of the garrison saw nothing amiss—if indeed they noticed at all. But that would change soon enough, as the ghosts drew nigh to drive their living victims to frenzy.

Time to halt their progress.

Varis's awareness flew to the crypt, there to issue commands. His own ghostly servants emerged; a wavering cloud of monstrous, vastly swollen figures. Such grotesque apparitions would hardly impress the spectral adversaries, but, at the proper time, were sure to spread havoc among Cerrov's troops.

The smoky haze issuing from the crypt flowed on to meet the white mist rising from the woods. They came together above the trees to the south of the castle. And while the cannon roared over the Ayzin Pass, the real battle went for a time unnoticed by all save sorcerous combatants.

Varis watched the two clouds meet and merge. His mind encompassed that impossible union, and the shock of it nearly broke his concentration then and there. He recovered, almost at once. An amorphous ectoplasmic fog seethed before him. The contending shades, melded for the moment into a single wildly unstable entity, vicariously engaged their respective summoners' minds. The contact was immediate and intense.

Varis sensed a disciplined, purposeful, collective consciousness pressing upon him. The force was not immediately overwhelming, but it was relentless. He had encountered it once before, but now it was worse; or perhaps his own recovery was less complete than he had imagined.

He flexed his mind, and the homogeneous cloud before him curdled into clumps, each comprising three or four convulsed individuals. Here a writhing limb or torso, briefly emerging from chaos; there, an agonized face, distinct for a moment, then lost again in communal being.

The mist swirled on psychic winds, and Varis's mind flagged for a moment like an overtaxed muscle. In that instant, the spectral figures began to resolve themselves, and there were the forms and faces of the antique mountaineers, the Bruzhoi tribesmen, the Narshk phantoms— all the Conclave's ghostly servants asserting identity, absorbing and assimilating their adversaries.

The monsters from the Haudrensq crypt were gone, their ghostly existence temporarily nullified. The Conclave's servants flowed on toward the Tollbooth.

Varis created transdimensional resistance, which they shattered without apparent effort. His mind shook under the blow, and the dimensions shuffled about him like playing cards.

A moment to regain control.

Done.

On they came. Only the discipline of years controlled the tremors rocking his focus. And on they came.

He had hardly exhausted his resources, however. The most potent of all still remained.

From his pocket he drew a wide-mouthed glass jar. Removing the cap, he regarded the opaline gelatinous contents. Crazy Clotl's extraordinary concoction. In all these years, never reproduced, and never equalled. The best of them all, now and always. There wasn't very much of it left, only enough for perhaps three moderate or two generous doses. Now, if ever, was the time to use it.

Tilting the jar, he shook half the contents into his mouth and down his throat. He paused briefly, then swallowed the remainder. The empty jar fell from his hand and shattered.

It took effect immediately. A sigh escaped him. It was even better than he remembered, life's zenith. The power and certainty rose within him, filled him, and he sent that force like a winter gale upon the advancing ghosts. He felt the collective will of the enemy necromancers break under the onslaught, and then the ghostly forms lost definition, blurred, and surrendered to chaos. Once again the ectoplasmic formlessness whirled and boiled above the trees.

It was almost easy now. The weeks of rest must have served him well, for he had never been stronger. With Clotl's marvelous gel to sustain him, he was for this moment invincible. Slightly altering Fornian angle, he channeled intention along the enemy blindnesses, slid through, and struck with all the strength of his mind.

The cloud below altered at once. The gigantically deformed Haudrensq ancestors reasserted themselves, obliterating opposition.

He took a moment or so to sharpen their physical-planar immediacy, then drove them south upon the hidden rebels, upon the alien sorcerers.

Not hard to find them. In their confidence, they had scarcely attempted concealment or mental shielding. He felt the encounter of ravening ghosts and enemy necromancers throughout his being. He experienced their united resolve, and for one instant, he caught some sense of who they were; foreigners—many yet one—dedicated, unworldly, devoted yet enviably dispassionate. A powerful collective will—but for now, not strong enough.

The Haudrensq ghosts descended. Their master had armed them with fang and claw, but these enhancements were largely symbolic. The significant weapons were intangible.

Ghosts and sorcerers met.

Varis strained his consciousness to the uttermost and beyond. Beyond. A great light filled his mind.

Shalindra stood in the shadow of the firs, watching the Conclave at work. The twelve members stood stilly linked about a jumping fire. Their faces were empty, their eyes identically lucent. Just so had she seen them merge their powers years earlier. Now they were grayer, and there were one or two new faces among them. Otherwise, little had changed.

The Conclave. Potent, united, formidable.

She believed them unconquerable, until she saw the clouds descend upon them; impossible clouds of dark vapor, settling where the warmth of the Conclave's fire, and the stirring of the atmosphere should have carried them aloft.

The clouds thickened and defined themselves, assuming distinct and terrible form.

Gigantic woman, quadruple-breasted; spurred of elbow, knee and heel; dragon-scaled and winged.

Huge man, goat-horned, tusked, curly-furred; countless small gargoyle faces sprouting from his back and chest.

Man, towering, vaporous cataracts issuing blackly from eyes, nose, and mouth.

Others, many others, equally monstrous. Initially soft-edged, but swiftly waxing in clarity and bulk.

For a moment, wonder eclipsed fear. She simply marveled. And then she was watching the phantoms darkening over them, claws knifing and tentacles coiling, and there was nothing she could do, nothing—

Almost to the last moment, she believed that the Conclave would somehow rally; believed it until she saw great talons close upon Under Librarian Oruno; until she saw the suffocating veils enshroud Assistant Librarian Jevuni. One after another, the librarians fell, dead eyes wide and staring.

The Librarian was last to go. At the end, she stood alone among her lifeless colleagues, erect and impassible as always. A swarm of grotesque forms enveloped her. Her will held them off for another minute or so, and then they closed upon her, and she fell.

The Conclave lay dead. Shalindra stood petrified. For a moment, the reality of the scene refused to register. Then the ghosts rose from their victims, terrible forms towering above the trees, and she met the lidless reptile eyes of the dragon-scaled woman.

All of it became real then, and the paralysis broke, and she was running through the woods, never daring to look behind her. But she felt their pursuit, and she heard their cries—

No. Ghosts were soundless, to the uninitiated. The screams, the wails—they came from Cerrov's men, now prey to mortal terror. The woods were full of fleeing, frantic human figures; and many of them were falling, and there the spectral forms converged—

Shalindra didn't let herself look. Lowering her head, she picked up her skirts and ran blindly.

Varis, motionlessly transdimensional upon the castle ramparts, perceived the destruction of the collective sorcerous entity that was his enemy. One by one, its individual components died. The last and strongest of them finally yielded, and steel discipline failed to suppress his rush of triumph. He could not afford such indulgences. His concentration was sure to suffer.

But it did not. That extraordinary inner light burned bright as ever. Brighter. It seemed that nothing would quench it. This morning surely marked a change. He had attained a new level.

Having crushed the alien necromancers, he set the Haudrensq shades upon the rebel soldiers, and for a time vicariously wrought carnage.

But the light in his mind yet waxed in brilliance, and now its intensity was almost disturbing. He blinked. The acuteness of his vision was actually burdensome. Too much. More than he could tolerate.

And still the radiance intensified, even to the point of pain. White-hot now, searing his mental vision. Overwhelming effulgence, like the sun inside him. Too much power, too sudden. He would have to learn to control it. Control it. Control.

He didn't know that he was tottering. When his hold on the distant Haudrensq ghosts failed, he didn't notice.

Light beyond comprehension. More than a sun; the inconceivable flare of a sun in its death agony. Light that consumed and annihilated—

Exploded in a soundless fury white beyond whiteness—

And vanished. Darkness fell like a headsman's ax.

His eyes still functioned. He gazed without comprehension upon an alien universe. Broken shards of recollection lay scattered throughout the mental wreckage, but he could make nothing of them. He was lost, mind useless as a broken limb, and the terror rose and grew in him until terror was all that there was.

There were uniformed figures about him, and strangers' faces with flapping puppet jaws, and gibberish was pouring out of them— *Ulor. Ulor* and there were hands reaching for him, clutching at him—

When he bared his teeth and snarled, they drew back, gaping, and he could breathe again. But only momentarily, for now there were others pressing close upon him, and snarls hardly frightened these new ones; these hovering, transparent ones.

These he knew, even now. They were his own kindred, after all; restored to their original forms, free of his command, but disinclined to leave him.

Their faces, their dead eyes—

Their voices, yelping, yammering—

Unendurable words.

Something exceeding them, drowning them out. Hoarse, incoherent cries. His own. Not good enough, he couldn't keep it up for long. Pause for breath, and they were still chattering, louder now, and mercilessly clear.

He struck out wildly, and his hand passed straight through them. Then he was running, moving in a clinging cloud of them, and through that ectoplasmic haze he dimly glimpsed the shocked faces of his soldiers—jaws wagging, gibberish gushing.

He ran, and presently the sky vanished. He was indoors, wandering a stone maze, battering himself against its walls, trapped and hopelessly lost.

But his feet seemed to remember what his mind did not, and his feet carried him down, down endless spiral stairs, down into darkness that was bright as day. The ghosts were no longer with him, he'd lost them somewhere along the way, but they might catch up if he didn't hurry—hurry—

. Down to the lowest subterranean level, and his feet carried him along a passageway to a door whose secrets his fingers remembered. The door opened, and he stumbled forth into a silent murky place, with an iron-barred gate, and daylight beyond the gate.

The way out.

Halfway to the gate, all sense of purpose suddenly left him, and he sank to his knees.

No telling how long he knelt there, consciousness all but extinct. At last, he became aware of another presence. A voice poked at him, apparently from the inside.

My star pupil. HEH!

Varis looked up into a smirking transparent face, with plaited beard and decorative scars. Fugitive, glinting splinter of memory. Cracked and buried. Gone again.

You took your own sweet time, boy. But I knew you'd get here in the end. I had faith in you.

Noise.

Nothing to say? Cat got your tongue? Don't be that way, it's not friendly.

Noise.

Oh, I see. Wiped out. Heh. WIPED OUT! As in— CRUNCHED. Eh? That's the way it takes us, sometimes. Eh? CRUNCHED. Like the rest of us. Heh!

Noise.

Well, don't take it too hard, boy. You'll get used to the change. We all do.

Noise. Comprehension undesirable.

And I'm here to welcome you to the club. Been looking forward to playing the host, ever since you killed me.

?

So, now what? Got a plan? Grand design? Inspiration? No? Never mind. I can help you out. Always glad to lend a helping hand. I can get you out of this.

Out. Severed-nerve twitch of intellect.

Eh? No, no thanks necessary. Happy to do it. My favorite pupil deserves no less. Come along with me, then. Come on, boy. Let me help. Clotl knows the way.

The ghost dimmed and receded. Eyes fixed upon the fading figure, Varis rose and followed.

Shalindra halted and looked around her. The woods boiled with running men and panicked horses. Of the ghosts, however, there was no sign. They were gone; vanishing suddenly as they'd appeared.

It took the better part of an hour to restore order. During that time, she repaired to her own tent. She knew, without asking, that the most helpful thing she could do was simply to keep herself out of the way. Moreover, the solitude concealed her tears, which welled each time she pictured the Fruce librarians falling one by one.

The entire Conclave, killed at a stroke, leaving Varis the clear victor—the inevitable victor.

But was he?

She became aware for the first time that the cannonfire above the Ayzin Pass had ceased.

There ensued a prolonged, nerve-chafing tedium; seemingly empty, yet in fact witnessing multiple exchanges of communication. Messages flew between Cerrov —up on the cliff with his artillerymen—and the officers on the slopes below; between Cerrov and the commander of the Tollbooth garrison.

In the midafternoon, Cerrov descended to join his troops, thereafter leading them from the shelter of the woods, up the sharply graded path to the summit of the western cliff. Before them rose the Tollbooth, its defenders visible upon the walls.

No fire from the castle.

Another exchange of messages. Shalindra, waiting in the midst of her brother's followers, endured another endless delay. And then her breath caught as she watched a white flag of surrender slowly rise above Castle

Haudrensq. Minutes later, the great central gates parted, and the rebel force marched in.

The soldiers of the garrison, having already laid down their arms, unanimously declared their willingness to swear allegiance to the rightful Ulor. This offer Cerrov accepted, forgoing all penalties and reprisals, provided his usurping uncle was handed over immediately, alive and in chains.

The garrison commander appeared uneasy. His trepidation was plain as he confessed that the usurper's whereabouts were unknown.

Cerrov requested particulars.

It seemed that the former Ulor—the usurper, that was to say—had, during the course of the early morning's artillery exchange, suffered a fit or a seizure of some kind. Distraught, delirious, or perhaps raving mad, the usurper had fled the ramparts. He had been observed to move in the midst of a cloud or a fog of some kind. More than one witness had noted the presence of hostile ghosts, although the commander himself could not personally confirm it. In any event, subsequent to that incident, the usurper had not been seen.

It has caught up with him. Shalindra suddenly felt the winter's cold.

Cerrov's expression was politely skeptical. Without directly impugning the commander's veracity, he ordered a squad of his own men to search the Tollbooth from top to bottom.

Shalindra's insides knotted queerly.

But an hour later, the squad returned to report its failure. The traitor Varis Haudrensq was nowhere to be found.

"He must be somewhere about. He couldn't have got out unnoticed. Try again." Cerrov's brows knit. He turned to his sister, who sat beside him at the table in the Tollbooth's council chamber. "Shalli, you were here for weeks.

Do you know of any way he might have sneaked out of this place?"

The tunnel. The crypt. The iron gate, and the deep woods beyond.

"Shalli?"

Shalindra met his gaze.

"No," she said.

20

NIGHT WITHOUT DARKNESS. Shalindra stood alone on a balcony overlooking the Zalkhash courtyard. A full moon shone overhead. The buildings themselves were extravagantly illuminated. Light glowed at every window, and colored lanterns dangled from the eaves. Beyond the high wall girdling the royal enclosure, the Rialsqui crowds still caroused in the streets. From time to time, bursts of fireworks scattered colored jewels across the sky. At each burst, cheering arose; a sound curiously shrill and thin.

At her back, the Grand Ballroom, with its crowds, odors, heat, and talk—its endless, empty, incessant chatter. She wanted none of it now. She took a deep breath of blessedly clear, chilly air. She wore only a velvet cloak over her ballgown of gold-spangled midnight blue, but she wasn't at all uncomfortable. She had quite successfully reaccustomed herself to Rhazaullean temperatures. And anyway, it wasn't really all that cold, not by native standards. Winter was over, and now was the short season of the Rift.

Cerrov—unchallenged Ulor of Rhazaulle since his army had entered a welcoming Rialsq, four months earlier

—had postponed his official coronation until this time when his subjects and allies might conveniently attend the festivities. And they *had* attended—Noble Landholders, untitled gentry, foreign dignitaries and their entourages—converging in droves upon the capital city. All of them eager to demonstrate their loyalty (a little belatedly, in some cases, but what of that?). All of them fulsome in their declarations, including more than a few Noble Landholders known to have occupied seats in the previous Ulor's own council. All of them seeking favor, security, advancement. All of them *smiling,* so indefatigably, throughout the ceremonies, celebrations, banquets, and receptions.

She was sick to death of them.

At last, only the strongest cub remains alive to become new Ulor, and bring winter to its end.

The old folktale.

A firm footstep sounded on the stone flagging behind her. Shalindra turned to confront a tall, broad-shouldered figure in a splendid uniform; handsome face, very blue eyes. Colonel Syun.

She suppressed a faint flash of irritation. Syun was a friend, of course; none better. Just now, however, she'd wanted a moment alone.

"I hope I don't intrude upon your Grace." He was smiling.

"Of course not," she lied, manufacturing a smile of her own. "And it's still Shalli."

"Still Shalli? Even as Duchess of Otreska? Even as heir to the Wolf Throne?"

She was growing used to the ducal title that Cerrov had conferred upon her. But it still sent an odd sort of thrill along her nerves—something of revulsion, something of hungry excitement—to contemplate her present position in the line of succession.

"Oh—that's a very temporary thing." She shrugged, pushing the thought away. "Cerrov will marry one day, and then there'll be a whole string of new little Haudrensq heirs."

"Perhaps, but for now——" He broke off as fireworks flared above, and shouting broke out anew in the street beyond the wall. The racket subsided. "Tell me, then—enjoying the taste?"

"Taste? Of what?"

"Greatness. Acclaim. Success. Triumph."

"Oh. Yes. Glorious." Another lie. For reasons that defied her power of analysis, the victory seemed terribly hollow; the glitter false, the cheering trivial. To her own ears, her voice sounded leaden. But Syun evidently noticed nothing amiss, for he was still smiling.

"You deserve it all, Shalli. And you suit your rank; you could be nothing less than a duchess."

"Kind words."

"I'm truly happy for you."

Happy? As easy as that? Did he see nothing, understand nothing? No, or he wouldn't be looking so simply, unreservedly pleased. Good and well-meaning, of course. But not particularly perceptive.

"Thank you," she heard herself reply. And then, because that wasn't enough, she inquired, "And is that what you came out here to tell me?" She'd aimed for the old teasing note, but it emerged sounding a little too acid.

Again, however, Syun noticed nothing. "But there are so many things I might tell you—out here," he suggested. A clear invitation to banter.

She wasn't in the mood. She waited in silence, her face very still.

After a moment, a look of faint trouble or puzzlement darkened his eyes, and he said, "Actually, the Ulor sent me to find you."

The Ulor. For an instant, her heart contracted, and then she realized that he meant Cerrov. "Nothing wrong, I hope?" she asked quietly.

"I think not. I believe he wants you to talk with that

tame Venerator—Colloquist—whatever title the fellow
applies to himself this week."

"Layo Burik, you mean?"

"That title, at least, doesn't change."

"What does Cerrov expect me to discuss with Burik?"

"Not sure. What is there to discuss with fanatics? Personally, I'd boot them clean out of Rialsq, but your
brother's not of my mind. I gather this Burik loon fancies
himself inheritor of the Frucians' cause, and since you've
personal knowledge of the librarians, Cerrov thinks it best
that you—"

He spoke on, but she didn't hear him. Layo Burik and
his Colloquist disciples. A motley fanatic band, crazed
zealots and misfits, most of them; but all of their considerable energy devoted to furthering the dead Conclave's purpose—mass spectral liberation. They were practicing and
proselytizing throughout Rhazaulle, and where they traveled, the crypts and graveyards and old haunted places
were cleansed. New converts daily swelled the Colloquist
ranks, and it seemed more than likely that the total population of Rhazaullean ghosts might achieve freedom in a
matter of decades.

All very humanitarian, laudable by any standards. And
yet she couldn't dam the swift dark current of her
thoughts—

Layo Burik and his people, trained by The Librarian
herself, possessed the secrets of Conclave magic; including,
no doubt, the formula of FSD107-N.

*I could get some from them. Fill up the locket again. Keep it
for an emergency.*

Only for an emergency.

*I'd be better, next time. I was starting to learn. I could
study, I could do it.*

"No," she said aloud.

"What?" Syun stared.

"No—trouble at all. I'll talk to Layo Burik."

"Oh."

No. No. No.

"He wants you to tackle the Aennorvi ambassador, as well."

"Oh, yes. There's King Dasune's proposed reduction of Rhazaullean tariffs."

"Dry stuff. Pointless, in any case. A conversation at a party accomplishes nothing."

He's not too clever, she thought, and was instantly ashamed. He was good and brave, loyal and gallant, kind, honorable, and quite sufficiently clever.

And ordinary.

Why had she thought that? So mean-spirited—so ungrateful—and she genuinely liked him. But it had popped spontaneously into her head, and there was no controlling it.

What's the matter with me?

"May I escort you in?" Syun offered.

"Umm—I'd just like another breath or two of fresh air. Could you please tell Cerrov I'll be there in a minute?"

"Yes, if you wish. Are you quite all right, Shalli?"

"Of course."

"I thought perhaps—" He frowned. "You're certain?"

"Entirely certain. No cause for concern, I promise."

"Very well. And there's another thing you must promise."

"What?"

"That you'll dance a Linniana with me."

"Oh. Yes. I'd be delighted," she said politely.

For another moment he stood eyeing her uncertainly, then bowed and retired, leaving her alone.

She drew a quiet breath of relief. A little more of solitude before she must face the crowds and noise again. Turning her back on the Grand Ballroom, she lifted her eyes to the full moon, round and golden as—

One hand rose to the locket at her throat. In her mind's eye, she saw again, for the thousandth time, the flash of sunlight on flying diamonds, the locket arcing through the air, and the tall figure poised at the far edge of the clearing.

Varis. Who had chosen to let her go.

"Why?" she whispered aloud.

Perhaps if she understood it, she could stop thinking about it.

Mad, Cerrov had opined, when she'd described the incident to him. *The first clear sign of his mental collapse. Uncle had no idea what he was doing.*

Oh yes he did, Shalindra thought. *At that moment, he knew exactly what he was doing.*

He'd known the consequences of her escape, and he'd permitted it, even assisted it.

A form of suicide? Deliberate self destruction? Or perhaps recognition and acceptance of his own impending doom?

Exhaustion? Despair? Indifference?

A merciful impulse? Had he simply pitied her? Or were there other feelings there?

And afterward—what became of him?

Cerrov's men had combed the mountains without discovering a clue. The usurper had vanished without a trace. Even now, the search continued, but each passing day lessened chances of success.

Where are you? Some part of her would always wonder. *Can you see the moon?*

Where are you?

In a clearing deep in the Bruzhoi woods stood an ancient hut with a crazy-hanging door and a partially caved-in roof. Such dilapidation suggested long vacancy, but the appearance was deceptive.

Within the hut, the air was hazed with smoke; foul with the stench of filthy bodies, excrement, and rotting food. The weak glow of a starved little fire reddened some dozen or so crouching forms. There were four or five

adults, and a gaggle of subtly misshapen, unnaturally quiescent children. Listless with hunger, an observer might
have supposed. But the eyes that gleamed through matted
elflocks held none of starvation's languor; they shone with
the unnerving brilliance of spifflication.

In a smudged-out corner farthest from the fire squatted a lone figure; long and gaunt of limb, gray-pale of
face, with lank black hair obscuring empty hazel eyes. For
hour upon hour, he sat there motionless. The insects
crawled upon him undisturbed. Almost nobody, seeing
him thus, would have known the former Ulor of
Rhazaulle. Certainly the patrols twice venturing into the
hut had failed to distinguish their quarry. He would not
have recognized himself; for he had no name, no past, and
little awareness of the present.

Most of the time.

There were moments, however, when the dreams
brought unwelcome recollections of a former life, real or
imagined. Faces, too vivid. So many faces to trouble the
calm of nothingness. Perhaps they were not dreams, for he
never slept; or else, he always slept. Usually, they were
silent. But one among them had a voice, impossible to
ignore. That one was with him now—again?—yet?—jabbering in his mind.

*So, how's it going, boy? Enjoying family life? Eh? Didn't I
tell you you'd fit right in?*

And there was a smirking transparent face, visible before him. Face and voice dispersing the fog, pricking mind
and memory.

*Always felt like a father to you, boy. Warms my heart—or
would if I still had one—to see you take my place as family
patriarch.*

He didn't want to hear. The words were so much gabble, but he didn't want to hear. Slowly he hauled himself
to his feet, and a startled chittering ruffled the spifflicated
tribe.

You MOVED! Haven't lost the old VERVE! I'm so proud of my boy!

Joints stiff as a rusted automaton's, he shambled to the door, opened it, and stepped out of the hut.

The voice ceased.

The ground outside was white. A sharp breeze sliced through his rags, but he never felt the cold. Overhead, the full moon shone round and golden as some piece of jewelry.

He stared at the moon. Memories stirred.

The night was still. Somewhere far away, a wolf howled.

Born and raised in Fanwood, New Jersey, Paula Volsky majored in English literature at Vassar, then traveled to England to complete an M.A. in Shakespearean studies at the University of Birmingham. Upon her return to the United States, she sold real estate in New Jersey, then began working for the U.S. Department of Housing and Urban Development in Washington, D.C. During this time she finished her first book, *The Curse of the Witch Queen,* a fairy tale for children that developed into a fairy tale for adults. Shortly thereafter she abandoned HUD in favor of full-time writing. She continues to reside in the Washington, D.C., area, with her collection of Victoriana and her almost equally antique computer.